MADELEINE BUNTING was for many years a columnist for the *Guardian*. Her first novel, *Island Song*, won the Waverton Good Read Award and was shortlisted for the *London Magazine* Debut Fiction Prize. She is also the author of many non-fiction books, including *Labours of Love: The Crisis of Care*, which was longlisted for the Baillie Gifford Prize and the Orwell Prize for Political Writing, *The Plot: A Biography of My Father's English Acre*, which won the Portico Prize, and *Love of Country: A Hebridean Journey*, which was shortlisted for the Wainwright Golden Beer Book Prize and the Saltire Non-Fiction Book of the Year. She is a Visiting Professor at the London School of Economics' International Inequalities Institute.

Also by Madeleine Bunting

FICTION

Island Song

NON-FICTION

Labours of Love: The Crisis of Care

Love of Country: A Hebridean Journey

The Plot: A Biography of an English Acre

Willing Slaves: How the Overwork Culture is Ruling Our Lives

The Model Occupation: The Channel Islands under German Rule 1940–45

Ceremony of Innocence

Madeleine Bunting

GRANTA

Granta Publications, 12 Addison Avenue, London W11 4QR
First published in Great Britain by Granta Books, 2021
This paperback edition published by Granta Books, 2022

A CIP catalogue record for this book is available from the British Library.

1 3 5 7 9 10 8 6 4 2

ISBN 978 1 78378 750 0
eISBN 978 1 78378 751 7

Typeset in Bembo by Avon DataSet Ltd, Alcester, Warwickshire
Printed and bound by CPI Group (UK) Ltd, Croydon, CR0 4YY

MIX
Paper from
responsible sources
FSC® C171272

For Luke Maurice

Turning and turning in the widening gyre
The falcon cannot hear the falconer:
Things fall apart; the centre cannot hold;
Mere anarchy is loosed upon the world,
The blood-dimmed tide is loosed, and everywhere
The ceremony of innocence is drowned.

W. B. Yeats, *The Second Coming*

LONDON
2018

1

Fauzia liked the office at this time of the morning, when the ranks of desks lay empty and expectant for another day of dramas. Before the rush, she could still think clearly, she could breathe without the tightness in her chest which gathered through the course of the day. Tapping keyboards were all that lay between her and the overwhelming rush of data; tapping which attempted to order and make sense of the world. She skimmed Twitter feeds, Instagram, she checked several competitor sites – the *Financial Times*, the *New York Times, The Times*; she had half an eye on *BBC World News* on a screen above the news desk. The first editorial conference was in ten minutes, and she needed to pull the foreign news list together: a bomb in Kabul, a British tourist in a minibus crash in Majorca, a political crisis in Italy. She was almost done.

'Fauzia, a call on line one – can you deal with it?' called Jack, the news editor. The ring of a landline was an unusual sound these days; the newsroom used to thrum with the ringing of phones and the murmur of voices, but that was twelve years ago, when she first started as a reporter. The screen was king now; voice calls took too long, and WhatsApp was safer and quicker.

Fauzia put on her headphones to take the call, and resumed typing the news list. A man was speaking so fast she couldn't follow, and she missed his name.

'. . . she had been studying for a PhD. She once told me she knew you . . . I think you had met through a family friend? She went to Cairo just ten days ago.'

Fauzia was searching through Twitter for the name of the dead British tourist in Majorca. The man's voice was educated, middle-class, but his sentences were fragmented, so it was hard to catch the significance. She paused her scrolling.

'You're saying she studied in London and has been here eighteen months. Is that right?' she asked. 'Sorry, who is this person? Who are you?'

'You met Reem Hameed – I think you knew her well?'

Fauzia stopped typing, alert. 'What's happened? What about her?'

Jack was calling her from the other side of the news desk, his face puckered with impatience. He needed the news list for conference.

'Hang on a moment, stay on the line,' she said quickly. No, no, not Reem. She forced herself to focus: the BBC were reporting that six British tourists had been killed or injured in the minibus crash. News was also breaking of a shooting in Louisiana, with two dead; she added it to the list and pressed save. Now Jack had the list, she switched her attention to the breathing on the other end of the line.

'What's happened to Reem?' she repeated.

'She went to Cairo and we haven't heard from her for several days. We've made various attempts to contact her, but nothing – no texts, emails, WhatsApp messages. It's not like her. She was in regular contact every couple of days, and now nothing.'

Fauzia tried to place the voice – was he a doctor? How did he know Reem? He was someone used to wielding authority, to being listened to without interruptions. Now that he had her attention, he slowed down and paused between sentences. He was making an effort to contain his anxiety.

'Disappeared? How long ago? What was she doing in Cairo?'

'She was vague. We last met at a seminar two weeks ago, and she mentioned in passing that she was going to Egypt. I didn't

4

think much of it, and we mostly talked about a paper she was preparing. I think she said something about meeting family or friends, but when I go over the conversation now, I don't know if I heard that or have added it in – but she was emphatic that she'd be back in plenty of time for a seminar yesterday, when she was due to present her paper. She was too conscientious to let me down without good reason.'

He paused. When he began again, there was a tremor in his voice and he had to clear his throat. 'Just before boarding at Heathrow, she emailed her phone number and gave the contact details for her hotel in Cairo. She said it was "just in case". I thought that was odd, but she's mature, she knows the Middle East well – she's told me something of her background, her father, and so on – and I reasoned to myself that she wouldn't run any risks.'

'Did she email or WhatsApp from Egypt?' Fauzia ignored Jack beckoning to her through the glass wall of the meeting room.

'A week ago she emailed to say that she was enjoying the sunshine and had pretty much finished the paper. She had a minor query. I replied and explained the running order for the seminar, and that we had an additional speaker. We've been trying to get the Foreign Office to help. They won't do anything – they say she is not a British national.'

'Who's "we"? And, sorry, I didn't catch your name.'

'I've got the university involved. I thought they would carry more clout. I'm Tim Blatchford, professor in international relations, and fellow at Corpus.'

Fauzia thought of when Reem had last come down from Cambridge. Reem had wrapped her thin, reddened hands around the coffee cup. She was cold – she didn't like the British winter – but she was cheerful. She hadn't said anything about an imminent trip to Egypt. Always that bright determination, and compact presence; her hijab neatly tied around her head, and her careful make-up. Reem had fired a series of questions at her about the Wilcox Smiths, Fauzia's former in-laws. Fauzia tried to answer, but Reem already knew more than she had ever done.

'I'm making headway. I've been piecing it together for over a year, and it's coming together. I found a letter – in a library in Cambridge – a letter from Phoebe Wilcox Smith. The funny thing is, she set the ball rolling,' she said thoughtfully.

'But it was her husband, Martin, who set up the business,' protested Fauzia. Her heart sank, Reem was still pursuing the subject.

'I know. I was surprised as well, but believe me, it all starts with Phoebe in Iran – she knew what she was doing. I've got some loose threads to tie up in the next few weeks, and then you'll see. I feel uncomfortable, though, digging all this up about Phoebe – I like her,' Reem went on, her forehead creased with a deep frown. 'She has been very kind to me. You know she paid for my grandparents to fly over for my graduation?'

'Yes, I'd heard something about that. It's the least she could do. Spare change,' replied Fauzia. 'I grant you that she is kind – but there is something about her which is unforgiveable.'

'That's too harsh. Last summer I really came to love her, and I know she felt the same way about me. That makes my research difficult, but . . .' She took a sip of coffee and there was a pause in the conversation as they both took stock of the implications of that phrase. 'I suppose you could say we're a bit alike.' Fauzia raised her eyebrows, surprised. 'We both know what we want and that makes us very determined.'

She had a few more questions about the family – ages, dates of marriages, children – and took notes. As they'd said goodbye, Fauzia reminded Reem that the Wilcox Smith family had always known how to keep things hidden, but Reem only laughed. 'Maybe not this time.'

Fauzia pulled her attention back to the voice on the other end of the line. Blatchford was saying, 'The Bahraini government won't help. The university asked the ambassador in London, but he said she no longer has citizenship. Her father was made stateless four years ago. It's got nothing to do with them.'

'She was definitely in Cairo? You're sure she didn't go anywhere else? Our stringer can look into it. What was her hotel address?'

Fauzia googled the hotel, and a shabby place in a back street on Gezira Island came up, popular with backpackers. A few years ago, she had stayed somewhere nearby on a work trip. She remembered the dust, the bedraggled tree on the corner where kids kicked a ball against a wall covered in graffiti, and the dull roar of traffic.

'What's your connection to her?' asked Fauzia as she searched Reem's Facebook page – the most recent posts were photos by the river Cam a fortnight before – her Instagram and Twitter.

'I'm her PhD supervisor.'

Fauzia stared down at her keyboard as she struggled with the possibility that Reem was not safe, that it might already be too late. Once the thought formed in her mind, it grew more solid, gathering a horrible, quiet certainty. Her mind fixed on the memory of Reem's thin wrists, how they protruded from the rolled-up cuffs of her big jumper as she reached up to fiddle with the single strand of small pearls she wore around her neck. Her hands were always restless as she spoke, making small adjustments to her hijab, shifting the loose gold watch round her wrist, smoothing down her jeans.

When Reem was awarded a place at Cambridge for her PhD, Fauzia had pressed her to find another area of research – something safer. 'Make a fresh start,' she had urged as they ate a quick lunch, 'and put the past behind you. Build a new life.' Reem had laughed: 'What do I want a "new life" for?' she asked, and Fauzia could think of so many reasons, she didn't know what to say. They had been in a cafe in Bloomsbury, celebrating the news that Reem's MA thesis had been awarded a distinction. Fauzia had been thrilled for her. She was on the point of finding a way in life, despite all that had happened.

'I warned her to be careful . . . but she is strong-willed,' Blatchford said haltingly. 'Perhaps too much so for her own good.'

'She had her reasons,' Fauzia replied, chewing a strand of hair. 'We'll see if we can find anything out.' She took his number.

★

'Not sure it's a story for us,' said Jack, preoccupied, as Fauzia recounted some of the detail.

'Hang on,' she urged, and pulled up a recent photo of Reem posing in her academic gown in a Cambridge cloister, smiling broadly, with her arm around a blond-haired girl. Jack looked over Fauzia's shoulder at the screen.

'She's pretty, I'll give you that,' he conceded. 'Perhaps we could put the picture up with a caption. It's a good image – risks to academic freedom and all that. See if you can find any more on her. If you knew her, there must be something you can dig up – was she saving babies or teaching street kids? Anything photogenic.'

Fauzia suppressed an inclination to roll her eyes, and nodded. She had worked here for long enough, and knew the rules: the story needed an angle or it was just another foreign student missing in a foreign country.

The conversations she needed to have were delicate, and she didn't want people eavesdropping. The desks were filling up as reporters arrived for the early shift, and Jack was back at his desk, within earshot. She picked up her mobile and what was left of her coffee; there was a stationery cupboard on the third floor where she could be alone.

She needed to make these calls – and others, to as yet unknown people in Egypt – to find Reem. She tried to imagine her sitting in a Cairo cafe, alive, sipping coffee, listening to her favourite

Arabic pop music, tapping her foot: surely, that could be possible? The image helped steady her.

As Fauzia reached the third floor, she saw a cleaner disappearing down the corridor. The cupboard was also used for cleaning equipment, and with luck she had fifteen minutes before the cleaner would be back. She opened the door and flicked on the light; metal shelves were stacked with boxes of notebooks, pens, Post-its, alongside spare desktop monitors and keyboards, cleaning fluids, and a watering can for the office plants. It smelt sharply of detergents and dust. She sat down on the floor and leaned against the wall under a narrow window. As she gulped her cold coffee, she scrolled through her contacts. She would call Kate first, and then Phoebe.

She dreaded the anxiety this news would cause Kate, the only one of the Wilcox Smith family who still mattered to her. The call to Phoebe would be awkward but less anguished; Fauzia hadn't talked to her former mother-in-law since a reception to launch Martin's biography three years ago at the House of Lords. In the crowd of politicians, business associates and family friends, they had exchanged a few words. Phoebe had been gracious, she said she was sorry that the marriage had not worked out, but her loyalty was obviously to her son, and as soon as she could she turned to another acquaintance. Since then they had once or twice been in the same place – Reem's birthday dinner last summer – but had only acknowledged each other from a distance.

Kate first.

'Fauzia, how lovely to hear from you!' Fauzia gritted her teeth at the warmth in Kate's voice. This was hard. 'I was going to invite you over for a birthday tea for – Sorry, hang on.'

Fauzia heard the babble of conversation and the words 'after school' and 'pick up'.

'Sorry, all done. I haven't got long – I need to get on the tube. What's up?'

'It's about Reem,' said Fauzia.

She heard muffled sounds, and a thump as if the phone had fallen. When Kate spoke again, she was mumbling incoherently. 'What about her? Is she OK? Where is she?' She was panicking.

'She went to Egypt and was due back two days ago for a seminar yesterday, but she didn't show up. Her PhD supervisor just called me.'

The cry was animal-like, as if something had been caught in a trap.

'Kate?'

'Not Reem,' Kate moaned. It was a horrible sound.

It inflated Fauzia's sense of foreboding and she felt a tightening in her chest. She leaned her head back against the wall's cold hardness.

'We don't know anything yet. Please don't panic,' Fauzia said, more sharply than she had intended. 'Kate, I need you to call Reem's mother.'

'I can't. She's back in prison.'

'Do you know of friends or other family we could contact? We need to find out what she was doing in Cairo. Who might know?'

Kate was crying. Too many things had gone wrong in her life, and Fauzia blamed the Wilcox Smiths for a large part of her misfortunes.

'You could call Aunt Phoebe – she likes Reem,' Kate finally said, her voice thick. 'She would know people who could help. They're close.'

'Let's hope so,' said Fauzia grimly.

'I have to go.' Kate was blowing her nose. 'I'm going to be late for work again. Fauzia, call me the minute you hear anything.'

Fauzia quickly agreed – she could hear the beeping of another call. It was Jack.

'I just spoke to the stringer, Ted, in Cairo. It doesn't look good. A couple of months ago, an academic was found dead outside Cairo. If this woman was asking difficult questions, she probably ended up the same way – did you know her well?' He sounded embarrassed and didn't wait for an answer. 'We can put it up on the site for a few hours, but until there's a body, it's not really a story. Can you get back to the desk asap? The dead in the Majorca minibus crash is now ten and counting.'

Fauzia put her phone on the floor. For a moment she listened to the air conditioning and the pipes gurgling as someone flushed a toilet. The opportunity for media coverage to help Reem was disappearing. She understood how her business worked, but Jack's brusqueness felt chilling. Reem was not British, she was some foreign student, and she didn't count.

She had to call Phoebe quickly before she went back downstairs. She listened to the distinctive ring of the old phone, picturing the big house, remembering those years of trying to win approval from her intimidating in-laws – all the weekends, dinners and theatre trips. Someone picked up the phone and, after a pause, Phoebe answered, hesitant at first when she heard Fauzia's voice, but then more at ease; she was used to negotiating difficult relationships.

'Such a dear thing. What could have happened? I'm sure she will turn up – perhaps she missed her flight.'

Phoebe's voice didn't waver. Her world, even after seventy-six years, had proved so predictable that she had no reason to panic as Kate had done, thought Fauzia, and she felt a rush of irritation at the Wilcox Smith complacency: their unshakeable belief that the world was well organized and safe; their wilful refusal to acknowledge its arbitrary, underlying violence. It brought out a savage desire to puncture Phoebe's complacency.

'Our stringer thinks she could be dead. Egypt doesn't much like academic researchers who ask tricky questions,' she said bluntly.

'A little early to jump to that conclusion,' retorted Phoebe. 'I heard from Reem only a few days ago. She was in Cairo and told me she had met by chance an old friend of Martin's. Lebanese, I think. Anyway, she was very cheerful, asking if I remembered anything about him. It seems he had visited Lodsbourne for a shooting party. He told her he admired our collection of Iranian miniatures. She was having a very interesting time, she said – she adores Cairo, you know. She promised to come down next week and tell me all about it. Very sweetly, she had even bought a box of my favourite dates.'

That call to Phoebe must have been just before she disappeared, Fauzia thought, as she caught the echo of Phoebe's voice in the high-ceilinged hall with its stone-flagged floor. She remembered the old-fashioned cream phone on the polished hall table.

'Did she say anything about why she was in Cairo? Did she mention anyone else she had seen? This friend of Martin's – do you know his name?'

'Goodness – so many questions. I think she said something about doing research in Cairo, but nothing more. She said she had seen some friends she studied with in London for supper.' Phoebe's voice had a slight edge of annoyance. 'I didn't catch any names, Fauzia. I can't offer anything useful.'

While Phoebe explained how she was planning to take Reem out for lunch when she visited, Fauzia's mind travelled up the Lodsbourne stairs, with the Iranian miniatures on the walls, to the first-floor landing, and then to the spare room ready for Reem's visit: the double bed under its old-fashioned quilt, the landscape painting over the fireplace, and the armchair by the window looking over the lawns to the park, and the downs beyond. She imagined how Reem would lay out her mat in the direction of Mecca for prayers. She snapped herself out of this reverie, and focused her gaze on the shelf in front of her, noticing that someone had hidden a packet of cigarettes behind some boxes. Phoebe was still speaking.

'I'm sure she'll call in the next couple of days to say she is back, safe and sound. You will let me know as soon as you hear from her, won't you, Fauzia?' After promises that she would, Phoebe rang off; she probably needed to talk to the gardener, thought Fauzia bitterly.

She stood up and ran a hand through her hair, before tying it with a band. She pulled out a pocket mirror and checked her mascara for smudging. Reem – of all people – would have known how high a price the truth cost. Fauzia was angry with her: she was too young and too clever to have lost the chance of a life.

She texted Jack: 'Coming. Nothing yet.'

Back at her desk, she turned her attention to the minibus crash. A relative was on the phone from Southend, complaining that the authorities were giving little information. While she was on the landline, her phone blinked – Kate was calling, and Fauzia extricated herself to answer.

'I blame myself. It's my fault . . .' Kate whispered hoarsely.

She must be at work, in the toilets, because the sound of rushing water was audible in the background.

'Kate, nothing has happened yet. Go back to your desk and concentrate on your job – you can't lose this one. I'll call when I have more news,' Fauzia said with quiet insistence, dreading Jack or anyone else overhearing. 'And, Kate, it's not your fault.' She hesitated, and then added emphatically, 'Plenty of others are to blame. Even Phoebe.'

Kate had no idea – she was the least of it, thought Fauzia. Kate could claim innocence, whereas she could not. And neither could Phoebe, despite having built a long life around the pretence of it. Perhaps she no longer knew what innocence really was; only the ersatz version of a determined refusal to know, an ability to shift her attention elsewhere – to her precious herd of cows, for example. For all her charm, Phoebe was capable of ruthlessness, Fauzia reflected.

★

Phoebe replaced the receiver. It was early – she needed breakfast. These days she found it harder to get up in the mornings, and sometimes she even allowed herself to sleep in until nine. Once, that would have been so unlikely, but the years were beginning to catch up with her. She had prided herself on her capacity to outrun her age, but she could see that in a short while that fiction would fade. She pulled her cardigan around her more tightly; the hall was always draughty. At times like this, she missed her dead husband keenly. Martin had served as an absorbing distraction throughout their long marriage: he'd had so many complex needs for her to manage.

She looked through the glass of the hall door down the gravel drive, and remembered the first time Reem visited. Most visitors made comments about the house, the gardens or the collections, but nothing overawed this small young woman. She had sat in the dining room at the family lunch as if such occasions were a matter of course in her life. Phoebe had deeply admired her sangfroid.

She gazed at the cherry trees which would be in bloom in a few weeks. Fauzia's call had left her uneasy; the confidence she had expressed on the phone came from an ingrained habit of maintaining the regular rhythm of life, an effort which had lasted decades, with only the occasional interruption. Now, though, she was tired of that effort and the continual small self-deceptions it entailed. Poor Reem and her unlucky family, Phoebe thought, as she made her way to the kitchen for breakfast.

TEHRAN
1969–70

2

Phoebe's taxi had to weave through the heavy traffic with its orchestra of irate car horns. The city woke early, and immediately a cacophony erupted as millions of people in the narrow streets and densely packed tenement blocks began a new day. She saw the crowd outside the consulate section of the embassy as soon as they turned the corner. She hadn't imagined so many would be here waiting for the doors to open. Joining them, she looked around at the young students and well-dressed middle-aged couples, and saw the anxiety in their faces. Some people had good reason to leave Tehran and get to the UK: young men keen to avoid national service, and those who had fallen foul of the Shah's regime and his secret police, the SAVAK. Street hawkers had spotted a business opportunity and were selling small glasses of mint tea, and offering to fetch fresh coffee. It was already hot, and Phoebe leaned against the high wall to catch a pocket of shade cast by a large tree that stood in the embassy's magnificent gardens. She had visited once and had marvelled at the calm, the perfectly clipped lawns and rose beds.

In front of her, people were jostling to be head of the queue. Suddenly there was a surge, and Phoebe found herself carried into the building as the double doors were opened. Officials were shouting in Farsi for people to get into line.

'British nationals this way, love,' said a burly British man, tapping Phoebe's shoulder, his sleeves rolled up already to cope with the hot day's work. He pointed to a roped-off area where a much smaller queue stood in an orderly line. Only three others ahead of her – she should be done by ten if the appointment was quick, so she wouldn't be too late for work. Surely it was just a bit of bureaucracy which the embassy would be able to sort out. She'd applied for a visa extension from the Iranian ministry two months ago, and had heard nothing. On a previous occasion, it had come back within a fortnight. Despite her employment at the royal court, all her efforts to chase the application had been fruit-less; telephones rang unanswered, and when she'd tried to speak to someone in person, the ministry was chaotic, with corridors full of frustrated people and overwhelmed, exasperated officials. The deadline for her visa was looming, and she had been warned of the problems if you overstayed. The tangled bureaucracy could take months to resolve.

The man taking details at the desk was British with a Birmingham accent which he had tried, and failed, to iron out. After Phoebe explained herself and handed over her paperwork, he sighed heavily and said he needed to check with a more senior official. He returned, looking concerned, and showed her into a private room. They would need to go over a few details with her, he said, adding, in a bid to reassure, 'It's routine procedure in these circumstances.' After an anxious wait of fifteen and half minutes – Phoebe was watching the hands of both the clock on the wall and her watch – a man arrived. Imposing and brisk, he introduced himself as Martin Wilcox Smith.

'I apologize for keeping you waiting, Miss Crowley. I'm the deputy ambassador here. I believe you may have attended one of the embassy receptions – I recognized your name, but we have not had the pleasure of meeting.'

'Is there anything wrong?' asked Phoebe, alarmed by his formality and seniority. A fan creaked overhead and notices pinned to the board rustled softly in rhythm. She was glad that, for once, she had followed her mother's advice: always dress your best for officials. She straightened the skirt of her pale-blue linen suit.

'We assume not,' he replied smoothly. 'I looked over the copy of your application, and I wanted to offer a word of advice, which might help with the visa.'

He coughed and straightened his tie, and she noticed he didn't look at her directly.

'I will be blunt: I understand you have a friendship with a talented young architect of the name Asil Farahmand?'

Phoebe stared at him, astonished.

'This is a beautiful – but difficult – country, Miss Crowley,' he continued when she did not reply. 'In order to help our citizens, we sometimes use the information that comes our way,' he added delicately.

'I have no idea what that means,' said Phoebe, thrown by the direction of the conversation.

'You've been here a year, I think. Perhaps there are some aspects of this country you have yet to understand.' Phoebe bristled at the patronizing tone. 'We have the highest regard for Mr Farahmand – he won a prestigious scholarship to study architecture in London, as no doubt you are well aware – but it has come to our notice that he has had a brush with the authorities in the past over a trivial matter. It seems he is under surveillance, and perhaps some of the company he has been keeping has been –'

'I don't see what this has to do with me or my visa,' interrupted Phoebe. 'Can we just sort out my affairs, and leave Asil out of it.'

Wilcox Smith's tone hardened. 'I'm afraid not. I gather the Iranian authorities are aware that you are spending considerable time with this young man and travelling outside Tehran in his company. I don't pretend to know the cause of their concern, but in the light of this, our advice is to suspend your friendship until your visa extension is granted – with luck in a few weeks. You are then free to ignore any further advice, although clearly this –' he hesitated – 'this association puts your presence in this country in some jeopardy.'

Phoebe stared at his crisp Italian suit and silk tie, his polished brogues and neatly trimmed hair. 'And if I don't take your advice?'

He sighed heavily. 'The matter is out of our control. At worst, they could terminate your visa, and if so, there would be nothing we could do.'

She began discreetly to bite her thumbnail – she couldn't help herself – as she tried to think through what he was saying – and not saying.

'Is Asil in danger?'

Wilcox Smith adjusted his collar. 'Possibly. It's always hard to tell how the authorities work. This can be a dangerous country. I would advise you not to speak to him – no contact, with immediate effect. I'm sorry, Miss Crowley. I understand you came to Tehran alone?'

Phoebe looked at him and this time he met her eyes, and, to her consternation, she could see genuine concern.

As she left the embassy, she resolved with a heavy heart to follow Wilcox Smith's advice. She felt guilty, as if she were somehow abandoning Asil, but she sent a message via his colleague, Monir, to explain. By way of response, a bunch of red roses was delivered to her flat with a card: 'I am waiting. A.' She yearned for their intoxicating love affair to resume – she missed his body beside her at night, their absorbing conversations, his brilliant, eclectic pattern of thought. On her bedside table sat his favourite cigarettes, which he'd left after their last night together, and a book he had been reading – Frantz Fanon's *The Wretched of the Earth*. They were waiting for his return.

★

Phoebe stood at the open window, her silk dressing gown loosely tied at her waist, a cigarette in her hand, staring at the point where the distant brown mountains beyond the city met the deep blue sky. She had fallen back into a deep sleep after the muezzin's call to prayer; she was at the lake with Asil, the surface of the water shivering in the breeze, the poplar trees rustling.

She slipped into the soft leather slippers that Asil had bought her in the bazaar – he had been a tough negotiator – and stepped out on to the balcony. She leaned over the wrought-iron railing to take a gulp of the city's hot breath, that distinctive mix of exhaust fumes and odorous drains, overlaid with the spices of their neighbours' fragrant cooking. Neither she nor Chantal cooked anything more complicated than scrambled eggs.

Chantal put her head around the door. 'Ça va, ma chérie? Coffee?'

Phoebe nodded and flicked her ash over the balcony, watching stallholders opening up for business in the busy street below. Tehran was sucking people in from the villages and mountains. Entangled in this maelstrom, the bewildered peasants scrabbled for purchase: a patch of street to sleep on, a few biros to sell at the crossroads, a packet of cigarettes to hawk singly around the busy cafes and restaurants. In time, they might graduate to a shack in the shanty towns on the outskirts of the city, which she passed when heading out for the weekend. From the car she caught glimpses of harsh lives: women carrying water from a standpipe, or balancing a child on their hip. When she went out for dinner, Phoebe tipped the small boys who sold her a cigarette, and Asil bought her the single red roses, even when he had little money to spare. Iranian roses were the best in the world, he boasted, and she agreed, their scent musky and sweet, their petals the texture of velvet.

A woman hanging out laundry on the rooftop across the street was staring at her and Phoebe tied her short dressing gown more closely, recalling her mother's disapproval. The shopping trip with her mother before she'd left London had been from another life. Mrs Crowley had come up from Reading specially, but was bewildered by the shops Phoebe insisted on visiting and the clothes she chose to try on.

'It's too short,' her mother had commented on the dressing gown, sitting in an armchair in the changing room. 'You're going to Iran, remember.'

'Tehran is a modern cosmopolitan city – you're out of date. It's not the forties; you don't have to wear pearls and floral-print cotton dresses any more. We're not running an empire – all that's over,' retorted Phoebe.

Her mother watched, appalled, as Phoebe reappeared in a jumpsuit and assessed her image in the mirror: it emphasized her waist and hips before flaring into wide trouser legs, the fabric a bold pattern of brown and gold. A prominent zip ran from pubic bone to sternum.

'It's never over; you should know that, you're British,' replied Mrs Crowley. 'You need a dress for cocktail parties. I can't think when you can wear –' she stopped, not knowing what to call the garment – 'that kind of thing.'

Phoebe was used to the tight pucker of disapproval – her mother had never been able, or willing, to hide her disappointment with her wayward daughter. She peeled off the jumpsuit and tossed it on the 'definite' pile. Next had been a black velvet bikini with ties at the hips and a halter neck.

'Oh, really –' Mrs Crowley was shocked – 'where would you be able to wear that? And look at the price! For a few scraps of fabric and some string.'

Phoebe added a cocktail dress to placate her mother.

Now, on the balcony in Tehran, she involuntarily shivered: no matter how 'difficult' – Wilcox Smith's word – some things were in this strange, beautiful country, she had no desire to go back to her life of damp bedsits and a patronizing boss in the Mayfair art gallery, let alone the petty strictures of suburban Reading.

'Breakfast,' called Chantal from the kitchen. She had been to buy croissants from the French bakery around the corner. The two women perched on stools at the small table in the sunlight to sip coffee, and eat the pastries.

'You should come with me,' mumbled Chantal through a mouthful of croissant. 'It will distract you from your lost love. It's not good to – what is the funny word you English use? Mope?'

They had been invited to a reception at the embassy that evening. Phoebe spread her croissant with a large helping of the cherry jam their maid had brought back from a visit to her family in the mountains. Chantal meant well, but Phoebe flinched at the words she used – her love was not lost: Asil understood, he wouldn't hold it against her, and once her visa came through, they would pick up where they had left off.

'I'll come – I might get a chance to ask one of the embassy people if they know anything about my visa,' said Phoebe.

Chantal lit a cigarette and exhaled slowly, mouthing smoke rings.

Later that day, the two young women dressed with particular care, sharing make-up, helping pin each other's hair up and swapping clothes. These receptions were useful for making contacts. Newcomers were pouring into town – Europeans and Americans, known as *khareji*, brought in to work on the Shah's ambitious projects for power stations, railway lines, fertilizer and cement factories. Chantal and Phoebe would listen politely to the engineers and oil executives, but found the designers, architects, curators, artists and musicians working for the Shahbanou – the empress – more interesting. Both of them worked in a design consultancy under contract to the Shahbanou's office, but they couldn't keep abreast of her plans, each more grandiose than the one before – a museum of contemporary art to rival any in the West, an Iranian equivalent of England's National Trust, a contemporary arts festival in Shiraz. They knew she had critics, but they were fascinated by her new notion of cultural diplomacy and her ambition to make Iran the meeting point between East and West. Phoebe loved her taste for the avant-garde. The Tehran they knew was intoxicating: the collision of cultures, the furious money-making and the attempt to reinvent a country unfolding all around them.

At the crowded reception, Martin Wilcox Smith nodded at Phoebe when their eyes momentarily met – he did remember her at least – but he was busy, moving from group to group, skilfully working the room: a word here, a handshake there. Despite two attempts, she failed to catch his attention. She fell into conversation with two dancers recently arrived from Paris, but kept an eye on Wilcox Smith. No one could describe him as conventionally good-looking: heavy eyebrows, the nose large and mouth wide, but the irregular features fitted well together. His hair was beginning to grey. Beneath the politeness, she detected a controlled intensity which was faintly intriguing, but he was too old – already middle-aged. At his side was his wife, elegant in Yves Saint Laurent. She came over and greeted Phoebe – they had not met before, but Phoebe had helped her to order furnishing fabric from London; now she repeated her thanks and they exchanged a few words on an upcoming exhibition of Iranian textiles. Phoebe wasn't important enough to warrant anything longer, and rather than being offended, she admired the woman's efficiency. Towards the end of the party, to Phoebe's surprise, Lavinia Wilcox Smith returned.

'We wondered if you might like to use the pool one Saturday morning – I'm usually out with the children at that time. I expect you would appreciate a swim?' Her hand briefly touched Phoebe's arm before she turned to say goodbye to the German ambassador and his wife.

Phoebe relayed news of the invitation to Chantal while they stood in the hall waiting for their cab to arrive at the gate. The embassy pool and gardens were an oasis of green in the city, and invitations were much sought-after amongst expatriates.

'But why would she ask me?' Phoebe wondered. It made her nervous.

'I'm glad to see you are bearing up, Phoebe. I do hope it hasn't been too challenging a time?' Martin Wilcox Smith had materialized beside the two young women, but before Phoebe had a chance to reply, he moved back to a group of American oil executives.

Guffaws of laughter filled the night air as Phoebe and Chantal walked down the drive. When Phoebe glanced back, she was puzzled to see Wilcox Smith standing in the light of the doorway, watching them with a distracted half-smile; he then turned, and putting a hand on his wife's back, ushered her into the house.

The cab wove through the heavy traffic to take them to a party in Shemiran. Chantal's strategy to take Phoebe's mind off Asil was to offer distraction, and she had promised dancing to new LPs recently arrived from New York: the Rolling Stones, James Brown, and Dionne Warwick.

'I may take her up on it,' said Phoebe, thinking of the embassy pool. 'But why be kind to *me*?'

★

After another two weeks, the brown envelope with the visa extension finally came through. Chantal poured them both Martinis to celebrate, but Phoebe wouldn't drink hers until she had called Asil. She ran down the stairs to the entrance of their apartment block, to the old-fashioned telephone hung on the wall. He was probably still at his office, finishing off drawings. She was so excited at the thought of hearing his voice that her hands were trembling as she dialled, her bare feet feeling the cool of the worn floor tiles. But the voice which answered was not Asil's. Thinking she might have dialled the wrong number, she rang off and tried again. This time the voice was impatient.

'Can I speak to Monir?' she asked, and heard the phone being handed over.

'Phoebe, I didn't want to call, I've been waiting to hear from you and to hear you have your visa. I'm so sorry –' the voice was muffled, as if Monir might be crying – 'Asil was arrested last week. He is in detention. We are all so –'

'What? How? Why?' Phoebe's voice was shrill with alarm.

'You must have heard about the protests last week – we think he was just curious to see what was going on, but he got mixed up in the melee. The police used tear gas and arrested dozens of people. I've been trying to help his father find out where they took him and whether he is all right. Some of the protestors were very badly beaten. We've heard nothing –'

'But someone must know where he is,' insisted Phoebe.

'It doesn't work like that here in Tehran,' said Monir flatly. 'Phoebe, it's best if you stay out of this – they could withdraw your visa. We will try and find him, and when we do, I'll call you.'

Phoebe climbed slowly back up the stairs she had run down only a few moments before, her heart so light and full of excitement. Now she felt nauseous and shaky, as if she had been punched. She sat down in the kitchen and stared at the Martini.

That evening, she and Chantal discussed the details, looking for clues: Asil wasn't involved in politics, insisted Phoebe, his passion was for architecture, for the work of Louis Kahn and Frank Lloyd Wright. Chantal didn't need to point out that perhaps he had friends who were involved in the protests; they both knew that could be enough for the SAVAK.

'He might have been released and left the country,' suggested Chantal, clutching at hope.

'He wouldn't do that without getting a message through to me,' Phoebe snapped. A tense silence sat between them for a moment. Phoebe apologized and Chantal put an arm around her shoulders. There were times she hated this country, with its warp thread of violence. She and Asil had only known each other for six weeks or so, and then nothing. Only a few reminders of their intense, short love: some dried roses, his precious new Bob Dylan LP, and a napkin covered with scrawled sketches of the hospital he wanted to build in Tehran. She could still see how the corners of his eyes crinkled when he laughed, how his thick black hair curled, how he gesticulated with his hands when he was trying to explain an important point, but they hadn't had a camera, nor imagined they had pressing need of one. She wished she had a photo.

After several days of waiting by the phone, Phoebe decided she had to do something herself.

'I'm going to take up that invitation to use the embassy pool tomorrow,' Phoebe told Chantal. 'The deputy ambassador might be able to do something. The way they treated me at the reception – that man and his wife – it was as if they already knew how things could turn out. The wife looked at me with *pity*.'

★

Phoebe's taxi drew up to the gates of the British embassy on Saturday morning. Her name was on the list of the day's visitors, and the keeper mentioned in passing that Mrs Wilcox Smith and the children were out. She wondered where Mr Wilcox Smith was.

Inside the embassy's high walls, Tehran's noise dulled into the background, it was another world: sprinklers were watering the green lawns under the shade of spreading trees, a gardener was at work on the rose beds, weeding and deadheading. The sun's heat would arrive as the morning wore on, but it would be filtered through the leaves, and softened by the damp lawns. As Phoebe made her way down the drive she had a sense that people were watching her, but she couldn't tell who or from where – the gardener? The maid? At the front door she looked around, uncertain where to go next, until a butler appeared and, without a word, led her round the back of the building to where a pool lined with dark blue mosaic shimmered in the shade. He pointed to the changing room and a pile of towels beside a lounger, and left. She changed into her bikini.

With any luck, Wilcox Smith would emerge when he heard her swimming. She dived into the water and did several lengths of noisy crawl. Then she lay back, floating in the fierce heat. She had the place to herself but for the occasional swallow swooping down to sip the water. Sometimes she heard footsteps – the kitchens must be nearby – and the gardener's snipping from behind a hedge. She had never imagined that this measure of calm was possible in the middle of this sweaty, dusty city.

The embassy was so quiet she began to imagine tiptoeing down corridors, past empty offices in search of Wilcox Smith. She got distracted imagining their family sitting room, even Lavinia's wardrobe, and Martin's bedside reading; in their very English way, they were too perfect to be true. Just once, she thought she might have glimpsed him through one of the windows.

She got out and lay and read for a while, a new novel, *The French Lieutenant's Woman*, sent by a concerned friend in London with an annoying note saying that Phoebe sounded depressed and should get some Valium. But she couldn't concentrate, and daydreams of Asil kept re-emerging in vivid detail: swimming in the lake in the Alborz mountains; then, when it was dark and the stars began to come out, they rolled out mats and lay on their backs identifying the constellations and describing their dreams of a grand future. She shook herself; those moments seemed a long time ago.

She heard a car engine, the slamming of car doors, and a male voice – perhaps Martin's? She remembered the edge of sympathy in that odd expression, 'bearing up', at the reception. She sat up, grabbed a towel and got dressed in the changing room. She checked her make-up in the mirror and ran a comb through her damp hair. She was going to look for him.

She went up the steps to the main entrance. No one was in the echoing hallway, but somewhere in the distance she heard a typewriter, and she headed in that direction. She passed a dining room and a plaque on the wall marking Winston Churchill's sixty-ninth birthday dinner. Despite her anxiety, she was taken aback: what was her mother's hero doing celebrating his birthday in Tehran in 1943? Further on she glimpsed a drawing room and a large vase of fresh flowers. She was now so far from the entrance, she was clearly trespassing, and she needed to find someone, a butler or a secretary. She opened a door but it was an empty office, she knocked on another and discovered a ladies' powder room.

'Can I help?'

Phoebe spun on her heel at the crisp voice. It was a woman of about her own age, English, probably Cheltenham Ladies' College: her voice could cut cake. Phoebe blushed but she braced herself.

'Martin Wilcox Smith is expecting me,' she lied.

The woman raised her perfectly plucked eyebrows.

'Well, that's odd, because he told me he had no appointments in the diary for this morning.' She surveyed Phoebe's acid-lemon minidress and sandals. 'Perhaps he forgot,' she added sceptically. She clearly thought Phoebe was more appropriately dressed for the beach than for an appointment with the deputy ambassador, but she took her back to the hall to wait, and reappeared a few minutes later with Wilcox Smith.

'It's Miss Crowley, isn't it? I hope you enjoyed your swim – my wife mentioned she had invited you.' Dismissing his secretary for the weekend, he led the way to a terrace in the shade.

'Your visa extension came through, I believe? Good. So, how can I help?'

'It's about Asil Farahmand. He got mixed up in the protests a couple of weeks ago and has been arrested. It's a mistake – he's not involved in politics, but his family have heard nothing. You mentioned that you got "information" when we spoke last, and I wanted to ask if you had heard anything.'

Wilcox Smith shook his head, and poured the lemonade that a servant brought on a tray. 'Do you have an address for his parents?'

'No. He didn't live with them, and he never told me his address. We met at parties, cafes, my flat.'

'It's unusual for the embassy to inquire about Persian nationals, but we have our channels – and I'd like to know. I met him a couple of times and he was obviously a very intelligent, talented young man.'

Phoebe could see his discomfort. She recognized the cough, the fiddling with his tie, as nervous tics. He looked away across the lawn to the rose bed.

'I don't want to worry you, Miss Crowley, but in this country, people are arrested and it's hard to track their whereabouts. You must know by now the more challenging aspects of this regime. With any luck, Mr Farahmand got out, was clever enough to go underground, and will manage to leave the country – let's hope tomorrow you get a postcard from Turkey – but none of us can be complacent. The wrong tip-off, a chance meeting, it can be as little as that.' He put his hands together as if in prayer, the fore-fingers resting lightly on his bottom lip. 'For now, we must be hopeful – I'll look into it.'

'Thank you,' said Phoebe, surprised. 'I hoped you might have heard something, but I didn't expect you to help.' She couldn't quite keep the tremor out of her voice. She bit her thumbnail again, and stopped herself, clenching her fist at her side; the nail varnish she had used to curb the habit tasted bitter.

Wilcox Smith stood up, and Phoebe took the cue. He walked her to the gate.

'Strictly speaking, it's not part of my job – but I take a bigger view: Asil Farahmand is the type of young man this country needs, and I don't want to see that talent wasted – he's benefited from a first-class education at the British taxpayer's expense for that purpose. When I hear, I'll be in touch – I should have your telephone number.' He took a notebook out of his jacket pocket and jotted it down.

'Leave it with me.' He reached out to shake her hand. Warm and dry. Comforting.

*

Phoebe rang the office to say she was ill. She was good at acting – the croaky voice, the hacking cough – and she knew the office could manage without her for a few days. There were others who could look through the art gallery catalogues and call dealers – when the international lines were working – to inquire after works by Jackson Pollock, Andy Warhol and Robert Rauschen-berg on the Shahbanou's long shopping list. She was holding on to Wilcox Smith's words and waiting for that postcard. She imagined Asil on the bus to Istanbul. After it came, she would go back to her job, or, if possible, book her flight immediately, borrow the money if necessary. Meanwhile she lay on her bed, sticky in the heat, and watched the bars of sunlight from the cracks in the shutters move across the floor, and listened to Bob Dylan's *Nashville Skyline* over and over, wearing the vinyl at their favourite track, 'The Girl from the North Country'.

Chantal cooked scrambled eggs or got food in, and in the evenings they drank cheap Russian vodka sitting on the balcony to catch the slight stir of cooler air. Phoebe talked obsessively of Asil, and Chantal, generously, patiently, listened, even when she had heard it all several times before.

*

The evening she first met Asil, the cafe had been crowded and Phoebe edged through the throng to get to the table where Chantal was seated with friends. She had been held late at work after a last-minute summons from the palace to meet with the Shahbanou's head of wardrobe. Above the jazz music and the hubbub of animated voices, Ehsan greeted Phoebe warmly and introduced his friend Monir and her colleague Asil. They moved up to make space. Phoebe assumed they were together, and turned to greet Chantal with a swift kiss on both cheeks. Ehsan was ordering fresh Martinis. The air was thick with cigarette smoke.

'Ma chérie! You look boiled. What did she do to you to keep you at the palace this long?'

Phoebe laughed, but felt her cheeks redden as faces around the table looked at her, curious.

'Why were you at the palace?' asked Sandy, a young American who worked for an oil company.

'Ah!' exclaimed Chantal, smiling broadly. 'Shall we tell all, Phoebe?' Her eyes were sparkling.

'Shsh, Chantal,' said Phoebe, laughing. 'I work on her wardrobe, that's all.'

'It's the party everyone wants to know about, not the dresses! Thousands of bottles of champagne, Maxim's to cater, I'm told, and the Queen of England heading the guest list.'

'I'm not supposed to talk about it but – listen, they want trees now – a forest planted around the Persepolis ruins, and hundreds of songbirds,' giggled Phoebe.

'The expats should get out now – backing the Shah will cost them, as the Americans and British will discover,' said a friend of Ehsan's, and he lowered his voice, 'The clever ones are heading to the Gulf or Hong Kong.'

Sandy remonstrated, and their argument became heated. Asil turned to Phoebe.

'Are you serious about the forest?'

Phoebe nodded, sipping her Martini. 'Parades, a tented city, a new airport in Shiraz. In 1971, to mark 2,500 years since Cyrus.'

'And what's your job?'

'Amongst other things, I'm researching traditional Iranian embroidery to send to Paris for the Shahbanou's outfits; sourcing some of the furniture for the tents, which have been specially designed in France. I gather that there weren't good enough hotels for the guests – every head of state in the world is to be invited.'

Asil half-closed his eyes in irritation. 'This kind of charade costs a fortune. A forest round Persepolis is pure fantasy – it's a desert.'

'It's not fantasy – it's really going to happen,' Phoebe insisted. 'The trees are being flown in, ready grown from the Netherlands or somewhere.'

Asil shook his head in disbelief.

'So how did you get to be advising the Shahbanou on Iranian embroidery?' He laughed, but his tone was gentle. Phoebe looked at him: the thick eyelashes, wide mouth, endearingly crooked front teeth, and the large dark eyes, kind, but mischievous.

'I was an assistant in a gallery off Bond Street. The Shahbanou was a regular customer, buying for her collection – we specialized in contemporary American art. They told me she liked my dress sense, and I was offered a job. I have an art-history degree, worked at Biba, spoke French, and so on. They paid the air fare. I'd only ever been abroad once before, on a French exchange trip.' She laughed. 'I'm afraid I had to look up Iran on a map – I had no idea where it was.'

Asil gave a deep, throaty chuckle, both sceptical and affectionate.

'Whisked from rainy grey London to Tehran on the whim of an empress! How do you like Iran?'

'Very much. The Shahbanou is buying my favourite expression-ists, and is planning extraordinary acquisitions – Gauguin, Monet, Pissarro, Degas. I'm part of a team building one of the greatest modern art galleries in the world. And she is such a global cultural icon – her sense of style is magnificent, on a par with Jackie Kennedy and Princess Grace.'

'But what about Iran?' he teased.

'I think she is dragging the country out of the Middle Ages. She's doing so much for girls' education, getting rid of the ghastly chador, proper healthcare. Progress here really means something – all those irrigation projects and fertilizing the desert –'

'It sounds as if you have been listening to too much court propaganda,' he said abruptly. 'Have you been outside of Tehran much?'

'Weekend trips.' He was irritating her.

'Come to my family's village. Many of the people in this country struggle to put the next meal on the table, but their lives are full of beauty. To understand my country, you must come with me to Taleqan.' He was in earnest, fixing his eyes on her.

'Me? But we have only just met –'

'What about this Saturday? We need a chaperone, or my cousin Fatemah will disapprove.' He ignored Phoebe's protests and turned to Monir on his other side. 'Monir, love, will you come with us to Taleqan this weekend?'

Monir, in mid-conversation, broke off long enough to say, 'For you, Asil, anything.'

He turned back to Phoebe with a broad grin. 'Monir is my colleague at the architectural practice – you will be safe with her. Everything is fixed. We'll hire a driver and pick you up.'

Phoebe couldn't help laughing. 'Do you make a habit of kidnapping *khareji* and taking them off to the mountains? Am I one in a long line?'

'I have never done such a thing before – I have certainly *never* taken a *khareji* to my village. And I want you to believe something, Phoebe –' he put his hand on his heart, suddenly grave – 'I am never going to do it again.'

Phoebe was startled.

'You want to know why? Because I am never going to meet anyone like you again. I know this already, in my bones,' he added slowly, smiling.

Phoebe laughed, bewildered by his switches from irritation to intensity to humour. She could feel his eyes taking her in – her thick long hair, her pale skin and grey eyes with their lashes thick with mascara. She met his steady gaze.

'It is not just your beauty: I see your spirit, and I know we will understand each other. We are adventurers.'

For the rest of the evening, they were buried in deep conversation, punctuated by laughter, sparring about meanings of progress, corruption, and the artistic significance of Rauschenberg and Pollock. Friends melted away, and they barely acknowledged their departures. When they finally looked up, they were the last in the bar, and the staff were waiting for them to leave.

*

That Saturday, as promised, Asil and Monir picked up Phoebe in a beaten-up Mercedes, and by 7 a.m. they had left the outskirts of Tehran and were heading up into the mountains north of the city, the car juddering as Samyar, the plump driver, shifted to second gear to negotiate the steep roads. Asil sat in the front and fell into conversation in Farsi with Samyar, and Phoebe only caught the occasional word. They appeared to be distantly related. After a few friendly questions, Monir fell asleep, leaving Phoebe to gaze out of the window, enjoying the cooler air of the forest pouring through the windows, though she flinched when the hairpin bends brought them perilously close to oncoming vehicles – the brightly coloured trucks driving at hectic speed and the heavily laden buses. Tall pine trees on the steep hillsides cast deep shade, and Phoebe caught flashes of water glittering in streams beside the road. Occasionally they passed villages where buildings crouched behind high mud walls between stands of trees. Children ran out of the compounds to stand at the roadside, waving and calling for a few coins.

By a gap in the trees they pulled over, and when Samyar turned off the engine, the distant rushing of a river could be heard in the stillness. They got out of the car to stretch their legs and enjoy the view. Asil was full of solicitude; did she need to eat? Was she comfortable?

She took a deep breath of the quiet. Since their Martini-fuelled conversation, she had been greeted each morning with a single rose, hand-delivered by a street boy. At work, Phoebe had found her mind wandering from the catalogues to Asil, apprehensive that when they met again, they would not be able to match the first evening's exhilaration. She looked over at him, and saw how the slight creases around his mouth had eased. He was watching her intently.

'My mother's family is from Taleqan and in the holidays we returned to my grandmother,' he explained, leaning on the bonnet of the car, as Monir unpacked the tea, fruit and biscuits she had brought for their journey. 'When I was very young, I spent several months there while my mother was working as a nurse. I remember the blossom of almond trees in spring and the irrigation channels which trickle through the vegetable gardens. They grow the best perfumed rice in Iran.'

Monir interjected, laughing, 'There's a competition for that title.'

'I helped herd the sheep and goats on the open pastures. At night, us boys slept on kilims spread on the roof under the stars, while in winter we slept on the *korsi* – it's a single brick platform covered with quilts, heated from below by charcoal.'

When they arrived at Fatemah's village, the car slowed down to navigate the pitted track and children ran alongside them, staring through the windows at the city strangers. Men who had been sitting in the shade came to greet Asil and offered directions on where to park, while dogs barked and chickens ran close to the car's wheels. They were welcomed into the family compound and ushered with great ceremony to a stone terrace, where a low divan was sheltered by an old vine. Dense bunches of small green grapes hung down amongst the foliage, and the divan's richly coloured kilims glowed against the soft ochres of the mud wall. On the table before them, plates arrived, heaped with bitter dark olives, crumbled cheese, warm flatbread and hot mint tea.

The men of the village clustered round to talk with Asil, and Phoebe was content to watch and listen. Occasionally he broke off to explain what they were discussing: water, crops, family members who had gone to Tehran for work, or further afield to the oil refineries on the Gulf coast. Monir took her into the house to meet the women who were preparing their food; they touched Phoebe's long reddish fair hair with wonder, and stroked her arm, exclaiming at her pale skin, their faces wreathed in smiles, breaking into frequent laughter – Monir explained they were enquiring about possible husbands and babies. Someone handed Phoebe a plump ten-month-old baby and he reached up to grab a fistful of her hair, chuckling with delight at his audience of adoring women.

Back on the terrace, they were brought plates of kebab and rice. Asil was profuse with thanks to the women, offering congratulations to one on her betrothal, to another on her imminent delivery. Small children gathered at the door, too shy to come closer, but Monir brought out a bag of trinkets, and they shrieked with delight over the coloured pens, whistles and beads. After the kebabs came baklava, peaches and coffee. Only after they had eaten handsome portions did their hosts agree that Asil could take Phoebe and Monir through the fields and down to the river.

'I studied for six years in London, and loved it – the bars of Soho and those squares in Bloomsbury – but I couldn't stay and leave all this. It was important you understood that from the start,' Asil said when they were sitting beside the river, and Monir had tactfully wandered further down the bank. 'I was offered jobs in London, but I had to come back. This is where I belong. One day, I will build my own house here. I have already found the site, up on the hill in the forest. My version of Frank Lloyd Wright.'

'Why me, why do I need to understand?' asked Phoebe, her heart beating with excitement at his reference to 'the start'.

He reached over and ran his hand through her hair. 'Can't you feel it too?' he whispered softly, and bent over to kiss her. 'Here –' he put his finger on her lip. 'And here –' he put his finger on the inside of her wrist, where the green-blue veins were visible through her white skin.

Phoebe put her hands on either side of his face, feeling the slight roughness of his cheeks, and kissed him.

'I daren't believe it,' she murmured, taking his hand and holding it tight.

3

A call came unexpectedly late one evening, their landlord shouting up the staircase. Phoebe was already tipsy on the vodka, humming along to 'The Girl from the North Country', and she suggested Chantal answer it. When her friend returned to the flat, distraught, she knew immediately. Martin Wilcox Smith wanted Phoebe to know that Asil Farahmand had died in unexplained circumstances in prison; his body had been released to the family and was due to be buried tomorrow. Chantal's voice fell to a whisper; he had apologized but said he did not think it was appropriate for Phoebe to attend the burial.

Chantal sat beside her for much of the night as Phoebe sobbed, and when she finally fell into a troubled sleep, lay beside her so that she would be there when she woke.

*

The grief was bitter and disorientating – Phoebe had now been without Asil for longer than the time they had spent together. She had been overwhelmed by his instant conviction in their affair – she loved him for it, and loved every moment they had shared – but she began to think that the intensity could not have lasted. The six weeks had felt unreal even as she lived them, even more so in the aftermath of his horrific death. At her most despondent, she feared that any future relationship would be overshadowed by this scorching, exhilarating passion; she couldn't – mustn't – try to look for it ever again. She would deliberately let his memory fade; she finished his cigarettes, threw away the dead roses, and gave his Fanon to an interested acquaintance, but she couldn't let go of the Bob Dylan. Very slowly, life resumed its familiar, pre-Asil patterns: dancing in Shemiran, and Chantal used her strategy of distraction, arranging a holiday to Isfahan to hear the poets sing under the arches of the famous bridge and to see the mosque, which Asil had insisted was the most perfect piece of architecture in the world. Phoebe immersed herself in the demands of her extraordinary job helping to organize the world's biggest party in Persepolis. After that was over, she dreamed of moving to New York – somewhere safe, beyond the reach of Iran's vicious violence.

But she resolved on one last step: she wanted to say thank you in person to Martin Wilcox Smith. Monir had told her that he had helped arrange the funeral at his personal expense, ensuring Asil had a decent burial plot. His parents were too poor to pay – Asil had been supporting them.

Phoebe stood at the embassy gates once again, and it was as if she had lived several years in the few months since her last visit. Inside, the gardens were exactly as she remembered, the drops from the sprinkler glistening on the grass. She waited in the hall, this time listening to the clatter of typewriters and the ring of telephones on a busy working day. The same assistant appeared, the sound of her heels preceding her down the polished corridor. She led Phoebe to Wilcox Smith's office. Its long windows overlooked the garden.

'I'm sorry to have kept you waiting, Miss Crowley. Can I offer you coffee?' he asked, as stiff and formal as the first time, but he came out from behind his desk and gestured her to a set of chairs. 'May I offer my condolences? It must have been a terrible blow.'

Phoebe realized this was the first time that anyone had recognized her grief – apart from Chantal. Her relationship with Asil had been all-consuming, and they had spent all their time together, so no one knew the seriousness of what they had shared. Only this strange man, this diplomat, had guessed.

'Thank you,' said Phoebe, squeezing in her clenched fist the handkerchief she had made sure to bring, determined not to break down in front of him. 'That's all I have to say, I won't keep you. I appreciated your calling me to let me know, and I gather you helped his family. Thank you.'

The coffee arrived and his assistant handed them each a cup. After she had gone, he replied, 'Miss Crowley –'

'Please, Phoebe,' she interrupted quickly.

'Phoebe, I did very little. It was unfortunate, but, sadly, these things happen in this country. It's poor government – messy – and only leads to more unrest down the line. I have suggested Her Majesty's Government make representations to the Iranian government. Asil no doubt had a wide circle of friends – perhaps one or two were involved in banned political parties, but it's not clear why the SAVAK picked on him. It may even have been a mistake, or the result of malicious information. If we hear anything, I will let you know, but in these cases there is often no clarity or resolution, and not a lot we can do.'

Phoebe nodded.

'I'd rather not know more –' her voice shook and she took a breath. 'It's nothing to do with us – their country and so forth – but it's changed my view of Iran. I'll leave after my work on the Persepolis party is done – I want to find a job in New York at the end of next year.'

She finished her coffee. 'I needed to come in person, to draw a line under it all,' she said, gathering her handbag and standing up.

He moved to open the door for her, and stopped. 'Phoebe, I wondered – when you felt able to – whether you would be interested in lunch one day? I'd like to stay in touch.'

He was nervous, and she wondered about Lavinia.

'Yes, I'd like that.'

He smoothed back his hair, and, as if reading her mind, added,

'Lavinia has moved back to London. She didn't like Tehran – too hot and dusty – and it seemed a good idea with the children at school there now. Perhaps in a week or so? I could send a driver round to pick you up.'

*

He chose an expensive restaurant with a terrace shaded by vines, and was already waiting when Phoebe arrived, seated at a table by the pretty fountain, dressed in a white linen suit. She hesitated at the doorway, and looked across the tables of *khareji* businessmen and their Iranian contacts, and knew she was arriving in a very different world, moving from the crowded bars, jazz clubs and cheap street cafes which she and Asil had frequented into the company of the powerful, moneyed and middle-aged. She wondered if any of them had listened to 'The Girl from the North Country' or would ever want to. And just as quickly she remonstrated with herself: keep an open mind, don't compare.

Wilcox Smith had noticed her, and stood up as she wove through the tables.

'Good to see you, Phoebe.'

He meant it, she could see that plainly. She greeted him, warily, and picked up the menu, curious: where, after lunch, would this go?

'I recommend the lamb and apricot. It's delicious, and to drink, I thought some champagne?'

Phoebe looked across the crisp white tablecloth, crystal glasses and expensive flowers, and wondered how old he was. She knew nothing about this man, and yet he was one of the few people who had understood the trauma of the last few months. His solidity and air of authority were reassuring; the stiffness she had once found off-putting was now, to her surprise, appealing. He was the sort of person who knew how to find his way through even the most brutal and unexpected turns of life.

'I know very little about you, Martin –' she hesitated over his first name. 'How long have you been in Iran?'

'Since '67 on this tour, but I was born here between the wars. My father worked for the Anglo-Persian Oil Company, BP to you, and I lived here until I was ten – I was sent to school in England in 1938. I had a Persian nanny and I grew up speaking Farsi and English, so in some ways this country has always felt like home.'

Forty-one, calculated Phoebe, a fourteen-year age gap, and she sipped her chilled champagne.

'You could say I was brought up inside out: England was a foreign country. My best childhood memories are of sunlight, the taste of pomegranate and spiced lamb, and a special jam made of young walnuts and cardamom. My Persian nanny was like a mother to me. In England I was cold and hated the boiled cabbage and grey meat. Food is very important to a young boy.' He sounded strained. 'Rugby, Latin, algebra, and hearty hymns: that's what England amounted to in 1938, and then war broke out. I felt I had been expelled from paradise and couldn't work out why, homesick for a place which everyone insisted was not my home. My dream was to get back – I came in 1951 for a short visit, and then again for my first tour in 1952, just as the whole regime was poised on the edge of collapse.'

Phoebe looked puzzled.

'You didn't know? The Shah fled to Switzerland in 1952, fearing a coup. We really thought he was done for, but here we are in 1969, seventeen years on, and he still has his crown, with a new wife and a batch of children. More champagne?'

'And where was home when you were in England?'

'Hampshire for the holidays. A handsome but crumbling pile of Georgian masonry – rather like the empire.'

'A strange parallel,' said Phoebe, surprised by Martin's blunt and slightly bitter honesty.

'The two things are bound up in my mind, since the house was built with the proceeds of sugar plantations in the eighteenth century, and now it is falling apart. My father's career was in the early days of oil, a few decades too early, and it's the Americans who are going to reap the benefits of his hard work. He has made it clear that he will leave the estate to whichever of his two sons has the means to do the place up. There's not much at the Foreign Office – unfortunately, we just help other people to make money – so it's all down to Lavinia and her family trusts.'

'You mean he has set you and your brother up as rivals?' exclaimed Phoebe, incredulous.

'He calls it healthy competition; when I was four, he started awarding weekly performance scores – he kept a tally of who won running races, who had the best marks in school, and so forth. My father is a bitter man. His generation made many sacrifices for their country – he lost two brothers at the Somme, and Lodsbourne was requisitioned in the First World War, and left in a pitiable state. Now Whitehall is selling us all down the river. We are scrambling to get out of places before we are kicked out – as we were in India and Aden.'

He leaned back and rearranged his neat tie. 'I don't want some rock musician to buy the place, so I can't divorce Lavinia – quite apart from the children – and I need a new job – one in which I make a lot of money. I'm afraid that is the sordid truth, Phoebe.'

He looked across the table at her, as if measuring her reaction to these revelations, then reached forward.

'I'd like to show you something of this country before you leave for New York, Phoebe. How about a trip to Qazvin, and then we could go on to the castle ruins of Rudkhan? I don't want you to leave Iran without understanding how the place creeps under the skin.'

'And Lavinia?'

He rolled a grape between his thumb and forefinger.

'Lavinia never liked it here, and I understand, it's difficult for a wife. She has been very dutiful. It's not that I miss her – she was never that sort of wife – but, as I say, I can't divorce.'

An affair then, thought Phoebe; she liked the honesty. She knew where she stood, and she thought of the Mayfair art dealer with whom she had had a dalliance before she left London. He had offered to rent her a flat.

'I would love to visit Rudkhan,' she replied, and leaned forward to briefly kiss his still lips. He looked at her intently, and she could see relief and desire in his hungry, lonely eyes.

★

Chantal and Phoebe made their way through the bazaar browsing in the antique shops.

'Do you still think about Asil?' her friend asked, taking her arm.

'I try not to. It only hurts.'

'Some people leave a print, however short the time you spend together,' commented Chantal, squeezing her arm sympathetically. 'It's horrible – the sensible ones get out, it's the only safe thing to do. They go to America, France or England, and campaign from there. The SAVAK are everywhere.' She spoke quietly. Even on the streets, passers-by could pick up a few words and relay them to the authorities to curry favour.

Phoebe fingered some fabric on a stall outside a shop.

'Since his death, no one mentions him. Monir says at the architectural practice they cleared Asil's desk and hired a replacement immediately. It was as if he had never lived. Maybe I need to visit his parents, just so that I will know he was real, not a dream.'

'Look, Phoebe, look at this silk!' Chantal beckoned to the assistant to roll out the brilliantly coloured cloth. 'And this Wilcox Smith? Is he a distraction?'

'Perhaps. I admit I'm surprised, but there's something appealing about Martin. It's more than desire – it's bigger. He needs someone to make sense of his life – I'm not sure how to describe it – as if he was orphaned and made homeless a long time ago. And he's trapped in his marriage.'

'Middle-aged man suffering post-imperial malaise by the sound of it,' mused Chantal absent-mindedly, her eye suddenly caught by some embroidered shawls on another stall. 'But if he keeps you distracted, good, and better still if he makes you happy,' she added. They were soon engrossed in bargaining over the exquisite craftwork they couldn't resist.

*

Phoebe and Martin arrived at the hotel in Qazvin just as dusk was falling. The lights in the courtyard blinked on, one by one, casting deep shadows in the arches of the old caravanserai. Palm trees were partially illuminated by tea lights in coloured glass. They left their bags to be taken up to their room and set out to explore the city and have dinner.

The bazaar was thronged with people: portly women laden with shopping bags, stall holders calling their wares, the piles of spices and herbs filling the air with their pungent smells. Martin steered them to the alleyways selling antiques and jewellery, the gold and silver glittering under brilliant electric lights. They marvelled at the exquisite ceramics and painted miniatures. At every corner, sellers tugged at their sleeves, promising good prices and the best quality. In one jewellery shop, he asked Phoebe to choose a pair of earrings and bought them for her – they were intricately worked, heavy silver. For dinner, he insisted they go to the Negarossaltaneh Café, famous for its brand of Qazvin's sweet biscuits. The lamplight flickered on its old brick domed ceiling, and Martin ordered dark Iranian red wine to accompany their aubergine tagine, and afterwards, the delicately flavoured biscuits.

'My Persian nanny told me stories and sang ballads every

night. She filled my head with the folklore of her region. We always celebrated the Zoroastrian feasts of equinox and solstice,' he recounted, in response to Phoebe's persistent questioning. 'At New Year, Noruz, everything in the house had to be scrubbed clean, and we sat at the table with seven symbols of springtime, each starting with the letter *s* – a goldfish, a mirror, a painted egg. It was such a rich world. By the time I came back in '51, she had died.'

'Why did you come back?'

He laughed. 'Ah, that's quite a story! I had just finished at Oxford after national service, and my tutor told me that a film producer needed a translator for a project in Iran. He couldn't pay anything more than the travel costs. We met in a pub off the Charing Cross Road to agree terms, and were joined by a morose, tubby Welshman, who nursed his pint of Guinness and said little. On the way to the airport, he told me he was a poet. I thought he was joking and he got very irritated. His job was to write the script on the benefits British business were bringing to the "poor, backward" country of Iran; he was badly in need of the cash because of a row with his wife over an affair. Can you guess who it was?'

'A penniless Welsh poet in 1952 . . .' pondered Phoebe. Then, incredulous, 'Not Dylan Thomas?'

'Well done. At your age, I'd never heard of him,' Martin said admiringly. 'He didn't like Iran, he was shocked by the extremes of wealth and poverty and the racism. He hated Abadan, with its rows of identical bungalows for the oil executives, its evergreen trees and lawns. On a camping trip to the desert, I picked out the sounds for him – jackals, camel bells, ibex – and after that he was more friendly. An Iranian in the office in Abadan knew all his poems – Ebrahim Golestan?'

Phoebe nodded. 'The film-maker, a critic of the Shah.'

'One evening Thomas and Golestan went for a drink, and I was allowed to tag along. I remember Golestan saying that since the time of Alexander, the buildings of Iran have been made of clay and mud, and they crumble back into the earth so there is nothing left to show of the history. In the twentieth century, that changed, of course, and now the concrete mixers work overtime.'

'I could write it up for you – if you give me the details – and send it to a Dylan Thomas scholar,' suggested Phoebe.

'I've never talked about it before – I didn't know anyone interested.' He put his hand over hers on the table, and his eyes were wide with surprise. 'I feel *understood*, and there's an astonishing feeling of liberation – I had no idea.'

They wandered back through streets still busy with shoppers, the cafes full of men smoking pipes and drinking coffee, and arrived at the hotel's imposing doorway set into the high brick walls. Inside, the garden, full of bougainvillea and roses, was splashed by a bright moon. The tea lights were reflected in the tiled pool of the fountain, its soft splash of water reverberating around the courtyard. They sat down at a table to drink a last glass, savouring the evening.

'Perhaps my obsession with Lodsbourne, this house in Hampshire, is a way to make myself feel rooted somewhere. It didn't matter so much when I was younger, but now . . .' He left the sentence hanging. 'My public-school education was designed to make the sons of empire as happy in the Solomon Islands as in Tanganyika. We were brought up to be nomads; home was a set of ideals. Now even those are disappearing.'

He picked an overhanging leaf and began to tear it into small strips.

'I have to say that the circumstances of Asil Farahmand's death were, personally, challenging – seeing his parents' grief. This regime is deeply corrupt and HMG's policy of pressure for gradual reform isn't working. The detentions, beatings and murders continue. I know some of that is unavoidable in this part of the world – a government has to keep a firm hand on things. But I used to believe that our presence helped push things forward, and that the empire was an engine of progress – the rule of law, railways, trade, and so forth. Now I'm beginning to think I was, at best, naive, at worst, wilfully blind, like many of my countrymen.'

Phoebe saw the lonely, rootless ten-year-old Martin still there, buried in this man.

'Do you still think of Asil?' he asked.

'No, I've put him out of my mind. We only knew each other for six weeks or so,' she replied, a touch too firmly, and he looked at her closely before picking up his earlier theme.

'My mother used to read me *Our Island Story* when I was young. It was old-fashioned stuff about the British empire, but now when I go back to London, my contemporaries don't know half of what I am talking about. They're preoccupied with Europe, the Common Market, and, of course, trying to keep up with the US. The change has been so swift, so complete – the forgetting of empire so determined and *energetic*. I sense the queen is as baffled as I am; she plugs away at the Commonwealth as if she is trying to salvage something, but it's a memento, an indulgence to HM. After she has gone, it will amount to nothing more than running races and poetry recitals in dusty African cities . . . I'm sorry.' He took a deep breath and pulled his shoulders back. 'Marital separation and a crumbling family house are routine –' he coughed loudly to clear his voice – 'but the end of an empire is not, and it is brutal, sooner or later, sometimes a lot later. I learned enough history at school to know that. My children will live through that final unravelling of imperial power; we're only at the beginning of the end.'

'Enough, Martin. Too gloomy.' Phoebe took his hands and held them. 'Do you know the poet Rumi? Did your nanny teach you any of his poems? Someone taught me one once:

'Come, come, whoever you are. Wanderer, worshipper,
  lover of leaving.
It doesn't matter. Ours is not a caravan of despair.
Come, even if you have broken your vows a thousand times.
Come, yet again, come, come.'

He joined in for the last three lines, and put his hand up to her hair to tuck a loose strand behind her ear. Smiling, he whispered, 'Perfect. It's a long time since I've heard it.'

It was still dark in the morning when they were woken by the call to prayer. They drank glasses of black tea from a samovar, and breakfasted on warm bread and cheese, watching the dawn break over the mountains, the sky a pale peppermint. They needed to set off early if they were to climb to Rudkhan castle, before the long journey back to Tehran. As they drove through the still dusky streets, Phoebe watched Qazvin coming to life: shopkeepers undoing their shutters and setting up their stalls of fruit and vegetables, cafes opening for their first customers. They left the city behind and the road wound through densely forested mountains. Martin asked Phoebe how she had come to be in Iran, and she told him how the Shahbanou's glance in Mayfair had led to her work researching acquisitions for the empress's new art gallery and organizing the celebrations in Persepolis.

'While she spends millions of dollars on clothes from Paris and expensive pictures, most of her subjects are hungry and illiterate,' he commented.

'That's what Asil said.'

'Well, I agree with him – and this party is absurd.'

She watched his profile, the set of his jaw.

'I'm not sure there is a secure future here. I've been looking at banking in Hong Kong – my brother is out there. I've been slow, others read the runes long ago and got on with making money. Plenty of men in my club in London have arrived from nowhere, and now seem to be in charge, with houses in Chelsea, and large property portfolios.'

At the car park, they put on walking boots, and packed bottles of water, bread and cheese in a knapsack.

'Ready?' asked Martin, straightening her sunhat. 'This is quite a climb.'

She laughed. 'I was netball captain at school.'

She looked at him, and was glad to see him happy. The previous evening, she had had a fleeting image of a man reaching out to catch a floating timber in the torrent. As for herself, she could see a project even more compelling and fascinating than the Shahbanou's schemes or a new life in New York. They began to climb the shallow stone steps up the hillside through the woods. Coolness lingered in the shade, but it was tougher than Phoebe expected, and she could feel the muscles in her calves straining with the unaccustomed effort. The sweat accumulated under the band of her hat and between her breasts. Every now and then, when there was a clearing, they paused and admired the valleys unfolding beneath them. When they finally reached the top, Phoebe was astonished at the drama of the ruined castle perched on this precarious ridge of mountain – the brick walls and turrets appeared to erupt out of the forest, and it seemed possible they could relapse at any moment, swallowed by the green canopy.

They ate their bread and cheese on a rampart, feeling the warm brick under their legs. They had the place to themselves, and Martin leaned over and stroked Phoebe's cheek, flushed from the walk and streaked with dust and sweat.

'You're very beautiful.'

She leaned forward to kiss him, and he separated out a strand of hair to smell and kiss. 'The hair of an angel.'

She pulled him towards her to kiss again, more deeply.

He took her hand – the nails were broken and muddy from scrambling over the ruined walls.

'I'm sorry I can't offer you more . . . My wife –'

Phoebe put a finger on his lips. 'Give me time,' she murmured.

He pursed his lips briefly, confused, and put his arm around her shoulders, pulling her close. 'Shall we go to the Caspian Sea next? A friend has a cottage,' he suggested, and she nodded.

'Phoebe, this time, it could be different, *I* could be different – with you –'

'I like you the way you are,' she interjected, tucking into him, smelling his aftershave and sweat after the steep climb.

'I don't think I could ever have described myself as close with anyone before – not with my wife, nor my children – dutiful, yes. I didn't expect this . . .'

'Well, we're agreed on that – nor did I. That first time I met you –'

'Formal?'

She grimaced. 'But a kindness too.'

'You were always beautiful. I saw you the very first time you came to the embassy.'

'Before I came about the visa?'

He nodding, smiling.

'So you went out of your way – for me?'

'Partly.'

Disconcerted, she jumped off the wall.

'Time to go back down. I want to wash in the stream at the bottom before driving back to Tehran,' she threw over her shoulder.

In what way did Martin think he could be different, she pondered, as they began their descent in companionable silence. Less of this end-of-empire gloom, for one thing, she thought. And as for money, it couldn't be that difficult. Plenty of people were getting rich in Iran, and if that didn't seem safe – the words of Ehsan's friend in the bar many months before came back to her – he didn't have to go as far as Hong Kong. Her uncle had done very well for himself in the Gulf, and her Aunt Edith was always keen to offer advice. She owed her a letter anyway, and Edith would love nothing better than a problem to solve like Martin's need for money.

In the months that followed they explored different regions they could reach from Tehran. Chantal murmured cautiously about rebound, but Phoebe dismissed the comment. When she and Martin had time off work, they extended their journeys. They went to the cottage on the Caspian, and walked along the shore, falling asleep to the sound of the waves breaking only a few feet from their veranda. In winter, they stoked up the log-burning stove, and talked in the candlelight. As the weather warmed, they went further afield, heading east, and stayed overnight in small coffee houses, searching out the new archaeological sites described by Phoebe's friends at the university. They would stumble over rough fields, follow unmarked paths, beg bewildered passers-by to guide them to the excavation site, and then they would wander round the ruins, marvelling at the extraordinary history, worried by their vulnerability to souvenir collectors, and the ravages of sun and wind. Golestan had been right: uncovered and with no protection, these ancient remains were disintegrating back into the soil. The excavations were a plundering of history, and they shared his frustration at Iran's nonchalance towards its past.

When they passed through the small dusty towns, they paused to visit the shabby shops and often found, under a pile of clutter, a painting, a tile, or a jug to buy. They never returned to Tehran empty-handed. There was little space in Phoebe's flat, but, regardless, they piled up the boxes of precious purchases. Uncertain that they could ever share a life, they laughingly agreed they could at least share pots, plates, fabrics and tiles. If necessary, Phoebe could take it all to New York, insisted Martin, and he would see it when he visited. They both realized that such a scenario was implausible for a myriad of reasons – tiny flats,

Martin too busy to visit, the end of their affair – but it didn't stop them buying, and Phoebe half-assumed that the collection would end up with a Manhattan dealer.

Once, as they were driving through Gilan province in the spring of 1970, they came across fields of wild tulips. Girls were bent over, picking the blooms, and others stood at the side of the road with full buckets. At the first stall, Martin bought the entire stock, and the girl's delight matched Phoebe's as he heaped the beautiful red and yellow, white and pink flowers on to the back seat. Looking at the heaps of flowers, an image came to her of Asil's single roses; just as quickly she put it out of her mind. A little further on at the next roadside seller, Martin did the same, and they drove back to Tehran that evening with the car full of tulips. Phoebe had armfuls on her lap and more at her feet; their scent mingled with the warm wind from the open windows which blew her hair wild and thick with dust.

4

'I've got a suggestion,' said Phoebe, holding the phone in the crook of her neck as she broke off a piece of her croissant. Still fresh from the French bakery, it was too good to waste, even for a phone call from Martin.

'Fire away.'

Phoebe wiped the crumbs off her desk swiftly with her handkerchief. A flake of the browned crust had fallen between the typewriter keys. 'My aunt and uncle, Edith and Roddy Grant, want to meet you and are visiting Persepolis when we're at the festival in Shiraz. My aunt thinks you have a lot in common with my uncle.'

Phoebe pulled the festival programme from under a mess of papers on her desk and flicked through the pages to find what was scheduled for the dates she had agreed with Edith: John Cage might be a bit avant-garde, but a modern Greek dance company and a celebrated Indian sitar player sounded more promising. Also listed was Cathy Berberian ('stretching the understanding of song and voice into new and astonishing territory' read the programme). She toyed with a pencil in the coiled phone wire as Martin broke off to talk to his assistant. She recalled her first sight of Persepolis at last year's festival, when she had seen Bizet's *Carmen* in the ruins, the pillars gleaming in the night sky under the spotlights. Chantal and Phoebe had stayed in Shiraz, enjoying evenings with artists, actors, musicians and bewildered Western critics in the bars, followed by lazy afternoons around the hotel pools with cocktails. She remembered how the crowds had stared at the cavalcade of international celebrities edging through the streets.

'What? Is the line bad? Can you hear me?' said Martin.

Phoebe pulled the pencil out and watched the coils spring back. 'Yes, I can hear. Edith and Roddy are heading home, they've finished up in Bahrain, and Edith wanted a last trip before Cheltenham, Salisbury or wherever they're retiring to. They've been in the Middle East for decades. What's that? Can't hear.'

'It's a bad line. I need to go — but I'd like to meet Roddy Grant. I've heard about him, he's an advisor on policing and security, I believe. He's very respected in Bahrain.'

From the other side of the office, Chantal was holding up a magazine open at a fashion spread; Phoebe tried to ignore her.

'We should visit them before they leave Bahrain. Edith works as Roddy's secretary but her real passions are birds and archaeology. She has a small launch and goes out on bird-watching trips round the islands — flamingos in the early morning, that kind of thing. By the way, when you meet them, you have to be very careful on the subject of birds: Edith watches them, Roddy shoots them, and they never mention the subject in front of each other — unspoken agreement.'

Martin laughed.

During the week, he was too busy to see her, with official functions, receptions and dinners with trade delegations. She had only these phone calls to remind her of their hot nights together at the weekend, when they lay in a slick of sweaty, tangled limbs under the creaking fan in his apartment. Phoebe put the receiver down and returned to the Yves Saint Laurent catalogue she had been looking at. There was a silk coat printed with a pattern of interlocking circles in green, yellow, black and brown. The length, on the knee, was modest, it had an elegant shawl collar, and the sleeves came to just below the elbow: perfect as a statement outfit for the Shahbanou's arrival at the Shiraz Contemporary

Arts Festival, setting the tone of the event as a showpiece of modern Iran, an equal to the West. She added a bookmark.

When Phoebe talked to Martin about her work, he sometimes suppressed a smile, teasing her that it was just frocks, or canvases covered with ghastly splashes of paint. She laughed gamely, but she was indulging him. He was a man who liked proximity to power – first-name terms with senior politicians and the executives in the oil, agribusiness and defence companies drawn by the pungent smell of money hanging over expatriate Tehran. Like many others in these circles, Martin hadn't grasped how television was transforming politics and diplomacy. He thought her work irrelevant, and her employer's tastes for lavish spending a dangerous liability for the regime. He would discover in time, Phoebe told him. Meanwhile the Shahbanou knew instinctively how it worked: the photographic shoots, wardrobes and exclusive interviews with lifestyle magazines and television stations were carefully calculated. She was crafting an international image of Iran, with an elegance which delighted and astonished her Western audience in equal measure. What it did for Iranians was not so clear – but perhaps that didn't matter, reflected Phoebe as she picked out a hat to match the silk coat.

*

Martin nodded at various acquaintances as they made their way across the restaurant in Shiraz to their table. She liked this public acknowledgement of their relationship. There was no need any longer for those discreet assignations at his flat in northern Tehran or at the cottage on the Caspian; people knew she was his mistress.

Phoebe greeted her aunt and uncle nervously, and introduced Martin – only she and Edith knew how much was riding on this weekend. Edith had always been a forbidding presence.

'We're delighted to meet you.' Edith held out a hand to Martin, and sceptically surveyed her niece's short black dress and knee-high white boots. 'We've heard a lot about you from Phoebe's letters.'

'It's time we had something decent to drink,' announced Roddy, scrutinizing the long list of sherries, cocktails, wine and spirits. 'The stuff in Bahrain has been boiled by the time it reaches us, and, I tell you, it is not the better for it.'

'Are you looking forward to retirement, to going home?' Phoebe asked, sitting down at the table.

Edith forced a tight smile. 'Home? I've not lived in England since I was young, but Roddy is staying on as a consultant in the Gulf, so I hope I'll be back every few months – air travel makes these things so much easier.'

'The woman has never cooked in her life – not even a boiled egg. We're going to starve in Salisbury unless she learns damn quick,' Roddy interrupted.

'I've enrolled on a cookery course,' conceded Edith, irritation evident beneath the forced cheerfulness.

Roddy knocked back his second sherry. 'London's policy in the Gulf has been a dreadful shambles. Humiliating for those of us trying to keep the flag flying, to be frank.'

Phoebe observed how deftly Martin drew her uncle out.

'After the mess of losing Aden to the Soviets, we were assured that there was no question of the UK pulling out of its bases in the Persian Gulf. There's oil everywhere, and HMG knows the stuff will make the place wealthy beyond all our imagining. It's hard to believe. It was just a collection of mud huts and some pearl fishing when I first arrived after the war – the Great War, of course –'

'Indeed,' said Martin. 'The decision is made now: the "End of East of Suez" next year. Plenty of questions were asked in Tehran as to why HMG was withdrawing, and we had a devil of a time smoothing things down – makes London appear unreliable as an ally.'

'I said as much in robust terms to the chaps I know at the Foreign Office, but they told me they are "managing decline".' Roddy was shrill with indignation, and he made an effort to drop his voice. 'I met the foreign minister when he came to Bahrain in November 1967, along with the rest of the British business community. He was promising lasting alliances in the Gulf states, but – can you believe this? – two months later, he was back saying precisely the opposite. It's chaotic.'

'Sterling is looking dicey and HMG has decided it can't afford empire,' said Martin. 'The foreign-policy priority has shifted to Europe and the Common Market.'

Roddy's face reddened. 'Utter nonsense,' he muttered.

The waiter arrived to take their order, then Roddy resumed, his forehead creased with frustration. 'I thought we won the darned war – why then do we have to creep into the Common Market, cap in hand? Britain used to stand for something in the world.'

He leaned over the table towards Martin, his voice lowered, and Phoebe had to strain to hear. 'The king of Bahrain wanted us to stay and he offered to cover all the costs of the British presence. It fell to me to tell him that HMG deemed the offer unacceptable – yet the Gulf is exactly where we need to be if we are to hold our weight in the world. The US simply won't take us seriously; we're making a mess everywhere. Palestine was bad enough – and none of these Arabs forget that. Suez was a catastrophe, Aden a bloody mess. Iran is the only hope of holding the Soviets at bay, or they will take control of the Gulf.'

'You've said all this back home?'

Roddy nodded. 'I thought it was Labour who were too stupid to understand, but this new Conservative government is as bad – they've forgotten what makes our country tick: it's the job of the ruling class to provide the nation with a purpose – one that is larger than selling widgets.' He spat out the last word with real contempt.

Martin nodded in agreement. 'I've become a salesman – diplomacy is an endless round of trade delegations and business promotions. Most of the time we are losing out to the Germans or the Americans; even the French get to some of the contracts faster. It's soul-destroying. There's money to be made here, but Britain is not getting its share. I'd do a better job of it than most of the sales directors they send out.'

The conversation was cut short by the waiter returning to fill their glasses with the champagne Roddy had chosen, and Martin, ever conscious of good etiquette, turned to Edith.

'Phoebe has secured tickets for us all for a performance of Cathy Berberian, an American mezzo-soprano, one of the highlights of the festival.' He smiled expansively as he slipped his hand under the table to rest on Phoebe's thigh. 'I gather her performance is a little odd – we may be in for a surprising evening.'

'Never much liked opera,' huffed Roddy, doubtful, but he glanced indulgently across the table at Phoebe. He was quite fond of his niece, despite her new-fangled ways – 'Damned pretty,' he had remarked to Edith earlier that evening.

'She's breaking all the boundaries of what we understand singing to be. She works with the most interesting composers,' offered Phoebe enthusiastically, as it dawned on her that her choice might prove contentious.

Bemused by her description, Edith changed the subject to Bahraini archaeology.

Towards the end of the meal, the conversation shifted back to Martin and Roddy's work. 'It seems to me that there's a way of doing this,' announced Roddy, his face red from the champagne and red wine which had accompanied his grilled lamb. 'We can still maintain a presence in the Gulf, keep ourselves in the game, without a big cost to HMG.'

Phoebe pricked up her ears: this is what Edith had hinted at in her letter.

'How?' Martin asked.

'It's quite simple. The ruler offered to pay HMG to stay, HMG said no, so who's going to do it? The Bahraini royal family are rightly very worried – the Shah makes no bones about his claims on the place, and the Saudis are breathing down their necks from the other direction. It is not just Bahrain – the Gulf shaykhdoms are sitting there, plump as pheasants in October waiting to be shot – the strategic and economic significance of the region can't be overemphasized.'

He paused, aware that he had Martin's full attention.

'If we don't provide security, someone else will: the Americans are likely candidates, and, given half a chance, the French. They'll be selling mercenaries, weapons, the lot, as soon as we've got the packing crates ordered. But we've a huge head start on both the French and the Americans – contacts, history – and we need to transfer all of that to private companies. If we can't maintain a British presence East of Suez as HMG, we set up an operation which is below the radar – nothing to do with empire or colonialism. Nothing those overexcited youngsters happy to spend their Saturday afternoons demonstrating will catch a whiff of.' He chuckled with satisfaction. 'Here's how it goes: we have the ceremonies, we haul the Union Jack down, the military band plays "God Save the Queen". We wave the ship off – and all the time we are recruiting the soldiers, security advisors, police and bankers into private consultancies, and they move back into the recently vacated barracks, offices, compounds and bungalows.'

Beaming with self-satisfaction, Roddy looked over his glasses at Martin. 'All change and all stays the same!' He pulled his napkin off his lap and dabbed at his thick moustache. 'I've lined up a job as advisor to a new company based in Trowbridge, in Wiltshire. It is very professional, and, I must say, well paid. I'm doing recruitment for the Bahraini police force already, and it's not hard; the best thing about dismantling an empire with such indecent haste is that there is no shortage of men with excellent experience looking for work. Men who were with me in Kenya, and so forth.'

'Suppressing the Mau Mau Uprising in Kenya was a tough business. You don't need that kind of experience in a sleepy place like Bahrain, surely?' asked Martin.

Phoebe saw that Edith looked unsettled. Roddy glanced at her briefly. 'The place isn't quite what it's billed; fine for foreign consumption – stable, peaceful – but there's another side of the story.' He lowered his voice. 'The villages can be troublesome. A few Shia –'

'Not a few, my dear,' intervened Edith crisply. 'Martin needs the full picture. It's not widely acknowledged, but Bahrain is perhaps sixty or seventy per cent Shia, and that makes for tension with the Sunni royal family. Loyalty is always an issue, all the more so, given Shia Iran's claim. And there are bigger challenges around political reform – more democracy. The royal family can be a little –' she hesitated, glancing at her husband – 'heavy-handed, and we help keep a lid on things.'

Roddy looked shifty. 'Edith spends time in the villages – the men she uses on the archaeological digs and on the boat are all Shia. Her Arabic is good, and she passes it all back. Useful intelligence, but no one in London has quite grasped that Bahrain has a problem with security long-term. The ruler will need help not just with defence but with policing. He's on a sticky wicket, and there are plenty of opportunities in the other Gulf shaykhdoms too. Saudi Arabia the biggest of all. This is how Britain reinvents itself.'

'It's how we got into empire in the first place – private business competing with the French to sell arms to Indian maharajahs,' said Martin. He was rubbing his jaw with his finger.

'You're right,' said Edith approvingly. 'Nothing important need change, we just have to be sure-footed. You could play an important role, Martin – I gather you're finding diplomacy limited.'

Martin looked at Phoebe, surprised.

'I mentioned in passing that you were looking for new opportunities,' Phoebe hastily explained.

'A man of vision could seize the challenge – someone with all the right connections in the region, liaison with HMG, the languages, the credibility to raise the cash in London, to broker the deals. Someone who knows how to keep things discreet. For the right person, the clients and contracts are right there, ready for the picking,' urged Roddy.

Martin nodded, thoughtful.

*

The sun was already streaming through the gap in the curtains when Phoebe woke the following morning, Martin's arm lying across her belly. She watched the sharp sunlight and his sleeping profile. She imagined what it would be like to be his wife; he was the sort of man who would be a full-time project. During the heady days of university, she had hoped her generation would do things differently, and women would have their own careers, but she had seen the options narrow and friends give up and marry. If you fell in love with an older, ambitious man, you had no chance – they expected too much from their wives. A life with Martin would always be eventful; he attracted powerful people like a magnet gathers iron filings. Was that enough to compensate her for abandoning the dream of New York and, one day, running her own art gallery? Unexpectedly, she had found that to be so needed in another's life brought a powerful satisfaction – it gave meaning and purpose to what had been a pleasurable but shapeless life. Surely that was more important than what she had briefly had with Asil: the exhilarating mutual recognition, that sense of being soulmates.

Almost two years on, she couldn't trust her memories of him, particularly given the terrifying aftermath. She still felt sick remembering the visit to his parents in the unfamiliar, shabby neighbourhood of Tehran – the smell of stale cooking on the shared staircase, and of rotting rubbish drifting up from the courtyard. His mother, her face stiff and exhausted, her eyes swollen and red from crying. His father openly weeping, the tears running down his cheeks, and the way he kept wiping them away with his large, rough hands.

Martin slowly opened his eyes beside her and reached over to stroke the curve of her cheek. He propped his head up on his hand to look at her, and kissed her nose.

'Marry me,' she whispered.

He leaned over and kissed her.

'You didn't answer,' she said later, lying sprawled across the bed, luxuriating in the aftermath of their love-making.

Martin traced the line of her neck and shoulder with his finger.

'Phoebe, you do know I love you?'

There was a pause.

'You're about to say "but",' she murmured.

He sighed heavily and finally said, 'Lavinia has asked for a divorce. It seems she has met an American corporate lawyer she wants to marry.'

Phoebe sat up, holding the sheet around her.

'I'm trying to negotiate an agreement whereby she takes on the house – a life interest – for the sake of the children. But my father is not keen – nor is she, for that matter.'

'So you could lose Lodsbourne?'

Martin nodded.

'Then you could come to New York with me and the pots,' said Phoebe with forced brightness. Something in Martin's expression filled her with foreboding.

'I'm not giving up the house yet. But it requires me to marry someone with substantial resources.'

She couldn't contain her fury. 'You mean, you're ending it! How dare you, Martin?'

He lifted a strand of her hair from her face but she batted his hand away.

'You fucking idiot.' Her voice was icy. She hadn't realized how much she wanted him – wanted his darned damp house, even.

Stung, he stood up and walked to the window. 'I'm sorry, unforgiveable.' He looked perplexed, standing there, naked, and put his hand up to push his hair back. Phoebe could see where a widow's peak was emerging. He looked his age, and she glimpsed the older man he would become, how the lines would deepen around his mouth and eyes, and saw his vulnerability.

'Take Roddy's advice, you fool. Make a fortune yourself, and we'll do up Lodsbourne.'

He spun round. 'Would you do that? Give up New York? Was that what this weekend was about?'

'It's that or I'm taking all our bloody pots to New York,' Phoebe retorted angrily. 'And selling them.'

★

Over drinks in the hotel garden that evening after the concert, Roddy made no effort to be polite about Berberian.

'Frightful caterwauling,' he complained as he fingered his tumbler of whisky. 'Bloody waste of time and money bringing her here.'

'Poorly judged,' was all Martin said.

When Phoebe protested, Edith pointed out that the audience had been bewildered. 'The screeching, the sneezing, the wailing. I'm afraid that kind of thing may be appreciated in London or New York in certain recherché circles, but it's absurd to impose it on a country still struggling to develop. I overheard one of the critics in the lobby just now, saying they need to understand Tchaikovsky first. He's quite right.'

'A conservative Iranian newspaper has hinted that the arts festival is un-Islamic, the mullahs are preparing to strike back,' added Martin.

'Of course it's un-Islamic,' retorted Phoebe, still angry with him after their argument that morning. 'Iran has a long pre-Islamic history. That's the point of the Persepolis celebrations. It's a diverse country with many traditions, and the Shahbanou is acting as an intermediary – between modernity and tradition, between East and West.'

'It'll cost them their fancy crowns one of these days,' commented Roddy. 'I'm afraid, Phoebe dear, that most of this country is still in the Middle Ages. The people listen to their ayatollahs – that's what you should be reminding your Shahbanou.'

'Phoebe has offered to help me buy a carpet tomorrow,' said Edith, changing the subject. 'Your taste is impeccable, dear, and these things are not my forte. We need a carpet for the drawing room in Salisbury. Shall we meet at eleven in the foyer?'

Phoebe nodded, quietly furious with her aunt and uncle, as well as Martin.

The following morning, niece and aunt set out for the bazaar. Edith knew of the best shop.

'The blue or the red?' she asked, seated on a low stool, sipping sweet black tea and surveying two large carpets.

Phoebe walked from one end to the other to assess the pile and how the colours shifted in the dim electric light of the shop.

'You know, Martin can make a lot of money in the Gulf,' Edith announced abruptly. 'Roddy likes him; he can help him with the right introductions and so forth.' She dropped her voice: 'This country is going to the dogs – and, to be honest, the antics of your team are not helping.'

Stung, Phoebe started to remonstrate, but Edith cut her off. 'You and Martin need to marry and get to the Gulf; he'll have plenty to do, and you can have babies. I sensed there had been a "domestic" yesterday evening, but you're a clever girl – use your head. Wait for him to come round. Men are always slower on the uptake. Like you at your age, I wanted to make something of myself. Martin will do nicely. Husbands are either interesting or kind, very rarely both, and occasionally neither. Martin is interesting and possibly kind.'

For a moment, Phoebe glimpsed the disappointment that had carved the deep lines in her aunt's face. Roddy had brought her a lifetime of travel, and considerable comfort, but little in the way of companionship or affection. Edith was of a generation whose choices had been painfully constrained.

She knelt down to stroke the luxurious pile. 'That's ridiculous, Aunt Edith – I'm not going to spend my time having babies.'

Edith got up to haggle over the price, and soon both she and the shop owner were smiling, and an assistant was rolling the carpet and wrapping it in brown paper. It would be sent to the hotel: the drawing room in Salisbury had its carpet.

They left the shop and made their way through the narrow streets of the bazaar.

'Don't take offence, dear. I've seen enough of life to know how these things go,' resumed Edith, taking Phoebe's arm. 'Martin is at one of those turning points in life, and there is a lot at stake: love, money, patriotism, duty, belonging. But provided you play it carefully, you can have Martin, and his house, if that's what you want. I've seen expatriate marriages founder in one way or another – through boredom, alcohol, temptation during long separations, or someone getting homesick. Martin will need your undivided attention – you will have to give up any nonsense about a career.'

Edith was interrupted by a particularly persistent boy selling scarlet roses. He was about thirteen, and he grinned, his teeth badly damaged. 'Please, please, fancy ladies,' he begged. Phoebe rummaged in her handbag for a few coins. She picked a stem and held it to her nose. The perfume was intense even here, amongst the bazaar's rich constellation of spices, incense and dozens of bodies. 'Thank you, thank you, pretty lady,' the boy said, hastily pocketing the generous handful of coins.

'As for Martin, he will come round – he's smitten with you – as soon as he sees he can make plenty of money. You'll be happy, believe me, once you get used to being his wife. Come and visit us, and Roddy will help . . .'

Roddy's help was part of what the weekend had been orchestrated to secure, and on that point, Phoebe was delighted, but, as ever, Edith offered her advice with sharp-eyed honesty. Phoebe reluctantly recognized some truth in what her aunt was saying about her aspirations to a career: the age gap meant that she and Martin had been born into different eras. So much had changed, so fast. On some things, Martin wouldn't be able – or want – to catch up.

*

Phoebe closed her eyes, feeling the heat of the sand through the mat that the boy had laid out for her. She pulled her straw hat over her eyes; the Gulf sun was fierce. Even through sunglasses and closed eyelids, there was a yellow-pink glare of light. After the cold of Tehran's winter, the warmth on her body was delicious.

'More lemonade?' called Edith from her deckchair. She was ensconced in the shade of a shelter rigged up with poles and bamboo matting.

She had a lifetime's experience of avoiding sunlight, Phoebe reflected, and smiled inwardly, recalling her aunt's expression when she'd changed into her bikini to sunbathe.

'Are you sure that's appropriate?' Edith had said, with careful emphasis, inclining her head towards the two boys resting in the meagre shade of the dingy. The yacht was anchored just offshore; the water was too shallow to bring it in any closer.

Phoebe shrugged. 'That's exactly what Mother said!'

Edith returned to her book.

The boys had helped them catch fish off the boat on the ride over from Manama. Phoebe didn't follow their instructions closely, instead she watched the breeze catch the sail, filling it to a gentle curve, and the boat's prow break ripples in the sandy water. She half-listened to Edith explain the history of pearl fishing, and the divers' extraordinary capacity to hold their breath, and how the tradition had collapsed in the space of a few years as cheap Japanese cultured pearls swept the market. Centuries of skill handed down, father to son, were rendered useless, she lamented.

On the boat one of the boys gutted the fish they had caught, washing the blood away with sea water, and throwing the innards back for the birds. After they pulled the dingy ashore, the boys built a small fire and the skipper grilled the fish with rough sea salt, pungent herbs and green, thick-skinned lemons. A boy laid a small table with napkins and crockery. The two women sat together in the shade, eating the delicate white flesh of the fish with flatbread and olives. The crew ate on their own, close to the boat.

If Phoebe opened her eyes a fraction, beyond her painted toenails she could see the grey-blue sea stretching out in the direction of the Iranian coast and its mangrove swamps. Somewhere over to the north-west lay the great Iranian oil refinery at Abadan, and further round the Gulf coast lay Kuwait, and the huge Ghawar and Khafji fields in Saudi Arabia. Behind her were a few scrubby palms and the odd clump of withered seagrass, but no sign of inhabitation. The water lapped sluggishly, and the air was heavy, laden with the smell of salt and mud. It was lethargic places exactly like this tiny island of Rubud Al Sharqiyah where huge reserves of oil and gas were being discovered, and making millionaires by the dozen. The rumours about the size of Qatar's reserves were scarcely credible, and it lay only a few miles away. Phoebe rolled over on to her front and imagined she could hear the roar of the black gold, deep under the sand and rock, waiting to erupt into these sleepy places and sweep them away in an oily tide. She fell into a light sleep, dreaming of black viscous liquid, glinting in the sun.

When she woke, she got up to sit beside Edith.

'Martin respects Roddy's advice,' Phoebe said, pouring them more lemonade from the thermos flask. Edith nodded, engrossed in an archaeological journal on the ancient ruins of Bahrain.

Back at Edith and Roddy's bungalow, the packing trunks were in the hallway, and their departure was imminent, delayed for a few weeks for this visit. While the men were closeted in meetings, Edith had kept Phoebe busy with visits to desert ruins and cruises, such as today's, to outlying islands.

Edith put down her book and looked at Phoebe over the top of her sunglasses.

'A friend in Hampshire knows a cousin of Martin. Apparently Lodsbourne is a lovely place, but in a dreadful state. It's going to need a lot of money, but Roddy speaks very highly of Martin. If Martin's father can just hang on a couple of years, you'll be in the clear. You will enjoy the house, I'm sure of it.'

Phoebe pulled on her dress and buttoned it up, bending her head to tie the halterneck straps. She scooped her hair into a knot.

'You would know how to bring a place like Lodsbourne to its full glory. You have an artistic eye – what fabrics to choose, pictures to hang. I envy you, to be honest,' sighed Edith. 'In my marriage, I've lived everywhere – and nowhere. I can't count the number of places I have tried to make home: the bungalow verandas, the gardens I have planted, the carved furniture, the trinkets I have arranged. But it's all stage scenery: deep down, we know we are interlopers, the latest in a long line of invaders and conquerors. We may do a better job of it than our forebears, offering impartial administration, law courts and a police service, a bit of education, but you can't live in any of these places –' she waved her hand vaguely towards the sea – 'without knowing all too well that even the most competent and efficient of empires crumble, and when they do, we will no longer be welcome. We may even come to be hated, as we were in India. I've seen it already in Iran, and perhaps even here in Bahrain.'

Phoebe had never heard her aunt talk like this.

'But it looks as if I might be offered a job in New York, starting next year,' she said. 'Perhaps I can persuade Martin to give up on the house.'

'Don't force him to choose between you and the house – he won't ever forgive you. We expatriates talk and dream of home all the time – that's the only thing we have in common. Otherwise we are a strange assembly of misfits – alcoholics, bullies, lost romantics – so it becomes an obsession.' Edith sucked thoughtfully on the stem of her heavy reading glasses. 'Come with him to Bahrain. You won't be able to stand it for long. After you've had a couple of children, you'll have exhausted the delights of swimming pools and country clubs. Then you can go home and mastermind the renovations, and, before long, Martin will be able to manage the business out of London. Run Lodsbourne as a gallery. Forget the career.'

Too many elements of Edith's scenarios were still unresolved. Could she really see that far into the future, Phoebe wondered.

The boys were preparing the boat for their trip home, and a slight breeze was picking up. Edith began to put the china back into the wicker basket.

'If Martin wants to feel virtuous as well, he can. I may have emphasized the money to be made here, but the place needs some judicious British intervention – keeping their legal system up to the mark, prisons, and so forth. They would be worse off without us.'

Such conversations left Phoebe uneasy – she sensed things she would rather not know. She recollected the reference to policemen with experience of suppressing the Mau Mau Uprising over dinner back in Shiraz. Kenya had been brutal, according to the news reports of the prison camps, and she thought of the chilling aftermath to Asil's disappearance – the emptiness of never hearing what exactly had happened or why. Was this the kind of police work Roddy was involved in?

Edith stood up and gathered her book and journals. Phoebe threw a light shawl around her bare shoulders, and watched the boys packing up the shade and the table. They avoided her eye and ignored her thanks. They made her feel uncomfortable. Perhaps the black bikini was best kept for the country club.

*

When Phoebe came down for drinks on the veranda that evening, Martin and Roddy were discussing their audience with the king. They both rose to greet her, and Martin gallantly took her hand.

'You look beautiful,' he said, kissing her.

He made her a cocktail. 'We attended the majlis,' he explained. 'It's like a reception for all sorts of businessmen and local Bahrainis with requests, and you usually have a few minutes to talk directly to the king. We had a very useful fifteen minutes – he's a man you can do business with.' The prospect of leaving the Foreign Office was giving Martin a new appetite for life. 'The king sat on his throne and beside him was his falcon on a tie. It was as if I was in a film about Lawrence of Arabia. When I came forward to speak to him, the bird fixed its beady eye on me. I was pretty much on a level with the damned bird – it didn't look friendly – it could have leaned forward and poked my eye out. Very disconcerting.'

Phoebe laughed, and picked out her cocktail olive.

Roddy turned to Martin. 'The other matter we discussed on

the phone is fixed, and he'll be here in the next few weeks. His wife is packing up the house in Nairobi and will join him after she has settled the children at boarding schools in the UK. He brings plenty of experience. He'll keep things in shape.'

Phoebe looked at Martin inquiringly, but he ignored her, and looked out across the garden to the blackness where the sea was chafing quietly against the shore. Edith had described it as a 'sea of subtle movements'. Phoebe felt a moment of unease between them, but then he leaned over and put his arm around her shoulders. She could tell he was very happy – excited, even; a new course had been set. Martin had seen the possibility of success, beyond anything he had ever imagined possible.

'It's time to announce our engagement,' he declared to the room, and turned to kiss an astonished Phoebe.

'I take it that's a yes?' he asked, laughing, and she agreed that, yes, it was. Yes. The kaleidoscope had turned, another pattern.

'I owe everything to my extraordinary fiancée, her vision, resourcefulness, commitment and patience,' said Martin.

Edith exclaimed with delight, and Roddy insisted on a bottle of champagne to celebrate.

'There's a house here that would suit us very well for a few months. I've arranged for us to look at it tomorrow,' Martin said to Phoebe, and raised his glass. 'To my Phoebe!'

'To us in Bahrain,' she replied, suppressing the twinge of regret, the loss of New York. 'And to Lodsbourne!'

LONDON
2018

5

Fauzia lay on her sofa, channel-surfing on her iPad, an empty wine glass on the table beside her. There had been no word now from Reem for ten days. At work, Fauzia was too busy to dwell on it, but she kept an eye on the Arabic sites for news. At home in the evenings, her mind kept coming back to Reem. She tried going out with colleagues one evening, but she had no heart for the office gossip. At the weekend, she eased the tension of her pent-up anxiety in a long workout at the gym, and afterwards she even managed to catch up on some sleep. When she woke in the late afternoon, bleary and disorientated, she couldn't face seeing her date that evening and texted to cancel. A furious reply came back. She barred his number; they had only met a couple of times and she hadn't been convinced. Online dating was a lucky dip, she and her friends agreed: a lot of sawdust and the occasional cheap toy. In the evenings after work she ordered in food, and watched films or did some online shopping – anything for distraction. She bought a white trouser suit she was unlikely to wear. The wine helped her switch off. As each day passed, that sharp, bitter foreboding grew stronger, and at times it made her want to vomit. If Reem disappeared, it could be her fault: her crazy carelessness, her cowardice.

The phone beeped, its light flickering on the ceiling. It was Kate, and she left it to ring. She couldn't keep up the pretence any more. She had tried to be reassuring and calm for several days, persuading Kate that Reem would reappear, insisting there was no reason to worry. Kate was fragile enough without all this.

Fauzia knew Kate had gone back to counselling – she still had flashbacks, nightmares, and sometimes woke screaming, soaked in sweat. The therapist had diagnosed post-traumatic stress disorder.

Fauzia had called the Cambridge professor the previous night and they had talked for nearly an hour. He told her that Reem had been researching British arms sales in the 1960s and 1970s; she had arrived at Cambridge very clear in her research focus: Britain's 'End of East of Suez' policy. Fauzia didn't follow the academic detail, but she liked listening to his voice. It had a calm authority, like that of a vicar; it reminded her of a visit she had taken once to Cambridge to meet Felix Wilcox Smith early in their relationship. Felix was at a conference and she'd agreed to join him for a night. It was late afternoon and raining, and as she walked past colleges, their windows glowing with warm light, she glimpsed rows of bookshelves, and the occasional gleam of a gilt picture frame. In such cosy rooms, clever men and women pondered the histories of nations, the great thoughts of philosophers and mathematicians, physicists and poets. In that moment on the shining pavements of Cambridge, she had deeply envied those detached observers, with their shabby armchairs and neat lawns. Here was the accumulated knowledge of centuries and its guardianship.

All this she imagined she could hear in Tim's careful, considered comments on Reem's whereabouts and his sensible interventions with the Foreign Office. He had even somehow got hold of her dental records. Slightly embarrassed, he pointed out that Reem had a small red scar below her left ear. He was right – Fauzia remembered Reem's habit of rubbing a forefinger over the spot as she straightened her hijab – but it brought her up short: how had he noticed such a tiny thing? He must have known Reem better than he was indicating, but there were more important things to dwell on. Fauzia told him she had forwarded photos for identification to the stringer, Ted, to pass on to the Egyptian

78

police, though she feared that he was too pissed half the time to do anything useful.

The phone flickered to life again: a WhatsApp message from Ted. She sat up and her fingers were shaking as she opened it: 'Body of young female found in Cairo suburb. Am talking to police. Will let you know asap.'

Fauzia took the empty glass to the fridge and filled it to the brim. She took a large gulp. Poor Reem. She hadn't pulled down the blinds and she could see her reflection, lit by the open fridge, in the large plate-glass window, merging with the view over the city, the red lights of cranes blinking in the dark. She wouldn't be able to sleep now. How could she kill this time? Her impatience felt murderous. Any minute the waiting would be over, and the last dwindling hope extinguished. It was past ten, and the middle of the night in Cairo. She thought of Ted ringing irritated, lazy police officials, with a bottle of beer beside him.

★

Fauzia first met Reem in 2016, shortly after Reem had arrived in London for her scholarship to study at the London School of Economics – she was living in Kate's flat. Fauzia hadn't expected her to be quite so beautiful, despite having 'met' her on FaceTime on Kate's laptop. When she took off her hijab, her hair was thick and dark. She didn't smile often, but when she did, it spread wide across her small face. She was petite, below five feet, but she had great presence, perched on the side of Kate's sofa, sampling her playlist of Arabic pop music on Spotify. She didn't seem interested in visiting the sights of London; Fauzia asked if she had been on the London Eye, or seen Buckingham Palace and Oxford Street yet.

'I'm not a tourist,' she replied coolly, and then she laughed, looking up from under her thick eyebrows. She was funny as well as clever. She referred to some of her fellow students from the

Gulf at the university as 'chicken nuggets', and when Fauzia looked puzzled, she explained, 'That's what we call kids who speak perfect English after a year in a private American high school and who are so well groomed – and woke.' She rolled her eyes. 'Yet they don't seem to understand much about how their own countries work.'

She became animated when she talked about her studies. She had switched her MA from business management to international relations on her first day.

'It was my plan all along,' she told Fauzia, as Kate prepared supper. 'I want to research the relationship between Britain and Bahrain – arms, security, horses, Formula One, everything.' She laughed, and then, serious, she flicked open her laptop and brought up a human-rights website with photos of prisoners who had been badly beaten in detention. 'There's some stuff here about a former London Metropolitan Police chief who came to my country after the 2011 unrest.'

Fauzia looked at the open door to the kitchen. Kate had her back to them, busy chopping onions. Khaled's 'C'est la vie' was playing, and Reem's body moved to the rhythm. Fauzia turned the volume up slightly, and leaned forward.

'You know that Kate's uncle set up a security company of some kind in the Middle East?'

Reem stopped moving, her mouth wide open, disbelieving. 'What?'

Fauzia shrugged. 'I know. Not what you would guess from someone like Kate. She has rich relatives down in Hampshire. Her uncle never talked about the company – a consultancy called ZSKa. It's been going decades. Look it up, see if it has anything to do with Bahrain.'

'What's his name?'

'Martin Wilcox Smith.'

At that point Kate came back to the room with drinks, swaying to the music, and Fauzia jumped up to join her in an impromptu dance around the sofa, giggling.

The following day Reem texted – as Fauzia knew she would – and asked if they could talk. They agreed to meet the following week, in a cafe in St James's Park, after a press conference Fauzia had in Whitehall. In the days leading up to the meeting, Fauzia debated with herself about whether to give her Martin's hard drive, and concluded it was too dangerous. Reem was only twenty-one; she wouldn't know the danger.

*

What was now making Fauzia retch with anxiety as she stared at the cranes' red lights from her flat was the fact that she had changed her mind. Inexplicably, impulsively, she had unlocked the drawer of her desk at the office and removed the hard drive, which had been lying there untouched for years, and stuffed it in her bag. Later, as she walked across the park towards the cafe, she could feel the plastic box bumping against her hip through the thin leather of her shoulder bag. She still hadn't decided whether she should give it to Reem. She didn't understand its contents, or their significance, but the Wilcox Smith family had gone to great lengths to recover it. They had something to hide, and somebody needed to get to the bottom of that damned family, and perhaps clever, determined Reem could – she was owed some answers. Fauzia's hunch was that, with enough persistent research, the hard drive would reveal the nature of the lucrative Wilcox Smith business, but her editor had refused to give her time off to investigate. She had thought she would get around to it, but life had intervened – first the divorce from Felix and its aftermath, then buying and moving into her flat. Digging into the affairs of her former in-laws had repeatedly been postponed; she had even considered throwing the hard drive away, but something made her hesitate.

'It belonged to Martin Wilcox Smith,' she told Reem, putting the hard drive on the table between them.

Reem's eyes fastened on the slim black box, immediately grasping its significance; she had already started researching Martin Wilcox Smith and his consultancy, ZSKa. She listened impassively to Fauzia's embarrassed account of how she had failed to do anything with it. She didn't tell her how she had got it, and Reem didn't ask. Fauzia urged her to be careful: only use it on a public computer, never keep it at home.

But she didn't tell her why she knew the information was sensitive, even dangerous. She couldn't bring herself to do that. Now, looking back, as she had done many times since Tim's first call, Fauzia asked herself how she could have put Reem at such risk.

*

The phone jerked on the glass coffee table. Another message: 'No identity papers but seems likely to be her. Early twenties, about 5 ft. Body badly beaten. No more info til tmrw.'

Should she call Tim? She could leave Phoebe until the morning, but Fauzia had promised she would ring Kate the minute she heard anything, and this mattered more to her than anyone. Kate had made it clear when Reem first arrived in England that she regarded her as family. Hot tears rolled down Fauzia's cheeks. She rubbed them furiously with the cuff of her dressing gown. The phone jerked again, vibrating on the table. Ted had sent two photos. Fauzia scrolled the confusing images trying to decipher what part of a bloodied body she was looking at, and whether there was anything she could recognize as Reem. In the dim light of the flat, the reds and pinks glowed harshly on her phone. She shivered, suddenly icy cold.

Tim answered the phone immediately, as if he had been waiting for the call, and pre-empted Fauzia's news.

'I know.' His voice was hoarse. 'I've been online all evening. The body was found this morning and reported on a local Egyptian news site at lunchtime. The report claims she was hit by a passing car. I've seen the images and contacted a friend, who is at the police station now. I didn't want to worry you until I had more information. No identity papers were with the body.'

Of course Tim would know. Fauzia imagined him messaging his contacts in Arabic from his study before going down to one of those ridiculous dinners in a hammer-beam hall lit by candles; sitting at a long, polished table before slipping back to his desk to decipher photos of a woman's battered body. Meanwhile she was looking at London's skyscrapers on a clear, cold night, and a body lay in an Egyptian police mortuary. What gave that body its precious, loved meaning lay in relationships scattered thousands of miles apart: in the dusty suburban street in Manama with her grandparents; in the prison nearby, where her mother must be lying in her cell; and here in Britain, amongst the friends and acquaintances Reem had made. These were the people who knew how brilliant and beautiful she was, how she had a remarkable life ahead of her, and how she was driven by her love for her father. Only in an Egyptian police station was all this unknown – and irrelevant.

'I'm sorry, Fauzia.' Tim must have guessed from her silence that she was crying noiselessly. Perhaps he was one of those stiff men embarrassed by tears. 'Let's speak in the morning. You or I may need to go to Egypt.'

After he had rung off, Fauzia splashed her face with cold water. She needed to be calm for Kate's sake. This could crush her. When Reem had won the scholarship, Kate had been so proud of her huge achievement. She was keen for Fauzia to meet her as soon as Reem arrived in London, and that first evening in the flat, the three women instantly found a warm camaraderie, despite their differences in life experience and age. Even Kate's son Art had been there, joining them to eat supper, if Fauzia remembered right.

She scrolled through her contacts and was about to ring Kate, her fingertip hovering on the screen, but she changed her mind: a call wasn't good enough. Kate needed company for this. Fauzia would go over to the flat and tell her face to face, and, if necessary, stay the night and help in the morning. She pulled on jeans and a jumper and threw a toothbrush and pyjamas in her bag.

Ten minutes later, she was in the lift down to the ground floor and the waiting taxi. As the car pulled away, she leaned back and fastened her seatbelt, hoping that the strong smell of air freshener wouldn't irritate her lungs. It was nearly six years since she had first met Kate at a lunch party at Lodsbourne on a hot midsummer weekend. She and Felix had spent most of the time in the pool, but she'd liked Kate immediately; her sincerity and unpretentiousness had been a refreshing contrast to the assembled Wilcox Smith tribe and their hangers-on. Fauzia remembered Phoebe fussing over napkins and flower arrangements, and for most of the lunch party Martin had been engrossed in conversation with the guests, a diplomat and his wife. Fauzia couldn't remember their names, only the chilly hauteur with which the wife had greeted her. Felix's older sister Dotty had been even worse. Afterwards, Fauzia had quizzed Felix about Dotty and he'd laughed. That was the problem with Felix: he'd never had much reason to take life too seriously. She didn't feel bitter about her ex-husband, just permanently, mildly irritated by his carelessness about things that mattered. Their divorce had been amicable enough. His redeeming feature was his loyalty to Kate; he was the only one who didn't treat her with condescension.

When Fauzia met Kate, she didn't know the history of her father, but over that weekend she sensed the discomfort Kate's presence provoked at Lodsbourne: a combination of guilt and irritation. Kate either didn't notice or didn't mind, happy enough that her son was enjoying the lavish hospitality. Fauzia would be the first to admit how seductive the whole Wilcox Smith set-up was – after all, she had fallen for it.

The taxi stopped outside Kate's block, and she felt a deep sense of dread, rather like being at the end of a high diving board. Or, even worse, like that time she did a parachute jump for charity in South Africa. She had clung on to the instructor's hand as she edged to the opening of the plane, and suddenly saw the tiny houses, the pattern of fields and roads below. She could already see Kate's future pain as if from a distance: how it would overwhelm her and remind her of past losses.

She pressed the buzzer. After a short wait, Kate answered, first husky with sleep, then alarmed when she recognized her voice. Fauzia climbed the two flights of steps, and above, she heard Kate undoing the bolts on her front door.

ENGLAND
2012–13

6

Kate looked quickly around her new flat. Boxes were piled along one side of the sitting room, but at least she had managed to clean and paint the kitchen since she moved in a month ago. It had made a big difference, and she was pleased with how the sunshine picked up the bright yellow. Before long the flat would feel like home. Her tenant would be here any moment. She glanced in the mirror and ran her fingers through her hair, smoothed down her tunic dress and wiped a smudge of mascara from under one eye. She was glad Art was at school; she knew how he scrutinized the interactions of adults. When she picked up the entryphone, the man also sounded nervous. She tried to sound confident and cheerful.

'Come straight up to the fourth floor.'

She opened her flat door and stood on the landing, leaning over the railing. The first sight of Hussain was the top of his head, and then he looked up and she saw his brown eyes, glasses, prominent dark eyebrows and his beard. He was carrying a large suitcase and a small backpack. He was moving in.

They had met two days before at the cafe near where Art was playing football. It was busy with parents and small children, and they sat at the end of a shared table. Kate felt awkward, as if they were on a date, and tried to be matter of fact, pulling up photos of the flat on her phone to show him. While he scrutinized the images, she tried to imagine what it would be like to live with him. He was slim, medium height, dressed in a cotton shirt, jeans and jacket. He was probably Middle Eastern, perhaps in his early forties. His fluent English had a slight American accent. He looked tired and pale, but he smiled a lot in an attempt to put her at ease. He had lines at the corners of his eyes, she noticed, from smiling or squinting into the sun. Kate's friend Shirin had put them in touch; she'd told Kate that he was studying in London, and warned that he was a private person and would be reluctant to talk about himself. When Kate looked quizzical, her friend had been evasive. 'He's a good man, very kind,' she insisted, 'trust me.' And Kate did – they had been friends for two decades – but she was still curious. Shirin wouldn't give any more information. 'Ask him yourself when you know him better,' she suggested. 'He will be the perfect lodger. Tidy, clean, respectful, and probably out a lot. He'll pay on time, and you are doing him a good turn. He needs a place fast,' she said, and added, 'He'll be good with Art.'

Sitting opposite him in the cafe surrounded by other families, Kate had been too embarrassed to ask him where he was from; it seemed intrusive. He didn't smoke or drink, he told her, and he needed a room as soon as possible – he wanted to move out of a shared house near King's Cross which was no longer suitable. He didn't explain why, and she didn't feel she could ask. He would pay the deposit and the month's rent in advance as requested. He said these things in a low, quiet voice, and Kate noticed there was a tremor in one of his eyelids. She recognized how anxiety hung heavily on every movement and interaction. At one point a child at a nearby table dropped a glass on the floor and Hussain flinched as it crashed into fragments. Kate thought of how the thousand pounds in rent would pay two months of mortgage payments.

She blurted out information about Art and the flat. She told him that they would have their separate lives but sometimes they might share a meal. His quiet listening was calming. He said he had a sixteen-year-old daughter. She mentally revised his age – perhaps he was in his late forties. His face softened, and he pulled a battered photo from his breast pocket and handed it over to Kate.

'It's very old but it reminds me of happier times.' It was of a young girl of ten or so, dressed for a party, in a wide skirt of white net sparkling with sequins, and pink slippers. Despite the festive occasion, she looked solemn, her heart-shaped face dominated by large brown eyes.

'She's very pretty,' said Kate, smiling, warming to this stranger. 'What's her name?'

'Reem.'

Kate looked puzzled.

'R–E–E–M – it means a gazelle.' He looked at the photo before he tucked it back in his jacket pocket. As he drank his coffee, Kate looked at his fingernails, bitten to the quick. Long fingers and a few wiry hairs. She often looked at hands when she had to make an important decision. They agreed to a month's trial, and that he would move in the day after tomorrow. He would come over first thing and Kate would go into work late.

*

'Can I help you with the suitcase?' Kate asked, but he shook his head. She led the way into the flat.

'I'm afraid I haven't finished unpacking – what with work and my son, there hasn't been time. At least the kitchen is painted, and I'm planning to get around to doing the rest of the flat eventually. I had hoped to decorate your room before you arrived, but I didn't have time, I'm sorry.'

Kate could hear herself talking too fast, filling up the silence as he looked around.

'It's nice. It gets sunshine and I like the plants on the balcony,' he said.

She saw for the first time how his face softened when the tension eased. She began to see why Shirin had been emphatic that he was a kind man. She glanced at the balcony, where she had managed to squeeze two chairs amongst the plants in pots.

'We had a garden where we lived before, and I managed to bring a few things with me. I'll show you your room. Perhaps you'd like coffee before you unpack?'

He carried the suitcase into the large double room Kate had prepared for him. She'd taken the small back room for herself, reasoning that if he had the bigger room, he would be comfortable spending time there rather than in the shared areas of the flat. Besides, he was paying a decent rent: he deserved it.

She poured coffee and he took a cup, but remained standing next to the table in the kitchen.

'Art is ten. He comes back from after-school club at about six, and at this time of year we often go to the park for an hour. We usually eat about seven thirty.'

He nodded, and sipped his coffee.

There was a pause and Kate began again, nervous of silences. 'Art's a complicated child – he has trouble with schoolwork and he had to change schools a year ago because he was being bullied. I think he misses his father, and it's hard being an only child. But he's better than he was, and we just have to hope that the move to secondary school in a year's time isn't too much of a challenge.'

He nodded again. Kate was floundering.

'Shirin said you were studying?'

'Yes, I'll be out much of the day. I'm a mature student. The room will suit me well.' He emptied his cup. 'I'll get on with unpacking and leave you in peace.'

'Of course,' Kate replied, disconcerted by his abruptness. 'I know Shirin said you might not want to say much about where you are from, but I'm guessing you are Middle Eastern?'

She could see he didn't want to answer, but she held his gaze. 'I'm from Bahrain.'

'It's a small place in the Gulf, isn't it? An island? Does it have oil? My aunt and uncle lived in the Middle East in the 1970s. They moved around a bit when they were younger – Dubai, Iran and, I think, Bahrain. They loved Iran.'

He shifted the weight from one foot to the other. 'There are a lot of British in the region,' he said stiffly. 'I had better get on. Could I have some keys?'

'I'm sorry, I didn't mean to pry. Of course, I got a set cut for you.'

'Please, don't apologize,' he said. 'There's no need. I think the English apologize a lot.'

'I can't help it – it's ridiculous, and I get teased about it at work, but I can't seem to shift the habit.' They both laughed, and Kate was relieved – it might work out. 'Art and I are away this weekend, so you'll have the place to yourself. We're going to my aunt and uncle in the country – the annual visit.'

'I'm out tonight. Perhaps I will see you before you go, but if I don't, I hope you have a good weekend.'

With that, Hussain retreated to his room, carefully shutting the door behind him. Kate could hear him moving around, opening and shutting drawers and wardrobe doors. A short while later, she heard him go out and the front door clicked behind him. She wondered how she was going to live with this reserved, quiet man.

*

Phoebe was on the doorstep, arms outstretched to greet Kate and Art as the car from the station came to a halt on the gravel drive. Two pointers at her side barked enthusiastically, and she shushed and called to them as they raced around the arrivals, their tails wagging. She gave both Kate and Art a quick hug, and Kate caught a snatch of her Dior scent. She was wearing a long, shabby apron, the pockets bulging.

'I'm a frightful mess. I've been with the cows, and I must smell dreadful. I'm so glad you could come for the weekend.' She laughed, and tucked a loose strand back behind her ear. Phoebe must be around seventy, but she still knew how to discreetly underline her best features: a small amount of eyeliner, the soft hair gathered with combs into a loose bun, cheekbones prominent in her lined face, and a pair of heavy silver earrings, no doubt purchased during the years she had spent in the Middle East.

'Cows?' asked Art, disbelieving. Kate's visit the previous year had been alone; Art had been in America with his father, and he had not been keen to come this time. He found Lodsbourne intimidating. The boy looked up at the grand façade of yellow stone with its rows of tall windows glinting in the evening sun. Kate understood his question: what do grand ladies do with cows? On the train, he had asked why people called Phoebe a Lady, and they'd had a conversation about titles – how people got them, how some inherited them – and it had left Art confused. Martin had been given a knighthood in the late 1980s in return for a handsome donation to the Tory party, Kate's mother had once told her.

'Yes, ducky. You see, in grand old age – and I am horribly old – ladies like me get interested in crazy projects: some take up needlework, and I have taken up cows. I have a herd of Jersey cows and they produce the creamiest milk in the world.' Phoebe put an arm lightly around Art's shoulder as she ushered them into the house.

'Do you milk them?' persisted Art.

'No, sadly not. I would have loved to, but it means you have to get up early, and I'm just not good at that. We have a room called a milking parlour, full of frightfully clever machines, and a Lithuanian man called Matis helps. He can show you how it works – you probably don't mind getting up early, do you? Maybe later Matis and I can show you my secret technique!'

Art looked puzzled.

'It's a cow-keeping secret, but we will let you in on it.' She gave him a conspiratorial wink as she led the way upstairs to show them their rooms.

'This is where you will sleep, Art,' she said, opening a door into a large bedroom. 'It used to be the nursery. And those are Felix and Dotty's old toys,' she added, gesturing to a tall cupboard, its shelves neatly piled with boxes of Lego and old puzzles. 'You probably won't have much use for them, they're too old-fashioned, but have a look and see if anything takes your fancy. The house rule is that you put them all back before you go.'

There was a pair of iron bedsteads in the centre of the room covered with faded quilts. Stuffed animals from several decades of the twentieth century were lined up on a chest, and standing in front of the window was a battered rocking horse, which had lost most of its mane. The window gave on to the walled garden at the back of the house, and Kate glimpsed rows of vegetables and fruit canes. Art was already rummaging through a stack of old comics.

'Your mum will be just opposite,' said Phoebe, beckoning Kate to follow. The landing was lined with family photos, and Kate glanced briefly at a portrait of Phoebe as a young woman. It was the style of photo which had fascinated Kate's mother in old *Country Life* magazines at the dentist: a head and shoulders portrait of a well-connected beauty. The slashed neckline of Phoebe's dress accentuated her neck and the distinctive earrings. Below, on a dark wood chest, sat a pile of ironed linen and a big vase of roses and delphiniums. This is what the calm of a lavish and well-ordered household looked like, Kate thought wistfully.

'Here is your room, Katharine – use the bathroom next door. I chose the pink roses because they have the best scent, and I knew you would appreciate them.' A collection of yellow and pink blooms sat on the bedside table. Phoebe put a hand lightly on her arm. 'I'm so glad you decided to come – the weather this weekend is going to be gorgeous. Unpack, have a bath or, if you fancy it, a dip in the pool. You've got time. It's only us for dinner, so we're eating in the kitchen – I hope you don't mind. Martin doesn't like it, but I thought it would be more relaxing for Arthur.'

'This is lovely, Aunt Phoebe,' Kate exclaimed, overwhelmed by the beauty of the room. On previous visits, she had been in the nursery or a room at the back of the house. Here, the double bed's embroidered bedspread echoed the colours of the wallpaper, with its swooping birds and flowers. Above the mantelpiece was an oil painting of the downs. Tonight, when Kate leaned back into the deep white pillows with their lace edging, she would drift asleep with the perfume of roses. Through the half-open window, she caught the cry of a wood pigeon as the sun dipped behind the copper beech.

'We got the grass cut today, because we've guests this weekend: our great friends Tom and Anne, and now Dotty is bringing the family over on Sunday, and Felix and Fauzia just called to say they might come after all,' said Phoebe, looking down at the lawn, where the dogs were sprawled in a last shaft of sunlight. 'I don't think you have met Fauzia before. The wedding in January was a small registry office thing – their choice. But we like her. She's ambitious and hard-working. You'll get on.' She laughed. 'I've got to see that supper is ready, so I'll leave you to settle in, but come and find me in the kitchen if you need anything – there's a pile of towels already at the pool. I need to get rid of the smell of manure – Martin can't bear it.'

Kate stood by the armchair looking out of the window: there were times when England could be forgiven for everything, she thought. Forgiven those endless days clamped under grey cloud when the weather does *nothing*; forgiven even for its inability to organize how people move – clogged traffic and ineffectual railways. When England put on its display of charms, it would be churlish to resist its particular beauty. Rarely dramatic, often beguiling: beyond the lawn lay the park, dotted with mature trees and the soft brown haunches of Phoebe's herd of Jersey cows, and beyond that, framed by woods on either side, was a sweep of chalk downland.

Phoebe had put Art at his ease – Kate could hear him clattering about in the nursery – and had piqued his curiosity about the dairy herd. Phoebe might be old-fashioned – who else talked of dressing for dinner or apologized for supper in the kitchen? – but she meant well. Kate even found it oddly reassuring that Phoebe and Martin had made so few adjustments to the twenty-first century in their domestic life, following old family traditions probably dating from their own mothers' upbringing nearly a century ago.

Through the door to the bathroom, Kate could see an enormous old bath positioned to give the bather a view out of the window. After dinner she could slip upstairs early, get Art to bed and then lie – perhaps even float – in the ancient bath as the sky darkened. The complications of life would fade: the conflicts with Art's father, and her nervousness over sharing the flat with her new lodger. After that she would lie between the ironed linen sheets in a bed made with the top sheet turned down over blankets and a quilt. It reminded her of childhood. Her adult life had been un-ironed Ikea duvets. She sat down in the armchair, putting her feet up on the window ledge, her eyes feasting on the view.

★

'Phoebe tells me you have moved?' said Martin, at the head of the table, looking over his glasses at Kate. His eyesight was fading, but his mind was as sharp as ever. She was used to these inter-rogations on her rare visits, but it didn't make them easier; she always felt her answers disappointed Martin.

'Hackney has become fashionable, I hear,' commented Phoebe, glancing at her husband before deftly switching the focus to Art. 'And what do you think of your new home, Art?'

Art looked rather lost amongst the silver and candlelight, and glanced at his mother before answering. 'Well, Mum and me will miss the old garden, but I've got my own room and the flat is near my school. I didn't want to change schools, and I have a friend who lives on the estate. We can play in the playground in the evenings, and Mum can watch from the balcony.'

'Estate?' repeated Martin, addressing Kate, his eyebrows raised.

She took a breath. 'It's a former council flat, a nice development from the 1950s. We were really lucky – and it has three bedrooms,' she explained brightly. It was true, she had been delighted to find it.

'We've got a lodger called Hussain who smiles a lot, but is very quiet,' added Art. 'I've only seen him once so far.'

Kate braced herself.

'It sounds just the ticket,' intervened Phoebe quickly, casting another meaningful glance at her husband. Talk was mercifully interrupted as plates were passed to Phoebe for second helpings of home-cooked ham and salad, and Kate hastily changed the subject by commenting on the set of old French plates they were using.

'I bought them on a holiday in Provence – it must have been the mid-seventies, I think. Is that right, Martin?' replied Phoebe.

Martin hadn't heard. His hearing appeared to come and go, and he dipped in and out of the conversation, so Kate didn't know if she was talking to Phoebe or both of them.

'We spent a week on the French Riviera, drinking too much champagne, and then we hired a car and drove through Provence, filling it with china, olive oil and, of course, wine. We were doing Lodsbourne up at the time, and needed crockery. Wonderful days, do you remember?' Phoebe's expression softened as she looked at her husband.

'The Riviera was beautiful then,' he said fondly. 'Before the crowds got there. Ruined now, like so many places on the Med.'

After ice cream and apple pie, Art was persuaded it was bedtime, and Phoebe suggested Kate join them for coffee by the drawing-room fire. Art and Kate climbed the wide wooden treads of the old staircase, pausing for Art to bounce on a particular creaky one, the timber shrill in protest.

'Are Phoebe and Martin really rich?' he asked.

'I suppose so, Art. I don't know, I don't ask questions like that,' laughed Kate.

'They must be millionaires with a big house like this, and cows, and that man Bill, who picked us up from the station. Might they even be multimillionaires?' Art's face was flushed with excitement. He was used to Kate frowning at the sight of bills, and was fascinated by money. Kate agreed they were probably multi-millionaires.

'Why are they rich and we're not?'

Kate was flummoxed for an answer. 'Martin's business has been very successful, I suppose.'

She urged him to get into his pyjamas, but he was still pondering the subject, and he paused while brushing his teeth at the sink in his room.

'I don't think it's fair. He's your uncle. We should have some of their money. I'd like to be rich: you get to live in a big house with a huge garden, and everyone likes you a lot.'

'Well, I'm not sure that last point is always true,' said Kate, folding his clothes on the chair and pulling down his bed cover. 'But you don't have to worry about things like gas and council tax, that's for sure.'

Art lay ramrod straight under the covers, and stretched out his arms. Kate leaned over to give him a hug. She could feel his thin limbs; he was growing fast. She was always pressing food on him, but he was a fussy eater. The doctor had reproachfully repeated that he needed to put on more weight.

'I want to live in a house like this,' concluded Art as she turned the light out.

Downstairs, Martin and Phoebe were on either side of the fire. A tray with a coffee pot and cups was perched on an ottoman; piled on the other end were art catalogues of recent sales and exhibitions in London and Paris. Lamps in various parts of the room created pools of light from under their pleated silk shades and illuminated bright kilims and embroidered cushions. Everywhere Kate's eye moved, it fell on some beautiful object – a collection of Persian tiles in turquoise and brilliant peacock blue on one wall, an ornate silver plate on another, a delicate Buddha sitting on one corner of the mantelpiece: all evidence of their years collecting treasures across Asia and the Middle East.

'It's Afghan, dates from around the time of Alexander the Great's invasion,' commented Martin, following the direction of her eyes.

Kate suppressed the sense of unease she felt surrounded by the Wilcox Smith's treasures; she couldn't help wondering whether they had acquired them legally or had bought them in suspect backroom deals and smuggled them through customs. Phoebe poured a small coffee and refilled Kate's glass of wine. Martin peered over his glasses at his niece.

'Katharine, why couldn't you do better than a former council flat? And why do you need a lodger?' The emphasis he used for both 'council' and 'lodger' indicated how rarely he had need of the words.

'I'm doing a friend a favour taking the lodger, but it is helpful with the mortgage. He's a very nice man, friendly, and keeps himself very busy, so I don't think we will see him much,' Kate blithely insisted. 'The flat cost quite a bit, so I have a big mortgage.'

Kate was being asked to account for herself; she knew from previous visits that this was how the Wilcox Smith family operated. She explained lamely that a council flat now cost hundreds of thousands of pounds, but Martin was too successful a businessman not to know.

'Couldn't Edward make sure you and Art had enough for a decent place?' he asked.

Phoebe looked anxious, but she was not coming to Kate's rescue.

'It is a very nice flat,' repeated Kate. 'It was complicated. Ed's parents owned the house we were living in.' Kate hesitated, hoping she could leave it there. She didn't want to talk about it, but they said nothing, waiting. 'When it came to the split, the lawyers said I didn't have much of a case, because we had not married. There was a legal tussle back and forth for eighteen months. In the end, his parents stepped in to make a settlement big enough for a deposit, and I took a mortgage for the rest. The lodger's rent helps with that. Art is having trouble with school work at present, and I didn't want to change schools. We haven't moved very far – it's only a few streets.'

'I could try talking to Ed's father. I used to know him well.'

Ed's father had not been the problem, reflected Kate bitterly. For the first time, she saw that Martin's capacities were slowly unravelling; this successful, very able man no longer understood the world as he had once, and it made him profoundly uncomfortable. He was used to mastery, and, for a moment, she almost felt sorry for him.

'No, it's all sorted. We've come to the end of a difficult patch. Art and I will be fine in this flat, I feel sure of it. The tenant is very easy. He comes from Bahrain – you lived there for a while, didn't you?'

Martin ignored the last comment, still intent on the issue of Ed's provision for his son.

'Where is Ed? Does he still see Art?'

'He's still in Washington, and Art visits him, and when Ed comes back to stay with his parents, Art can spend time with him there. They talk on the phone sometimes.'

Kate winced at the memory of the last transatlantic call: the long silences and how Art had been confused by the slight time delay in the conversation, which meant sometimes he and Ed began speaking at the same time. Then, his frustrated, angry conclusion afterwards: 'Mum, he didn't listen to me.'

Martin harrumphed; there was no other word for the combination of snorting and shifting in his chair which eloquently expressed his disapproval.

'Who's the lodger?'

'Martin, Kate's got her own life,' Phoebe remonstrated gently. 'Kate, I think you've done very well in the circumstances. I'm sure the flat will be lovely when you have settled in, and I can't wait to come and see it. You are such a fighter.'

'You're welcome to visit any time,' said Kate remembering her manners, but inside she quailed at the idea of Phoebe arriving at the local station and walking down the high street past the pound shops and fast-food outlets to reach the flat. What would Phoebe make of the smell of disinfectant on the block's staircases? She preferred to keep Phoebe down here in the midst of her magic, on her beautifully designed stage, playing the part she had chosen for herself, as exquisitely as always. Kate finished her wine, relieved that the interrogation was suspended. At least there had been no questions about Ed's new girlfriend, and Phoebe had deflected the questions about the lodger. She thought longingly of the bath upstairs, and suggested she would head to bed.

'Of course, what a good idea: an early night.' Phoebe put down the tapestry she was stitching, and held up her cheek like a child to be kissed. 'Breakfast is at nine, and you'll hear the gong, but if you'd like a cup of tea in bed, there'll be a pot on the landing at eight as usual. I hope Art gives you a lie in.'

After Kate kissed Phoebe's cheek, Martin held out his hand to her and when she took it, he squeezed it. 'Good to see you here,' he murmured with unexpected warmth.

Walking slowly up the staircase, Kate examined the succession of framed Persian miniatures on the wall, and admired the delicacy of the figures and the vivid colouring. She remembered a diary item she had once read in the *Evening Standard* about the opening of a new room in the British Museum dedicated to Iranian art, which had been named after the Wilcox Smiths. They had donated several pieces, and the article noted that the Wilcox Smiths had one of the finest private collections of Persian art in the country, each item top in its class.

The bath was so long that her feet only just reached the taps. She floated in the warm water, scented with bath salts. The label described them as white tea, and their perfume filled the bathroom. She thought of Art's comment that it was not fair. It was true: that much she had long understood, although the details of why her grandfather had left Lodsbourne to Martin, the younger son, had never been fully explained to her. Her father had been very angry about his father's decision, her mother once said. Kate had only hazy memories of her father – after her parents' divorce, he'd come back twice from Hong Kong to take her on holiday, but had died when she was nine. Now her mother was dead too, and there was no one else to press on why Martin had inherited everything. A little bit of the Wilcox Smith family's vast good fortune would have been useful, she reflected ruefully, but their lives were so distant, so exotic, compared to hers, she could barely think of them as her family, let alone feel entitled to a part of their wealth.

She lay there, gazing out of the tall window, watching the pale lemon sky fade and darken to dusky blue, and the shadows under the copper beech grow thick. The quiet was astonishing, soft and precious like silk velvet. The nearest road was about half a mile away, and that was a narrow lane with little traffic. She was used to London's night, pierced by sirens, those screams of horror and fear, emblems of breaking lives. Here, only the cry of an owl was audible. Kate added more hot water. A bright moon was rising behind the copper beech: already she could see the glitter through the leaves, and in a few minutes it would emerge. She waited for it to cast a shaft of light through the window into the bathroom, catching the white of her body in the water. Finally it broke through in all its brilliance, almost a full moon, and Kate lay back to moonbathe.

Life could start again now that she was finally in her own flat. Ed had been gone five years; it was time to put that behind her. Here, surrounded by Phoebe and Martin's lovely life, she could begin again. By a process of osmosis, she would simply absorb into every cell of her body their immense good fortune and taste: rural England in the midsummer sun; Phoebe with her love of cows, Persian tiles, Indian jewellery and dogs. Art could learn about milking, and it might even help him find multiplication comprehensible. When they returned to the flat and their quiet lodger in London, she and Art would both be different people. She slipped further down into the silky water and balanced with the tip of her toe on the end of the bath. It would be a rebirth, she promised herself, and smiled.

*

Kate heard the dogs barking and guessed that the guests had arrived for lunch. She was preparing salad in the kitchen and was not inclined to join them. Under instructions from the housekeeper, Sue, she had picked the lettuce leaves and the ripe tomatoes from the walled garden, and washed them in the pantry. Sue pointed out bowls and knives, and they chatted about Art, and Sue's grandchildren. She had been with the family since Dotty and Felix were small, and although Phoebe was the one who accepted guests' accolades for the cooking, it was Sue who ensured the Wilcox Smith table was well provisioned with fine food.

Outside on the terrace, the long table was laid for lunch with an Indian printed cloth and the sun sparkled on the glasses. At intervals down the table stood vases of wild flowers, the sprays of pin-bright forget-me-not echoing the colour of the plates. Everything Phoebe touched had this effortless beauty, as if arranged for an exclusive lifestyle magazine, reflected Kate. It was inimitable, literally so: the fabrics, crockery and furniture all dated from decades before their like had become fashionable. They had the patina of age – a chipped plate, sun-bleached fabric, a small stain; nothing was garishly new, but spoke of years of loving use, like the rest of Lodsbourne Hall – carpets were worn through in places, sofas sagged, and some armchairs had fraying edges. Phoebe was unconcerned about the ageing of things, as she stepped in time with her belongings, accumulating layers of rich memory.

Kate placed the large bowls of salad on the table, and then absentmindedly began straightening the cutlery. Through the open drawing-room windows she caught fragments of conversation.

'Kate is Martin's brother's daughter. He died when she was young, and then her mother died about ten years ago. She's a dear thing, and much nicer than either of her parents. Quiet but very easy. Things have been difficult for her recently: an awful cad has left her with the child –'

Phoebe broke off, perhaps to serve drinks. Kate could hear the popping of a cork. She was not surprised by this account of her presence to the guests, having heard such biographical summaries from Phoebe and Martin before; it was part of how, as hosts, they orchestrated the interaction between their guests. 'Giving people something to go on' was how she had once heard Martin phrase it. She had never heard herself described before, and she didn't like Phoebe's cutting remark about her parents. Meanwhile, Phoebe had moved on to Fauzia. 'My daughter-in-law is coming with Felix. She's very beautiful – and doing so well at the newspaper. A gutsy young lady – grew up in Wembley, I believe, very modest background. Parents came over from India. Muslim, but reasonable. She drinks and so forth.'

Kate flinched at the casual prejudice, and then Phoebe appeared at the French windows, carrying a bottle of wine in each hand, the guests following, and Kate was introduced. She ducked Tom's attempts to establish whether they had met before, using the excuse of helping Sue to bring food to the table. (They had, once, at a drinks reception early in her relationship with Ed.) Before long, everyone was seated, with Art amongst several other children at the end of the table. Martin and Tom were discussing Egyptian politics and Libyan oil companies, and then Ann turned the conversation to the imminent Olympics, discussing the tickets she had bought for the children. Martin made an attempt to draw Kate in, asking how close the stadium was to her new flat, and Tom's eyes registered his surprise at her familiarity with the geography of east London. Thankfully, the conversation switched tack again as Phoebe pressed Art for an account of his visit to the milking parlour that morning. She promised the secret ingredient would be revealed at milking time that evening.

Lunch was well advanced when Felix and Fauzia finally arrived. Felix greeted his mother warmly, before coming around the table to give Kate a hug.

'Kate, you must meet my wife,' he said proudly, and introduced Fauzia. She was wearing a long orange linen dress, which set off her dark hair.

'I know we are going to be friends,' Fauzia said, squeezing Kate's arm. 'Felix has told me so.'

Turning to the assembled family and guests, Felix offered an account of traffic jams out of London by way of apology for their late arrival, which provoked great amusement around the table. Fauzia rolled her eyes as she held his hand affectionately. Felix had published a short, witty book on traffic jams a couple of years before, which had been surprisingly successful, winning him a spot on Radio Four's *Start the Week*, where he had expanded eloquently on the cultural symbolism of England's traffic congestion – a metaphor, he argued, for the country's political stagnation. Felix's fortunes had been transformed; once an obscure academic, he now had a Twitter following in six figures, another book contract and was regularly asked to opine on radio and television. The career somersault had bewildered his father, and Kate noticed that Martin was the only one not amused. In return, Felix gave his father the barest of greetings.

Phoebe managed the rearrangement of places smoothly, with exclamations of sympathy for motorway travails, reinforcing the sense of convivial ease in this peaceful idyll. Felix sat down beside Kate. A debate on traffic jams ensued around the table, with Dotty complaining that other densely populated European countries such as Belgium and the Netherlands had efficient transport systems, while Tom described the remarkable mass-transit systems he had seen in China on their last visit.

'South-east England is now the most crowded region in Europe,' Martin pointed out. Tom and Ann nodded vigorously in agreement. Kate looked up from her plate at the stretch of downland just visible beyond the copper beeches: there wasn't another house in sight.

'It depends how you analyse the data,' rejoined Felix, looking at his father. 'We will never match Monaco or Malta – let alone Bangladesh. According to the most meaningful measure of how population is distributed, known as "lived density", we are behind the Netherlands and even behind a highly urbanized country like Spain –'

Dotty retorted that her brother's forays into geography should stick to holiday research, and Kate caught Martin's irritable mutter, 'What on earth has Bangladesh to do with it?'

She looked down the table, laden with food and flowers, the guests eating and discussing subjects as diverse as cows and Libya, how to grow salad and the Muslim Brotherhood, and felt a sharp stab of discomfort. It was not so much that she was an imposter, but that their lives were so replete, encompassing details of English country life as well as global politics, all within an imposing pattern of domestic contentment and public engagement. By contrast, her life was makeshift: a fragile construction with too much happenstance. The thought made her uncomfortable, as if she were incompetent at life, while those around her were enviably at ease with the world. In the middle of this painful sequence of thoughts, she heard Felix asking her a question about a recent film which she had not had time to see.

'You must go,' he insisted, and although he meant well, the pressure only confirmed the private fear that she couldn't keep up with any of them. She noticed how Fauzia was talking intently to Martin and Tom about the Arab Spring and the politics of the Egyptian elections. Judging by the way they responded to her comments, she was well-informed, yet she could only be in her early thirties. She and Felix made a striking couple.

Ann leaned towards Phoebe, her voice lowered. 'Tom and I are thinking that I should move back to London. Cairo just feels too tense. It's never been an easy posting for a family. It's very hot in summer and, even with the club pool, the kids get fed up having to spend so much time indoors with AC.'

'That was the decision Martin and I took back in the mid-seventies when we were in the Gulf. He stayed on for a while, but I came back to Lodsbourne to oversee the renovations. I went out a few times a year to join him – I still had some clients out there – but Martin was working very hard, I'd have just got in the way.'

Ann and Phoebe exchanged notes on keeping marriages and families together over thousands of miles, with long periods of separation: husbands abroad, children at boarding school, and wives tending the familial shrine in the country. Kate's attention drifted. Art had got up from the table and was chasing the dogs around the lawn with Maisie, Dotty's daughter; the two children were laughing as they raced across the wide lawn. They would be back for pudding, a large bowl of Eton mess, piled high with fruit and cream.

'So, what keeps you busy, Kate?' asked Tom abruptly, cutting across several other people to address her. He was the sort of man who was used to getting answers.

'I work for an aid agency, a children's charity,' said Kate hesitantly. 'I'm the office manager.'

'Not much money in that, I imagine,' commented Tom with a cheery grimace.

Kate stiffened. 'I manage.' She tried not to sound too defensive – that was bad form in these circles – but she intensely resented his intrusiveness.

'There are new opportunities opening up around the fragile-states agenda. Aid and security go hand in hand. Let me know if I can offer any pointers.'

Kate was taken aback. There must have been a more extended briefing before lunch than the one she had overheard. This was how pity worked. She felt her cheeks flush and her voice sounded strained. 'I'm not looking for a job, I love my work.'

'Of course, just a thought. Let me know if you change your mind. I can see you have big responsibilities coming down the line.' Tom's eyes were on Art, who was sitting at the end of the table again, eating pudding.

'Got plans for education, Kate?' interjected Martin.

Kate knew where this would lead. 'Yes, I have, actually. The local school is good.'

Conversation around the table suddenly stilled. No one there had ever sent a child to a 'local' school; they went to boarding schools with old family associations. This was how it went at the Wilcox Smiths: a sudden change of subject and a chasm yawned open, and she was left stranded as an outsider, without the opportunities, advantages and experiences they took for granted.

Kate saw Dotty at the other end of the table lower her sunglasses to look at her.

'Local? You mean in Hackney, Katharine?' asked Martin, trying, and failing, to keep the scepticism out of his voice.

Before Kate could answer, Phoebe intervened. 'We need the cheese. Kate, can you be a dear and help me bring it through?'

In the kitchen a cheese board was ready on the table alongside a plate of biscuits. 'Sue only does mornings at the weekend,' explained Phoebe. Kate paused for a moment's relief, then picked up the board and followed her aunt back out to the table.

Tom and Fauzia were in the midst of a heated discussion about whether Islam had ever had an enlightenment. Kate liked how Fauzia held her own in this company, even though she found her combination of confidence and beauty terrifying. Kate longed for the whole thing to be over; she looked at the hammock swaying in the breeze under the beech tree. Her aunt and uncle saw her as a problem to solve: she had too little money and a child to educate. Perhaps that was even part of why Tom was at this lunch – so that he could help Kate find a more lucrative career. Not only money but a currency of favours made Phoebe and Martin's well-connected world go around; a contact here or there, and they assumed every crease in life could be ironed out.

Once in the hammock after lunch, the murmur of voices at a safe distance, Kate finally relaxed: she had narrowly missed a mauling over the school issue. Between half-closed lids, she could see Art's hair catch the sunlight as he lay on the lawn by the yew hedge. He and several other children were constructing something with the Lego they had brought down from the nursery. The garden and house had the well-fed quiet of a hot summer afternoon. Occasionally, from the end of the garden, she heard the splash of water and laughter from Felix and Fauzia at the pool. Martin and Tom were sitting in deckchairs in the shade, talking. It was remarkable how Martin managed to keep an interest in his work – he must be about eighty-four, if she remembered right. She watched Tom, thirty years his junior, explain something and listen carefully to Martin's responses. Phoebe and Ann had disappeared. Above her a pattern of leaves shifted in a kaleidoscope of oranges and scarlets where the sunlight caught the plum-coloured leaves and whispered as a breeze moved through the branches. She would get up to swim in a while.

She must have drifted off to sleep, because she was woken suddenly by the loud clattering of a machine; the sound swelled into a roar. Shocked, she jerked upright, swinging her legs over the side of the hammock, and looked around. Art was running towards her, looking wildly up at the sky. The noise was now deafening. Martin and Tom had stopped talking and were scanning the sky. Two Chinook helicopters appeared, one after the other, blades whirring furiously as they passed overhead, appearing to skim the roof of the house before heading up over the hill. The windowpanes were rattling, and Kate could hear breaking glass somewhere. The ground reverberated under their feet, and the top branches of the copper beech tossed wildly. The helicopters were so close it was possible to see the pilots peering down at them. They had gone in a few moments, but no sooner had the sound of the engines faded than it began again. The roar strengthening, another helicopter appeared, slightly higher in the sky.

Kate held Art tightly, his breathing was fast – they were both trembling. One of the other children was screaming. As the noise receded and the quiet regathered, she got up, still shaky, and walked over to Martin, holding Art's hand. A glass had fallen off the table and smashed on the stone flags.

'What was that? It was terrifying.'

'Just exercises on Salisbury Plain – always a lot of them this time of year. Nothing to worry about,' said Martin comfortably, adding, in an aside to Tom, 'The Chinook is still a damned good machine.'

Tom nodded in agreement.

Kate was unnerved by the looks they exchanged. Both of them were used to war, she realized; they weren't really civilians. They were soldiers at heart, albeit the armchair variety these days. Martin had been in Palestine in the 1940s on national service, and on some kind of Foreign Office secondment to Aden. She had never paid much attention to his cryptic references. Tom had been in Northern Ireland, the Falklands and the Gulf War, he had told her the first time they'd met. Between the two men, they had experience of several generations of British warfare and its machinery, and saw it as nothing out of the ordinary for a Chinook to scrape the roof tiles on a hot Saturday afternoon.

At that moment, Felix and Fauzia came running from the pool, still in their swimming costumes.

'Blimey, that was close,' gasped Fauzia, her hair dripping on to the terrace.

'It was horrible,' declared Felix. 'Can't you get the army to give us a wider berth? We're several miles from the plain. You know the people in charge, Pa – can't you pull a few strings?'

Martin didn't reply.

'Time for tea,' announced Phoebe, appearing at the terrace door. 'Sue has made a wonderful cake especially for you, Felix – and of course for you too, Art. How many want tea?'

Lodsbourne always entailed plenty of food; the rituals of eating kept everyone busy. The Chinooks disappeared from the conversation, but they had left Kate on edge. She couldn't shake off the sense of unease, provoked not just by their clatter but by Martin's insouciance. Something had come into sharp focus for the first time – he was a man used to dealing with violence – and now she had seen it, she couldn't easily forget it, however much she might try.

The helicopters flew over again several more times, only now they were further away and their noise had faded to a muffled roar. Had Martin made a call, as Felix had suggested? Kate hadn't noticed him going inside to the phone, but she could have missed it. Phoebe had asked her to help bring out the tray of crockery and a chocolate cake decorated with strawberries and dusted in icing sugar.

7

There was a moment first thing when Kate woke and found herself disorientated by the new flat, her eyes searching the bare white walls, the brown carpet with its stains, the boxes waiting to be unpacked. The flat didn't yet feel like home; it was partly lack of time, as she had explained to Hussain, but it was also a reluctance to fully arrive. The account she had offered at Lodsbourne had entailed a degree of bravado, for the benefit of her aunt and uncle; in truth, she was struggling to accept how she had ended up as a single mother in a shabby flat. That part of her which was her mother peered into her life with dismay, and then she hated herself for exhibiting the snobbery she had inherited.

While the coffee brewed, she looked out of the kitchen window at the back of a row of terraced houses which bordered this side of the estate. Most had built up their garden walls and topped them with barbed wire or metal spikes to stop people climbing over. Behind these barricades, the gardens were cleverly designed, and some of the houses had extensions with large panels of glass revealing their open-plan kitchens. In the evenings, she could look straight into several families' homes, their supper tables and wooden floors glowing under stylish lighting. She could even see what they were eating. It was unlikely they spared a thought for their unwitting spectators in the block of flats, beyond their dark windows. A mother at Art's school had mentioned that the houses on that street each cost several million; Kate would rather not have known. She didn't like the role of witness to these fortunate lives. She had pondered on whether to hang baskets of plants to screen the view, but they would block the light.

She heard a step behind her and turned, surprised to see Hussain offering her a cup of coffee before he disappeared back into his room. What on earth did he do during the day and in the evening? Once – and she felt very guilty – she had looked in to his room. They had run out of milk, and he had offered to go to the corner shop to get a pint. He usually kept the door shut, but on this occasion, it was ajar. A few of his belongings were laid out on the floor: a Qur'an, a prayer mat, a first-aid kit, and a small washbag beside his bed; on the back of the door, he had hung a suit, crumpled and slightly dirty, but well made. She had picked up the Qur'an and flicked through the pages of Arabic text and found a small photo of a woman and a little girl of about four or five; they were sitting on what was perhaps the terrace of a house, leaning against a balustrade, smiling at the camera. The girl was Reem, with her father's big brown eyes and his broad smile; the woman was presumably his wife.

'What are you doing in here?' Art had demanded, his voice fierce with accusation, hovering on the threshold. 'This is Hussain's room. Why are you in here?'

Kate blushed. 'I just needed to look for something – I thought it was in here.'

Art was suspicious. 'You could have waited and asked Hussain.'

'I'm sure he wouldn't mind – anyway, it's not here.'

Kate came back into the main room, shaken by Art's policing.

'What were you looking for?' he persisted. 'There's nothing in that room.' Then he added, gesturing at the sitting room, 'There's nothing in any of these rooms. It doesn't look like a home – it's just bare walls and empty shelves.'

Kate, startled, looked at him, standing defiantly in the middle of the room. She didn't know this boy: her baby was adoring and unquestioning, not this truculent, challenging character.

He was growing up, but there was something else: he was defending Hussain. He had only met the man a few times, usually on Hussain's way in or out. Just once, Hussain had helped with a maths homework.

'I'll get around to unpacking, I promise,' Kate said. Art threw himself on the sofa, and she assured him, 'We'll get your bed built very soon, and straighten out your room.'

That had been several days ago, and now it was Saturday. She braced herself to deal with the challenge of Ikea construction. Art had chosen a wooden bed frame on stilts, with a ladder and a desk tucked underneath, but it was still in its packaging and he was sleeping on a mattress on the floor – he had a point. Kate put the painful confrontation out of her mind and turned her attention back to the sun, which had risen above the treetops. She closed her eyes to feel its warmth. For the first time, the three of them would be together for the weekend. Kate wondered if Hussain would go out – he couldn't stay in his room all the time.

Art had come into the kitchen and was eating breakfast, engrossed by a cartoon on the back of the cereal box.

'We'll get your room sorted today. Get posters on the wall, build the bed.'

He didn't answer; he didn't believe her.

She dressed and set to work, pulling the boxes into the centre of his bedroom, and began to cut the ties and cardboard with a Stanley knife. It was blunt and she was hacking away with increasing irritation at the plastic ties when she felt a sudden sharp stab of pain, and couldn't contain a yelp. The knife had slipped and cut her thumb. Kate bit her lip at the pain. Art came running, and stared with horror at her hand.

'The blood – look at the blood, it's going everywhere.' His voice rose – he hated blood.

Kate held her injured hand, trying to stop the blood falling on the carpet. 'Bring some kitchen roll, tissue or loo paper. Quick,

Art, anything.' The cut was bleeding profusely, and Kate dreaded the thought of a visit to A and E.

Art wailed, his eyes fixed on the blood.

The next moment, Hussain was kneeling beside her with a drying-up towel. He swiftly wrapped both her bloodied hands, and led her through to the sink, clearing the breakfast dishes with one hand, while he ran the tap with the other. He unwrapped her hands and pulled them into the flow of tap water. The water ran red in the sink.

'Stay here.'

He came back with the first-aid kit she'd seen in his room. 'I think it needs a couple of stitches.' He wiped his hands with disinfectant and began to thread a needle.

'Stop, Hussain, careful – do you know what you're doing? I can go to A and E.' Kate's voice was panicky.

Hussain looked at her, astonished.

'Trust me – I know what I'm doing, Kate.' He said it with such authority and force that she nodded numbly and looked away – she wasn't much better than Art about blood. She felt the prick of a needle.

'That's done,' he said a short while later, and she heard the snipping of scissors. 'Do you have any bandages?' he asked.

'They are packed in one of the boxes somewhere.'

'I'll look – which one should I start with?'

'Maybe the big one over there?' she said. 'They should be amongst the bathroom stuff.'

'I can help,' said Art, reassured by Hussain's calm practicality.

The two of them opened up the box and started lifting out its motley contents – clothes, books, toys and kitchen equipment, but no bandages. They started on another box.

'I'm sorry, it's a bit chaotic,' said Kate from the sofa, immobilized by her hand.

'At least we will finally have to unpack now. We can't put this stuff back,' said Art, pleased to see some familiar computer games re-emerging.

Kate giggled. 'You're right, we'll sort everything out – we can't leave it all over the floor.'

'Hussain will help. You can just lie there on the sofa, Mum, and give us directions. We'll do it all, won't we, Hussain?'

'Hussain can't do that,' she interrupted quickly. 'He might have other things to do.'

'I'm happy to help if you like?' He looked at Kate, his eyebrows raised.

'Hussain could build my bed – you're rubbish at Ikea plans anyway, Mum,' said Art breezily, handing the instructions to Hussain and adding, with his most winning smile, 'Can you?'

Hussain touched Art's shoulder affectionately and nodded, and Kate watched, incredulous at Art's familiarity with the man. With a start, she realized that she had not given much thought to what Art would make of Hussain living with them. She had been preoccupied with keeping her own careful distance, and now she saw that Art liked Hussain: her wary, reserved son really liked this man.

'Here we are,' said Hussain, pulling a package of bandages out from amongst towels and washbags. He held Kate's hand steady as he bound it with a bandage. He did it with practised ease – he knew how. 'You can't do much with that hand, but Art is right, you can direct us.'

Hussain set to work on the bed, studying the assembly instructions, and enlisted Art to help work out which bit belonged where. Two hours later, the bunk-bed frame was fixed, the bed made, and Art was arranging his favourite things on his new desk below. Hussain came back into the main room, where Kate was sitting, working her way through a pile of books with one hand, trying to decide which to give away. He picked up a set of saucepans.

'Where shall I put these?'

He sorted through another box of kitchen equipment under her direction. Then he started on the books, putting them on the shelves according to Kate's instructions. Art came to help and Kate managed to do a bit, unwrapping some ornaments from their packaging and placing them along the shelves, and Art unpacked a rug.

'We need a hammer and some hooks for the pictures,' said Hussain as the room began to look like a home.

By lunchtime, the pictures were up – a painting by a friend and several drawings of Hong Kong by Kate's father when he was a young man. They were her favourite possessions. It was good to see them back on the wall, like old friends turning up.

Unexpectedly, there was a loud knock.

'Could that be a friend, Art?' asked Kate, surprised, as she went to answer it.

A woman was on the doorstep – a round freckled face with brown eyes, greying hair and a cautious smile. 'I live over the way.' She gestured to the front door on the other side of the landing. 'I've been meaning to catch you to say hello, but you never seemed to be in. I've met your other half a few times. I'm Jackie.'

'Kate,' she replied.

'Well, just wanted to be neighbourly. I heard the hammering – you must be settling in. Any time you need anything – sugar or something – just knock.' She was looking past Kate's shoulder into the flat. 'Just the one, then?'

'Oh, yes – this is Arthur, Art for short.'

Jackie laughed. 'Funny name – my grandfather was called Arthur, but I don't know many others called that these days. I've got three myself, they're almost off my hands. The oldest has moved out, so it's just the two left at home. And your other half?'

Kate, flustered, didn't know how to reply.

'What's his name?' Jackie asked, her eyes still looking past her into the flat.

'Oh, Hussain, he's the lodger –' Kate came to a stop.

Jackie looked disbelieving. 'Well, anyways, I'd better be off, but give me a knock anytime if you fancy a cuppa or anything,' she finally said, disappointed that Kate had not asked her in.

'Thank you, yes, of course.' Kate shut the door and leaned against it in the small hallway, and took a deep breath. She had not thought about what other people might think of Hussain moving in. A block of flats was not a place to keep secrets.

'Just the neighbour,' she said as she came back into the sitting room. Hussain and Art were looking through one of Art's old comic books. 'She said she had met you, Hussain?'

'There's a woman I've passed a couple of times on the landing. She asked me where I lived, so I told her, that's all,' said Hussain. 'She wanted to know where I was from – she's curious.'

'Yes. I can see that – nosy, more like,' commented Kate, irritated by the woman's curiosity.

'No, just interested,' he replied gently. 'It's natural, people who live nearby want to know about each other.'

'What did you tell her?'

'I said I was studying in England.' He gave a shrug of his shoulders, and that soft, sad smile.

'Studying what?' Art looked up.

'You, England, London's strange ways,' replied Hussain, ruffling Art's hair. Art wriggled, but Kate could see he loved it. Then he flopped back against Hussain, the two of them leaning against each other on the sofa. Kate stared, uncomfortable. She owed Hussain thanks – for the first aid, for the unpacking, for his care of Art – but she felt uneasy and she couldn't put the words together: who was this man she had invited into their life?

*

'For God's sake, Kate, this is sheer madness – insane. You're telling me that you have picked some asylum seeker as a lodger? Someone you know nothing about – some Iraqi or Syrian – he could be a terrorist, for Christ's sake,' hissed Ed.

Even for Kate, well used to Ed's intermittent Skype outbursts critiquing her care of Art, this was too much. 'Not every Muslim asylum seeker is a terrorist,' she said with fury at his bobbing face on the screen. He was on an exercise bike in Washington.

She hadn't intended to tell him about Hussain, suspecting that his views had become even more right-wing since working at the think tank, and had suggested to Art they keep it secret, but he must have let something slip on a call.

'He's a kind man, Shirin has assured me, and I've known her for years, and trust her,' Kate added angrily.

'Trusting *her* is one thing. Trusting this stranger around my son is quite another.'

'He's *our* son,' she snapped.

'He could be a paedophile, he's probably illiterate – he might have a disease.'

Kate took a deep breath and clenched her fists so tightly the nails dug into her palms: she needed to be calm. She kept her voice low to ensure that Hussain couldn't hear; the walls of the flat were thin.

'He is highly educated and very respectful. He's a father. He has even started coaching Art in maths – and Art likes him.'

Ed groaned.

'I'm not continuing this conversation,' she said icily, and hung up.

She came out of the bedroom, shaking with rage. Art was absorbed in a computer game on an iPad, but Hussain looked up at her, and she knew he had overheard. She sat down at the table, and he got up and wordlessly made tea, placing a cup beside her. She took a sip gratefully. It was black and very sweet.

'This is how we like tea at home,' said Hussain stiffly. The way he said 'home' was as if he were lifting some enormous burden into speech. Kate felt deeply embarrassed; those were terrible things for a proud man to have heard. But even worse, he did not look shocked – perhaps he was used to such insults.

'I'm sorry,' she whispered. She was apologizing not just for Art's execrable father, but for the humiliations and deprivations which she suddenly realized might be familiar to this man. Hussain had only been in the house a couple of weeks, but Shirin had been right: he was a good man.

'I don't want to be a source of conflict between you and Art's father. I can leave.'

Kate gulped the black tea and whispered so Art could not hear through his headphones. 'That man has caused enough disruption in my life. He now lives in America, and is not involved in much of his son's life, so he is not in a position to tell me what to do.'

She heard herself and was astonished by the clarity of her response. Hussain looked troubled, and busied himself with cooking.

Before Hussain moved in, they'd agreed on a month's trial. But even if she did want to avert more conflict with Ed, how could she ask Hussain to leave now that she knew him? Their acquaintance had been slight, amounting to little more than him unpacking that Saturday, the odd exchange over a cup of tea, and a couple of shared meals. The problem was his kindness to Art; he had helped him several times with his homework, and had even picked him up from the after-school club once when she had to stay late at work. He was uncannily sensitive in judging when to disappear to his room. When she came home from work, he left her alone with Art, only emerging to prepare his supper. He was learning how to cook, he told her, and she noticed how he looked up recipes on his phone. Sometimes he took his plate to his room, but twice Kate had offered to cook for them all and suggested they ate together. Conversation at the meals was stilted; they were both trying to keep their distance. He noticed all the ways she kept the house and copied them: cups, bowls, plates, crockery, wooden spoons all went back into their usual places; he was careful even about small things. One evening after Art was in bed, Kate asked him how he had learned such neat domestic habits. He looked surprised. 'I like things to be tidy,' he said with a shrug, adding that he had studied in America, and had lived in a college dorm. It explained the slight American accent to his English. She didn't ask any other questions, remembering Shirin's advice: 'Leave it a few weeks. He has been through a very difficult time.'

They eased nervously into their new life. Early in the morning, she heard a muted alarm call, and it puzzled her, until she guessed he was praying. Afterwards he would make coffee, leaving some ready for her, and return to his room so that she and Art had breakfast alone. One evening when Hussain was helping Art with homework, she looked at their heads leaning close together, Hussain's thick black hair and Art's blond mop, and she felt a sharp ache of sadness: this stranger was filling the gap his father had left.

One evening Hussain came back to the flat, his beard shaved off.

'It's much nicer, isn't it, Mum?' exclaimed Art, catching her surprise. 'He doesn't look like a Muslim any more.'

Hussain and Kate exchanged looks, and she grimaced apologetically. Hussain laughed, resigned. 'He's got a point.'

They were all chuckling now, for different reasons, and the humour eased her anxiety.

Kate revised some of her assumptions about Hussain; perhaps he wasn't the intensely pious man she had been imagining. In truth, Kate didn't want to know more about him. She assumed he had some awful story to tell about why he was in London with his meagre belongings, but she had enough of her own troubles to deal with: one flat could contain only so much human suffering. She liked how he stayed in his room, how his presence in the flat was often barely noticeable, beyond his love of coffee and the smell of the spices he used for cooking. She liked his lack of curiosity in her; it made everything much tidier. It was exactly how she wanted to keep things.

*

'Is that you, Kate? Martin here.'

She was taken aback: it took her a moment to stammer an answer. Martin had never called her before.

'Phoebe gave me your work number. There's something I want to discuss with you – Phoebe and I have talked it over. Can you come to my office in Mayfair on Tuesday? The company still set aside an office for me when I'm in town. Could you drop by at 5 p.m.?'

Martin's telephone manner was more direct, but he shared with Phoebe the assumption that the world could be shaped exactly as they wanted it. Kate was too startled to say no. It would mean leaving work early, and she would have to ask Hussain to pick up Art from the after-school club. If the meeting was short, she wouldn't be too late back. What on earth could Martin want?

On the Tuesday, she left work early as planned, and headed to Martin's offices near Green Park. Once she emerged from the tube, she walked briskly, nervous of being late, down the quiet side streets of freshly painted houses, their window boxes brimming with flowers. It was hard to recognize that this was the same city as her neighbourhood in east London. She arrived, breathless and sweaty, at the black door with its gleaming brass doorknob; above the bell was a plaque engraved with the company's name, ZSKa. She rang the bell and waited, casting her eye over the manicured plants in the window boxes; she examined them in search of a single dead leaf or damaged petal, but the white begonias and variegated ivy were perfect. She was about to reach over surreptitiously to check whether they were artificial when the door buzzed open. In the marble-floored hall a staircase curved elegantly upstairs, its mahogany handrail curling to a stop at the carved newel post. A young woman sat at a desk with a laptop, and greeted Kate by name.

'Sir Martin will be just one moment. He is expecting you.'

The house was extraordinarily quiet, the sound of the traffic muffled by double glazing. Kate sat down on a plump, upholstered sofa, and stared at the John Piper print on the wall opposite. What did ZSKa actually do? Her mother had once spoken of Martin having worked at the Foreign Office, and tartly added that he had made a lot more money after he left. All that Kate knew was that his career had been in the Middle East, and that he was fluent in Arabic and Farsi. On the low table in front of her were copies of the *Financial Times* and the *Economist*, and glossy brochures for property developments in Dubai, but nothing as brash as a company catalogue. The place breathed discretion – its business could be simply anything. It didn't look much different from a private art gallery that Kate had once visited around the corner.

'He'll see you now. If you will follow me.'

Martin was sitting at a honey-coloured desk in a large light room. As Kate walked over to a chair, she felt her shoes sinking into the immaculate cream carpet as if she were paddling in clotted cream. A silk Persian rug ran across the centre of the room, and on the walls hung two bold abstract paintings. Martin slowly got up from his desk to greet her, gesturing to leather armchairs by a window overlooking a courtyard of palm trees in pots.

'Good of you to make the time,' he said, proffering his cheek for Kate to kiss. 'I'm only up once a month these days, but I like to keep an eye on things. We've got a good team in place, and they know how to run the show.' He paused. 'I'll come to the point, I know you are busy. Phoebe and I have been talking it over. We were delighted that you enjoyed your weekend with us. It was good to see you and Art so relaxed.'

There was a pause, and a clock chimed on the marble mantelpiece. Kate waited.

'The thing is, there's a cottage on the estate . . . An aunt of Phoebe's lived there for some years, but she didn't want anything done, so it hasn't been touched for a while. I'm afraid the plumbing is a bit dicey, and there's no central heating: *Cold Comfort Farm* type of thing. It needs doing up – but we can't afford to do that right now.'

Kate couldn't imagine where this conversation was going. What did 'can't afford' mean to people like Phoebe and Martin, she wondered.

He cleared his throat. 'But there's a good garden, with a nice view. A path at the bottom leads through the woods to Lodsbourne.' He paused. 'We wondered if you and Art would like to use it at weekends, holidays and so on.'

He was looking down at his hands. Kate couldn't think what to say; she could barely cover the mortgage, let alone rent a cottage.

'Uncle Martin, that's kind, but –'

'No rent needed. The running costs are minimal and we can cover those – bit of council tax, water, electricity, wood. Maybe you do the telephone and TV licence if you want one,' he ploughed on. Kate was surprised to see that he was finding this difficult. She imagined he usually left this kind of thing to Phoebe.

She had noticed the row of farm workers' cottages on a walk early one morning at Lodsbourne a fortnight ago. A yellow rose was in bloom as it climbed up the faded pink brick of the end cottage, obscuring the windows, the narrow strip of garden was overgrown. Why was Martin doing this?

'I can't possibly,' she burst out. 'It's much too generous an offer. What about Felix? Couldn't he use it?'

'Felix has no use for it. He stays at the house – when he comes, and that's not often. Dotty has her own place, of course, with her family. Perhaps you want to think about it?'

Kate imagined how she and Art could ramble through the woods and on to the downs; he could experience a freedom unavailable in London; he could climb trees, build dens, sledge in the winter. For herself, she glimpsed a relief from the scream of sirens, the blaring of car stereos and the arguments of noisy neighbours. Weekends in the country would even ease the strain of having a lodger. If she had breaks, she could manage the necessary politeness and the conversation at mealtimes with Hussain.

Another elegant young assistant appeared, putting down a tray with tea cups and a plate of small biscuits. She poured the tea, and left the room at a gesture from Martin. He took a sip and then placed his cup in his saucer with deliberate care; it was the gesture of an old man, trying to control his movements.

'This is more than kind –' stumbled Kate. 'Art would love it.'

He waved away her thanks. 'We won't live in each other's pockets, but if you are inclined to come up for the odd meal, Phoebe and I would be happy to see you both, but I don't want you to feel obliged.'

'Let me at least pay the bills,' said Kate, knowing well that she couldn't afford any new costs. Ed's maintenance payments were erratic.

Martin shook his head. 'I'll tell Phoebe this evening that it's agreed. She will want to get it cleaned.' He smiled briefly at Kate but quickly glanced away rather than meet her eye. She wondered if he needed to get on to his next appointment. She kept her eyes on the table between herself and Martin. There was a neat pile of magazines beside the biscuits and tea cups: *Jane's Defence Weekly* was the title of the top copy, its cover a photograph of a drone.

Martin stood up, and as they walked to the door, he put a hand on her arm. 'Come as soon as you like. Call Phoebe to arrange it, and she can get some produce cut from the vegetable garden. And, Kate, one other thing –' They were standing in the middle of the room on the luxurious silk rug. 'I've included a legacy for you in my will. I hope it will be useful for Art's education. He's a Wilcox Smith, after all; I gather from Phoebe he doesn't have his father's surname. No more need be said on the matter now. My solicitor has your new address, and she'll be in touch. She just needs to be notified of any future moves.' He stooped to kiss Kate on the cheek. 'Right, I mustn't delay. I have to be at my club.'

Kate retraced her steps across the marble floor, opened the heavy door and stumbled into the street. Life had, all of a sudden, become extraordinary. The will she could dismiss as no more than a kind gesture, but the cottage was real, and it could even start this weekend. This was Phoebe's doing, she was sure, and typical of her to arrange things so it looked like Martin's idea.

She travelled home on the tube, exhilarated: this was an unexpected stroke of good fortune, the first for a long time. She had something to give her son: freedom, adventure, fresh air and space. She envisaged the walks and bonfires, roasting marshmallows and cooking sausages. It would be a reworking of the best of her own childhood, when she and her mother had had a brief spell in a rented cottage in Surrey, before she went to boarding school and her mother moved into the flat in Dorking. As all of this tumbled through her mind, another set of thoughts nagged alongside: why lend her the cottage? They could have rented it out. Was it guilt? She remembered the bitter comments her mother had made about Martin and his success, and how Phoebe had always been a woman who knew what she wanted. Her father had never talked to her about his brother or her grandparents – or if he had, she'd forgotten.

'Art!' she cried as she unlocked the front door. He was sitting at the table next to Hussain, a maths book spread out in front of them. 'You'll never believe this.'

Her dreams came pouring out, one after the other, as she described all the things they would do together. Her enthusiasm was infectious, and Art pestered her with questions: could he take his friends down? Could they now get a dog? Could they build a den? Could he hang a rope swing?

'No dog, but yes to everything else!' She was laughing and the two of them danced around the sitting room.

'Can Hussain come too?'

Kate hesitated. He had got up to start preparing supper in the kitchen. Through the open door, she saw his back turned to them, and the flat was filling with the smell of their imminent supper. She couldn't tell whether he had heard, but she didn't want to offend him.

'He may not want to come. He may want some peace here on his own.'

'No, no!' cried Art, now rolling around on the sofa. 'He must come too. He will like the cows. I'm sure of it.' Art ran into the kitchen as if half-demented, and Hussain turned, a wooden spoon in his hand.

'They are multibillionaires, Hussain, and they have a huge house, and Phoebe plays music to her cows at milking time and says it's her secret ingredient. It makes the milk better, and there's a swimming pool.'

For the first time Kate saw Hussain smile with real feeling. He looked at her, and their eyes met briefly.

'He can come one day, if he wants to,' she said lightly, laughing as Art flung his arms around her to give one of the old hugs, now rare. The country would be good for him, she felt sure. Hussain turned back to the cooking.

★

Kate and Art pushed open the unlocked door and found themselves in a low-ceilinged sitting room. Phoebe had asked the cleaner to air the cottage, but it had not shifted the musty dampness. Kate's eyes adjusted to the shadows and picked out the low beams and small windows. Logs were piled in the fireplace. There were a couple of sagging armchairs and a sofa, their flowery upholstery worn through in several places, and Phoebe had hung a couple of watercolours of some vaguely Middle Eastern scene – a mosque minaret in one.

'It's a bit smelly,' said Art doubtfully. His mother's excitement had led him to imagine something better.

'Do you want to choose your bedroom? The smell will disappear after we've had a few fires – you'll see.'

Art brushed past her and stomped up the wooden stairs. Kate made her way into the kitchen, where a basket of vegetables from the walled garden at Lodsbourne sat on the small table. She admired the home-grown lettuce, beans, tomatoes, courgettes and even a few apricots. The kitchen was old-fashioned, with a small gas cooker and a worn pine dresser. The washing machine looked as if it hadn't been replaced since the 1970s, but the place was clean, and she liked the window above the sink looking down the long narrow garden to the downs.

She could hear thuds upstairs. Art was rearranging the furniture.

'I want the bed by the window,' he announced as she arrived at the top of the stairs. 'I want to lie in bed and look at the stars.'

'Fair enough,' she agreed, moving a bookcase out of the way, its shelves full of old James Bond novels.

The larger room next door had a view of the narrow country lane, and fields beyond. The mattress was a bit lumpy, but when she opened the window, she heard the reassuring call of wood pigeons. This could be home, she told herself, and she lay back on the bed, her arms spread out. Through the old floorboards came the sound of Art rummaging through a cupboard downstairs, chattering to himself. He still did that sometimes – and always hotly denied it. The cottage was compact enough that she would always hear what he was up to, but large enough to give each other room.

A home of their own, and no one to tiptoe around.

★

Kate was woken early the following morning by chaffinches pecking vigorously at the bird feeder hanging at her window. It sounded like someone knocking on the door. She lay still, watching the birds come and go. They thrust the bright beads of their inquisitive eyes this way and that, and their soft breast feathers pulsed with the beat of a small heart. Last night, Phoebe had rung to welcome them and ask them to lunch on Sunday. 'Dotty is bringing the children over and Maisie is begging Art to come.' She knew that made it impossible for Kate to refuse; she had probably also noticed that Kate kept well clear of her formidable daughter. Phoebe liked to joke that Rebecca's nickname had been a complete mistake: there was nothing dotty about her. Kate had reluctantly accepted the invitation – it was churlish to refuse when they had been so generous – but today was free, and they could spend it how they liked. She must have drifted back to sleep, because the next thing she knew, Art was standing beside her bed with a cup of tea.

'I wasn't sure what to do with the tea bag so it's still in there,' he explained as he gingerly handed it over. Kate was touched, peering at the strong lukewarm brew. 'That's perfect, my love. Just how I like it. What a treat.'

Later, they took their breakfast into the garden and sat down on a bench beside a pond, thick with weeds. It was a morning of high white clouds scudding across the sky, and sunshine breaking through the trees on to the garden's overgrown shrubs and ragged lawn.

'I want to dig all these plants out of this pond and put some new fish in it,' said Art between mouthfuls of toast.

'Mmm . . . that's hard work, Art,' said Kate sceptically, aware that his projects had a way of petering out. 'Are you sure you want to do all that digging?'

They discussed reeds and fish and even a fountain, but Kate was only half paying attention. She was looking back at the old red-brick cottage, the rambling rose and its lemon-yellow blooms, as large as saucers, with dark yellow centres. A high hedge separated the garden from their neighbour, and on the other side was woodland. She loved being enclosed in walls of greenery; here, no anonymous faces could appear at nearby windows. It was private, and she could dance from one end of the long garden to the other, unobserved, if the fancy took her. She and Art could build their fantasy garden in this narrow rectangle, with a winding path through the long grass and under the crooked old apple tree. She resolved not to bother with a lawn mower, and if a plant wanted to self-seed, then she wasn't going to get in its way.

★

'Would you like seconds, Kate?' Phoebe was carving the lamb. The fresh homemade mint sauce was passed down the table with the new potatoes. They still tasted of the earth from which Kate had dug them an hour ago, at Phoebe's request.

'Art, what a good eater you are!' Phoebe heaped up a second plate for the boy.

The dining table was crowded with Dotty's family, an old friend of Phoebe's, and another couple who knew everyone well. The hubbub of chatter was broken only by occasional exclamations or laughter.

'The move into the cottage went all right?' Dotty asked Kate.

Dotty had made a lot of money in her banking career and was about to take over running ZSKa, or so Kate understood.

'And Art is all sorted for the summer holidays?' she pressed.

'Yes, all sorted,' said Kate, hoping that she sounded confident enough to pre-empt any more questions.

Dotty would have had her children's summer planned by the end of January, Kate thought, as she listened to her cousin detail the family's summer schedule: a holiday on the Med, then the children were off to a sailing school on the Isle of Wight, followed by a week at Lodsbourne while Dotty and her husband had a holiday alone, then they were signed up for a summer music school. Dotty's next question was where Kate and Art were going on holiday.

'Art and I are coming down to the cottage for a fortnight. We might have a night camping in the woods. Then we have plans for the garden, so we might do some digging on the pond,' replied Kate.

There was a moment's pause as Dotty took the information in.

'You're so – game,' said Dotty, carefully landing on the word. 'You don't find the cottage too crumbly?'

Kate assured her she didn't, and Dotty laughed and turned to talk to her father.

Later, after lunch had been cleared away and Art had disappeared with the other children, Kate found herself in the drawing room on the sofa opposite Dotty, who was reading the Sunday papers. Kate picked up an arts section. A light summer rain had closed in, and she was waiting until it passed before heading back to the cottage.

'Someone in this family had to make some money, you know,' said Dotty suddenly, lowering the top of the business section she was reading. Her tone was oddly defensive.

Kate looked up, surprised.

'They're leaving the estate to me. I'm the eldest, and besides, Felix said he didn't want it – it was settled years ago.' She put the paper down and Kate did likewise, aware that Dotty wanted to make a few things clear. It had never occurred to Kate to wonder who would inherit the house.

'I mean, Pa is not going to live for ever, and if I am to keep the place up, I have to earn a lot. This place eats money: roofs, gutters, repointing – all those tedious things you don't even see. It may look pretty, but it's a wonderful ruse to inveigle hundreds of thousands of pounds out of your investment portfolio.

'Felix is useless. He would prefer us to sell the place, but I want to see the Wilcox Smiths make another century here. We've only got a decade to go, and then we are over the finishing line, so to speak.' Her laugh was harsh. 'Or we could go for a second century!'

Kate nodded with what she hoped was the right combination of interest and sympathy, but she was wondering how to extricate herself from a conversation she had no interest in. She would prefer to be in front of the fire at the cottage, flicking through one of those James Bond novels.

'By the time I was twenty-two, Pa and I had sorted it out. I had twenty-five years to make enough money to be able to live here when he died. He has done his best, and there is a bit set aside to help.'

Kate thought of the thick carpet in the Mayfair office, and the way it had muffled her steps. 'A bit set aside' might be an understatement; she was sure that she and Dotty estimated sums of money very differently.

'I'd like Maisie and Tom to be able to bring their children here. I'm old-fashioned like that. Not many families get a long innings – wealth has a way of leaking as it shifts down the generations. What was the word that dull prime minister used? Some nonsense about waterfalls . . .' she paused as she searched her memory. Kate looked blank. 'That was it: John Major wanted money to "cascade" down the generations – do you remember?'

Kate didn't, and Dotty explained how it had led to a proposal to reduce inheritance tax.

'You have to go to such lengths to sort things out these days: offshore trusts, gifts seven years in advance, all that stuff.'

Kate wondered if Dotty needed to unburden herself. She had drunk quite a lot of wine with her roast lamb, and it was hard to imagine her husband, the handsome James, doing much listening – he was fond of the sound of his own voice. He and Kate had never got beyond a brief greeting or farewell.

They were suddenly interrupted by the children arriving in a mob, loud with giggles and argument, to settle on the floor in front of the fire. Phoebe followed.

'We have a game to play,' announced Art, his cheeks flushed with excitement from their game of hide and seek around the house. Kate feared she was about to be dragged out of her deep sofa.

'It's called Happy Families – it's a card game,' added Maisie, pulling up the low table and pushing aside the pile of Sunday papers. Dotty groaned.

Phoebe settled down on the sofa. 'They found the Happy Families cards I made when I was young, and insisted I teach them how to play.'

Art started dealing the cards. 'Are you playing, Mum?' he asked, and Kate agreed. She loved seeing Art's confidence here. Dotty slipped out of the room with the paper, probably retreating to the library.

There was quiet as they each studied their hand: which mother and father could be matched with which daughter or son, which sister or brother?

'These are beautiful cards,' exclaimed Kate. They were hand-drawn in pen and ink, cartoon images of flying airmen, scout-masters, atom scientists and political figures from the 1950s and 1960s, such as Mao Tse Tung.

'Who was Mossadec?' asked Maisie, bright and sharp like her mother.

'An Iranian prime minister,' replied Phoebe. 'I got the spelling wrong, I'm afraid. And you have just given away the fact that you have one of the Mossadegh family! Now, we need to get on with the game.'

'Concentrate, Mum, play the game,' instructed Art.

'I drew them for fun when I was teenager. I bring them out on rainy Sunday afternoons,' laughed Phoebe.

'They are so inventive,' said Kate admiringly. 'I never knew you were so good at art.' She knew little about Phoebe's life before Lodsbourne.

'Well, it didn't really lead anywhere. I pottered around for a while, then I went to university and did art history,' said Phoebe brushing off more questions. 'Now, who has Master Atom, the scientist? Art, I think it's you.'

Art whimpered with mock despair. 'How did you know? You're a magician, you can see through cards.'

Dotty's strange confidences faded in the delight of the card game as the children tried to guess who had what card, and to remember who had asked for what.

Happy Families, thought Kate, drawn by a young Phoebe a decade before she produced her own happy family. She looked over at her, with Maisie perched on one side and Art on the other, and the pointer flopped across her feet. Phoebe was surrounded by love and admiration here at Lodsbourne. Even Dotty, so different in temperament, and every bit her father's daughter, adored her mother. How could one not adore someone who had such an uncanny knack of creating a sense of place? Kate marvelled at how she had imagined her life into being through a card game.

8

Art pushed the baked beans around his plate.

'Eat up,' snapped Kate, tired after the train journey from London. They were sitting in the cottage kitchen, bags of shopping still at their feet. She was already thinking of her bed.

The summer holidays had arrived and they had a fortnight stretching ahead of them. The last few weeks in London in the hot weather had been difficult; pavements sticky in the dusty, dry heat, the grass in the park dried to a crisp pale brown, and the tense manoeuvring around Hussain in the flat. The month's trial had come to an end, and they had agreed that the arrangement would continue with a month's notice on either side. The rent was too useful to let him go.

Kate's voice was sharper than she had intended, and Art dropped his head. She looked at him, noticing absent-mindedly that his hair needed washing. She was too tired to coax him into the damp bathroom tonight.

'Eat up,' she repeated more gently, trying to curb her impatience. Her own plate had long since been emptied.

'I don't like beans.'

Kate sighed. 'Well, you did up until yesterday. You've eaten them all your life very happily – what's changed?'

He twirled his fork in his hand. 'My tastes have changed,' he declared. 'I like Hussain's food – the things he makes me when I get home from school called falafel.'

She looked at her son, bewildered. Until Hussain's arrival, Art's diet had been limited and predictable, and baked beans had been one of the few things he was guaranteed to finish.

'I like Hussain's food better than yours,' he said. He looked up, his eyes squaring up to hers. She could see how he was trying to provoke her, and it made her feel like crying; her boy was pulling away from her – and it hurt. He was lavishing on this quiet man, Hussain, his frustrated adoration for his father. It worried her, because Hussain would leave at some point. Everything about him was transitional; he was travelling light, and he would move on again before long, he had made that clear. She thought of that bare London bedroom with his one suitcase. He would be with them for a few months and then off, and she probably wouldn't know where, just as she still didn't know how he had arrived. How could she explain any of that to Art?

'Fine,' she replied grimly, clearing the table. 'You'll just have to go to bed hungry.'

He had made his point and he was now going to press it home. 'I think Hussain should come down here. He needs a holiday too.'

Kate had her back to Art as she washed the plates, and suppressed her irritation for the second time that evening: how could Art possibly know what Hussain would like, or whether he needed a holiday? The man barely spoke. She tried to keep her voice level.

'Hussain has his own life in London. He has things which keep him busy – he doesn't want to sit around with us in this damp cottage.'

She turned towards her son, leaning back against the sink as she dried her hands on a towel. Her comment infuriated Art.

'How do *you* know?' he demanded, standing up and staring at her across the small kitchen. 'You don't know him like I do. You don't talk to him when you get back from work – I do. I know him – and I *know* he needs a holiday.'

Kate was taken aback. Her son was right, she didn't talk to Hussain – but then he didn't talk to her either. She busied herself with the kettle, Art's eyes boring into her back. He wanted an answer, so she tried a different tack.

'Art,' she said, her voice more gentle as she turned to face him, 'why do you think Hussain needs a holiday?'

Art looked uncertain, his eyes fixed on the floor.

'Art?' she repeated. He was holding back something.

'There was a call – he asked me not to tell you – he was crying. I saw the tears. Then he told me not to say anything.'

'A call – on his mobile?'

'He spoke in a language I didn't understand. It was after school one day, and he was sitting in his room on his bed, but I heard the sobbing through the door.'

'Sobbing?'

'I knocked on the door but he told me to go away. When he came out of his room, he washed his face in the bathroom. I asked him what the matter was, but he said he couldn't talk about it. I kept asking and finally he said he missed his daughter. He had just said goodnight to her on the phone.'

Kate slowly poured the hot water into a mug for tea. There was an awful symmetry, she could see: just as Art was transferring his affection for his father to Hussain, the latter was doing something similar to Art. A fierce protectiveness – perhaps also possessiveness – surged inside her; she didn't want Art hurt by the disappearance of another father figure. She reproached herself; she should have thought of this earlier. She took a breath.

'Art – you do know that Hussain will leave us some time, don't you? His staying is a temporary thing. He could leave us at any point – he is just waiting for papers.'

Art didn't trust his mother. 'What papers?' he asked suspiciously.

'Well, when you are an asylum seeker – someone running away from your own country to be safe – you have to apply to the government and fill out lots of forms. They decide whether to let you stay or send you home. That's probably what Hussain is doing now, and when he has papers, he can get himself somewhere to live and a job.'

'*Probably?*' repeated Art. There were times when her son could instantly cut to the quick. 'You don't know for sure.'

'I don't think Hussain wants us to know. He needs privacy.'

Art was relaxing his guard. 'Well, I think he might get lonely in London. Why can't we ask him to come down here, and if he doesn't like it, he can go back?'

'OK, we can do that,' said Kate, playing for time, and hoping that Art would forget about the idea.

'Promise?'

'Sure,' she said, offhand, and began to unpack the bags of food. Art headed up to bed. She was deeply troubled by his sharp comments; he was right, she didn't know anything about Hussain. She had given him the room on the strength of a friend's recommendation, and Shirin had been right – he'd been very kind. But some of his behaviour was odd: there were times when she heard him slip out of the flat late at night. Should she be worried? She had mentioned it to Shirin, who had reassured her. He never woke her when he came back, and he was always there in the morning. What she hadn't allowed for was that Art – her shy, nervous son – might form a deep attachment to him. As for the idea of Hussain coming down to Lodsbourne, that was clearly ridiculous – how on earth would she explain him to Martin and Phoebe? She dreaded the thought of a silent Hussain at Phoebe's lunch table, fending off questions.

She switched off the lights and opened the front door briefly to take a gulp of country air. She smelt the thick dust of the harvest; the combines would be out early in the morning if this weather held. Art was calling. She locked the door and went upstairs to say goodnight. Only the top of his head was visible, he had burrowed down under the duvet, so she kissed his hair. He put his arms around her neck and pulled her close. He smelt of school and sweat, and she made a mental note that he needed a bath before he went up to the Hall in the morning.

'Thanks for inviting Hussain,' he murmured, half asleep.

Kate's heart sank.

★

Kate spent the next morning pulling up brambles and nettles, dressed in an old apron and leather gloves she had found in the garden shed. She loved the exertion, her face flushed and sweating, and the satisfaction of wheeling barrows of cut vegetation to the bonfire pit at the end of the garden in the hot sun. Art had gone to play at the Hall. By lunchtime she was satisfied with her labours and retreated indoors to the cool cottage. She ran a tepid bath and stepped in gingerly to scrub the dust and sweat off. The cool water was exhilarating.

'Phoebe said to tell you to come over for tea,' Art shouted up the stairs, and helped himself to the sandwiches she had left on the kitchen table. He sat on the step outside the bathroom to explain between mouthfuls that he had been building a dam in the stream with Maisie, and he was heading straight back to finish it.

After Art's flying visit, Kate spread out a blanket on the grass and lay down with one of the dog-eared Bond novels, but even the antics of 007 couldn't allay the anxiety of the previous evening. How would she protect Art from getting too attached to Hussain? Her only consolation was that the annual visit to his father in Washington was well-timed; in two weeks' time, he would be on a plane, and with any luck his father would take a few days off to spend with his son.

★

'Kate, I hear from Art that you have invited a friend down,' said Phoebe as she unloaded the tea tray, putting out the cups and cake. A cloth had been spread on the table under the shade on the terrace.

'Art said that his name is Hussain, and that he's your lodger,' she added, cutting the cake.

Kate got up from her deckchair to come over to help, hoping that the conversation could be just between them, but it was too late: Dotty, lying on a lounger nearby, had overheard.

'Did I hear Art say the lodger was a man called Hussain? Is he British? Is that safe, Kate?' She put her hand to her forehead to shield her eyes from the glare of the sun as she looked up at her.

Phoebe saw her daughter was preparing to interrogate Kate, and intervened.

'Where's he from, Kate?' she asked, assuming that the question would be easy to answer. She poured the tea.

Kate kept her voice low. 'A friend introduced us.'

'I've forgotten the sugar,' exclaimed Phoebe. 'Dotty – would you be so kind?' Dotty sighed and grudgingly got up to get it from the kitchen.

Phoebe had given Kate a reprieve. 'You're sure he's trustworthy?'

'Yes,' replied Kate as firmly as she could. 'Art wanted to invite him down, but I really don't think it's appropriate. I'm sure Art will forget – he's off to Washington to see his father in a fortnight.'

'Exactly. But if you do decide to invite him, it will be quiet at the end of the week. Dotty will be in the south of France by then, and Felix isn't due. There wouldn't be tricky questions – I know how these things can sometimes be.'

Phoebe smiled conspiratorially.

'It's not what you think,' Kate whispered vehemently, horrified at her implication.

'Well, maybe it should be, Katharine, dear.' Phoebe laughed slyly. 'Don't look so alarmed, I'm only teasing. Mind you, a love affair would do you a power of good. I should take you shopping somewhere – a well-cut dress, some nice sandals, even a manicure. It must be a long time since you've had the time to make yourself pretty.'

Kate gulped, feeling suddenly acutely self-conscious of her faded jeans and old cotton shirt.

'Phoebe, the last thing I want is a man,' she insisted sharply.

Dotty returned with the sugar and Phoebe switched tack. 'I'm delighted that you're enjoying the cottage. Once you have dug up the brambles, let me treat you to a few summer clothes. You are doing us a favour, clearing that overgrown garden, it's the least I can do.'

Phoebe and Dotty moved on to other matters, and Kate concentrated on eating her cake, quietly smarting from Phoebe's double-edged generosity and her skill at extracting information. She didn't have the bluntness of her daughter, but in her roundabout way she was just as inquisitive.

'One other thing, Katharine, Martin has some guests on Monday – clients. It's all rather tedious, they need entertaining – the gates will be shut and there will be a lot of people around. Best to keep well away . . .'

'A lot of people?' repeated Kate, confused. Lodsbourne was always full of people; what was different about these ones?

'Security types – usual thing for the company, but hush-hush,' Phoebe said, tapping her nose with her finger. 'We've got caterers in to help, Sue's having the day off.'

Kate couldn't follow what Phoebe was saying – why caterers? Why hush-hush? But at that moment Art and Maisie arrived from the pond, dripping with weeds and mud. Squealing, they pretended to chase their mothers across the lawn. Phoebe's mysterious guests slipped out of Kate's mind.

★

The birds were quieter now as July gave way to August. At midsummer their song had been intense. The exuberance of these small creatures was infectious, and they had given Kate a surge of energy to embark on renovating the old garden. The paralysis of not even being able to unpack her boxes in the London flat was a thing of the past; she was amazed by her determination and stamina. Meanwhile Maisie was keeping Art happy and occupied. Sometimes he spent the day at Dotty's house, a couple of miles away, and the nanny dropped him back in the car, but once Kate offered to walk over the fields to fetch him. Thankfully Dotty was in London, and Kate could wander around the place unobserved. The old farmhouse had been demolished to make way for a contemporary open-plan structure, with a kitchen of gleaming white and steel; a wall of glass overlooked the landscaped garden. A wooden spiral staircase dominated the two-storey hallway, with an astonishing creation of glass and light bulbs running the full height. Kate had to drag Art away from the basement cinema with its widescreen television and adjacent games room.

When he was home at the cottage, his main interest was food, and Kate delighted in this new appetite and how his thin face was visibly filling out. One teatime, Kate suggested pancakes, and the two of them set to work, cracking the eggs and beating them. Art laid the table with jams and honey from the pantry. Kate loved the domesticity of these moments and she heaped up Art's plate with fluffy pancakes.

'When is he coming? Are we picking him up from the station?' asked Art in quick succession.

'What?' Kate said, immediately alert. This was the first time he had mentioned the subject of Hussain for several days.

'Have you asked him?' Art looked up from his plate, his eyes fixed on Kate's face. 'I really wanted him to come. We could be a real family then – not just you and me.'

Kate flinched both at the comment and at the quantity of jam he was heaping on to his pancake, but restrained herself from responding to either. He had said something rather similar about 'a real family' back in the winter, and she had pointed out other single parents at the school, but once Art had fixed on a subject, there was no budging him. His persistence could infuriate her.

'Have you asked him?' he repeated peremptorily. At times, his manner was akin to that of a high-court judge. 'You haven't – I knew it!' Art was shouting now. He stood up, his face reddening with indignation.

'OK, I'll call him,' said Kate reluctantly.

He took her hand and pulled her into the hallway to the phone.

'What, right now?' parried Kate, as Art picked up the receiver and handed it to her.

Hussain was surprised by the invitation; Kate knew she sounded awkward, and added with unnecessary emphasis that it had been Art's idea. Despite that, he agreed to come. 'Say thank you to Art for his invitation. I'd like to see a bit more of England.'

After they agreed to meet his train at the station, Kate and Art sat back down at the table with the leftovers of their cold pancakes. Satisfied, Art finished his plate, but Kate had lost her appetite. She told herself that Hussain was only coming for two days.

'Mum, why don't you just marry Hussain? Then he would be able to stay in England – that's what asylum seekers need – Jackie said so to Hussain.'

This was a new direction, and Kate was speechless. Jackie?

'He is more handsome than Dad.' Art was licking the jam off his knife.

'Art, I'm not going to marry Hussain – he's married already.' She remembered the battered photo in his Qur'an.

'It's pointless if a wife lives millions of miles away and you never see her.'

'Well, perhaps someday Hussain's family can come and join him. He just has to get asylum. Once he has permission to stay, he can bring his daughter and wife. I'm sure that's his plan, Art, so don't start imagining that he will be part of our family. He has a family.'

'Well, Muslims are allowed more than one wife – you could be his second wife.'

'Thanks very much, Art, I think that's where we end this conversation.'

Art was humming. It was his way of telling his mother that he had made his point.

Kate tried to keep her tone even. 'What was Jackie saying?'

'Oh, she's a chatterbox, always wants to talk to Hussain and me when we come back from school. Boring stuff, mostly.'

'Like what?'

'I dunno – stuff about Hussain staying in England. He never says much.'

Kate tidied the kitchen, unsettled by the inquisitive Jackie, and by Hussain's imminent arrival at Lodsbourne. She just had to ensure that Hussain didn't meet Martin, and then get him back to London before the weekend, so that he didn't have to face Dotty's exacting appraisal.

When Art was in bed, she thought she should check the room where Hussain was to sleep, and make sure it was at least clean. The door to the study was kept shut to reduce draughts, and Hussain would be their first guest; she had only given the room a cursory glance when they'd moved in. The walls were lined with bookcases, and at the window was a large desk, covered in piles of papers and files. In a corner of the room, a bed was heaped with folded blankets. Kate sat down at the desk and ran her fingertips over the ink-stained leather. She pulled open one of the desk drawers – ink pens and rusty staples – and in the next were old passports. She took out the top one and flicked through the pages, reading the stamps: Port Said, Damascus, Basra, Nairobi, Mombasa, Bahrain, Dubai. The passports all belonged to one woman, Edith Grant. The most recent had 1968 as the date of issue and a photo of a severe, elderly woman. She had been born in 1902. This was presumably the aunt of Phoebe's that Martin had mentioned.

Kate laid the passports out on the desk, a record of changing styles, their corners clipped to indicate they had expired. Several were water-stained and creased – they had been well used. Intrigued, she pressed open the passports at the photo, and compared the images. Here was Edith as a young woman with a dark bob – not beautiful, but she had a striking face. Every ten years a new passport told how she aged, the lines gathering around her mouth and eyes, and the open expression of her youth fading, gradually replaced by a grim determination. In the last passport she looked defeated, as if life had proved a disappointment. Kate gathered them up and put them back in the drawer.

She cast an eye along the bookshelves, which sagged under the weight of tomes on the Second World War and the Gulf. They could be an overspill from Martin's shelves, or perhaps they had belonged to Edith Grant: histories of Persia, Iraq, Oman and Afghanistan, archaeology, and a lot of books on birds. She ran her finger over the tops – they were thick with dust. She needed to do some cleaning before Hussain arrived. The rest of the clutter would have to stay; there was nowhere else to put the papers and the medley of ornaments. She opened the windows to get rid of the musty smell. She had assumed that the cottage's watercolours of Damascus, Petra and Isfahan were Wilcox Smith cast-offs, but perhaps they had belonged to Edith Grant and her life of travelling.

*

Hussain walked down the station platform in his trainers and sweatshirt, already smiling at Art. He didn't seem to notice, or care, that other people were casting furtive, curious glances at him. Kate realized it was the first time she had seen someone at Lodsbourne who was not white English. Hussain stood out here; he didn't wear 'Hampshire clothes', as she and Art described them: ubiquitous linen, men in striped shirts, tweed jackets, red corduroy trousers and panama hats.

Art ran down the platform to greet him.

Hussain smiled apprehensively at Kate. 'It's nice to be here.'

'Well, Art was very keen to show you everything. I don't know what you will make of it – the cottage is a bit dilapidated –' Kate was stumbling over her words, embarrassed. The cottage had become precious; she didn't want anyone judging it harshly.

'I'm sure I'll like it, the countryside air is good, and I will appreciate the quiet at night.'

The three of them walked up the lane, and Kate dropped behind as Art and Hussain fell into easy conversation. As they arrived at the cottage, Kate suggested they eat dinner outside in the back garden. The previous evening Art had put tea lights in old jam jars and arranged them in a row along the low wall beside the table, and now he set about replacing those that had burnt out. Over supper Art was particularly talkative, as if trying to keep everyone happy. He described dens, walks and Maisie's house to Hussain, who nodded with interest. Kate said little. She occasionally shot a quick glance at his face and saw how his eyes caught the glow of the candles; he looked more relaxed. After Art had gone upstairs, they sat in silence for a short while before she started to clear the plates. When she went up to check that Art was in bed, she discovered the window still open above the garden table. He had been trying to eavesdrop.

'I just wanted to make sure you were both happy.'

Kate leaned over to kiss him goodnight.

'I know you like him. You try to pretend you don't, but you do,' he whispered.

'Of course I like him,' said Kate smoothly. 'He's a nice man and we are very lucky to have him as a lodger.'

'Not "like" in that way – in the love way.'

'Don't be daft, Art,' she said firmly.

When she came back downstairs, Hussain was still sitting at the table outside in the dusky light. Kate hesitated at the back door.

'I wanted to say thank you,' he said. 'You and Art have been very kind to me. You have made me welcome, and I'm grateful and –'

Kate interrupted quickly. 'You've been kind to Art, thank you.'

'He's a lovely boy, and you've been kind,' he repeated.

'Well, anyway,' Kate said, trying to conclude the conversation. Art was probably eavesdropping again.

'You haven't asked me questions, you have taken me on trust. That is a very generous thing to do.'

Kate stood there, hesitant, watching the candlelight flickering in the light breeze.

'I'm sure there are things you wanted to know, but didn't ask. I miss my wife and daughter very much, but being in another family has helped.'

Kate shifted her weight to lean against the door jamb. 'I'm not some saint or something, it was just a way to manage, and you've been a help with Art,' she said grudgingly.

'If there is anything you want to know about me, I can't promise to answer but I will try.'

'I can ask? Now?' asked Kate, surprised.

'Anything, and then we leave it.'

'So, it's sort of time-limited?'

Hussain laughed.

Kate stood there, searching her mind as to what was the most important question. Why was he an asylum seeker? Where did he go at night? How long would he need to be with them?

'How many questions do I get?' She sat down at the table.

'One, two? Three at a push.' A sad, brief laugh.

Kate took a breath. 'What did you study in America?'

'Specialist training in surgery.'

'Surgery?' That explained the confident stitches when she'd hurt her hand, but she added quickly, 'That's not another question.'

'There is one other thing I wanted to make clear. I told Shirin

I needed to get out of the house in King's Cross. The place is run by critics of the regime in Bahrain, and they post many photos of events. If I was seen in one, it would be difficult for Maryam, my wife. That's why Shirin suggested your flat, but I can go back if you need me to, or find somewhere else.'

Kate stared at one of the candles, feeling profoundly uncomfortable. She didn't like his gratitude; she was the one who should be thanking him.

He smiled at her. 'Thank you, from the bottom of my heart.' He put his hand on his heart and bowed his head.

'It's nothing,' she said briskly, and looked away. There was such kindness in his eyes.

*

The next morning, Kate woke late and heard the clatter of cutlery in the kitchen below and the murmur of conversation. Hussain must be making Art breakfast. It was a luxury to be able to pull the pillow over her head, turn over and go back to sleep. She couldn't remember the last time she had had a lie-in.

When she finally came downstairs, there was a note on the table.

> *I'm taking Hussain to the magic tree on the downs. We've made a picnic. You can have lots of peace and quiet and do your gardening. Love, Art.*

She chuckled to herself, folding the note up to tuck into her diary later. She had the rest of the morning to dig the flower bed she was planning. Out of the window, she could see patches of blue sky and the trees moving in a brisk wind.

Several hours later, she was rummaging in the shed amongst the piles of old tools for secateurs when she heard the phone ring. There was an old-fashioned fitting on the outside of the cottage which ensured you could hear its loud ring everywhere in the garden. It was probably an irritating marketing call, but just in case, Kate ran back into the hallway in her apron and wellingtons.

'It's me,' said Ed.

His voice could evoke a paralysing fear in her, even now. He only called when he wanted something. She didn't know he had the cottage number.

'It's me,' he repeated, sounding preoccupied, as if he were reading a screen at the same time.

'I heard the first time.'

Ed's tone hardened. 'I want Art to come over earlier. Work assignments have changed and I can't make the dates we suggested.'

'They were not "suggested", they were *agreed*,' wailed Kate.

He sighed heavily and there was a pause – he had been distracted by something, she could tell. She heard typing in the background.

'Well, whatever – agreed, suggested – I can get Art on a flight on Thursday.'

'Thursday?' she exclaimed, furious.

'What's the problem? What difference does it make? This way I can spend some quality time with him. We've planned a trip to the sea. Is he there? Can I speak to him?'

Kate sat down, speechless; the man still had the capacity to wind her. Who was this 'we'? And how could they have already planned something before she had agreed to move the dates for Art's trip to the US? Ed, as usual, assumed he could rearrange her life whenever he wanted. She tried to breathe deeply as the therapist had advised her; this was how the panic attacks started.

'He is on holiday with me at the moment and we have plans. His flight is booked for a fortnight,' she cried hoarsely.

'That's OK, I've changed the flights – it was lucky. I got one of the last seats on Thursday.'

'But you can't do this – you *can't.*'

'What? Can't do what? The line isn't good. Listen, Kate, you said you wanted me to spend more time with Art, and this way I can spend five days uninterrupted at the sea with him. It's what you said you wanted. He'll be back on the plane to you a week later.'

'Just as *my* holiday finishes,' she replied sharply.

'Well, OK, that's a shame,' he conceded, 'but you are just in that damp cottage – he goes there a lot, right? You can take him down for a few extra weekends to make up. You said you needed time alone, and this way you get it.' He repeated, 'It's what you said you wanted.'

Kate didn't know how to explain to him the complicated sequence of plans she had put into place for childcare over the summer: the play dates, the few days away with one of Art's friends, and her own holiday allocation.

Ed took advantage of the pause. 'He's booked on the 5.30 p.m. from Heathrow. He will be escorted on the flight, and I will email the tickets.' He added condescendingly, 'Don't worry about packing, I'll take him shopping. The stuff you pack doesn't suit Washington.'

After the annual holidays with his father, Art returned with a new wardrobe – T-shirts with bold, witty slogans, expensive trainers, shorts and hoodies. For a few weeks he was very proud of his new outfits, and then he slowly reverted to clothes Kate found for him in charity shops, or the cast-offs from Dotty's children. She looked through the open doorway as Ed talked. Today was Wednesday; Art would be gone by tomorrow afternoon. Most of her holiday down here would be alone: none of the walks, picnics and swimming in the river they had planned. There was never anything to say to Ed. He conducted conversations entirely for his own purposes, saying what he believed was necessary to say and listening to himself saying it. It had a crippling effect on her; she was left with nothing but undignified responses such as shouting, weeping or pleading.

'Kate? Are you there? We'll meet him at the airport.'

'Who's we?' asked Kate shakily.

'My fiancée – we're engaged. She has a ten-year-old daughter, actually, and we think the kids will get on. We're taking them both to the beach. By the way, we're planning to marry at Christmas – but don't tell Art. We want to tell him.'

Art finally had his 'real' family – even a sister – and he would love it. Kate felt hollowed out with loss; Art would be absorbed into this American family. Her imagination ran away with her as she saw some beautiful woman who would produce more siblings, and all these brown-legged, blond-haired children would end up as a happy tribe.

'It's a good time to give you the heads up. We're getting married in Key West – off Florida – and, as I said, we will want Art there. The ceremony is booked for Christmas Eve so that we can have a holiday with the children instead of a honeymoon – I thought you would approve.'

Kate didn't know which bit of information to respond to. Ed had always insisted he would never marry; he had certainly been adamant about never marrying her. Even worse, the idea of a Christmas without Art was shocking.

'It's only fair. I haven't had Christmas with him since he was small.'

'Fair? I can't agree to this now!' Kate was dangerously close to crying; she could hear the plaintive tone of her voice.

'Oh, God, Kate, I have to go, something has come up. We can discuss all this later. Art will be on the plane tomorrow, won't he?' He hung up before Kate had answered.

After the phone went dead, she replaced the receiver, and wandered into the front garden. A thrush was now perched on a low branch, and she stood still watching as it turned its head from side to side. Damn the man. He did this with bad news, sending her into a spin with a sequence of announcements, all of which were upsetting, knowing that the overload would overwhelm her. Then he had the knack of extricating himself from the conversation before her anger had gathered force.

She went up to Art's room to pack a few of his things for the journey in a small knapsack. Long ago she had vowed to herself that her son would not grow up with her fury at his father; she had had enough of such shadow emotions towards errant men when growing up herself. She had to put him first. But she would be bereft, alone for the rest of her holiday. All the pleasure of the garden was premised on Art's close proximity. Time on her own changed its quality entirely when he was with his father in America. Ed could easily outstrip her in parental competition, lavishing money on treats for Art. Suddenly she felt acutely aware of the shabby cottage; it symbolized the makeshift arrangements she had constructed for Art and her life, and, in particular, with this kind stranger, Hussain. Makeshift was bad enough, but now she felt something worse nagging at the edges of her mind: her life was beginning to feel precarious – it was to do with Hussain – in ways she couldn't articulate, only dimly sense. It made her nervous.

9

Art clutched his knapsack, excited and anxious, and Kate put her arms around him to whisper goodbye. Then, with a brave grin, he disappeared through the Departures gate with the air steward. Kate stood and watched until she could no longer see any part of his familiar body, then the tears streamed down her face. She tried to brush them away, but her whole chest heaved with sobs. She crumpled inside, the last twenty-four hours of tension emerging in waves of fury and sadness. She suddenly felt Hussain's arms around her. For a fraction of a second she held herself stiff in his embrace, but he pulled her close, and she leaned into him, burying her face in his sweatshirt, feeling the damp cloth on her hot cheek, smelling the sweet scent of him – an unfamiliar Arabic brand of soap he must have found somewhere in London. He was stroking her hair to soothe her, and whispering in her ear. It was the sound of his voice she listened to; the words were secondary. In the midst of the bustling crowds of passengers at Heathrow, they were immobile, locked together, and everything else was irrelevant: she and Hussain, the still centre, a place of intense sorrow.

He lifted her chin and wiped her cheeks with a tissue. 'He's coming back – it's only two weeks,' he repeated.

Kate was sobbing too hard to speak. There was too much to explain to this stranger, and how could she even try? It wasn't just Art's departure for this holiday; she was terrified she was losing at least half of her son. That was what Ed said he wanted: his share. But he was a greedy man and he would buy more with treats and excitement. This was the worst part: he would succeed by creating the family Art so badly wanted. Art had been thrilled at the idea that he was going to have a seaside holiday in what he called a 'normal' family of two parents and two children. He'd chattered enthusiastically about the photos he was going to take to show friends. The panicky fear erupting now in Kate was that she would lose him, and become a pitiable figure, similar to her own mother. She was struggling to breathe, and her gasps came fast and shallow.

Hussain kept his arm around her, and led her to a cafe, where he sat her down at a table. He brought her a cup of tea and urged her to drink it. Sitting down beside her, he held her other hand, damp with tears and sweat. Slowly the sugary tea took effect and her breathing slowed. She was overcome with embarrassment as she blew her nose and vigorously wiped her eyes with another tissue. A pile of used, damp tissues accumulated on the table in front of her.

'I'm sorry,' she whispered.

He was silent for a moment. 'I know what it is to miss a child,' he said quietly.

Her eyes filled again, horrified at the dissimilarity of their stories. 'But . . . but it's not like you –' She no longer knew if she was crying for him or for her. She could see tears in his eyes now, and squeezed his hand in sympathy.

'Can you come back to the cottage, just for tonight?' she whispered.

He looked confused. At breakfast, she had suggested that they part at Heathrow after dropping Art and that he take the tube back to the flat. He had packed his bag.

'Come back to the cottage – please, just for tonight. I don't want to be alone.'

He hesitated. He was torn, and she understood.

'Please,' she whispered again, and he nodded. Their carefully maintained distance of the last six weeks was crumbling.

The train back to Hampshire was crowded and hot, but someone noticed Kate's distress and offered Hussain a seat so they could sit together. Kate could feel the heat of his leg against hers, and it helped steady her. The tears had left her exhausted and her head dropped on to Hussain's shoulder as she stared out of the window at the parched fields, burnt brown in the summer heatwave. Hussain remained upright, and after he'd reassured her that he would look out for their stop, she fell into a troubled, light sleep. As they approached their station, he gently shook her awake, and they got out with a few commuters. They headed up the hill away from the village towards Lodsbourne, and she reached out to take his hand again. She sensed his reluctance, but she didn't let go; she found the touch deeply comforting. It was a long time since an adult had touched her. The green shade of the trees swallowed them up, a cool relief after the hectic movement and noise of Heathrow. She felt ragged from the intense emotion, her eyes sore and swollen from the crying.

Back in the cottage, she saw some of Art's games and clothes scattered on the sitting-room floor, and the sharp sense of loss swept over her again. She was still holding Hussain's hand and she pulled him close, her mouth searching for his. Now she had been touched, she wanted more: the feel of his body, its weight on her. Astonishingly, she felt a surge of unrecognized desire welling up. He had his hands on her shoulders as if holding her back.

'Kate, this isn't right.'

He was staring at her, and she couldn't bring herself to look at him, aware that her need was blatant.

'Kate, I can't. My –'

She reached up and put her fingers on his lips to stop him.

'I know, I know. You love her, but . . .' She didn't know how to finish the sentence, how to explain that she only wanted a small part of him, that she understood he was Maryam's.

He sat down heavily, his bowed head in his hands.

'It's not right for me – it's not right for you,' he whispered.

She knelt on the floor in front of him. 'It *is* right for me. I know it is.' She surprised herself with this sudden certainty.

'I thought, all these weeks, that you wanted to keep well away – and I understood. I felt the same, and it felt right. But now . . . how can we do this?'

'How can we not?' she whispered, amazed at herself, confident.

'I can't make any promises . . . It cannot last.' He looked away.

She gave a small smile. 'I know, Hussain.' She leaned forward and kissed his still lips. He didn't respond, but he didn't move. She pressed closer, her arms around him, her lips searching for a response, and she felt the tension ease. Gently he held her head in his hands to kiss her, hesitantly at first, then with a sudden urgency. She was pulling at his clothes, slipping her hands underneath to find his warm skin as he undid the buttons on her shirt and pushed her bra up to cup her breasts. He kissed her neck and throat, his dry lips tasting her skin as his hands caressed her body. She led him up the stairs to the bedroom, stopping halfway to kiss, both of them now overwhelmed by their unexpected desire.

The warm evening slipped by, and occasionally Kate noticed the light of the setting sun catch the wardrobe, and then the thickening dusk. In a pause, Kate got up to open all the windows so that, as they lay intertwined on the bed, they could hear the last of the birdsong and the garden settling to an evening quiet. Later, she slipped down to gather the tea lights from the garden and placed them around the bedroom, before returning to their caresses, each stroking the other's satiated body in the dim glow. Then they resumed their love-making, less urgent and desperate now, luxuriating in the slow touch of the other's body.

Next morning, they took breakfast back to bed, propping themselves up against the pillows to drink coffee and hungrily eat toast, intermittently chatting, and then quietly content. The long spell of hot weather had broken, and the patter of raindrops falling from the low eaves lulled them into a rhythm of making love and light sleep. The room was cave-like in the dim light, and life had shrunk to fit into the low-ceilinged room for these hours. They lit new tea lights, and Kate rested her head on Hussain's chest, feeling the soft fall and rise of his breathing. He stroked her cheek.

'Thank you,' she murmured, lifting her head to look at him. He kissed her shoulder.

The phone sitting beside the bed burst into life, a shocking intrusion.

'Leave it,' suggested Hussain, running his fingers down her arm.

'It could be Art.' She leaned over and picked up the receiver.

'Mum!' His voice was shaking with excitement as he told her about the films on the plane, the food, the nice air steward, Daddy's new girlfriend, Mona, and her daughter. He had his own bedroom, and they were going off to the seaside that day. He was talking so fast Kate struggled to follow; she forced herself to keep her voice at the right pitch of encouragement and enthusiasm.

'That sounds terrific, my love.'

Finally, when Kate's throat was dry with the clenched artificiality of her responses, Art asked if Hussain was there, and whether he could speak to him.

'Of course, I'll hand you over.'

She lay back and listened to the chatter start again. Hussain handed the phone back to Kate to say goodbye.

'Mum, where are you?'

'Where?'

'Where in the cottage?' Art repeated. 'It's just that it sounds as if you and Hussain are sitting very close together. You can't both be in the hall – there isn't room.'

Kate took a breath: his quickness. 'Yes, we are!' she insisted cheerfully. 'We were just on our way out. We are setting off for a walk. It's lunchtime.'

'For a moment I thought you might be both in the bedroom.' He started giggling. 'Have a nice walk, Mum.'

Kate put the receiver back on the phone and turned to Hussain, her hand over her mouth. They laughed out loud, and he leaned over and kissed her.

Once again, the piercing ring of the phone, and this time it was Phoebe.

'Kate, I gather your friend is still here. Someone saw you at the station yesterday. I am so pleased. Why not bring him for tea this afternoon? It's just me, and it's dreadfully dreary in this rain – I need cheering up. Sue has made a delicious cake. See you around four?'

Kate rolled on to her back. She hadn't said anything beyond hello and goodbye; Phoebe, in her inimitable way, had engineered the conversation, swiftly achieving the outcome she wanted.

'She invited us for tea?' asked Hussain.

Kate nodded, grimacing. 'She will ask questions – she has a roundabout way of doing it, so you don't even notice.'

'I can manage,' he said, tucking a strand of Kate's hair behind her ear.

'We've made things more complicated, haven't we? she said.

He sighed heavily and nodded.

'I don't regret it. I'm just not sure what happens now – after this?' Kate turned on to her side to look at him.

Hussain shrugged as he stroked her arm. 'I don't know either. Anything. Everything. All that could have happened before and more?'

'That sounds like a riddle,' she said, smiling.

'We didn't know what was going to happen before, and we don't know now,' he said, lying on his back and staring at the ceiling. 'I know very little from one day to the next. I have learned to live like that – well, sort of live. I cannot dwell on my hopes – it's too painful that way. My dreams are full of Maryam and

Reem . . . but when I'm awake, I try not to think about them. It's not easy, I admit. Now you are with me, it will be a bit the same for you – you cannot hope. I didn't want that, I wanted to protect you, but it hasn't worked out that way . . .' He trailed off.

'You dream of Maryam?'

His nod was barely perceptible.

'One day, when you get asylum in the UK, you can get a job again,' suggested Kate, propping herself up on her elbow and reaching out a hand to trace his sternum with her finger. She remembered how she had told Art that Hussain's family would join him.

'I'm not applying to the UK for asylum. I'm trying to get to the US, and I'm waiting for a visa. I have an uncle there, and Maryam has relatives there too – they are trying to sort it out.'

Kate sat up, frowning. 'Why the US?'

'I only arrived in the UK because I had no choice. I'm on a multiple-entry visa. It was the best option at the time, but my stay cannot be longer than a hundred and eighty days – I arrived at the beginning of May. I have to leave before it expires, or it will make my chances of getting into the US harder. I become illegal.'

Kate counted on her fingers. 'Three more months.' She was silent, absorbing this painful announcement. 'I see,' she said bleakly, and she rolled over and got up.

She ran a deep bath and lay in the water, looking out of the window at the rain falling on the climbing rose. She thought about how long three months was – long enough to get Art back to school, long enough to get them to October half-term. Then Maryam could have all of him back – she was only asking for a short loan. She sank down under the water to wash her hair. It was a holiday romance – at home.

★

'I do love Persian tiles, don't you?' said Phoebe, leading them into the drawing room. The rain was driving against the tall windows, the lawns and copper beech misty in the downpour. She had had the fire lit and the air was thick with the scent of lilies in the vases around the room.

Kate glanced at Hussain as he looked at the Persian tiles. He had that familiar air of calm reserve, but she knew now what lay behind it. He had clung to her with a hungry lust mixed with despair. He had shaken with repressed sobs in the early hours of the morning, waking her, and when she'd put her hand out to touch him, she'd felt his sweat-drenched skin. 'Nightmares,' he had explained, rubbing his eyes, and then turned over to hold her tightly.

Phoebe sat down and gestured to Hussain to sit opposite, the tray between them. 'Why not sit here, next to the fire?' Catching Kate's surprise at the lavish flower displays, she added, 'They're magnificent, but rather overdone. The company ordered them for the clients' lunch. I do hope you like the cottage, Hussain? I'm afraid it's a little shabby.'

'It's charming,' he replied politely.

'Ah, I've forgotten the milk, I was too preoccupied with the cake. Why don't you come and help me, Kate – and Hussain, perhaps you can cut the cake?'

Once they were in the kitchen, Phoebe pounced. 'I am so pleased for you – no, don't deny it: it's written all over your face. You're glowing!'

Kate blushed a deep red.

'No need for that. I may be old, but I was never a prude. I walked down the lane at lunchtime, and saw that all the bedroom curtains were still closed – a good sign, I thought!'

She poured milk into a jug. 'Besides, he's so handsome. A good love affair is exactly what you needed. Enjoy every minute – even if it can't last.'

'Yes . . . no . . . well, exactly . . .' Kate found herself stumbling out useless words. She took a deep breath as Phoebe watched her confusion. 'I'm worried about how Art will deal with it.'

'Don't worry about that – children are very adaptable. I'm sure he will be delighted. He obviously adores Hussain. That's good enough for me: a man who is patient and kind with a child like Art has my approval.'

'He won't answer questions, Phoebe. Don't ask him anything. He doesn't want to talk about why he came to the UK.'

'Fine, we can talk about Art, then.' She picked up the milk jug, and suddenly paused. 'He reminds me of someone I once knew . . .'

Kate expected her to continue, but, with a sigh, she straightened her shoulders and headed back to the drawing room.

The three of them sat before the fire, drinking tea and discussing Art's call from America and his father's holiday plans. Phoebe managed to keep the conversation flowing with Hussain. Her experience of corporate entertaining stands her in good stead, thought Kate; she does small talk so well you are not even aware of it.

Kate was still upset by Phoebe's comments. They were intrusive and too early in a new love affair which was so unexpected in every way. They had been enjoying its privacy – just the two of them – which could only ever last a fortnight, until Art's return. The conversation turned – perhaps Hussain had asked Phoebe a question when Kate's attention had drifted. Phoebe was talking about her time in Iran.

'I went in 1968, recruited by the empress, no less,' she chuckled, her face lighting up at the memory. 'I was twenty-seven and very naive. I knew nothing about the place beyond romantic nonsense such as *The Arabian Nights*, but we had so much fun. I have memories of so many wonderful people, the parties, and our travels around that beautiful country.'

'Travels with Martin?' asked Kate, curious about Phoebe's life before her marriage.

Phoebe smiled mischievously, and Kate glimpsed the twenty-seven-year-old who had arrived in Tehran with the poise of a young woman, well used to attracting attention.

'Yes,' she replied, but there was a slight hesitation in her voice. 'And before I met him . . .'

Kate laughed teasingly. 'Before?'

Phoebe got up to add more logs to the fire. 'Tehran was full of foreigners – Italians, French, Americans – and the city was awash with money. The champagne and cocktails flowed all night. Looking back, it is shocking what went on, but I didn't pay much attention to the politics at the beginning. I was too busy with my work for the empress, and I suppose I accepted the royal court's version of events.'

She broke off to poke the fire, and small showers of sparks exploded in the grate. 'I travelled to Mashhad, Tabriz, Isfahan, Shiraz, Qazvin and Yazd. I was collecting, you see – carpets, tiles, textiles, ceramics, metalwork – alongside my work for the empress. It was a sideline, and a lucrative one, I admit. Some of what I collected was exported to a gallery in Paris, and the rest is here,' she said with a flourish, her heavy rings glinting in the firelight.

'Did you change your mind about the royal family?' asked Hussain.

'Yes, I did in the end, but I was slow, and I missed things. After the revolution in 1979, there were books and articles I read which made more sense of that febrile atmosphere in Tehran a decade earlier. You couldn't imagine the luxury villas in northern Tehran, in Shemiran, and the absurdity of the Shah's projects in the midst of the poverty. Did you ever hear about his party?'

Kate shook her head.

'The extravagance of it: chilled champagne and food flown in from Paris for dozens of heads of state to feast on in the middle of a desert. I was part of the organizing team, and helped the empress choose her wardrobe. It was utter chaos, and half the time I was terrified and the other half I was hugely enjoying it all, I'm ashamed to say. Working through the nights in the final frantic weeks, rushing by taxi from air-freight depots to seamstresses and then to the palace for fittings. My strongest memory of the actual event was sleeping on the floor of a friend's room in a very crowded hotel in Shiraz, and watching it on a small black-and-white television. But I did join the crowds on the streets when the first limousines came through from the airport – I maintain I caught a glimpse of Princess Anne, but it could have been any of the VIPs, since the car windows had dark glass.' Her face stiffened. 'I thought it was a bit of a joke – thousands of young men dressed in nylon tunics in imitation of ancient sculptures – but the fear in that country was never funny. I didn't notice it at first. The *khareji* – that's what the foreigners were called – were insulated against it, but once you stumbled across it, you could never forget. I was very glad to get out when I did.'

'Fear?' pressed Kate.

'The Shah's police – the SAVAK.' She paused before continuing, 'I knew a young man who was arrested. He was an architecture student. He'd won a scholarship to London, but he returned to Iran, keen to help build a new country. If he had stayed on in London, he might still be alive . . .'

Phoebe left the sentence hanging. Perhaps it was the melancholy of the wet afternoon or Hussain's presence that had prompted her to speak. After a moment she resumed, 'I haven't spoken about him for years. We only spent a few weeks together, and then –' Phoebe's voice was suddenly thick – 'then there was nothing.'

'Nothing?' echoed Kate, puzzled.

'Once someone was arrested, people were frightened to ask where they were. Asil died while in prison but no one dared to ask what had happened. Afterwards even close friends didn't refer to him, for fear of the SAVAK informers, who were everywhere. My Iranian friends lived with that fear all the time; sometimes they were proud, so they hid it from the *khareji*. I visited Asil's parents, and they couldn't understand why their clever son had died. Years later, I read the stories of what the SAVAK had done to thousands of people arrested on spurious allegations – the torture was horrific.'

Phoebe was staring at the fire, her eyes glittering. It was hard to tell if it was with tears, but Kate watched her profile, strangely collapsed with sadness; she glimpsed a different woman, with a history of a lost Iranian love. Hussain was silent.

'Did Martin know Asil?' asked Kate.

Phoebe blew her nose briskly, and regained her usual cheerful poise. 'I think they met – Martin was at the embassy and scholarship students got an invite to a reception for their send off. That's all. Martin was very good. I didn't know him at the time but he paid for the funeral expenses. My relationship with Martin started a few months later. I'd asked his advice about how to find Asil, and he called to tell me he had died. I don't think he was surprised. He said it was not our business to get too involved; by then, he had lost faith in the Shah's regime, and, more importantly, in British diplomacy. He said that the British had developed a habit of backing the wrong horse. He hated the extravagance and the lavish projects. We once went to an arts festival in Shiraz –' she added, her voice lighter – 'Martin had no time for the empress's taste for avant-garde art. He said it deeply offended the clerics, and he was right about that.'

'When did you leave Iran?' asked Hussain.

'Late 1971, after the Shah's party in Persepolis. That was the final straw, and Martin decided to leave the Foreign Office. He had been looking at other opportunities, and I introduced him to my uncle Roddy. Everything fell into place. He signed a big contract very quickly and set up ZSKa, we left Iran, spent some time in Bahrain, and then moved to Dubai. I got pregnant and we married, and Dotty arrived in 1972. Martin maintains it wasn't just our lives which were decided in 1971, but the fate of Iran, the future of the Gulf, and Britain's position in the new global oil economy.' She laughed, and added deprecatingly, 'He was rather dramatic about the whole thing.'

It was the first time Kate had heard Phoebe talk of having lived in Bahrain. She looked over at Hussain, but he quickly glanced away and asked Phoebe, 'How long were you in the Gulf?'

'A year or so. I came back to have Dotty here, of course. Martin set up his main office in Dubai, but the Gulf was rather dreary – country-club type of thing. Too many expats for my taste.'

One of the dogs came over to Phoebe and nuzzled in her lap. She absent-mindedly stroked its head. 'She needs walking – she's been waiting all day for this rain to stop.'

Kate and Hussain were being gently dismissed. They stood up to leave, and it occurred to Kate to ask, 'Do you have any old photos?' She was curious about this chapter of Phoebe's life.

'Dozens of mouldy albums upstairs, full of photos of drinks parties, barbecues and a lamentable taste in swimming costumes,' replied Phoebe, with a forced buoyancy. She picked up the tray and added, half to herself, 'I missed Tehran for a long time – its brittle edge was dangerous, but full of possibility.'

Hussain paused in the hall to look again at the Iranian miniatures, while Kate followed Phoebe into the kitchen, carrying the cake.

'Kate, dear, he's not Iranian, is he?' Phoebe asked, taking a sharp breath, as if the idea had only just come to her.

'No, he's from Bahrain, but he doesn't want to talk about it,' replied Kate, hoping that by giving this one detail she would forestall more questions. 'Phoebe – who was Edith Grant? When did she live at the cottage?'

Phoebe's face softened fondly. 'My aunt. A fascinating character. She married Roddy after the First World War and followed him round the Middle East and Africa to Iraq, Iran, then a stint in Kenya and back to Bahrain and Kuwait. She was passionate about archaeology and birds. She was in Iraq before the Second World War and was involved in some of the archaeological excavations there. She was a very clever woman, and these days she would have been an Oxbridge don, but for her generation, that wasn't an option. They were travelling for half a century and when they retired to the UK, he took to drink. She was often bending Martin's ear about something or other, but he was fond of the old girl, as I was. She was something of a plotter – but some of her plots were surprisingly successful. She always knew that there were useful things for Martin to do – he used to say she was suffering from post-imperial stress syndrome: power-lessness. That generation found it hard to give up on empire. Why do you ask?'

'I found her passports in a drawer of the desk in the cottage.'

'How odd. I thought Martin had cleared out all her papers after she died. She left a lot of stuff to an archaeological institute in Cambridge, if I remember. Martin was her executor and had to go through everything and sort it all out. He put a lot of time into it. Very conscientious.' Phoebe took the cups off the tray and stacked them in the dishwasher. She put the cake in a tin in the pantry, and as she came back into the kitchen, she added, 'Edith was a powerful character when she wanted to be. She was the one who got us to Bahrain, and that was the start of Martin's business.'

'Do you have any of her things from Bahrain? Books? Photo albums?'

Phoebe tidied the drying-up cloths on the Aga rail. 'Now you mention it, I think there's a box of her papers upstairs in a cupboard – Felix promised to take them up to Cambridge at some point, but what with the wedding and so forth, he has been dreadfully slow. It has more of her writings on archaeology, and an archivist in Cambridge wanted to have a look. We can dig it out if you like – it might be a distraction from this rain if Hussain is interested in archaeology. Then I must take the dogs for a walk.'

'It could keep us busy for an hour or two,' agreed Kate, glancing outside. She was intrigued by this Edith. Hussain waited by the front door as Phoebe and Kate went upstairs. The store cupboard was lined with shelves from floor to ceiling. Every shelf was stacked with neatly labelled boxes. It was as big as Art's bedroom back home, thought Kate, her eye falling on labels such as 'Table Clothes (white)' and 'Table clothes (Provençal)'; one box was marked 'Martin's Evening Suit, 1995', and another, 'Spare blankets'. The cupboard reeked of moth balls. On the floor was a box labelled 'Edith Grant, Cambridge', and another, 'Baby Clothes'.

Phoebe looked a little embarrassed. 'I know it's ridiculous, but I didn't have the heart to throw the baby clothes out. I hoped that Dotty or Felix might one day enjoy dressing their children in their old smocked dresses and sailor suits. Here, this is the box – I expect most of it is about crumbling desert ruins.'

Kate crouched down to pull it out.

'Let me know if you find anything interesting. Martin didn't think it added up to much, but then he didn't have time for Bahraini archaeology.'

The three of them stood on the front doorstep, and Phoebe put the dogs on leads. The rain had eased slightly. She turned to Hussain suddenly. 'Kate is one of the family, you know. She's a dear person and she has been badly treated. It's been such a shame, but she's putting all that behind her.'

Kate winced. They both knew what Phoebe was indirectly telling him. Then she headed off, in her long mackintosh, with the dogs, towards the downs, and Kate and Hussain walked back across the lawn and through the copse to the cottage, carrying

Edith's box. The air was fresh and laden with moisture after the heavy rain, the leaves of the beech trees glittered, and the mast, sodden underfoot, was a deep rust.

'What did she mean?' asked Hussain. 'Badly treated?'

'Who knows?' Kate bit her bottom lip. 'I don't really understand Phoebe – she's charming and kind, but I never know how much of it comes from pity. Sometimes I feel it's an elaborate performance. Hearing her talk about Tehran, and that young man, Asil, was interesting, because the performance slipped for a moment – she would never talk like that if Martin were there. Most of the time she floats through life on a combination of charm and self-belief.'

She was annoyed at the thought that Phoebe might see her as a sad offcut, someone who had not really found her way in life; she didn't want it to be quite so obvious.

'Art's father left you – is that what she meant?' persisted Hussain.

'I suppose so. We split up when Art was five. I was young when I met him and we fell in love for the wrong reasons.'

'And your parents? Are they alive? Do you have brothers or sisters?'

'I'm an only child. My parents divorced when I was about seven, and my father returned to Hong Kong; my parents met and lived there for a while before I was born – he was trying to make his fortune, my mother said. After the divorce, he came back to England twice to take me on holiday to Cornwall. He died a couple of years later, in Cambodia, of an infection, my mother said, when he was travelling on business. She was my only source of information about my father; I gather he needed money so badly because my grandfather had decided that whichever son could afford to renovate Lodsbourne would inherit it – Martin beat him to it.'

'That's a painful story. And your mother?'

Kate shrugged and looked up at the branches of the trees overhead.

'I look at old photos of her and I can't connect the young woman she was with the person she became. The mother I knew always had health problems of one kind or another; she was often in bed or in hospital. We were short of money, and she hated that. She died shortly after Art was born. I know I irritated her. I was never the beauty she had been, and she couldn't understand how a woman made her way in the world without beauty and money.'

'I see you as beautiful,' Hussain said as he opened the gate into the cottage garden.

Kate stopped and stared at him, laughing.

'You must be mad.'

He cupped her face in his hands and kissed her.

'No one – *no one*,' she repeated with emphasis, 'has ever said that to me.'

Hussain smiled and she reached up to kiss him.

10

The rain resumed and for the next twenty-four hours it barely paused; Hussain was astonished by its relentlessness. He opened the back door and stared at the water falling from the heavy sky, and the thick, wet greenery of the garden: the dripping leaves and the sodden flowers. Kate banked up the fire to hold off the damp, and turned on the lamps in the sitting room. Beyond the windows, the light glowed a murky green. She took down another thriller to read, but Hussain was restless, frequently getting up to check the sky for a break in the clouds.

'I'm sorry – even after three months in England, I don't think I am used to this kind of rain.' He sat down next to Kate on the sofa. 'In the summer in Bahrain the temperature is forty-five or fifty degrees and the humidity is eighty per cent. Here it is cold – it can't be more than twelve degrees. More tea?'

Kate shook her head. 'How about we look through Edith's papers?' she suggested, putting down her book.

He didn't answer and just stared at the fire.

'It's dark even in the daytime in your English summer,' he said with a harsh laugh. Kate shivered. Perhaps they should return to London; at least there, the noise and bustle of the city might distract him.

She went upstairs to the study where they had put Edith Grant's box. The room was dark and she switched on a desk lamp and the fuse blew. Undeterred, she turned on the overhead light. The papers were yellowed with age. She picked out several monographs on an archaeological site in Iraq, then her eye was caught by an article, from 1990, about a red kite breeding programme in the Chilterns. It had escaped Martin's sorting and got bundled up with Edith's papers on archaeology. Kate paused to skim read, curious about these birds of prey, which often accompanied her on walks over the downs, hovering above as if she were possible prey before they circled away over the fields. When she disturbed them in the hedgerow, their white markings were clearly visible on the underside of their wings as they soared into the pale Hampshire sky. Their beauty had caught Hussain's eye, and she hoped he might be interested.

In a folder on the migration patterns of birds in the Gulf, Kate flicked through aged photos of flamingos, magnificent in their pale-pink plumage against the bright blue water. She turned to a wad of hand-typed notes on the ancient Dilmun civilization in Bahrain and its role in trade between the Indus and Mesopotamia, thousands of years ago: ivory, pearls, lapis lazuli, carnelian and gold were exchanged for silver, olive oil and timber. She found herself engrossed in an account of how in some versions of the Sumerian myths, the deified hero of the floods is taken by the gods to live for ever on the island of Dilmun, described as 'the place where the sun rises' and the 'land of the living'. She studied a map of Bahrain marked with numerous Dilmun burial mounds. A closely typed article discussed the evidence for Bahrain as the origin of the Phoenicians, citing Strabo and Herodotus. At the back of this folder were a few letters in Arabic on sheets of pale-blue airmail paper; she set them aside to show Hussain.

At the bottom of the box, Kate rifled through used Jordanian, Iraqi and Bahraini stamps, carefully steamed from their envelopes, and found a folder on which had been scrawled, 'Private. Roddy's papers. Misc. 1963–'. The first few pages, stapled together, were labelled 'Speech to Private Industrialists Confed. mtg by John Stonehouse, 1964'. Kate flicked through the pages and her eye was caught by a paragraph which had been underlined:

the old idea that ministers and civil servants should keep at arms-length from the squalid commercial world is a nonsense. Selling Britain's products is a noble task . . . this Government is behind you all the way in promoting British aircraft overseas; you must regard all of us in the Ministry as an extension of your own selling organization.

She had to reread it to be sure she had understood it properly. What an extraordinary statement, that a ministry should be seen as an 'extension' of a 'selling organization'. Who on earth was this John Stonehouse? The next piece of paper was a carbon copy of a letter, dated July 1966, addressed to 'Mr Wortherton, The British Embassy, Tehran', from 'Director of Army Sales at the DSO, Harold Hubert'. Kate scanned the short letter, her eye landing on the final startling statement: 'I am not keen to educate the Persians in virtuous ways. My task is to sell British equipment.' What did Edith have to do with any of this?

Next were more carbon copies, the blue lettering blurred; it was a long time since anyone had used carbon paper to duplicate documents, Kate thought. On one side were notes on an archaeological dig but on the back was a form. At the top of each page there was a name in English and Arabic, followed by a date and place of birth. The forms were filled out by hand in both English and Arabic, and were dated – all from the first few months of 1970. They appeared to be case notes, with a printed summary detailing arrest, imprisonment and charges. The men were young – several of them were teenagers. Some of the forms had photos attached with rusty staples of badly beaten faces; she noticed several were initialled 'RG' in blue ink at the bottom. Martin would never have given these pages to Cambridge; they had slipped through his sorting. She gathered them back into the folder, and carried it downstairs. Hussain had banked up the fire and was on his phone, scrolling through Arabic news sites.

'These seem interesting – they were in the box,' she said as she put the folder and the airmail letters in Arabic on the low table and sat down beside him on the sofa. She handed Hussain a few of the duplicate forms, and watched his intent expression as he read.

'You know these people?' she asked.

'No, but I recognize some of the names – Bahrain is a small place,' he said, still absorbed. 'I know their villages.'

Kate watched him.

'How come Edith had these papers? What did she do in Bahrain?'

'I don't know,' said Kate slowly, thoughtful. 'But look at the other papers – a speech by a man called John Stonehouse and a letter – they are shocking.'

Hussain read the letter and the whole of Stonehouse's speech, then he put down the papers and stared at Kate. '"A noble task" . . . "not keen to educate the Persians in virtuous ways"?'

He jumped to his feet and started pacing the small space between the sofa and door. 'This is terrible stuff.' One clenched fist beat his palm. 'That's the thing about this country – the remnants of empire are everywhere, tucked away in every corner of your country: in houses and museums, in the street names and public monuments, and now, here in this cottage – this imperial garbage. Selling British arms is cast as a "noble task".' His voice was heavy with sarcasm.

Kate nodded, uncomfortable at this anger. She thought of Phoebe in the kitchen the day before saying that Edith had helped Martin get his business started. Kate hadn't mentioned it to Hussain, and was glad of it now. She sensed that something delicate was hanging in the balance: could this unexpected anger turn on her? She was British, she was a Wilcox Smith.

'I'm not even sure where Bahrain is,' she said, as lightly as she could manage, even though her mouth felt dry. She picked up her laptop and brought up a map of the Gulf and then focused in on Bahrain. She clicked on Google Street View, and followed a dusty back street in the capital, Manama. She angled the laptop screen to show Hussain, but he didn't look.

'That's the luxury of empire. You don't need to know where Bahrain is – better even for you not to know,' he said abruptly.

He took a breath. More gently, he continued, 'Bahrain has always been useful to Britain. Just across the water from Iran, and within reach of a large part of the world's oil and gas reserves. After the official departure of the British in 1971, they slipped behind the scenes – training the army, providing private security, oil engineers, property developers, public relations – and developed their military bases.'

'I didn't know,' she said apologetically, and looked back at the screen, meandering down some more back streets, past what looked like an Indian shop and some nondescript office blocks to a vacant lot of sand and a dusty palm tree. 'You could show me the street where you lived – maybe even your home?' she suggested.

Hussain frowned, and Kate blushed. 'Oh, God, I'm sorry,' she blurted. 'I suppose it would be strange seeing your home on a laptop on the other side of the world.'

'Very strange, yes. Seeing a home I can't return to, looking at a front gate I can't walk through,' he replied sharply.

'That was a stupid suggestion.' She was embarrassed at her tactlessness. 'Martin would know about what you're saying.'

Hussain turned to face her, suddenly insistent: 'What exactly is his business?'

Kate picked up her mug of tea and fiddled with the handle. 'I don't know – property or something. I went to his office in London a few months ago; brochures about luxury developments in Dubai were on a table in reception . . .' The image of *Jane's Defence Weekly* on his desk came to mind but she said nothing about it.

One of the girls at her boarding school had lived in Bahrain, Kate remembered. Her accounts of riding in the desert, swimming pools and tennis parties had made it sound like it was a holiday camp. Kate knew there had been riots last year, during the Arab Spring, but Art had been bad then, and her own life had felt so chaotic that she had struggled to focus on the anguish of other people far away.

She steeled herself; she needed to know now. 'What happened to you? How did you end up here?' she whispered. She had glimpsed during their lovemaking the red welts on the soles of Hussain's feet, and the fretwork of scars on his back.

The room felt suddenly close and quiet, the only sounds the snapping of the flames and the occasional shift of a log in the grate. Hussain was looking at the hearth and, after what felt like a long silence, he reached out his arm to put it around her shoulder.

'I can see the pain of your life, and the struggle you have. You seem so alone with it, but when I am at home, I have brothers and sisters, parents, many cousins and uncles, and a grandmother still. When I go back to my village, I know everyone and everyone knows me. It is only in the last year that I have had to learn to live alone, and yet it feels to me that there is something in you which has always been alone. I'm not saying this to dodge the question, but to explain my hesitation in answering you.' He paused and Kate waited, winded by his observation. 'How do I help you, I ask myself. I can't answer that beyond the next few months, and it worries me. I will leave you and Art, and that will be another broken relationship. Perhaps we were right when we kept at a distance – perhaps I should leave now before we get any closer. I can find somewhere else to live –'

'*Could* you leave now?' she asked, her voice trembling. 'Could you stop us now?'

'I have learned that I *can* do many things I never thought possible. I can survive solitary confinement, I can survive a crowded noisy prison cell – and worse.' He cleared his throat abruptly, and knelt down on the rug to throw a log on the fire. He stayed sitting on the floor, and faced Kate. 'I don't want you and Art on my conscience. I'm fond of you both, but I love my wife and our family. I can feel this tearing me in two, and it is so painful. Our lovemaking is beautiful, but it was a mistake, it brings us closer all the time. Knowing your body – all its beautiful details – brings the desire to know and understand you, and to be understood. That brings complications, and my life has enough of them already.'

Kate's voice was unsteady. 'We've only just begun, Hussain – you can't end it now. I know what I'm doing, I've made my choice. That means I want to know what happened to you. How does a doctor from Bahrain end up in London as an asylum seeker?'

'You're being brave, but I can offer you nothing: no security, no commitment – all I will bring is pain,' said Hussain harshly.

Perhaps he was right, but she had begun to hold on to some fantastic possibility that there could be some way in which they had a future, only she couldn't tell him that. He had told her hope was painful, but it was also precious. She suspected that any hope he had managed to sustain was focused on his wife and daughter, and a life in America. She couldn't ask for a share.

'It's a holiday romance – at home,' she said. Her voice sounded forced.

Hussain gave a bleak laugh. 'And does an account of my arrest, my time in prison and my escape come within the terms of a holiday romance?' His eyes were serious as he asked the question: he was telling her that she didn't have to know the details.

'Tea?' She suggested, unsure, and needing time to prepare herself.

Hussain nodded, staring at the small flames licking the new log.

In the kitchen, Kate stood by the window as the kettle boiled, watching the rain. Would it be possible to live with this man for the next three months without knowing? She had bumped up against his story so many times already: the daughter, the job, the country, the mysterious disappearances at night in London. Above all, the sense of deep anguish which he kept carefully concealed behind his composure. It did frighten her – what horrors had he experienced or witnessed? – but she had passed the point when she could pull away. She had felt the texture of his skin, listened to the rhythm of his breathing as he slept, and the quick gasps as he reached climax. She felt bound to him already: a reckless sharing of fate which thrilled and terrified her.

She carried the pot through and put it down on the table with the mugs and milk.

'When the rain eases, there's a walk I want to take you on. You can borrow wellies.' She handed him a mug and added, 'I want to know everything.'

Hussain was silent. When he looked up, he had tears in his eyes.

'My family are Shia Arab, but we have never been involved in politics. We worked hard and kept our heads down, and that was how we managed. Bahrain is a difficult country for my community, but we look after each other. My father was a businessman and he made sure that my siblings and I got a good education. I studied hard and did well at medical school – that's how I got the study leave in America.' He paused and took a sip of tea. 'I liked my job as a general surgeon – I was good at it. Every day was different; there were terrible times when the victims of a car crash were brought in and we lost someone, but I knew I was doing something worthwhile.'

'And Maryam? Your marriage?'

'I married at twenty-five, in the middle of medical school. Our families had known each other well for a long time. Maryam had trained as a nurse, specializing in paediatrics. Those years were very busy – I was training and working long hours, and then Reem was born.'

Kate nodded thoughtfully. 'Tell me about your life, your friends? I want to understand how you lived.'

'We had a good life – comfortable houses, good friends, and I loved my work. We saw our families often, or we might go away for the weekend – drive to Kuwait for the excellent seafood, or even fly to Dubai to do some shopping, or go out on a friend's boat to one of the islands. We liked Fasht al Jārim – it's not far, and the water is very clear – or for a longer trip, Hawar is very quiet. Sometimes we went to Al Dar – it's only ten minutes by boat from Sitra. I used to love scuba diving, but the coral reefs around Bahrain have mostly been destroyed. We had many friends who were expatriates – Australians, Brits, of course, and a lot of Americans. I look back and can't believe that life; it was so ordinary and secure. We saw a future stretching ahead in which we would have lives much like our parents', and, in time, build a good-sized house near our families. Maryam and I planned our garden and the house. We wanted a big terrace and barbecue – Maryam loves to cook for friends and family, especially seafood. We had a neighbour who would call us up when he had a good catch on his boat. We were very blessed with Reem: she is a remarkable person, intelligent and loving. No more children arrived, but she is enough.'

Kate nodded, waiting. 'And then what happened?'

'Through all this time, I ignored the fact that the country was built on lies and decades of corruption. The Al Khalifa, the ruling family, and their allies run everything. I knew the education system was stacked against us Shia, even as a child – you couldn't avoid it. I was bullied and the headmaster didn't dare step in. You learn young that, at every stage, you will face discrimination, and that many routine decisions, such as job applications, business permits and building permission for a home, were more difficult for us. I saw how the royal family took the best land for their own commercial developments, and, of course, for their palaces. We lost access to the sea near our village for one luxury development, and other beaches were privatized. Now only three public beaches remain, and they are very shabby. During my lifetime, the coastline has been ruined; the real-estate developments have reclaimed land, smothered it in concrete and piled it with artificial boulders. It's hideous. Protesting against any of this is hard. Occasionally, there were disturbances in Shia areas such as Sitra and in the villages, and men would come into the hospital suffering from injuries caused by birdshot or tear gas. I knew the police were brutal. As I grew older, I heard of corruption allegations against the royal family and their associates, and that many of them were paid allowances by the government; I began to see the poverty and frustration of my community as a consequence of how the royal family runs the country in the interests of a Sunni minority. I saw how Sunni Pakistanis were recruited for the police, and how the army was almost entirely Sunni.

'When protests developed across the Arab world in 2011, it was inevitable that the unrest would reach Bahrain. I could remember the "uprising of dignity" in the mid 1990s and the repression which followed. In 2011, the place was waiting to explode. What was different this time was that the demonstrations were well organized and peaceful. Pearl Roundabout — it's a traffic junction, a major landmark in the capital — was crowded with people of all ages and backgrounds demonstrating and asking for change: families, young women and children. It wasn't about sectarianism — we were united across boundaries of faith and ethnicity, despite all the lies that have been told since. The atmosphere was exhilarating. Maryam and I visited one evening after work with Reem. It was a bit like *iftar*, with people sharing food, and strangers falling into long conversations about the reforms the country needed. Then on February seventeenth, the army moved in to clear the protestors and four people died, but the protestors returned. The demonstrations which followed were the largest in Bahrain's history – it was estimated that about half the population of the country took part. In mid March, the crackdown became brutal. With help from the Saudis and the United Arab Emirates, the Bahraini security forces tried to clear the streets. Hundreds of injured protestors poured into the Salmaniya Medical Complex.'

Hussain sighed heavily. Kate was quiet, she didn't want to interrupt him.

'That day I had a shift at the hospital, but Maryam and Reem were at the Pearl Roundabout. Maryam was more involved than I; she felt passionate about the possibilities for reform, for anti-corruption measures and democracy.' His voice was a whisper. He coughed. 'At the worst points of that day, I feared they had both been hurt, and it was months before I knew for sure they were safe. Thankfully, Maryam was warned by a text from a friend that the army was on its way, and she and Reem took refuge in a friend's flat nearby. They were just in time, and watched from the balcony as the police and army broke up the demonstrations with tear gas.

'At the hospital, cases began to arrive in private cars with all kinds of injuries – the police wouldn't let ambulances through. Everyone was suffering from the effects of tear gas, but more serious were the rubber-bullet wounds and birdshot. For several hours, we worked almost continuously, only pausing while the theatres were cleaned. When I went outside to get some air at the back entrance of the hospital, I could hear the repetitive crack of gunfire. As we worked, we had time for brief exchanges, and someone told me they were using live ammunition to clear demonstrators at the Pearl Roundabout. I knew Maryam and Reem had been there and I dreaded that each new stretcher might be carrying one of them.'

Tears were running down Hussain's cheeks, and Kate reached out to hold his hand, clammy with sweat.

'You really want me to go on?' he asked.

Kate nodded. 'Please, everything.'

'The injured were all ages; later, they said the demonstrators were young men, unruly elements, but I saw that elderly men, women and children had been indiscriminately attacked. The beds were filling up, people had to sit or lie on the floor, and we worried the hospital might run out of blood. The staff were exhausted, but no one went home at the end of their shift. By night, every corridor was full, and you could hardly move between the people lying on makeshift mattresses, and new cases were still coming in. They were the worst injured, with multiple wounds and broken bones. They were mainly men, and I presumed they had been resisting the police. Some needed complex operations to save their lives.

'We kept working into the following day, surviving on coffee and adrenaline. I didn't have a chance to sit down and eat. Whenever I had a spare few minutes, I checked my phone and called Maryam, but there was no text and she didn't pick up. I had to focus on my work, but all the time I was frantic with worry. I called my mother and my sister, and they had heard nothing. When they went round to visit our house, there was no answer. Later, Maryam told me that they didn't dare venture on to the streets, and stayed at the friend's flat until it was calm. In the chaos escaping Pearl Roundabout, she had dropped her phone.

'At about 2 p.m., I was in the operating theatre when I heard a lot of shouting and screaming outside in the area where patients are prepared for surgery. We pressed on, hurrying to stitch up a young man, when the doors burst open, and several armed police came in. We protested, telling them this was an antiseptic environment, but they said they were arresting all the healthcare staff who had assisted revolutionaries. It was absurd: I was standing there in gown and mask trying to finish the stitches while arguing with the police. They pushed me aside and put handcuffs on two of the nurses. Everyone was shouting, and one nurse was screaming. I was arrested, along with the trainee surgeon who was working with me on that shift. We were pushed into a van, still in our scrubs.'

Kate's eyes were fixed on him. He was shaking.

'We were taken to the CID – the police station in Manama – where we were blindfolded. More people kept arriving. For hours, we waited to be interviewed. I was desperately hungry and thirsty, but there was no food or water, until eventually, that evening, I was given some water and rice. From the police station they took us in batches by van to prison. For the first few weeks, they interrogated me every few days, but then nothing; it was as if they had forgotten about me. I was in solitary confinement for over four months – I kept track of the days on my wall. Then they put me in a cell with three other men who had criminal convictions, and I was not allowed any reading material except one book: the Qur'an. I have never read it so closely as I did in those months, and it helped me cope with the fear and anxiety. After three months, Maryam was allowed to visit, and when I knew that she and Reem were safe, my relief was enormous. After that, I felt I could cope with prison. I've heard since that many other doctors and nurses were arrested for treating demonstrators. Some are still in prison.

'The response of the West was muted. The Bahraini government maintains that it protects the region from Iran's ambitions. The Saudis subsidize the government in Bahrain, with some help from Kuwait and the Arab Emirates. These countries didn't want a democratic uprising, neither did the British or Americans: we were ranged against some of the most powerful regimes in the world. We didn't have a chance. Now the British deflect the allegations of human-rights abuses in Bahrain with promises to help reform our police and judiciary. The island has too much strategic significance for them to fret about human rights.'

'And your release – how did that happen?'

'The full story isn't clear to me, but I believe that my older brother and uncle helped publicize my case, and there was international pressure from human rights and medical organizations. All I knew was that after eleven months and twelve days, I was suddenly taken from my cell, and there in the prison waiting room were my father and brother. My father wept as we embraced. I had lost a lot of weight. As they drove me home, they said there was a risk I might get rearrested, other doctors had been convicted on spurious charges of promoting the downfall of the regime and inciting sectarian hatred. The terms of my release were very harsh: I had to report daily to the police station, and I was not allowed to work. They advised me to leave the country, and explained that they had arranged for me to be smuggled across the border into Saudi Arabia. From there, the plan was to fly to America to my uncle and claim asylum. They had booked me on to a flight in two days' time. Once I had asylum, Maryam and Reem could join me. I knew it would mean many more months of separation before we would be together again, but my father convinced me I had to leave – it was too risky to stay, and this way, we had a chance of another life in exile. The government was beginning a new strategy of stripping people of their citizenship, and after that happened, it was impossible to work or own property. Citizenship is conferred through the father, so if I was made stateless, it could affect Reem's education and future. I felt I had no choice, and agreed to go into exile. It was the hardest decision of my life. My brother had found a man who would drive me across the border that night. I saw Maryam and Reem for an hour and said goodbye . . .'

He paused as he struggled to stem the tears, and wiped his eyes with his cuff. When he resumed, his voice was steady again.

'I was hidden in the boot of a car. The driver took me across the causeway to a safe house in Saudi, where I was to stay for a couple of days while my US visa came through. The Bahraini police had taken my identity papers when they searched our flat after my arrest, but my father had persuaded a cousin to give me his passport for the flight. We are about the same age and similar in appearance. The plan was that I would use a US student visa to leave Saudi, and claim asylum on arrival in the US. My uncle lives in Maryland, and I would stay with him until I won my case. My family and Maryam had planned it as carefully as possible.

'After I got to Saudi, things went wrong: the US visa didn't come through and I missed my flight. We had thought the passport was in order, but restrictions on those travelling to the US from the Gulf had been tightened. We have various cousins in Iran, and some of them have been involved in politics . . .' He hesitated. 'This, at least, has been our guess. My cousin's mother is Iranian, and I think this has been the problem for American immigration. In the end, I used a cousin's multiple-entry visa for the UK instead, and that's how I ended up here.'

'And Maryam – has she been safe since you left?'

'She lost her job when I was first arrested, because she was married to me. She moved back to her parents' home with Reem, but they are safe, and she tells me she is hoping to start work again soon. They need nurses too much to lose someone of her skill. Maryam says Reem worries about me, but we speak when it's possible, and I've encouraged her to focus on her schooling and be patient. We know most of the social-media sites are monitored, so we can't communicate easily. I don't want to make things more difficult for them.'

'You lost everything,' Kate whispered. 'I'm so sorry.' It was one thing to read about this kind of story, but to hear someone she knew describe it was of a different order. She was overwhelmed with grief.

'It has been very painful, I admit: to go from a successful, comfortable life as a respected surgeon to being a fugitive, hiding in car boots, and dependent on handouts from other Bahrainis in London and the money my family can send. I've known humiliation and despair, but also the extraordinary courage and generosity of people who have helped me. This last year has been an education as demanding and challenging as my surgical training. I tell myself I must stay strong and hopeful for the sake of Maryam and Reem.'

Kate stood up and moved around the room – the pain of his story made her restless. 'And when you go out at night in London? What are you doing?'

Hussain was sitting on the sofa. He shifted, rearranging a cushion, embarrassed. 'I had thought I was quiet enough not to disturb you.'

'I find it hard to sleep, and sometimes I hear you leaving.'

He sighed. 'People in London heard that I was a doctor. They are homeless or on the run for some reason – I don't know their stories, only their pain. But some don't dare go to the NHS, afraid they will get tracked by immigration. They began to ask for my help; I could diagnose and suggest medication to buy on the internet. I felt useful again, even though some people are too ill for me to help much. The worst cases are tuberculosis, and sometimes they don't have the money for the medicines they need. One case led to others, and I started visiting the places where these homeless people sleep – under motorway bridges, and in derelict buildings. There may be a dozen people living in squalid conditions – sometimes just sleeping bags on concrete floors. Some are British, some Eastern European, some African or Middle Eastern. Often they get illegal work, but for little pay and are exploited by gangmasters. They are well hidden, and I need guides to take me. I do what I can.' Hussain rubbed his forehead. 'It's a crazy world – to know the pain of men and women who are just metres away from a motorway, where the cars stream past, their occupants oblivious to the suffering, preoccupied by their busy, secure lives. I was once one of those in the cars, now I've flipped into this other world; the two realities are so close – and yet so far apart. This may be a rich country, but it's a cruel one; too many use their privilege to avert their eyes.

'A couple of weeks ago I treated a man who had broken his leg. We managed to make a splint and reset the bones, but it was a bad break and he was screaming with pain, and we didn't have enough painkillers. We worried that the sound might be heard by the people in the cars, but they were entirely sealed off, rushing to their jobs or back home, while this man was desperate.

'Without my faith, I would have been lost this last year. When I was young, I thought Islam made no sense – this Shia pre-occupation with the deaths of the grandsons of the Prophet – Peace Be Upon Him – a thousand years ago – but now I see that the world is a brutal, unjust place, and all we can hope to find is solidarity and the mercy of Allah.'

Neither of them said a word, and they listened to the murmur of the fire.

> '*Tis all a Chequer-board of nights and days*
> *Where Destiny with men for Pieces plays,*'

Kate recited quietly. 'Omar Khayyam – my father used to recite it, and one holiday I asked him to write it out on a card for me. It's one of the few things I remember about him, and I kept the card for a long time. Bleak, isn't it?'

'It's a philosophy of despair, in which everything is a matter of chance. There is a harshness at the core of the West's so-called civilization,' Hussain commented wearily. 'I prefer the lessons I learned from my mother as a child, and from the mosque, and on the pilgrimages we made to Shia holy places, like Mashhad in Iran, and Karbala in Iraq, before the war. The Shia have a long history of injustice and martyrdom, and now I'm part of that.

'"The noblest of riches is the abandonment of desire," said Ali, the first Shia imam. That's what we say to each other to encourage *zakat* – the giving of alms – but it applies to all desires. In the last eighteen months, I have had to give up everything – my work, family, safety, country, even my name. Hussain is the name of my cousin. I'm Tahir.'

'Tahir?' exclaimed Kate, and he nodded.

'Best to keep to Hussain – it's too confusing for Art. I'm getting used to Hussain. Only now do I understand the wisdom of the Prophet, Peace Be Upon Him. My life has been in the hands of Allah, and one of his names is the Most Merciful. That is all there is for me to trust in.'

She had never seen this fervour in Hussain before. This was what lay behind his sad gentleness: this fierce, austere faith.

Hussain took her hand. 'For now, Allah has brought me to you.' He spread out his other hand to take in the cottage – the embers glowing in the grate and a watery sunlight just visible through the window.

'You can trust me, and trust my love,' Kate found herself urging. 'I won't let you down.'

He squeezed her hand tight, but she could see reserve in his eyes: either he wasn't sure he believed her, or that love was relevant, she couldn't tell which. She had surprised even herself: she loved him.

*

After lunch Kate found boots for Hussain amongst the cast-offs in the back porch. He was bemused by the idea of walking in the drenched countryside. He remonstrated that he played squash in a gym when he wanted exercise in Bahrain, and the idea of strolling aimlessly around the sodden fields struck him as an odd pastime, but Kate was insistent. She wanted to show him her favourite walk up to an Iron Age fort on the down, where a wizened hawthorn had been sculpted by the wind.

They emerged from the cottage, almost blinking in the light as the clouds slowly lifted, and every leaf and blade of grass gleamed wet, polished in the bright air.

'I needed this,' said Kate, and she pushed back the hood of her raincoat, despite the fat drops of water still falling from the branches overhead. They walked out of the back gate on to the fields, where the view opened up across the valley. In the distance hung purple-grey clouds, swollen with future showers, but they were moving away to the north. The pale blond stubble glowed in the moisture-laden light.

'Isn't it lovely?' exclaimed Kate, shaking off the tension and darkness of their conversation in the cottage.

Hussain's eyes were softly indulgent, struggling to share her appreciation. 'It looks a bit grey to me – and flat.' Laughing quietly, he added, 'But you are lovely – the fresh air has brought colour back to your cheeks and there are drops of water in your hair.'

She smiled gratefully, but she was aware that his story had both brought them closer and put new distance between them. So much of it was beyond her ability to imagine: the injustice, the violence and the faith. There was only a sliver of this man that she could really understand, and the rest had to be taken on trust: he believed in a god, and she believed in him. She slipped her hand through his arm and they set off down the muddy track, swerving around the large puddles. Overhead, the delicate stems of the ash trees danced in the light breeze.

'You didn't tell me much about your time in prison,' she said hesitantly. 'I wondered . . .' She was thinking of the scars on his feet.

'There are details you don't need to know,' he responded quickly.

Kate plucked a tall grass from the verge, and nibbled its sweet green stem as she pressed on with her questions. 'And Maryam? What would she make of us?'

'She is a generous woman, and I hope that she would understand and forgive. My father had two wives for several years, and I am the child of the second marriage, so I know these things are possible. Westerners don't accept polygamy, but I find their infidelity and divorces more cruel. They leave broken hearts and homes, and children without proper parents. I never thought I would have a second wife, but I never thought many things, and yet they have happened –'

'So I could be a second wife?' interrupted Kate, with a mixture of amazement and amusement.

'I'm not saying that,' said Hussain quickly, adding, 'But in a way, you are already.'

'A second wife?' Kate laughed.

'When I next get a chance to talk to Maryam, I will ask her permission.'

'Permission?' she repeated, startled.

'Yes, I need her to accept our relationship.'

'Even if it's a holiday romance?'

'Yes, even then.'

'Is that how you square our relationship with your faith?'

'I suppose so – each marriage makes many demands. We are allowed to take a second wife, but it brings responsibilities also.'

Out here in the sun and space of the hilltop, some things became possible, even the idea of being a second wife. In the cottage, she had felt real terror, a coldness clenched in the pit of her stomach at the cruelty of the world. It was different from the casual indifference she had suffered in her life; this was about the ruthlessness and violence with which people pursued their objectives, regardless of the suffering.

A surge of protectiveness towards Hussain – his reserve and his shy stiffness – now carried her along with a sudden buoyancy. She would do whatever she could to help him. Shirin had been right: he was a good man, and she felt his goodness in a way she had not experienced before in somebody. He had a sense of honour, principle and commitment.

They were walking up a steep incline. The track was scored deep into the chalk, and the banks rose up on either side, dotted with pale-blue field scabious and bright buttercups. She pointed out the flowers to Hussain, and they watched a red kite hover above the steep scoop of the chalk valley, searching for prey, its wings outstretched as it glided over the fields.

11

The daily routines of school and work had changed, and each now was charged with the exhilaration of being in love. The most ordinary of moments were magical: waking up and finding Hussain's warm body curled around hers, then drinking coffee together in the kitchen before Art was awake. During the day at work, Kate relished the thought of returning home and cooking together, and how they would linger over supper, their hands intertwined, talking. Hussain loved experimenting, searching for recipes online, and both Kate and Art developed a taste for Middle Eastern food. At the weekend, they went over to Edgware Road, to one of the cheap Lebanese restaurants for Saturday lunch, and did some shopping in the Arab supermarkets for the spices and ingredients Hussain needed. They usually bought a box of pastries, dripping with syrup and ground pistachios to eat with the bitter coffee Kate had learned how to brew. She loved how they were evolving into a family, as their habits and tastes developed to fit around each other. Hussain introduced Art to Arabic pop music, and Art introduced Hussain to his favourite computer games – which they spent far more time playing together than Kate thought was healthy, screaming with delight and punching the air at their victories, lamenting with anguish when they lost.

On one restaurant outing, the waiter made a reference to them as a family, and Art squirmed with delight. 'He's my stepfather,' he said, putting his hand on Hussain's arm possessively, and then added, 'I have a father in America and a stepmother and sister.' The waiter looked a little taken aback at this rush of information, but congratulated him on such a big family. Art had the number of relatives he had always wanted. The complexity of his family, spread across two continents, was irrelevant, and he refused to consider the uncertainty of Hussain's continued presence.

As autumn encroached, Kate noticed the leaves turning and felt a sense of foreboding. At the end of October, Hussain's visa would run out. Seize the moment, Kate whispered to herself continuously, but the leaves shifting to buttery yellow on the tree outside the flat were a sharp reminder that the days were passing swiftly. They explained again to Art that Hussain was going to live in America, and he already had a family, but Art was impervious.

'We'll come and stay with you when I am visiting Dad,' he insisted.

'It's more complicated,' Kate concluded limply, and he ignored her.

Sometimes, when Hussain was out at night and she couldn't sleep, she lay in bed with her laptop, making her way slowly through the Amnesty reports on Bahrain, detailing torture, arrests, hunger strikes and rapes. On human-rights websites, she read about the arms imported by Bahrain's security services from America, Germany and South Korea. She found a list of huge contracts with public-relations companies based in London and New York, presumably to sustain Bahrain's image as a stable and peaceful country. She read the coverage of the Bahrain Grand Prix back in April, when Formula One faced down calls for the race to be cancelled in the light of continued unrest; the *Independent* described the decision as 'one of the most controversial in the history of the sport'. As she read, she kept expecting to come across the name of ZSKa or even Martin Wilcox Smith, but there was nothing.

Hussain had translated the letters written in Arabic which they had found amongst Edith's papers, but was reluctant to pass them on to Kate. Some contained lengthy descriptions of archaeological discoveries by a Bahraini professor; in others, one of the boat skippers who used to take Edith out on trips listed bird sightings, but his letters also included references to a clever son. It emerged that Edith had taken a close interest in the boy's education and supported him through university. On graduating, he set up a property business and prospered, but there was some wrangle over land, he was arrested and, according to his father, falsely accused of fraud and sent to prison after a sham trial. An anguished letter from the father begged Edith for help; in the margin, in a different pen, she had noted, 'Ask Martin.' Another letter, a few months later, informed Edith that the son had died of mysterious injuries in detention. Kate understood why Hussain had been so slow to let her see his translations; his suspicions of Martin sat between them, unspoken. Neither knew how to broach the subject.

Hussain began doing his own research when Kate was at work. One evening, after they had had supper and Art was in bed, he told her he had discovered what the initials 'R.G.' on the forms stood for.

'Edith's husband was called Roderick – or Roddy. He worked in the Bahraini police force in the 1960s and 1970s. He trained many of Bahrain's senior police and he initiated the policy of recruiting Pakistanis. It was a classic imperial technique to bring in a loyal minority to provide law enforcement. Does Phoebe know anything about this uncle?'

'Who knows, and if she did, would she tell me?' replied Kate nervously.

'Grant is quite well known – let's just say his methods were rough. He got the job after suppressing the Mau Mau rebellion in Kenya. He got kicked out of Kenya after independence. I guess the British empire found such men useful, and they were passed from place to place. He ended up in Bahrain, and no doubt made a small fortune there. One historian I emailed suggested that his wife acted as his secretary. You should ask Phoebe about her aunt and what she was doing in Bahrain. Or ask your cousin, Rebecca Wilcox Smith – I found her profile on LinkedIn. Ask Dotty what ZSKa really does.'

His tone was sharp and Kate was taken aback. 'They're my relatives – I can't quiz them,' she replied defensively.

'Why not? Because they lent you the cottage? They invite you for meals?'

She had never heard him talk like this.

'And I found out about that John Stonehouse: he was "parliamentary secretary" – whatever that means – to a Roy Jenkins in the Ministry of Aviation in the Labour government in 1964. As for the other letter, I researched what "DSO" stands for: the Defence Sales Organization was set up in 1966 within the Ministry of Defence to market British arms overseas. The Shah's Iran became the UK's biggest customer.'

'It's awful, but it's not my fault,' pleaded Kate. 'I feel like you are blaming me.'

After a while, Hussain sighed and looked down to answer a text on his phone. Kate, biting back tears, got up to clear the kitchen. Shortly after, he followed her and put his arms around her as she washed up.

'I don't want to get you upset – let's leave it,' he said.

Relieved, she turned around and leaned against him. 'I don't want to get mixed up in all this ZSKa stuff. It scares me.'

He stroked her hair. 'Sometimes it's not about what we want,' he replied softly.

Later that night, lying in bed next to him, Kate thought about her visit to Martin's office and the magazine cover's sinister image. She had found no comfort in her own internet searches on ZSKa; the company's website was strangely unsettling, with photos of luxury apartment blocks and swimming pools in brilliant sunshine, and descriptions of bespoke security services for 'individuals, brands and reputations', online and offline, 'Leaving you, your employees and your family to sleep peacefully at night.' One section of the website, illustrated with images of neon electrical circuits, talked of web surveillance, information gathering and dissemination, but it only offered obscure generalities about security, and a contact form for enquiries.

A fortnight later, Kate found herself next to Dotty at a lunch at Lodsbourne and plucked up courage to ask about the company. Dotty was immediately wary.

'Has Hussain told you to ask?' she said sharply. She had not met him yet, but no doubt Phoebe had given detailed reports of the lunch to which she had persuaded Kate to bring Hussain during the summer. It had been a daunting affair, but Hussain insisted that he had found it interesting. Kate didn't like his choice of adjective.

'No, he hasn't,' lied Kate, flustered, and repeated her question. Dotty's reply was vague and dismissive: 'Public relations and the usual.'

On another occasion, Kate tried Martin, and he was equally unforthcoming. 'A type of estate agent, bit of property security,' he told her.

'What does the acronym stand for?' she pressed.

'Ah, that was Phoebe's aunt's idea. Z stands for Ziusudra, the hero and last king of the ancient Sumerian town of Shuruppak – that's the S and K – which is Tall Fa'rah in modern-day Iraq, on the banks of the Euphrates. The Sumerian myth of Ziusudra is that he had a vision before the flood which led him to build a boat to save himself. The "a" is for "analytics" – we handle data for some clients.' He chuckled before asking her view on his preferred topic of conversation: the shortcomings of the European Union.

One of Kate's favourite activities on the nights when she couldn't sleep and Hussain had gone out was to go on to Google Street View and wander around Bahrain, moving slowly down dusty side streets bordered by high walls where the overhanging greenery hinted at private gardens, or along the highways teeming with traffic. On Google Earth, she was fascinated by the palette of grey and brown of the cities of Manama and Sitra; only in more prosperous neighbourhoods were there patches of green and the rectangles of brilliant blue swimming pools. She watched the allegedly live coverage on YouTube of the King Fahad causeway snaking its way over the sea and sandbanks to Saudi Arabia, sixteen miles away. She began to notice that the same white cars repeatedly drove up to the passport kiosks in a mesmerizing loop. She tried to imagine herself there, driving in the heat from Saudi across the water towards Hussain's home in the suburbs of Manama. Then she switched back to Street View to continue searching for that distinctive balustrade she had noticed in the photo of Maryam and Reem.

She told Hussain nothing of this, and he told her little of what he was finding out. Once she looked at the search history on his laptop when he left it open on the sitting-room table, and saw a list of defence companies and Arabic news sites. She feared he had managed to find out more than she had about ZSKa, but she didn't dare ask. If he looked at her search history, she wondered what he would make of its muddled wanderings. But neither talked of their internet journeys; instead, when they had time, they whispered about the progress of his visa application and his uncle's efforts with US immigration. They could only talk freely after Art was in bed, nervous of what he might relay to his father on a phone call. Hussain was trying to get reliable advice about the best course of action if the US visa didn't come through. One contact suggested he get a visitor's visa and claim asylum on arrival in the US, another urged he claim asylum in the UK, and yet another maintained that Canada or Australia might be better options, given his medical skills.

As September came to an end, and heavy winds began to bring

the leaves down, Kate became insistent that he try to claim asylum in the UK. They spent several evenings ploughing through websites detailing UK immigration rules, and forums offering advice. Kate was horrified at the complexity. She became alert to every government announcement on immigration, and the radio news was now a regular accompaniment to morning routines.

'"Hostile environment"?' repeated Kate at breakfast, outraged by an interview with Theresa May, the Home Secretary. 'How can they make asylum seekers into criminals?'

'What are asylum seekers?' asked Art, his mouth full of cereal.

'They're people who have to flee their country because it is too dangerous,' said Hussain. 'Like me.'

Kate looked meaningfully at Hussain; she thought they had agreed not to tell Art too much. Art stared at Hussain, fascinated. 'Too dangerous? Like someone might want to murder you?'

Kate swiftly intervened. 'It's time for school – is your bag packed? PE kit?'

'Might they come and kill you here?' persisted Art.

Hussain tried to make light of it, laughing as he packed Art's lunch. Kate mouthed silently to him over Art's head that she didn't want any more of this discussion on the way to school.

In one of their late-evening conversations, Hussain told Kate he had spoken to Maryam about their relationship; she had been very upset, immediately fearful that she and Hussain would never be reunited, and he had done his best to reassure her. Kate felt a sudden stab of guilt: the poor woman. He used Kate's phone sometimes when he was out of credit, and she would hear him in the sitting room, murmuring in Arabic. It was the least she could do, Kate told herself; she had Hussain, while Maryam had thousands of miles of distance and this excruciating wait. Kate knew that at any point their positions could be reversed, and she tried to imagine what that would feel like. She didn't feel possessive – she just wanted a share; she would take whatever part of him he could offer her. Their love was so rich and so far beyond her experience that it couldn't be tucked into conventional categories, she insisted. She had been in one relationship with a man who refused to marry her; being in a relationship with a man who couldn't, but whose love she trusted, was a significant improvement, and hence a cause every day for wonder.

Two or three times a week, Hussain went out at night, usually after Kate was asleep. She would stir in the early hours and, reaching out her hand across the bed, find it empty. She had got used to his rhythm of praying – the soft whisper, the occasional crack of a knee joint, and then his return to bed. But this was different: he hadn't come to bed in the first place; the sheets were cold and the duvet still smooth. He left the flat, shutting the front door so silently that it never woke her. It was safer at night for the people who came to him for advice, he told her. When he returned, slipping into bed as quietly as possible, she rolled over into his chilly arms and sought out his face to kiss – his mouth, his nose, his eyes – warming him with her body, and she could feel the tension ebbing from him as he settled to sleep.

★

'Kate? This is ridiculous.' It was Ed on the phone. 'I'm coming to London to get him.'

Kate's phone had rung just as they were about to sit down to eat, and she should have left it. Ed was incandescent with rage. She retreated quickly to the bedroom and shut the door so that Art would not overhear.

'Art told me that he is going to become a Muslim. This is insane – it's the influence of that boyfriend of yours. He is totally unsuitable. How dare he try converting my son? He's dangerous – are you sure he's not a fundamentalist?'

Ed was gabbling furiously about custody.

Kate, incensed, tried to keep her voice low. 'Don't *you* be ridiculous. Hussain is a doctor, an educated and good man, and Art has developed a deep affection for him. His faith is entirely peaceful.'

'How can you be sure?' sneered Ed. 'You were always so naive. He could be taking you for a complete ride. He's got a cosy place to hide while he plots some ghastly bomb attack.'

'How dare you!' Kate exploded furiously. 'I'm in love with him, and I am going to marry this man, so don't ever – ever – speak of my future husband in this way!' She hung up, shaking.

When she opened the bedroom door, Art and Hussain stared at her, different forms of anxiety written over their faces.

'You're not arguing with Dad, are you?' asked Art. 'I *hate* it when you argue. I want Dad to like Hussain – and I want you to like Mona. I want everyone to *like* everyone.' Then he added, worried, 'Dad was asking all these questions. I don't know, maybe I didn't say the right thing . . .'

Over the top of Art's head, Kate looked at Hussain, frowning and twisting her mouth in a grimace. Was Ed vengeful enough to contact the police or social services? After all these years, might he try and get custody of Art? She felt the grip of incipient panic.

Hussain came over and gathered both of them in his arms, whispering reassurances. As Kate's breathing calmed, he suggested they resume supper, but Kate couldn't swallow. She sensed Art's anxious eyes fixed on her hesitating knife and fork. Hussain tried to distract him, proposing games after supper, and before long they were chatting. Kate was able to gather her thoughts; she needed to phone Ed back as soon as possible – she wasn't sure she could trust him. She would have to use all her meagre powers of persuasion, and Hussain would have to promise no more discussion of conversion – if there ever had been any; it could quite easily have all been in Art's head.

When Hussain and Art were ensconced on the sofa, their eyes fixed on a screen, she went back to the bedroom.

'Ed, it's Kate.' There was silence on the end of the phone.

'I want to explain – make things clear. Hussain and I are getting married. His asylum application is well advanced, and in due course he will do the test and register so he can practise as a surgeon in the UK. He is a very good stepfather to Art, and has brought a lot of stability into both our lives, but there is no question of anyone becoming a Muslim. Hussain is not religious, he drinks – all that kind of thing,' she lied. 'He is very Westernized, he studied in the US.'

She listened to her concoction of fact and fiction, and hoped it sounded credible. She also hoped that Hussain couldn't hear.

'Shit – this sounds like shit. You're being taken for a ride. Art tells me he already has a wife and a daughter somewhere in the Middle East. You're an idiot, and I don't want my son mixed up in it all.'

Kate took a breath, bitterly regretting the notion of being honest with your children. 'They are estranged – they have not been together for years – he is divorcing her,' she lied desperately, adding sharply, 'Since when have you been such a prude? These kinds of overlap happen sometimes, you know that.'

Her tone was wrong, so she reined herself back in and started again: 'Let's not argue about this – Art gets so anxious when we are at odds. He loved the time with you in the summer, meeting Mona and her daughter. He is beginning to settle and his school work is going much better. Let's keep this on an even keel. He can be a loved part of two families,' she urged. 'We need to be grown up, and accept that each other's lives may be complicated at times. Hussain and I are working things out – we are really committed to each other.'

She could tell that Ed was listening closely, but he wasn't saying anything, so she ploughed on, drawing in everything to support her case: the waiter's comments in the restaurant and Art's pride in his growing family; the photo of his father and Mona he had put in pride of place above his bed. Slowly, she felt she was making headway.

'Well, I'm still sceptical – some bits of what Art tells me don't stack up with what you are saying, but, for now, I'll give you the benefit of the doubt,' Ed said grudgingly. 'But I'm quite prepared to get Art to come and live over here – I want him safe. I don't want him mixed up in any Muslim nonsense – just so you know. I suspect I could put a good case together in a family court with a decent lawyer. Remember that.'

Kate squeezed her eyes tight shut to keep herself from bursting out with rage at the threat. He rang off before she could reply.

She sat on the bed, stunned. At any time, an inadvertent comment of Art's could trigger the catastrophe of a struggle over custody, the involvement of social services, and then perhaps the immigration authorities. How could Ed still destroy her life? Here was this precious, brief chance of happiness – and he was capable of destroying it.

The threat of Ed, the imminent departure of Hussain: both preyed on her mind almost continuously. She found it hard to concentrate at work, and at night she struggled to sleep. Only when Hussain was back home in bed beside her could she drop off for a few hours. The doctor prescribed antidepressants to help her sleep, but they would take a while to kick in, Hussain said. She was losing weight, and at night Hussain's hands stroked her hip bones and ribs. He didn't say anything – he didn't need to; they knew the anxiety each was carrying. Once, in the grey light of early morning, when they were both trying to catch a last hour of sleep, he turned over and said, 'I'm sorry.'

But she put a finger on his lips, and shook her head.

★

These days, Art scuffled the piles of leaves on the way to school. Kate was back in her winter coat, and one morning she needed gloves in the chilly air. She had tuned her ear at night to the sound of the leaves of the big plane tree outside the flat: the soft murmur of early summer had been replaced by a dry rustle. When it was windy, the sound was like the roar of a wave withdrawing on a pebble beach. She didn't ask Hussain what he was going to do; she waited for him to tell her, but he said nothing. She kept expecting him to announce that he had booked a flight to the US.

They had not been able to get down to the cottage for a few weeks, because Art had started a music workshop on a Saturday morning. Kate had too many things on her mind to miss her visits. Phoebe rang to ask how they were, and asked after Hussain. Kate managed to sound cheerful.

'It's wonderful,' she told her. 'We are settling into the routines of family life together. Hussain is learning to cook, and Art is doing well at school.'

Phoebe professed herself delighted, and tentatively asked if Hussain was going to get a job.

'Oh, yes,' Kate assured her. 'He's going to do a test – the PLAB, professional and linguistic assessments – and register in the next couple of months. After that he can look for jobs,' she lied blithely. Now she had started, she surprised herself with how easily the falsehoods could slip out, and how naturally she could embroider her circumstances with wishful thinking and her internet research: she had looked up the process for international doctors and checked that his qualifications were recognized.

One Saturday, she suggested the three of them went to the park. Art wanted to teach Hussain how to fight with conkers so they packed string, scissors and a penknife. It was a fine autumn day, the reddening leaves vivid against the blue sky. Other families were out, enjoying the mild weather, and Hussain bought them ice lollies. By an avenue of chestnut trees, Kate sat down on a bench to crack open the prickly green chestnuts. Once they had a good pile, Hussain set to work with characteristic precision to pierce and thread them on string. Before long, both Art and Hussain had several strings. Kate watched as they danced around each other, trying to flick their string of conkers at the other's. Hussain was laughing so much the tears were streaming down his face, and he cried out that he could hardly see through the blur. Neither managed to hit the other's string, and Kate leaped up and joined in, carefully manoeuvring so that Art made a direct hit – a conker cracked, and he yelled with delight. Kate, now suffering from a stitch from the combination of running to escape Art and laughing, sat back down, gasping for breath.

An elderly man was sitting on the other end of the bench, and Kate nodded at him.

'Good to see the youngsters playing the old games.' He watched, wistful. 'His stepdad is good with him, isn't he?'

Kate tried to see what this man was seeing: the stark difference in hair and skin colour made fatherhood unlikely. She imagined what a child of hers and Hussain's might look like: his brown eyes and her white skin, or her grey eyes and his skin the colour of pale honey. She loved the thought, and for a blissful moment she let herself indulge in the delicious fantasy of growing big and round with Hussain's baby, of him stroking her tight stomach, him holding the baby girl in his arms, and bringing her home. How they would hover over her basket, and watch her limbs strengthen so that, in time, her plump legs would kick out as she chortled on the changing mat. It all unfolded in her mind in an instant: complete in its utterly ordinary perfection.

'Lovely times, these,' said the man, watching her. 'Life doesn't get better, does it?'

She nodded, unable to speak, her heart brimming.

*

At half-term, they went down to the cottage, but the shooting season had started and there was none of the quiet Kate had envisaged to soothe her nerves – Hussain had only a few days left to decide. In the morning, the volleys of shots would start up and he flinched at the sound of the guns, which was followed by the furious flapping of wings as the outraged birds protested, rising above the woods to escape. What chance did those overfed pheasants have? Kate thought. They had been in pens with overflowing grain feeders, and then released, crowding the hedgerows with their raucous cries, and now they would be ruthlessly slaughtered. The birds were still innocent of their imminent death, and assumed this village and its fields were their playpen, sauntering down the lanes and up the garden paths as if they owned the place. As they settled at night, their cries echoed across the valley, a reminder of those dark spaces high up in the trees beyond the reach of predators.

They were Chinese chickens, she joked with Art, and promised him a large present if he could catch one of the lazy birds. That kept him busy: he would dart out of the kitchen in socks or bare feet every time he spotted one strutting across the lawn, and give chase. Just as it appeared he had it within reach, the canny creature escaped, reluctantly levering its weight off the ground into a neighbouring shrub or tree, leaving Art with nothing but the occasional feather, iridescent green and blue, or flecked with honey brown. He had accumulated a considerable collection.

One morning, a fleet of Land Rovers and SUVs purred up the lane, presaging a large shooting party. Kate, making the bed, glimpsed flashes of chrome metalwork as the vehicles caught the sun through the trees. The sight felt strangely ominous. She watched the cars park, the men and dogs spilling out, and wondered where the three of them could go to escape the shooting. She didn't want Hussain to spend the morning wincing at each shot again. She could see the tension in his face these days; new lines were appearing around his eyes and mouth. He had resumed smoking, shutting the door behind him when he went out on to the balcony at the flat, and going down to the end of the garden at the cottage. He was distant and uncommunicative, and his jaw was hard with determination. Kate tried to keep her voice gentle, but she couldn't bear the way he kept his distance. What decision was he making? Would he leave for America or overstay his UK visa?

★

Most of the birds would end up as landfill, Martin casually remarked over a lunch of roast pheasant at the Hall. Killed in their thousands, their meat was too meagre for contemporary tastes, so those feathers, bones and guts were tipped into mass graves, he explained. Kate found her mouthful of meat and roast potatoes sticking in her throat.

'Most of the estates around here sell the shooting – it's lucrative. The company runs our shoots,' he added, and then commented to Phoebe, 'I gather Champing uses helicopters to bring them from Heathrow now. A day's shooting, and then off they go back to the Gulf or Germany, or wherever, leaving the gamekeepers with a pile of carcasses to dispose of.' Martin chuckled.

Kate could see Art's eyes fixed on Martin. She didn't dare look at Hussain.

'Poor pheasants,' she murmured below her breath, but Martin heard.

'Oh, I don't know. Their life may be short, but they have more food than they would ever find in the wild. As it happens, we have clients down next week for some sport,' he added. 'You'll have gone fortunately –'

'The usual palaver,' interjected Phoebe, and threw up her hands in mock horror. 'Flowers, caterers and the rest!'

★

By 27 October Kate couldn't keep quiet any longer. They had only three days left before Hussain's UK visa ran out and he became illegal. He had insisted she stay out of it, but she had waited long enough. She found a solicitor on the web who specialized in immigration cases, and worked out how she could take out a loan to cover the cost. After Art was in bed that night, she proposed that they go to the solicitor together. She had a high enough income to bring in a spouse legally. She wanted to know if they could marry in another country and then bring Hussain back into the UK. She could buy them flights with a loan. She didn't get as far as suggesting any of this to Hussain – it would entail divorcing Maryam. He stayed up late, emailing friends and contacts across the world, trying to work out what his best option was and whether the application process might be easier for a doctor in Canada or New Zealand. They had two days left.

On 29 October, when Kate got in from work, she sensed he had decided. She tried catching him alone in the kitchen, but Art interrupted them, full of news about a school project. Kate switched to discussing Halloween costumes until she insisted it was bedtime, having surreptitiously reset the kitchen clock.

'The advice is confusing,' said Hussain. 'I'm trying to understand the immigration systems of three countries – New Zealand, Canada and the UK. Everyone seems to have a different opinion on what I should do. Most of the Bahrainis I know have had no problem claiming asylum here and in other countries, but something seems to have held up my application in the US.' He looked broken. 'I don't want to use your money, and I don't want to leave you, so I'm caught between the two –'

'Stay here and let's work it out. Forget the money – that doesn't matter.'

He gave her a wan smile. 'Kate, you have been too generous

to me already – with your love, yourself, your home, your son . . .' He rubbed his creased forehead and sighed. 'But I know what you want and I can't give it – one day I must be with Maryam, and I am yet to find an immigration system which is prepared to accommodate two wives. I'm not just choosing my best chance of where I can make a new life, but also choosing between two women. I can't bear it.' His voice cracked.

Kate put her arms around him.

★

The solicitor was tight-lipped. She could take the case, but warned that it would be difficult. Hussain should have claimed asylum in the first country he arrived in, she reminded him. In turn, he pointed out that it would have been no safer for him in Saudi Arabia than in Bahrain. When he said he wanted his wife and daughter to join him as soon as possible, she arched her eyebrows, glanced at Kate, and pointed out that his daughter needed to be below eighteen for the rules on family reunion to apply. That gave them just under nine months; Reem was eighteen in August. The solicitor suggested a down payment of £2,000, and Kate gave her bank details.

Afterwards, they sat in a cafe while Kate arranged an overdraft on the phone. Hussain promised he would pay her back as soon as relatives sent the money. The next day his visa would run out, and the solicitor had been emphatic: if he came into contact with the police, he was at risk of detention, and even deportation. He had heard of the detention centres where people could spend months while their cases slipped into bureaucratic limbo. Worse, the solicitor had warned him that once people were in the system, the immigration authorities could sometimes move too quickly for her to have time to intervene; he could find himself on a plane within a couple of days.

He poured the sugar into his espresso and stirred it vigorously.

Kate put her hand around his to still the clatter of the teaspoon. 'Keep hope. I have never loved anyone like I love you,' she whispered, her eyes full of tears.

He looked as if he was about to say something, but he stopped. He just about managed to smile, but it didn't reach his wary eyes.

*

The night of Halloween, the neighbourhood was full of small groups of children looking for sweets on trick-or-treat expeditions; their screams and costumes of dripping blood and masks only added to Hussain and Kate's edgy anxiety. Hussain could see no better option than to stay in the UK, and hope the lawyer could help him claim refugee status. His uncle in the US had not given up, he added. 'One or other option will work out,' he said, but there was no conviction in his voice. On Bonfire Night, Kate offered to take Art out alone, and suggested that Hussain watch football with earplugs to avoid the sound of fireworks. After she got back and they settled down to try and sleep, the small explosions still reverberated around the neighbourhood, reminding him of the shooting in Manama during the protests. After a while he got up, and Kate heard him pacing up and down the living room. He often woke, trembling and sweating, in the nights which followed. Kate stroked his forehead and his hair, murmured into his ear, and, eventually, he would drop off. In the morning, he didn't refer to his disturbed sleep.

More and more lay unspoken between them. They both tried to reach across the widening gap, but their efforts were stymied by what they could not, or did not want to, speak about. For Art's sake, they chatted at mealtimes and afterwards they sat on the sofa together and watched television in a show of family time which Art loved, snuggling between them with his arms tightly tucked into theirs, as if holding them together. To make matters worse, Ed had confirmed that he was having Art for

Christmas, and had booked the flights; Kate was steeling herself for his absence.

What brought Kate and Hussain close again was entirely unexpected. One night Hussain slipped into bed around 3 a.m., and Kate, still awake, turned over to put her hand on his arm. Unusually, he described his night visits – he had been to see a Moldovan man who had broken his ankle; Hussain had been able to fix it with a splint, and give the man painkillers, but what troubled him was that he was very hungry.

'He was malnourished,' he whispered, 'after months of poor diet, and he was not the only one.'

Kate lay in the dark, alert.

'Could we take food?' he suggested tentatively.

'Of course,' she replied, and kissed his shoulder.

The following day, they planned to make a thick soup, and when Kate got home from work, they chopped the vegetables Hussain had bought in the market. Kate found two large plastic containers, and he went off that night with a backpack and two big bags.

'Did it go down well?' she asked sleepily when he returned.

He stroked her arm. 'Yes, much appreciated.' Kate couldn't see his face in the dark, but she could tell he was smiling. When he got into bed, he rolled over and put his arm around her, and she shifted into the curve of his body.

Art was even roped in to help after school, carrying bags full of shopping back from the market, and then peeling potatoes and carrots. He was proud of his efforts, and relayed to his mother the explanations Hussain had given him about the homeless people with nothing to eat. Hussain started to take food with him twice a week. He visited three different places, each about an hour away by bus amongst the industrial estates and goods yards on the fringes of London – places Kate had only ever passed in a car or train on her way out of the city.

A few weeks into this new regime of running a part-time soup kitchen, Art had a sleepover with a friend one Friday.

'Can I come and help you tonight?' Kate asked Hussain suddenly, when they were eating supper.

Hussain frowned.

'Why not? I can help carry the stuff.'

Hussain refused to meet her eye. He took a breath. 'I don't know these people I feed – who they are, or what they are up to. I just know they are desperate.'

'What difference does that make? Is it because I am a woman?'

'In part, yes. Many of those I see are men, but other things –'

'I'll be all right if I'm with you,' she interrupted.

'Some are illegal, some have probably been trafficked and escaped. There are people looking for them – criminal gangs, that kind of thing.' He shrugged his shoulders. 'Maybe I have watched too many movies, but it feels dangerous sometimes.'

'But I can carry some of the bags,' she persisted, sounding more definite than she felt.

He got up to start clearing the table. 'That's true,' he said reluctantly. 'If you are sure, you could come tonight. It's organized by an older man, Khalid, who ensures everyone behaves – no drink or drugs. It should be safe. You can carry the bread – I got leftovers from the Turkish bakery. I admit it would be nice to have the company on the bus – the journey can feel long.'

At about midnight, they left the flat, well-wrapped in scarves and coats against the bitter cold. Kate was carrying two bags and Hussain another two, along with the backpack. On the stairs, they passed Jackie on her way home, and she stopped to chat about her trip to the cinema, but Kate apologized, saying they had to get on. She found her intense curiosity disconcerting as Jackie glanced at the bags and backpack.

The pubs were emptying, and the streets were busy with young people making their way to clubs and bars. Sitting at the bus stop, Kate observed this night-time world, and remembered how she had once been part of it, when she and Ed went out with friends. But she was so much happier now, Hussain's purposeful body against hers, bags clustered around their feet, and she took off her glove and slipped her hand into his, inside his pocket. He squeezed it.

The bus took them beyond anywhere familiar to Kate, past betting shops, convenience stores and fast-food joints along a main arterial road east. They changed buses at a stop where cars streamed past a major junction. The next bus was nearly empty; its route ran along residential roads and past large warehouses. Kate was sleepy, and found her head slipping on to Hussain's shoulder. He woke her to get off at a stop near a dual carriageway, and they took a path which ran along a perimeter fence. Through the chain-link wire, Kate could see the buildings of City airport. The tarmac was gleaming in the light rain, reflecting the lights of the runway. Occasionally, a vehicle moved around the quiet terminal. She imagined the airport in a few hours' time, full of travellers arriving for the first flights of the day, their well-organized lives running to timetables and schedules.

After about ten minutes, the path left the airport, and Hussain used the torch on his phone to guide them, shining it carefully at his feet so she could follow. They came out into an empty car park where only one street lamp was working, and in the dim light Kate picked out a row of old garages. They were covered in graffiti, and several had had their doors smashed in. Rubbish was piled up on the concrete forecourt, but there were signs that the place was used, and a path had been cleared through the rubbish to a door.

'Careful where you step,' whispered Hussain. 'There are needles.'

Kate nodded. In the small patch of light from the phone torch, she saw the glint of silver and a used condom. Hussain's calm confidence was reassuring; she felt safe with him. He knocked twice on a battered metal door. After a pause, they heard someone undo a chain, and a young man, with a hoodie pulled so low Kate could see little of his face, beckoned them in. As she squeezed past with her bags, she glimpsed his thick beard, but he didn't look up to meet her eye. She heard Hussain murmur to the man in Arabic.

Hussain had told her on the bus that he would describe her as his wife, and she had moved a ring to her wedding finger. 'That way, it's simpler all round,' he said, adding awkwardly, 'and not completely a lie.' Kate squeezed his arm.

'Not completely a lie,' she repeated to herself silently as she followed him down the corridor to a second door. It opened on to a large space dotted with concrete pillars, and it took a while for Kate to get her bearings in the low light. Old furniture had been salvaged and arranged in one area, where three men sat on a sofa, the upholstery ripped and splashed with paint. They looked very young, barely out of their teens. In a corner, various boxes served as storage, and Kate could see rows of old tins and some kitchen equipment – plastic bowls and saucepans. They had an old Calor-gas cooker, with a bright orange canister to one side. Candles had been stuck into jam jars and gave weak pools of light. It was cold, but dry. One man was sitting at a table on a broken chair, his face lit up by the computer screen he was reading intently. Several phones were plugged into a car battery on the floor at his feet. There must have been about a dozen men in different parts of the garage – a couple of bodies were lying on mattresses on the floor, but it could have been piles of bedding – and, apart from the one on the computer, all turned towards them, their faces expectant.

'*Assalamu 'alaykum*,' said an older man coming out of the shadows and greeting Hussain with a big bear hug. 'What's for supper, doc?'

'*Wa 'alaykum assalam.*' Hussain nodded in greeting.

The sharp contours of Hussain's jaw had eased, and as he sat down at a table and started opening up his bags, he joked in Arabic and both men laughed. Khalid took the plastic boxes and emptied their contents into large saucepans and placed them on the Calor gas cooker, breaking off repeatedly to chat with Hussain. Kate watched and thought he looked more relaxed here than she had seen him for weeks. Several of the men went outside, and through the open door Kate glimpsed them taking turns to stoop over a plastic bowl to wash their faces and hands, before they came back and sat down in a circle on a piece of old carpet. The saucepans were placed in the centre. Khalid used the ladle Hussain had brought to serve each one with a paper cup of the thick soup. Hussain was always 'the doc' and she heard herself referred to in English as 'the doc's wife'. Khalid gestured to a place on the carpet for them to sit. Kate looked round at the group of men, the candlelight illuminating details of their tracksuits, ripped jeans, and padded jackets with frayed cuffs. Most of them were in bare feet or socks, their toenails poking out of large holes. Their muddy trainers were lined up by the door.

The men paused briefly with the food in front of them, some prayed, while others waited. Then they began to eat, tearing off bits of the flat bread to dip into the soup and dig the potatoes and lentils out of the paper cups. Soon Khalid was ladling out second helpings. Kate could see their pleasure in the food.

Some of the men were speaking in Arabic, others in a Slavic language she didn't recognize. Occasionally one looked at a mobile phone, and the meal was punctuated by the quiet ping of a text, and a glimmer of light on a phone screen. These men had almost nothing but their phones. Hussain managed to get to this garage once a week, he had told her, and he visited another place in Tottenham on the edge of the marshes, and a squatted house in Walthamstow for his other 'surgeries'. The men felt they were safer at night, and, besides, many had casual work during the day.

When the food had been eaten and cleared away, a few moved over to sleep under the bedding on the mattresses. It was time for the surgery and Khalid took charge of organizing the slow sequence of consultations. He held the queue of people, men and women, arriving at the door, while Hussain spoke quietly with each person on the sofa, taking notes in an exercise book. He had a small stock of antibiotics and painkillers as well as dressings and antiseptics. Kate sat on the other side of the room by the cooker in a slightly damp armchair, waiting. She had already packed the empty containers back into their bags. She closed her eyes and several times she drifted into a light sleep. When she woke, she glanced over at Hussain, bent over, talking to a patient. Kate had never seen his blood-pressure cuff or his stethoscope before. He still had secrets.

One woman came over and sat down beside her.

'Have you children?' she asked Kate in a thick Eastern European accent.

Kate nodded. 'One.'

The woman smiled shyly. 'I have two – at home. I came to England to earn money for them. But now I may be pregnant.'

She bit her fingernails. A strand of her blond hair fell over her face as she hunched over.

'A friend told me the doctor might help me.'

Kate put a hand on her arm. 'I hope you get the help you need,' she whispered.

The woman nodded, nervously wiping her cheek as she got up. Hussain was available, and she went to sit down next to him.

About two hours later, he had seen perhaps as many as twelve patients. He stood up and signalled to Kate he was done, it was time to go home. Those who were still awake got up to shake his hand and thank him. There was no doubting their sincerity, but

Hussain was embarrassed, brushing aside their gestures as he zipped up his jacket.

Kate and Hussain made their way back in the dark, retracing their steps along the fence. The airport was now largely dark but for the runway lights winking red and green. At one point they almost stumbled over a bedraggled fox; it appeared as astonished as they by the encounter. The animal had a suppurating wound on its back, and slunk off nonchalantly into the undergrowth.

Finally, they arrived at the bus stop, with the dull roar of the traffic on the dual carriageway nearby. Kate sat in the orange sodium glare of the street lights; she knew now a part of what lay in the darkness on either side of the road, its hidden life. On their journey home, the bus driver careered past the empty stops. They were accompanied some of the way by a tired office cleaner setting off for her shift in the centre of the city. Kate watched her face crumple into deep frowns as she slept, disturbed by unknown nightmares. She herself slowly succumbed to sleep, assured by Hussain that they wouldn't miss their stop. Disturbingly, her sleep was of a dream in which she was walking over a carpet of silver needles, her feet bleeding with the pain, tears pouring down her face.

*

Kate woke late the following morning, and when she got up and pulled back the curtains in the sitting room, the night before felt like a dream. She looked out of the small kitchen window at the plane tree's bare branches. Someone was putting out their rubbish, and a couple of children were riding their bikes. She could hear steps in the flat above and a murmur of voices: the normal routines of city life, yet now they felt fragile, knowing that a couple of bus rides away, human lives had come to rest temporarily in hidden edge-lands, where the city petered out and deposited its waste of smashed cars, rubbish and sewage. It made her feel deeply uncomfortable; she had been too preoccupied with her own life to see the cruelty. A line from her A-level English class on *King Lear* came back to her:

> '*O, I have ta'en*
> *Too little care of this! Take physic, pomp;*
> *Expose thyself to feel what wretches feel . . .*'

She couldn't remember how it went on. She woke Hussain with a cup of coffee the way he liked it, black and very sweet. One meal every few days was not enough for these people, she explained – they could do a crowdfunding page. She had friends who would contribute, and perhaps some would even cook a meal. On a piece of paper, she was writing down ideas, names and plans before Hussain was even properly awake. He had never seen her so full of energy and determination this early in the morning.

By the time Art returned, grumpy and tired, from his sleepover, they had drawn up an appeal on a Facebook page, and had even had their first donation: the 'Secret Kitchen' project was launched. The time they spent at the computer, shoulder to shoulder at the table in the sitting room, was a reminder of their easy warmth back in the summer. Absorbed in their task, they shared the collaborative spirit of suggestion and counter-suggestion. They wanted more volunteers, but they had to be careful that they didn't inadvertently expose the locations to the immigration authorities. Kate's name was the contact point, and Hussain was not mentioned – they both agreed that was safest. Money was to be transferred into her bank account. She kissed Hussain and he stroked her hair. 'You're a good person,' he said gently, his eyes soft with appreciation.

12

'Thank you, Kate. It's a terrible shock. I hoped we had a few more years together, but neither of us was young, and we knew our time was running out.' Kate thought she heard Phoebe's voice crack, but it could have been the telephone line. 'He was a wonderfully interesting man to be married to. I was lucky for forty years.' She was blowing her nose. 'Please come down the day before the funeral, and help me to decorate our church,' she went on, her voice clearer; organizing was something she was good at. She would arrange the perfect funeral: tasteful, moving and dignified. 'I want you to myself. Can't Hassan – or is it Hussain? – bring Art down the following day? I have worked out what I want: a church full of greenery – branches of yew, ivy, laurel, holly from the estate. I gather the company are doing the flowers – white roses and camellias.'

Kate imagined the shock to such flowers – probably the roses were grown in Kenya at this time of year – emerging from their tissue paper and boxes into the sharp cold of an English church.

'The flowers will arrive in the afternoon. Dotty will arrange the greenery. Come down that morning, will you? We can have lunch before we start decorating the church.' She rang off. Kate would have to take a second day off work.

Martin had been ill since Christmas, when a chill had developed into a chest infection. Kate had phoned one weekend she was down at the cottage, and Phoebe had said it was best not to visit. Since then, she had called once and Martin had come on the line; he had sounded frail, but still his old self, asking yet again where

Art was going to secondary school. Phoebe had assured Kate that he would shake it off, but she had been wrong. Kate thought of Martin at Christmas a month ago, as reserved as ever, but she had been touched that he'd sat down next to her to give their presents: wellies for Hussain, a new lawn mower for Kate and for Art, a thick puffa jacket and a pair of designer trainers to greet him on his return from his visit to his father. Both were the right brand to please Art, and Kate detected the advice of Dotty.

She tried to imagine Lodsbourne without Martin. He had kept a clear distance from Hussain – she didn't think they had ever had a proper conversation beyond a few pleasantries about the weather and Hussain's studies in America. Kate had never found him an easy person to talk to, and had always avoided sitting beside him at meals, or in the drawing room. The conversation usually included questions about Kate's 'career', as he insisted on calling it. She had tried once asking him about his childhood in Iran, but he was evasive, and she didn't know how to press him.

*

Kate stood by the Aga to warm herself after her walk from the station while Felix laid the table. The kitchen was the only room in Lodsbourne that could properly be described as warm in cold weather. Dotty was texting on her phone. Now that Martin had died, Kate wondered if various formalities of the house would fall away; she couldn't imagine Phoebe hosting dinner at the long dining-room table on her own. The glamour of the place was going to fade. The funeral could be the dramatic finale – not just to Martin's life and his great career but to a whole way of life at Lodsbourne. Phoebe already looked diminished. It took Kate a while to realize that she was not wearing her large silver earrings. Without that signature of her bold, flamboyant style, she looked smaller.

'We heard there were going to be sub-zero temperatures and

possibly snow, so we had to find gravediggers immediately, or they wouldn't have been able to dig the grave,' Phoebe explained as she served cottage pie to Dotty, Felix and Kate. 'The undertakers got them in from Portsmouth – some Rumanians, I believe.'

'They seem to have done the job,' said Felix. 'I was down there this morning. The grave is ready, with mounds of earth on either side as hard as rock.'

'How will they fill the hole?' asked Dotty, alarmed.

'God, you're right. I didn't think of that,' said Phoebe.

Felix was laughing. 'He might have to just lie there in the hole. For once, he might have to wait for something.'

Dotty and Phoebe looked at him with a mixture of irritation and distaste.

'This isn't a laughing matter, Felix. It could be unpleasant, having the coffin sitting there in the churchyard, waiting for a thaw,' snapped Dotty.

Kate began to clear the plates as the siblings bickered.

'Right, Kate,' said Phoebe, getting up. 'Let's leave these two to sort that one out. We have work to do. You'll need a coat – the church will be cold. The heating is going on at seven tomorrow morning to make sure we don't all freeze during the service.'

A few minutes later, Phoebe and Kate set off down the drive. Phoebe looked extraordinary in a set of mink – hat, muff and coat. She took Kate's arm to keep steady on the icy ground.

'I must look ridiculous in this get-up, but it is wonderfully warm. It was a present from one of Martin's clients. You will just have to put up with me looking as if I am about to appear in a Russian novel,' said Phoebe. Kate could see the tiredness in the blush of mauve below her eyes.

Kate laughed, and stroked the softness of the muff lying next to her own worn parka. She was carrying a basket, containing two pairs of secateurs and scissors. She looked up at the grey sky, heavy with the promise of snow. The trees stood silent, as if waiting for something – no breeze stirred the branches, or twigs snapped in the business of a field mouse or hare. The stillness was stolid, unbroken by a single cry, as if the throats of the birds had frozen.

'How come you call it "your" church, Phoebe?' asked Kate.

'Well, because it is,' said Phoebe, offhand. 'It is ours, I mean.'

'Part of the estate?'

'It wasn't originally. We never used to go, but Martin heard it was falling down and bought it for a nominal sum – a few pounds, or something absurd – but a condition of the sale was repairing the roof, and that cost a *fortune!*' Phoebe said the word with the relish of someone with a healthy respect for both the possessing and spending of vast quantities of money. 'The roof wasn't the end of it – there was the guttering, and some awful damp-rot problem in the vestry. It was Martin's most expensive hobby by a very long way.'

'It could have been a yacht in San Tropez or a golf course on a Scottish island,' mused Kate.

'Mmm . . . well, that's a thought. I should have tried persuading him of the first, but the golf I could never be doing with,' Phoebe replied, smiling.

'Could you have persuaded Martin of something like that – a yacht in Saint Tropez?' asked Kate, curious as to how their marriage had worked, the inner mechanisms of who made the decisions.

'Goodness, no. I never persuaded Martin of anything, not even at the end. I tried to keep him going. I told him it wasn't time to give up yet, but it was no good.' There was a catch in her voice, but after clearing her throat, she continued, 'Martin made his own decisions – though sometimes I could arrange things in such a way as to make the necessary decision obvious. And when things didn't matter to him, he let me decide.'

'Like what? What didn't matter?'

'Oh, I don't know – Dotty's schooling,' said Phoebe airily. 'Wallpaper in the bathroom, nannies. Got some things wrong, of course: Dotty is the one who takes after Martin – as good with money as he was. By and large, we left each other to get on with things – I never really understood the business, and he never understood wallpaper or curtain fabric. I know that sounds silly, but actually it wasn't. We both hugely appreciated the outcome of what the other did, without needing to know the details of how or why.'

Kate absorbed this statement, the gravel crunching under their feet, before she returned to the subject of the church.

'But why did Martin pour money into a damp country church?' She had only ever seen it from the road, where it looked incongruous, as if it had been towed from some respectable Victorian suburb and abandoned in the middle of a field. 'It's not like it was a beautiful medieval building.'

'I think he did it to salve a guilty conscience.' Phoebe gave her a faint, puzzled smile, which managed to convey an indulgent fondness, and an indication that the conversation stopped there.

They arrived at the church and Kate lifted the latch on the heavy wooden door. Inside the porch was a tall stack of expensive cream cardboard boxes.

'Excellent, the flowers have all arrived,' said Phoebe happily – more comfortable with flower-arranging than discussing guilt.

She directed Kate to carry the boxes into the church. She cut the tape of the first box, lifting off the lid. Inside were perfect white roses, wrapped individually in white tissue. The florist's thick card, edged in gilt, lay on top. Under Phoebe's direction, Kate brought brass vases from the vestry filled with water, and they set to work.

Kate picked up their conversation from earlier. 'What did Martin have to be guilty about?'

'Umm . . .' Phoebe responded absent-mindedly. Then she

stopped, secateurs in hand, and stood there, looking at Kate. 'Well, you for one.'

'Me?' said Kate, startled.

'Isn't this just divine?' Phoebe was holding a waxy cream camellia with stamens the colour of egg yolk.

'Phoebe?'

'What?' She looked up. 'Oh, darling, don't make a fuss about it. You must have known.'

'Hang on, Phoebe, I'm confused.' Kate felt her face flush.

'Well, you could have been the one to inherit Lodsbourne.'

Kate looked at her, but she was busy snipping the rose stems with her secateurs.

'Your mother must have said something – or your father, before he died? It was a ghastly business, but it can't be helped. Your father tried his business in Hong Kong and Singapore, but Martin was more successful. Your grandfather was monstrous to set the boys up against each other like that, but he got what he wanted – Lodsbourne is in good shape for Dotty to inherit. Roses here?'

'Roses.'

'I never met Martin's mother, she died shortly after we married in Bahrain, and the old man went gaga in a home for the last couple of years. But she did her bit identifying heiresses for her sons to marry. As adults, each of them had to submit their financial circumstances to the family solicitor every year. Awful bullying, really,' said Phoebe, standing back to admire the magnificent standing display she had constructed. 'It was nasty, but Martin played by the rules. I'm sorry that your father took it so badly but, well, there we are –'

'Badly?'

'The suicide – your mother told you about that surely?'

Kate stood with camellias in her hands, remembering the night she was woken by her mother sobbing in the hall, holding the phone. Kate had come to the door of her room and overheard her repeating his name: James, James. Kate had seen so little of her father, she'd felt nothing: one blank was replaced by another blank. She had never known how to grieve for a father whom she had barely known.

She shook her head, her lips pressed tight to hold back the sudden urge to cry. 'She said it was an infection. Years later, when she was dying, she admitted he had a drink problem.'

'That's true, and drugs, I gather. Poor James – he just couldn't cope with failure, and he fell apart.'

'And Martin had a guilty conscience?' said Kate, more sharply than she intended.

Phoebe spun round. 'Kate, there's no point getting upset now – Martin worked very hard building up the business. Lodsbourne's renovation and upkeep has cost him millions. Your father would never have managed that, and the estate would have ended up being sold. It worked out for the best, in my view – at least in terms of the estate. My father-in-law was not a good father, I admit, but he wanted to save Lodsbourne.' She turned back to her flower arranging, pursing her lips as she leaned back to survey a new display. 'But, yes, it's true, I think Martin did have a guilty conscience about poor old James. That's why the legacy will help. He told you about that, didn't he?'

Kate remembered Martin mentioning his will at that odd meeting in his office. So that was what it had really been about.

'I told him to tell you the whole story, but he never liked talking about any of it. As I say, their father was a bully – beat them both, and so forth. Anyway, the legacy will help with Art's school fees.'

All Kate could muster was a rather clipped reminder: 'I don't have school fees.'

'Not yet. Now, can you help me with this branch of yew? I want it behind the altar.'

Kate installed the branch as instructed while Phoebe opened a box of church candles. 'I want these on the altar. I will bring more scented candles down in the morning.'

They worked in silence for a while: there were displays for every window, and several for the altar. Kate was trying to remember what her mother had once said about Martin being ruthless.

'The undertakers will put flowers on the coffin.'

Kate nodded, but didn't reply.

'You're not going to be difficult, Kate, are you?'

For the first time, she noticed a coercive edge to Phoebe's tone. Kate knew she had to settle this now: hanging in the balance was a resumption of their easy, if guarded, friendship – or a corrosive distrust. She suddenly saw the single-mindedness, usually well hidden, which had enabled Phoebe to construct her beautiful world.

She hesitated, but then said, 'Of course not,' with what she hoped was credible conviction, adding tightly, 'It's a long time ago, water under the bridge.'

Phoebe looked pleased. 'Exactly, I couldn't have put it better myself.'

They did not return to the subject, but finished their work, only exchanging the occasional comment about roses and trailing ivy. As they walked back down the drive in the dusk, Phoebe took Kate's arm, and said she would leave Kate the magnificent furs in her will. Kate thanked her – as she knew she must – but pointed out gently that wearing such furs in east London was out of the question: she would make herself a target for animal-rights activists. They both managed to laugh at that.

'Sit near me in the front row tomorrow,' urged Phoebe as they arrived at the front door of the house.

'Of course,' said Kate, knowing that she had no intention of doing so. Hussain was bringing Art down. He had said he wanted to pay his respects to a generous host and a relative of Kate, and the three of them would sit at the back somewhere. Dotty had told her that hundreds of people were expected. It was a good thing the Victorians had built their churches with such optimistic self-confidence. There was plenty of room.

★

The next day, Kate made her way over to the Hall early, as requested by Dotty. In the kitchen, a pot of tea on the table was still warm, but there was no sound of anyone about; the house was becalmed, full of anticipation. Kate wandered into the hall. More boxes from the florist had arrived and were stacked up waiting to go down to the church. Fauzia appeared briefly, greeting Kate with a flustered kiss, and hurried upstairs to dress.

'They're all hyacinths – we have to add them to the flowers in the church,' said Dotty, coming down the stairs, already dressed in an elegant black suit. 'Mummy mentioned to someone in the office that it was a shame the flowers weren't scented, so they ordered another delivery. I've got to get them down to the church soon to have a chance of scenting that cavernous place – Mummy needs to be able to smell them.'

'Right' said Kate vaguely. Her mind was not on hyacinths.

She was finding the news of her father's suicide hard to absorb, and it lodged itself in her thoughts, huge and incomprehensible, painfully reminding her that she had known very little about him. Last night, after she got back to the cottage, she had built up the fire and sat up late, thinking about both her parents. Phoebe's casual remark that her grandmother might have singled out her mother as a suitable heiress had cut her to the quick; had her mother stumbled into the trap of a loveless marriage? Kate had dim memories as a child of her parents' terrifying arguments, usually about money. They had had little in common. She felt she understood a little more about her mother's anxious desire for

227

status: she had been trying to catch up – or keep up – with the Wilcox Smiths.

Dotty led the way into the kitchen. She was wearing high heels and the soles of her black shoes were scarlet. Her appearance was always striking, in a conspicuously expensive way.

'I'm sorry for the loss of your father,' said Kate. Dotty looked narrowly at her.

'I adored Daddy, and I will miss him badly. I suppose you don't really remember the death of your father?' Kate flinched, but Dotty's tone changed and she moved swiftly on: 'Let's go over the will in the study, we'll be out of the way. Daddy made me an executor, and wanted me to understand all the implications.'

No one had ever been allowed into Martin's study when he was alive. During a game with the children, Kate had once tried the closed door to discover it was locked. She was being invited into sacred space. The room was one of the most handsome in the house. A desk in front of a large bay window overlooked the rose garden; glass paperweights sat on neat piles of papers. A desktop screen had been removed – the leads lay across the keyboard as if recently unplugged. Martin had been a rare octogenarian, taking to email and the internet with relish, and, right to the end of his life, had been capable of mastering new technologies. Kate remembered one of the conversations last summer at Lodsbourne when he had talked animatedly to the man from Cairo about cyber surveillance. He had kept up with business associates all over the world, as well as with financial and business news on an almost hourly basis. He used to arrive at lunch or dinner talking about stock-market movements, even though Dotty was the only one who understood.

The walls of the study were lined with bookcases, and Kate's eye instinctively flicked along a shelf: many were in Arabic or Farsi. He must have had a lot in common with Edith, she reflected drily.

Dotty sat down in her father's old leather armchair by the fireplace, and Kate took a chair opposite. 'I won't bother you with all the detail. Obviously Daddy's financial affairs were complicated, but I'll go through the paragraph which relates to you and Art.'

'That's fine,' said Kate, sensing Dotty's edginess.

'Well, I suppose the first thing to point out is that Daddy paid your school fees after your father died, and an allowance at university.'

'Really?'

'I assumed you didn't know,' said Dotty tartly. 'I think that was your mother's approach. Anyway, water under the bridge. Just so you know.'

Kate winced at the use of the saying twice in twenty-four hours. Why was she being told this now? Was she being manoeuvred into position? Had Dotty and Phoebe talked all this through, even planned it? Her mother, she remembered, had led her to believe there was some sort of 'family money' that paid for her education.

'Daddy wanted Art to be properly educated, and has left you some shares in ZSKa – they are currently worth about a hundred thousand – for that purpose. It will help – unless you are planning on sending him to Eton,' said Dotty, laughing, then added, 'But you're a bit late for that.'

. 'A hundred thousand . . .' echoed Kate, genuinely shocked.

Dotty looked directly at Kate for the first time. 'It's very generous, isn't it? That's Daddy for you.'

'I thought when Uncle Martin mentioned a legacy, he meant a few thousand pounds. I never imagined this – I'm astonished.' Kate couldn't take it in: what was she going to do with £100,000? Pay off a chunk of the mortgage?

Dotty seemed to read her mind. 'Daddy couldn't specify that the money was to be spent on Art's education, but he makes it clear in the will that this is what he wanted. Look, here, in this paragraph.'

She handed the pages over, and Kate looked at the words, but couldn't focus. Dotty was sorting through some other papers in her lap, and Kate's glance quickly slid off the legal terminology. On the table lay copies of *Jane's International Defence Review*, along with the *Spectator* and an old *Financial Times* and *Wall Street Journal*. The shelf of books closest to her was filled with thick tomes on Second World War battles in the USSR and the Pacific, and other conflicts of which she had only a dim knowledge. *The Necessary War, A Bright and Shining Lie, Fields of Fire* – just the titles on the spines depressed her. She found Martin's interest in warfare disturbing – grotesque, even – as if he had porn in his desk drawer. She remembered his comment on that sunny afternoon when the helicopters had flown over the house, that Chinooks were 'damned good machines'.

'That's understood, isn't it, Kate?' Dotty repeated. Kate had not heard her.

'Daddy intended the money to be spent on Art's education – *private* education,' she emphasized.

Kate found it bizarre that this middle-aged woman still called her mother and father Mummy and Daddy. It sat oddly with the sharp efficiency of her voice. She was fiddling with one of her earrings as she watched Kate. For the second time in the space of twenty-four hours, Kate knew her relationship with this family hung in the balance. At risk was all that she had found at the cottage: a place where she felt at home – the long evenings by the fire watching the logs tumble in a small shower of brilliant sparks, the close intimacy in the shadowy room, the hoot of owls hunting on the hills outside. She couldn't risk losing any of that. So she made a promise she was unlikely to fulfil: a promise she resented, imposed by a dead man haunted by his brother's tragic, failed life, and enforced by a cousin who displayed a patronizing indifference in all her dealings with Kate.

'Of course, that's understood,' she lied brightly.

'Good, then we're done,' said Dotty, draining her coffee cup. 'I really need to get on with the hyacinths and the problem of how we are actually going to bury Daddy.'

'Bury him?' Kate had momentarily forgotten the Rumanians and the frozen ground. 'Ah, the frost, of course.'

'I've told Felix to go and buy plenty of bags of compost from the garden centre. At least then the coffin will be covered.'

Dotty stood up. 'I'll get round to sorting this room out at some point,' she said as she looked around. 'I want to redecorate it as my study – get rid of all these books.' Then she added hastily, 'Once Mummy is happy to leave, of course.'

Back in the kitchen, Felix was at the table, eating toast. Fauzia was making them both coffee.

'I've dropped twenty bags of compost at the church, Dotty. There were a couple of men hanging about in tracksuits – they were presumably the Rumanians. I asked them to empty the sacks by the hole,' he said cheerfully, between mouthfuls.

'Did you explain exactly where?' asked Dotty sharply.

'Well, I waved in the general direction. It's pretty obvious.'

'Oh, for God's sake, Felix,' she snapped, grabbing her coat from the back of a chair and her car keys from the table. 'I'll have to sort it out.' The door slammed loudly behind her.

'That woman!' exclaimed Fauzia. 'She's impossible.' She turned to Kate, giggling. 'Sometimes these in-laws drive me nuts.'

Felix looked at Kate, a wry grin on his face. 'Hard work keeping the peace between wife and sister. Both are highly combustible.' Fauzia laughed and poked him sharply in the ribs.

'Pa was monstrous in a very English way, wasn't he? All that uptight professionalism, that sense of importance and patriotic duty, popping up to London to advise cabinet ministers on the defence of the realm . . .'

'Well . . .' equivocated Kate, unsure of what to add, her thoughts still full of the announcement of Martin's generosity.

'I thought it was all self-aggrandizing warmongering. His huddles in clubs around the Mall. Very discreet, and manipulative. It's empire stuff. God, I couldn't stand it. Fauzia finds it fascinating; she can't get enough. I have sometimes wondered if she just saw me as a way to dig it all up for her journalism.'

Fauzia snorted into her coffee, and put an affectionate hand on Felix's shoulder. 'Father-son stuff. The old man was not so bad – and generous. I'm going upstairs to get my handbag, and then we need to be off. Dotty says we have to be at the door to meet and greet. Did you say that Hussain is coming?'

Kate nodded. 'He wanted to support me, and he says it's a respect thing, a gesture of appreciation for the hospitality.'

'I'm surprised he would want to hang out with Martin and Phoebe's crowd, but it'll be good to catch up with him after it's over,' said Fauzia. 'Any news on the application yet?'

During a supper at Kate's flat in London, Fauzia had bluntly asked Hussain about his immigration status. Ever since, she had insisted they relay detailed accounts of the solicitors' meetings, and had even managed to get a contact in Bahrain to find another witness statement to support Hussain's application. Felix had offered to ask his godfather for advice – he was a judge in immigration cases.

Kate shook her head, and Fauzia put a hand on her arm sympathetically. After she had gone, Kate looked over at Felix. She had never seen this dark, sharp humour in him; something had been liberated.

'It's OK, I hated Martin, and he hated me,' he said. 'It was managed in a very English way, without a word said, but he didn't like my choice of career. He was always polite, but I could see the concealed contempt. And he didn't much like Fauzia; he believed ambition was something to be kept hidden at all times.

He was of a generation whose understated sense of entitlement was a sign of good breeding. Fauzia saw the entitlement and loathed it – and I don't blame her. I love her energy: she was born to smash things up.'

'Blimey. I could see that you didn't get on, but this –'

'Well, at least I inherited discretion from my father. I don't like histrionics – best to keep it all below deck in rough seas.'

Sue had come back into the room, and Felix gestured to Kate to keep quiet.

'You have to read a bidding prayer,' he said, switching subject smoothly. 'I've got a reading. We agreed Dotty would do the eulogy – she was more of a son than I ever was, heir apparent and all that.' He picked up an order of service Dotty had left on the table.

'*Dear Lord and Father of Mankind*,' sang Felix from the booklet, tied with a red silk tassel. 'Priceless. I haven't sung this in years. *Forgive our foolish ways*, da da da . . . di da . . . *In purer lives, Thy service find*, da, da . . . Ah, here, look at this line: *and let our ordered lives confess the beauty of your peace.*'

'I'm impressed that you remember the tune,' giggled Kate.

'Of course – Father paid handsomely for the lasting legacy of a public-school education: knowing the hymns at weddings and funerals. I have my uses.'

'Felix, will the black mourning thing be very strict?' asked Kate nervously. 'It's just that my best coat is dark red.'

The front door slammed. Boxes were being moved. Dotty was directing the catering company. Someone was asked to take the hyacinths to the church. In the midst of her instructions, she opened the kitchen door.

'Felix, you need to help.'

'Right, oh. Just showing Kate her bidding prayer. She was asking about black –'

'What about it? It's a *funeral* for God's sake.'

Even Felix looked taken aback by her irritability. 'She's only got a red coat,' he explained.

Dotty looked bewildered.

'I've got a black dress, but it will be too cold not to wear a coat. I had hoped I would be at the back, but . . .'

Dotty arched her eyebrows and closed her eyelids for a second in suppressed exasperation.

'I'm sure it will be fine. Martin would not have minded,' interjected Sue, with quiet firmness.

Kate followed Felix into the hallway, and overheard Dotty muttering under her breath, 'Since when does the cook decide mourning etiquette?'

As they carried the boxes of hyacinths to the van waiting outside, Felix commented quietly, 'Dotty is assuming power, and she has not yet learned to carry it with grace. She'll get better at it. It's a role which doesn't usually pass to daughters, but let's hope she works it out.'

'And what happens to you, Felix? How will you cope under her reign?'

Felix laughed. 'I'll keep a careful distance. Daddy left me with enough dosh not to bother her. Not as much as her, but then she has all this to prop up for the next half century.' He waved at the façade of the house. 'She's welcome to these crumbling bricks and bug-infested timbers.'

*

Kate was waiting on the platform as the train pulled in. She watched Hussain and Art get off at the far end, and walk towards her. They were in the middle of a conversation – Art was talking, and Hussain was nodding his head in his considered way. Even from a distance she could see that Art's words could not come out of his mouth fast enough, interspersed with those vital links, 'and then . . . and then . . .' – the breathless flow of words designed to forestall any adult interruption. She saw them as a stranger might, and they made for a sharply contrasting pair: Hussain solid and calm while Art was like Japanese porcelain: he looked so pale and skinny that a winter gale might throw him scuttling along the railway tracks like a dead leaf. On the other hand, his vibrant energy was like electricity sparking from a broken telegraph pole, a sight she'd seen once in Delhi, many years ago – a storm of sparks spraying the street. Hussain had a composure which both Art and she had come to depend on.

Art was hopelessly, inappropriately dressed. He was wearing faded green jeans which were ripped at the knee and were too short, stopping above his ankles to reveal odd socks. He was wearing his big blue puffa jacket, the Christmas present from Martin and Phoebe. Hussain was wearing his thin suit, and looked very cold.

'Mum,' cried Art, spotting her, and he darted forward, his face split by a huge grin. It had only been twenty-four hours since she had left him, but reunions always provoked this form of rapturous greeting.

Kate wrapped her arms around him, and whispered through the hood of his coat to where his ear might be, 'Sweetheart, lovely to see you. Was it all right missing a day of school?'

Art wriggled free. 'I'm missing maths and PE!'

She greeted Hussain with a hug. He was shivering. 'I brought a coat from the cottage; it's a bit faded, but you will need it. It's freezing down here. I have finally managed to get the cottage warm, but I was buried under two duvets last night,' she said, laughing.

Hussain put his hand on Kate's arm. 'You look a bit tired – everything all right with the family?'

'Is it that obvious?' Kate murmured out of Art's earshot, and tried rubbing her cheeks to give them a bit of colour. 'I'll explain later.'

The church was a twenty-minute walk from the station, along the lane past the Hall. They found themselves squeezed on to the verge by a succession of cars destined for the funeral. Kate noticed some diplomatic number plates, and then a Daimler with darkened windows crept silkily past them. The car park was already full and a long line of cars was parked on the narrow road. Art pointed out the smart makes of car – Porsche, Rolls, Audi – while Kate wondered how the large vehicles would manage to turn around in the lane.

'Martin had a lot of rich friends,' commented Hussain, as he and Art playfully competed to be the first to identify the make.

Dotty was standing at the church door with her husband and children, greeting guests. A dramatic black hat decorated with feathers was perched on top of her blond hair. She had inherited her mother's grace and tact: a small word here, a handshake there.

'Ah, Kate, family on the right, take the fourth pew back,' murmured Dotty. It was as if she had a map of the seating arrangements in her head. 'First wife is here. She's third row back with Anthony and Pandora, Daddy's children by his first marriage. My advice is not to engage beyond the necessaries.'

The church was nearly full, apart from the rows at the front reserved for family. Over the sea of heads, Kate saw the spectacular displays of flowers. The church was lit by dozens of candles, and the air was heavy with the scent of hyacinths, beeswax and expensive perfumes. Surrounded by this opulence, Kate, Art and Hussain looked like misfits: red coat, green trousers and Hussain's faded country tweed coat. There was nothing for it but to brave the curious glances as they walked down the aisle.

The organ started up. Kate could hear the shuffle of feet at the back of the church. She was two rows back from Felix, but she could hear his strong voice, and she smiled to herself at the memory of his rehearsal in the kitchen a few hours ago. She found the swell of voices deeply moving, with their poetry of human frailty and fear, and to her surprise her eyes filled with tears, but they were not for Martin. They were for her own parents, and their frustrated lives.

Phoebe in her mink followed the coffin of dark glossy wood heaped with white roses. Dotty gave the eulogy: her father's national service, commended for bravery, his time as a brilliant linguist at Oxford, as a young diplomat, his business in the Gulf since the early 1970s and how it had expanded across the world and led to lasting friendships – she bowed to the congregation in recognition, and thanked those who had come a long way on this chilly January day to pay their final respects. Kate cast her eye over the pews: amongst the country Hampshire types, she could see several men of Middle Eastern appearance, and presumably these were the object of Dotty's gratitude. She went on to talk of Martin's love of Lodsbourne, the estate and his country, England, and his formidable energy and determination to protect its interests; she expanded on his generosity to the church, to many charities, and in particular the endowment of a chair in Arabic studies at Oxford. She spoke proudly of his knighthood. Above all, she concluded, he was a family man, a devoted husband and a loving father.

As the organ began the next hymn, Hussain leaned over and whispered, 'I need to leave. Can I have the key for the cottage?' The urgency in his voice forestalled any questions, but she frowned as she handed it to him. 'I can explain later,' he added, and left by the side aisle. When Art turned questioningly towards Kate, she put her finger to her lips. A soprano was singing a haunting solo, but she was too confused to concentrate. Hussain had insisted on coming; why, then, had he changed his mind? It was her turn next to read the bidding prayer, and she slipped off her offending coat to walk up to the lectern. The church boiler had been hard at work, but she shivered in her black dress. Dotty had written the prayers: for the prospering of Martin's country;

for his grandchildren – that they might find their way in life to achieve fulfilment – and finally for peace, good government and co-operation across the Gulf. As Kate read out this last prayer, she looked up, and her eye was caught by two men standing by the entrance wearing earpieces. As she walked back to her seat, she noticed how their eyes flicked from one side to the other, scanning the pews and the doorway. They were thickset, dressed impeccably in black suits, ties and overcoats. Of course, realized Kate, they were security men. Those diplomatic number plates, the Daimler with darkened windows: powerful, rich people were here.

Outside the church, the crowd of mourners formed a procession to wind through the graveyard, frosted with falling snow. They gathered on the uneven, hard ground around the grave. The priest's voice sounded thin, out in the open, and a queue formed to throw a handful of the compost on to the coffin. The security men were standing on either side of a man in a smart cashmere coat; Kate could tell the quality of the cloth, falling in a silky sheen, even from a distance. He was putting on sunglasses. It suddenly dawned on her that Hussain might not want to be seen by some of Martin's former associates, and immediately she felt stupid for not thinking of that earlier. Art was asking her something, but she was preoccupied, exasperated with herself for not foreseeing this possible risk to Hussain.

'Where is Hussain?' hissed Art again.

'Shsh . . . he's back at the cottage.'

'He walked there? He only had thin shoes, and his feet were cold even on the train,' whispered Art hoarsely.

Kate thought of him trudging through this snow. She hoped the cottage would warm him. Phoebe and Dotty were getting into the undertaker's black Rolls for the short ride back to Lodsbourne. Several chauffeurs had the engines purring already to pick up their masters, and a stream of cars began to set off for the Hall. Kate and Art followed behind on foot, slipping on the icy road.

By the time they arrived, the house was full of people and lights blazed from every window in the grey winter light. At the open front door, waiters stood with trays of champagne, while others moved among the guests to refill glasses and offer canapés. Art disappeared to find Maisie.

Kate was downing her second glass when a woman worked her way through the throng and stopped in front of her.

'You must be Kate. I'm Lavinia, Martin's first wife. I was in Tehran with him at the embassy. I knew your parents back in the sixties.'

Non-committal, Kate nodded.

'Martin was not an easy man to be married to – Phoebe was welcome to him, as far as I was concerned. Obsessed with this damned house. Phoebe had useful contacts, I gather, but he got into a nasty business, I heard: brokering arms contracts and so forth.' Her bluntness, combined with the champagne, ensured Kate couldn't scramble a response before she continued, 'Oh, don't worry, it's all tucked away behind the property portfolio. I gather that you will get a few crumbs of the family wealth – not before time. Nothing was going to stop Martin winning; James never had a chance, poor man, and once he got on to the drink, it was never going to end well. Dotty is a chip off the old block, and now she has finally got her hands on the tiller. Although I think Phoebe will hang on to the house for a while.'

Another tray appeared and Kate took a glass. She needed it.

'It was a mad time in Tehran. Looking back, it's obvious that the whole thing was going to blow up. I don't think I have ever drunk so much champagne and eaten so much Beluga caviar, but it was fun. Beautiful place, and I loved the people. Martin couldn't get his hands on any of the money, though, and it made him miserable.'

Lavinia took a bite of roast-beef canapé. Kate noticed the perfect white teeth, the coiffured hair, the diamond brooch.

'I'm sorry about your mother,' Lavinia went on. 'She stumbled into this mess with her money and ended up losing it all – husband and money. I always felt the family treated you both shabbily.'

Kate felt another wave of intense sadness. 'I've been coming down at weekends – they lent me a cottage,' she said, trying to shift the conversation away from her parents.

'Yes, I heard about that. It's the least they could do, given that this pile could have been yours.' Lavinia put her hand on Kate's sleeve. 'I'm glad we have finally made contact, you should meet your cousins – my children by Martin – Anthony and Pandora. Anthony is Martin's *real* son – made from the same mould, not like Felix. He is in public relations, and worked with Martin on some of his recent contracts. Rightly speaking, he should have taken over at ZSKa, not Dotty. They are here somewhere . . .' She turned around to scan the room.

'Come on. Let's find them.' She took Kate's wrist and began to pull her away from the corner which had provided some shelter from the maelstrom of noise and bodies, but they were intercepted by a tall man who loomed over Lavinia with exclamations of delight. In the midst of their greetings, Kate was able to slip into the crowd – she had no interest in meeting anyone else. She was desperate to get out of the room, out of the front door, and down the drive to the cottage and Hussain. She felt like she might be sick.

First Kate raced up the Hall stairs, two at a time, to find Art. He was watching a film with Maisie and her friends, and was happy to agree that he would come home before dark. Descending by the back staircase, Kate reached the kitchen, bustling with catering staff loading trays with food and drink. Ducking between them, she made for the back door and slipped through the rhododendron bushes to get to the drive, unseen. She had left her coat behind, but the cool was a relief. She gulped the icy air as if it were sparkling water. Her head began to clear as she walked briskly, almost at a run, away from the house. She had nearly reached the gates when she heard the soft roar of a luxurious engine behind her, a car rolling over the now packed snow on the drive; it crept up alongside her, and the back window slipped down, revealing a thick-set, pasty man. He inquired if she would like a lift – he had a strong Russian accent. She shook her head vigorously. He nodded and the window silently closed, the car's pace quickened and it headed out of the gateway, turning back to the main road. Someone else was in a hurry to leave.

13

Kate sat down in the kitchen, shivering in her smart funeral dress, trying to put Lavinia's comments out of her mind. She was thrown off balance again – the world a giddy place. Was Lavinia trying to settle old scores with Martin, with Phoebe? Her mind bounced from one train of thoughts to the next: from Lavinia's reference to 'arms deals' and the security men, to the silky cashmere coat, and the man in the back of the car on the drive: Martin's business connections terrified her.

Hussain was in the sitting room on the laptop. She had glimpsed him through the window when she got back to the cottage, his face illuminated by the screen, crouched forward in the armchair close to the fire. She called out as she came in, but he did not reply, so she made herself coffee and sat down at the table, trying to sober up. The ruthlessness of the Wilcox Smith family had created Lodsbourne, and its beauty was now recast in her mind, no longer the lavish gift of a beneficent universe to the lucky, but the result of their determined grasping. And she was implicated.

'You might have warned me.' Hussain came in and stood by the sink. He was angry.

'I'm really sorry, I should have thought. Did you recognize someone?'

He nodded curtly.

'The church was full of them!' he hissed, turning to her. 'Merchants of division – these are men who deal in death.' He slammed his fist on the table, making the leftover breakfast plates rattle. 'Those pews were stuffed, row after row, with the hypocrisy of the British ruling class. Were your eyes not open? Politicians, defence-company executives, diplomats – if you had blown up that church, you would have ripped a massive hole in the British establishment, with its penchant for influence in some of the most hideous regimes in the world.'

Hussain swept his hand across the table, and hit a mug. The china shattered on the tiled floor, and the old coffee splashed the wall.

Kate shrank back, staring at him. 'I didn't know –'

'That's the point,' interrupted Hussain. 'No one has any idea in this goddamn country! You look away – you have built an entire culture out of averting your eyes, and it's lasted centuries. *Centuries.*'

Kate nodded dumbly. She had been drawn into the web of charm, patronage and generosity of the Wilcox Smith family; that ghastly phrase kept coming to mind: the same flesh and blood.

Hussain drummed on the wall with his fists, swearing. Then his fists fell to his sides, he was trying to calm down. When he spoke again, his voice was level, but deeply angry.

'I recognized a member of the Bahraini royal family who has a senior position in the army. It's alleged that he ordered the shooting at Pearl Roundabout. Then I saw the bodyguards and realized the security was tight because there were serious potential targets – the kind of men who can't travel anywhere in the world without protection. Protection probably arranged by ZSKa,' he added sarcastically, 'so Martin profits even from his own funeral. No wonder the company was happy to buy the flowers to ensure a good show: put it down as a business expense.'

Tears silently ran down Kate's cheeks, but Hussain didn't notice; he was staring out of the window at the drifting flakes of snow. He spoke more quietly now, but his tone was frightening, and Kate dropped her face into her hands.

'When I came back here, I looked up two of the other faces I thought I recognized: one of them is in the Saudi defence department, in charge of weapon procurement. All Martin's wealth is *blood* money,' he said with contempt. 'The fancy collections of Persian artefacts, the nicely kept house – it was paid for by having some part in deals for tear gas, rubber bullets, water cannons and armoured vehicles in the Middle East over the last forty years, to maintain corrupt regimes and suppress opposition. Did he sell the stuff? Introduce people at shooting parties? Or make up the press releases? I don't know, but I'm going to find out. And then there are the wars. All the equipment needed to kill – *millions of people*. Start with the Iran–Iraq war, the one that Westerners don't even remember, despite having made so much money out of it, and then the two Gulf wars. A region plundered for its money and oil by the West. Now these Western companies make it their job to spin myths on behalf of corrupt regimes about "reform, modernization, stability", and "open for business". ZSKa might broker the multimillion-pound contracts with public-relations agencies in London and New York which come up with the ridiculous euphemisms. I suppose running the British empire gave people like Martin plenty of experience; the country managed to concoct a myth of Pax Britannica out of piracy, drug dealing, and the manipulation of puppet regimes.'

He turned to Kate as if she might provide an answer.

'I don't know,' repeated Kate.

'Yes, but *why* don't you know?' he persisted, leaning over her. 'Why do you know nothing about all of this?'

She was sobbing. 'I don't know, I don't know . . .' How could she be held responsible for the bloody empire, she wanted to plead, but her desire to placate his anger overrode any impulse to defend herself. 'Please, Hussain, please. Don't do this . . . you're scaring me,' she stammered.

He stared at her, then threw up his hands in a gesture of bewilderment. It was as if the temper he had kept on a tight leash for so many months had finally slipped loose. All the frustration of the slow legal case, living as an illegal, and the months of uncertainty had reached an explosive pitch. He looked at her with disgust – there was no other word for it – and then left the cottage, banging the door behind him.

Kate went to the sink and leaned over it, taking deep breaths to calm herself, but her chest was so tight it felt as if it had been bound. The thought that Art could come through the door at any moment forced her to calm down, and she splashed cold water on her face. She needed to clear up the kitchen. Her hands shook as she swept up the broken china with a dustpan and brush, and wiped the wall.

Afterwards she sat by the fire, wrapped in a blanket. She stirred once when the phone rang: it was Dotty's nanny calling to say Art wanted to stay over. He came on the line, and Kate tried to sound cheerful as she reminded him to ask for a toothbrush. She was relieved that she didn't have to rally herself for his return, and the routines of bedtime. The fire died out, but she didn't have the energy to relight it, and she just stared at the ash and charred logs in the grate.

Hussain had offered evidence of what she had not wanted to probe too deeply during her Google searches. How come Edith had scribbled on that letter from the father with the son in prison, 'Ask Martin'? Ask Martin what, and why did Edith think he could help, and had he tried? The son had died in detention. Edith was not the only one needing to ask Martin. Kate had allowed her questions about his business to be brushed off with one-line answers about property development, and now it was too late.

Then there was beautiful Phoebe with all her kindness. What part had she played over the years? How much had she known? Or chosen to ignore? Kate had taken Phoebe at face value, admiring the home she had created and the steady stream of guests who played their appreciative part. The sense of entitlement was so deep and pervasive in the life of the Wilcox Smith family that people understood it instantly on meeting any of them. Such security of place and identity were the most expensive of luxuries, Kate reflected. It required the domination of political institutions, and the creation of a specific culture of deference over centuries. A social system had been designed to forestall challenge by ensuring people either 'knew their place', or were crippled by the sense that they had no place. She had fallen in the latter category, she thought bitterly; she had been cast in the role of grateful, dependent relative. This system could not be bought: all the bespoke security contracts in the world could not provide it. Here in England, an entire social order had been constructed to ensure that the wealthiest could securely enjoy their large houses, art collections and swimming pools, *and* be admired for their privilege.

Their forebears had travelled the globe without passports – speaking English and some guns had been sufficient to gain entry almost everywhere – and now their descendants glided past the threats which plagued most people's lives, in their air-conditioned vehicles on their way to luxury hotels, their safety secured by satellite tracking devices to ensure they got to their beaches, yachts and exclusive boutiques. At the other end of the scale was the garage where Hussain saw his patients, only a few hundred yards from the passengers waiting for their flight in the airport terminal. A playground for the elite sat precariously in the midst of everyone else's *insecurity*. She could understand Hussain's anger. She felt it herself. She thought of the men in the garage who ate the food she and Hussain cooked; they had no security of any kind – no homes, no money or medical care, often no family, certainly no laws or police. Some of them had no country. They had nothing but each other, and sometimes not even that.

She was still sitting by the fire when Hussain returned. The front door closed quietly. It was too cold to stay out for long in this snow, and there was nowhere for him to go; the last train had left for London. She sat alert, trying to interpret his emotional state from the sound of the door shutting, the click of the latch, and his footsteps. He came into the room, grey with cold, despite the thick coat he had taken.

'Come by the fire,' said Kate as she got up to rekindle it.

He sat down beside her. 'I'm sorry. I just couldn't take any more after those speeches at the funeral.'

Kate put her hand on his leg and rubbed it, feeling the chill through the thin fabric, and nodded. They listened to the embers shift and collapse quietly in the grate as the flames took hold. He put his cold hand over hers, and in turn she put her other hand on top to warm it. She would use her inheritance to pay Hussain's legal costs and clear her debts, she resolved, but there was no need to tell him. She would sell her shares in the company as quickly as she could, and that lawyer might begin to take more interest in their case now that she had money.

*

By late spring, there was some progress on Hussain's case. His application should be sufficiently advanced by August to ensure Reem could get asylum too. The solicitor, Ruth, warned them not to get their hopes up, but Kate began to feel more positive. The money was making headway. Dotty had explained that the inheritance would take a while to come through because of probate, but knowing that it was on the way gave Kate the confidence to take out another, bigger loan. At the cottage, the daffodil bulbs that Kate had planted the previous autumn burst into bloom, their fragile yellow trumpets bravely defying a cold March. Kate remembered how she had planted them, praying that Hussain would still be with them to see them flower, and he was.

In the evenings at the flat in London after Art was in bed,

Hussain showed Kate the research he was doing on British security firms operating in the Gulf, and the network of arms contractors and public-relations agencies. What particularly concerned him was an information war he was tracking on social media; automated programmes on Twitter were using false information to fan sectarianism between Sunni and Shia across the Gulf region. Twitter bots made absurd allegations about Iranian plots in Bahrain and Shia links to terrorism, stoking fear. It would tear apart the fragile coalition in Bahrain that was pressing for human rights and political reform, he explained. Kate suggested Hussain collect the research and give it to Fauzia for a story. Such insidious tactics of divide and rule needed to be exposed; she knew that he was trying to establish if Western PR agencies were involved in devising the programmes. It was hard to prove. Sometimes, they sat in front of the laptop together, reading, discussing and following new links. After Hussain emailed Fauzia a couple of times, she suggested they met to go over what he had found.

Late one night, Kate, remembering Phoebe's reference to the Shiraz arts festival, googled it and stumbled on a rich seam of material, with academic articles and contemporary footage. Together in bed, she and Hussain watched an interview with the empress of Iran as she talked of how Iran could be a meeting point of civilizations. A documentary included interviews with Western music critics by a swimming pool; one suggested that Tehran's orchestra needed to work harder on their Tchaikovsky. Kate winced at the condescension, and protested vehemently at the frequent camera close-ups of the slim legs of the young Western women. She looked at their faces carefully, pausing the footage several times, curious as to whether one of them might be Phoebe. The documentary moved on to a pair of dancers rehearsing a passionate erotic duet against the dramatic backdrop of the Persepolis ruins, before interviewing bemused Iranians. 'We think we should keep our traditions untouched by the West,' one young woman in a headscarf sternly remonstrated. But the commentary concluded that it was inevitable that Iranian culture would be swept away by modern technology and progress.

'That pretty much explains the Iranian revolution, right there,' said Hussain, fascinated by the old footage. 'No one likes the idea of inevitability, particularly when used by the powerful.'

'Mmm . . .' said Kate, scrolling through a Google search on Persepolis. 'The Shah had a party in 1971 with sixty-two heads of state, two hundred and fifty bullet-proof limousines,' she read out. 'This is the party Phoebe was talking about: did you know about this?'

Hussain nodded. 'It was an absurd extravagance, and it helped destroy him.'

They looked through clips of military parades with soldiers in costumes in the style of ancient Persia.

'Twelve thousand bottles of whisky and twenty-five thousand bottles of wine. Sixty-year-old vintage champagne and Château Lafite Rothschild from 1945,' announced an American reporter to camera, surrounded by curious Iranian bystanders. In a more recent documentary, Iranian officials were interviewed, admitting to the vast expense.

'Fifty thousand birds – sparrows from Spain – imported to fly amongst the fully grown trees planted in the desert, and they dropped dead in the heat,' exclaimed Kate.

The commentary explained how every need had been accommodated in the guests' tents, as the presenter demonstrated the kitchen, bedroom and sitting-room suites. The camera panned round the furnishings. 'There!' Kate hit pause as the camera focused on a tray inlaid with ivory or bone in a pattern of delicate arabesques. 'The same tray is in the drawing room at Lodsbourne – Phoebe kept a souvenir!'

Hussain laughed. 'It might just be a coincidence.'

But then the documentary continued with an interviewee who

said that everything from the tents disappeared in the chaotic clear-up after the party – the telephones, the mattresses, the furniture, all spirited away by staff.

★

Once a fortnight or so, when Art had a sleepover, Kate accompanied Hussain to one of his surgeries. He was glad of her company and the help. What with looking after Art, shopping, cooking for the Secret Kitchen and the hours of web research, they were busy, and the weeks slipped past with an unfamiliar speed. Kate was used to time dragging, but now it had a headlong tilt she did not recognize. Sometimes, to help Hussain out, Khalid came to the flat to collect food and medicines. The sense of usefulness buoyed Kate up, and at the back of her mind she believed in Ruth's cautious optimism: Hussain's asylum case would work out.

It helped that Ed didn't call; ever since Christmas and the wedding, his calls had been erratic. Kate imagined his new wife and step-daughter were taking up a lot of his spare time. She had gathered from Art's cryptic responses that the wedding beach holiday had not been as idyllic as everyone had hoped. Mona and Ed had argued, Art told her, without going into details. Ed texted to say he was working on a big project, and sent Art his love. At least it meant that Art couldn't inadvertently cause problems with revelations about his new home life, in particular the amount of cooking and shopping they were doing. Kate was troubled, though, when she came back one evening to find Art and Hussain praying, side by side. She made it clear to Hussain that that was too dangerous for all of them: if Art mentioned Islamic prayers to his father, Ed would be incensed and there was no knowing what he might do.

'His father is Islamophobic. I'm sorry, but we have to be sensible,' urged Kate.

Hussain was quietly furious. He had looked Ed up online and read the comment pieces he had written on the Iraq War in 2003 as a prominent apologist for the invasion, with passionate declarations about the 'clash of civilizations'.

'It was Art's idea, not mine,' he said defensively.

Kate told Art it was not a good idea to pray with Hussain because his father wouldn't like it. 'I just wanted to see if I could hear Allah,' Art replied. She didn't hear about prayers again.

As the weather warmed in April, Kate and Art went down to the cottage alone. The Hall was quiet and Kate found the shuttered windows a relief. Phoebe had gone to the south of France for a holiday over Easter. Dotty was skiing. After the funeral, there had been a couple of tense telephone calls; Phoebe had rung to say something important had gone missing from Martin's study, and that Dotty had hired private investigators. Kate was to expect a call. Phoebe assured her that she just needed to answer a few questions, and that it was all routine box-ticking for insurance purposes. Kate had thought little of it, and when the man rang, she was able to answer his first question easily: no, she had never been in Martin's study on her own – she had only been in once with Dotty. But she was unnerved by his next questions: had Hussain ever been to the Hall alone? Did he leave the cottage for unexplained periods of time? She got irritated and was emphatic: Hussain had last been at the Hall at Christmas, before Martin was ill, and he did not attend the reception after the funeral. She didn't like the implications behind the questions nor the man's persistence, and she decided not to tell Hussain. She suspected Dotty was behind that line of questioning. She could have confronted her cousin, and tried to straighten out the misapprehension, but she couldn't face it. Some part of her even felt vaguely guilty over their late-night internet research on ZSKa; Dotty was now managing director, after all. She was as implicated as her father in whatever the business did.

After the funeral, Hussain had told her he never wanted to return to the cottage, let alone the Hall; he didn't want to have anything more to do with Kate's relatives. She hoped that in time he would relent, but through April and May she visited the cottage alone with Art. She watched the fresh green horse-chestnut leaves explode from their sticky buds, and her favourite, the beech leaves, emerge in soft furred pleats, and in the morning she listened to the mad intensity of the birdsong again. Before long, it would be a year since that memorable first visit in June. On these weekends, Kate rang Hussain when she needed a break from her digging and planting. He explained what he had been up to, and she talked about what she was doing in the garden. He found her pleasure in gardening peculiar, and teased her. 'At home, we have servants for that kind of dirty work,' he laughed, as she showed him her mud-encrusted fingernails on FaceTime. 'But I like the way your cheeks go pink in the country air.'

As the summer half-term loomed, she and Art both begged Hussain to join them at the cottage. He said he would think about it. The weather forecast was for good weather, and Kate felt he was beginning to relent; she promised him that they didn't have to visit the Hall. They were standing in the kitchen of the flat as she offered this reassurance, and she put her arms around him.

'Please come.' He stroked her hair, brushing it off her forehead and taking a curl in his fingers. 'We can leave Khalid a key and he can make the soup here if he needs to,' she urged.

'I'll come,' he agreed reluctantly, kissing her on the tip of her nose.

The three of them took the Friday-afternoon commuter train, and for some of the way Hussain had to stand, while Art sat on Kate's knee. Arriving at the small station and emerging from the stale air of the train was a relief: they smelt immediately the rich scent of early summer. The light was thickening on their walk up the lane to the cottage, the new leaves of the copper beech were darkening to plum. The verges were brimming with the frothy cream of Queen Anne's Lace.

In the morning, they woke late and Kate went downstairs to make coffee. Art had left a note on the table; he had gone up to the Hall already. They were alone. They made love slowly for the first time in several weeks. Recently, Hussain had sometimes turned Kate's overtures aside, pleading tiredness, but this morning his passion was like at the beginning, urgent, overwhelming. He buried his face in her breasts and thrust deep into her as she wrapped her arms tightly around his back, sinking her nails into his shoulder blades, and moving with him as the birds sang in the trees outside.

Afterwards, Hussain lay with his head on Kate's stomach, and they talked of childhood memories: he used to have a kite which he loved to fly on the beach, and once, when he was a teenager, they had visited his mother's family in Mashhad, Iran.

'It's a beautiful pilgrimage city, full of restaurants and cafes, with the best pastries,' he mused. 'One day I will take you there. Our idea of pilgrimage is more celebratory – we like to pray, but also to eat and spend time with those we love.'

Kate listened, loving the idea of a city near the Afghan border where she could eat pastries with Hussain. She knew it was fanciful – there were so many obstacles before such a thing could happen – but for a few minutes, she could indulge herself in the dream: they would stroll down the streets amongst the crowds, their hands occasionally brushing against each other, before stopping at a cafe to sip coffee and watch passers-by. The ordinary stuff of a holiday.

In turn, Kate described a school camp when she had walked the South Downs Way. Hussain was incredulous at the idea that teenage girls carried heavy backpacks with their tents and sleeping bags, and spent the nights out on the hills.

'But the stars – they were beautiful up there on the top of the downs, with the glow of cities in the distance, like Brighton,' said Kate, chuckling at his horrified amazement.

'Stars?' Hussain was sceptical. 'To see stars properly, you need to be in the middle of the desert, far from street lights. Then you can see how millions of pinpricks of light crowd the night sky.'

His face softened, and Kate pushed back a lock of his hair as she tried to imagine his stars in the desert. She could dream of this too – the day when they might both stare up into such a sky. She had plenty of dreams these days, and she let them flourish and take on new detail: of Hussain at work as a doctor, and of living as a family. She couldn't help herself. One dream Hussain had flatly rejected: a baby. She'd even suggested that it might help his case, but he was adamant that it was not the right time. She wanted another child, *his* child, but, even if he were willing, she was nearly forty-one, and she had struggled to get pregnant with Art, so this was a dream she guarded against, only indulging occasionally in the delightful fancy before dismissing it from her mind.

Hussain was showering and Kate was making pancakes for brunch when Phoebe arrived on the doorstep with her dogs, a trug of early peas and lettuce from the greenhouse, and a bunch of red tulips.

'I'm so sorry, I've interrupted you – I'll leave you be, but come for supper this evening. Dotty and the kids will be there with a few friends. It would be lovely to feel the house full of people and life again.' As ever, Phoebe was impervious to their polite refusal. 'Felix and Fauzia might turn up too.' She hovered on the doorstep. 'That's a delicious smell. I haven't had pancakes in ages, could I have a small one?'

Kate set out another plate and Phoebe ordered the dogs to sit outside and came into the kitchen, still in her coat and wellingtons. Hussain joined them, and Phoebe appeared ill at ease. She praised Kate's gardening, admiring the row of green shoots emerging in the vegetable patch, and her choice of tulips, the last of the season, blooming in the front garden.

'They're one of my favourite flowers. There were fields of them in Iran –' commented Phoebe. Before she could continue, Kate interrupted.

'We came across a film of the Shah's party in Persepolis on the web the other day.'

'Really?' Phoebe said vaguely, between mouthfuls.

'The camera panned around the guests' tents and we saw a tray just like the one you have in the drawing room for the sherry.'

'You're becoming quite the detective, Kate!' laughed Phoebe, with an edge of irritation. 'It must have been something I picked up after it was all over. I did help them find the tents – they were French, if I remember. A few of us went to Paris to sort out menus, choose champagnes, arrange fittings for the empress's clothes.'

There was an strained silence, broken only by the tap dripping in the sink. Phoebe glanced nervously at Hussain. 'It was a terrible waste of money, I realized later. There were huge blocks of ice flown from Paris which just sat there in the desert melting. No one knew what they were for, until one of the catering staff suggested they went in the ice buckets. I never claimed I understood the country, I was just doing my job.'

She got up suddenly and Kate accompanied her to the front door. Phoebe put the lead back on the dogs, and as she straightened, she said quietly, 'You know, the Iranians on the organizing committee for that terrible party were told they would be shot if they didn't get it right. They were terrified.' Then she called out in the direction of Hussain, 'See you for drinks at seven.'

Kate returned to the kitchen, puzzled. She told him what Phoebe had said. 'It was odd – why whisper it like that, just to me? What's she afraid of?'

'Her guilty conscience?' he said, shrugging his shoulders.

'No one has worked out who to blame for empire – everyone, or no one?'

Kate was distracted, putting Phoebe's flowers in water. 'Empire? What's that to do with it? Iran wasn't in the empire.'

'Mossadegh? A couple of centuries of meddling?'

Kate looked up. 'Mossadegh is one of the characters in Phoebe's Happy Families cards, but I've never been sure who he was.'

Hussain compressed his lips. 'An Iranian democrat, a prime minister who tried to nationalize Iran's oil, and was toppled by the British and the Americans for his efforts.'

'When was that?'

'Early 1950s, only a decade after the British had toppled one Shah and installed his more malleable, twenty-year-old son in the middle of the Second World War; on that occasion, their ally was the USSR. It was a pattern of British interference which began in the nineteenth century, and the discovery of oil only made it worse.'

Kate had come to recognize this tone of Hussain's: sarcastic and irritated by her ignorance. She had taken out some books on the British empire from the library; she wanted to understand better, but by the time she got round to reading late at night, she found it hard to concentrate. She couldn't tell whether he apportioned her some part of the collective blame by way of her nationality or her relatives. He guessed what she was thinking, and reached out to squeeze her hand.

Relieved, Kate changed the subject. 'I'm afraid it's dinner at the Hall tonight.'

They looked at each other, and, for the first time in a long time, they laughed, really laughed, from deep down. Phoebe was an absolutist monarch, and they were serfs with no option but to obey.

*

They spent the afternoon in the garden. Hussain was on Kate's laptop at the rickety table while she was busy weeding a flower bed. He had met with Fauzia twice, and now they were both pursuing leads, investigating companies who were specialists in disinformation and web surveillance. Hussain had contacted a Bahraini friend with more computer expertise for help.

'Are you hacking British security-company websites from an English country garden?' Kate called out merrily. Everywhere in the garden there were tasks needing her urgent attention: weeds sprouting between the stone flags of the path, and ivy threatening to strangle the shrubs she had planted last autumn.

'Far less exciting,' Hussain laughed. 'Hearings of a US congressional committee on cybersecurity – it's dull but important.'

Companionably, they worked alongside each other, occasionally pausing to exchange a remark, Kate pointing out a bird's nest, or Hussain commenting on a new detail of a commercial transaction or government policy. It was an odd combination of interests, Kate thought, but then perhaps it wasn't any different from that time when the Chinooks had flown overhead last summer. The helicopters were a fixture of life, she now knew, part of regular army manoeuvres up on Salisbury Plain. The English countryside was riddled with the nation's history of warfare, she had come to realize, ashamed of her own blindness all these years: the bunkers down by the railway tracks, memorials from many wars in the churches, and the grand houses built from the proceeds of slavery and piracy. Felix used to joke about it, but since meeting Hussain, it had come sharply into focus.

Art appeared around teatime, arriving by the back way at the end of the garden, bringing news of a den he had built with Maisie. He had developed a wiry strength in the year since they had first visited, Kate noticed with pleasure; his long rambles and adventures with Maisie in the grounds of Lodsbourne and on the downs were good for him. His confidence had grown. After several slices of cake, he turned his attention to fishing, and Hussain closed the laptop to help him make a rod. They found a length of hazel and Hussain bent a pin for a hook. Kate joined them on an expedition to the pond at the bottom of the lane. It was half-covered with brambles and broken branches, but Art managed to crawl along a fallen tree to perch over the algae-covered water. Kate and Hussain offered encouragement from the bank until the sun dipped behind the hill, and Kate announced it was time to scrub themselves clean of mud and algae for supper.

★

Kate looked down the table, lit by a line of candles, with relief. Hussain had been seated next to Fauzia and was happily engrossed, and occasionally she heard him laugh. He was far enough away from Phoebe and Dotty for either to be able to eavesdrop. Felix was next to Kate. A friend of Dotty's had brought her children. The lamb was delicious, and the wine was plentiful; Martin's cellar was still providing a fine selection. Felix kept refilling Kate's glass and she was beginning to feel slightly tipsy. She slowed down, knowing how much Hussain disliked people drinking too much. He was no puritan, and drank occasionally himself, but he strongly disapproved of the continual emphasis on alcohol in England. As Kate anxiously looked down the table at him, Hussain glanced at her and smiled. He was managing, and might even be enjoying himself.

The children slipped away, leaving the adults to talk over coffee. Just as Kate was thinking it was time to collect Art and head home, Dotty came back to the table.

'I can't find Maisie or Florence – the other kids are in the TV room, but they say they haven't seen them since supper.' She was irritated.

There were various suggestions – garden, back bedrooms, attic, the greenhouses – but Dotty shook her head vigorously. She had looked everywhere. She was tired and cross, and had certainly had too much to drink.

'How about everyone has a walk around the garden – a bit of shouting and hallooing and they are sure to turn up,' said Phoebe brightly.

The guests duly rose to their feet, several taking their glasses with them, and trooped out into the chilly summer night. Kate grabbed someone's coat at the front door and offered it to Dotty, who was shivering. It was too cold for the children to be out. They fanned out across the lawn, and as Kate plunged into the shrubbery, she could hear the others' voices calling the girls' names. Florence had a fierce wildness about her – she didn't look like the sort of child who obeyed anyone; she must have led Maisie astray.

Kate found herself in a far corner of the woods, where the trees thinned out. She could see the dim outline of the fields stretching away into the valley. The Hall lights were blazing through the trees, and intermittently she could see someone's torchlight, but in front of her it was dark; she looked up into a sky sprinkled with stars and again imagined standing with Hussain and Art under a desert sky. In North Africa perhaps, next year, on holiday. She cherished the lovely thought. An owl swooped silently down over the field in front of her, so close that as it rose again into the air, she could see its prey hanging from its claws. Its strong wings beat slowly as it pulled up and away through the tops of the trees and out of sight. She was cold. 'Damned Florence,' she muttered to herself.

Back at the house after a fruitless search, she found the dining room empty, the chairs pushed back, napkins thrown on the table. Someone had ushered the children up to bed in the nursery. Phoebe was by the fire in the drawing room.

'I'm too old to be tramping around the woods in the dark, looking for stray children. They will turn up,' she said. 'Forgive me, but I'm tired, I'm off to bed.'

Kate was inclined to agree, and envied her the chance of bed, but a few minutes later Dotty arrived back with her friend Camilla, Florence's mother, and both were deeply alarmed. Protesting that the girls' behaviour was out of character, they insisted that everyone keep looking, and the search be widened to include neighbouring fields, the valley and the pond. For the next hour, the six adults tramped up and down hedgerows and along the nearby tracks, calling the girls' names again and again. At one point, the other children were woken and interrogated by Dotty on the girls' possible whereabouts. Various suggestions were followed up with no luck.

It was past one in the morning when a few of them congregated back in the kitchen. Fauzia and Felix were finishing the remains of a bottle of wine. Kate made a pot of tea. Dotty arrived, her face drawn with worry. Camilla was outside, going through the garden sheds for a second time. Dotty said she was almost hysterical, and threatening to call the police. Felix looked alarmed and insisted that wasn't necessary. He recognized the danger immediately for Hussain, and exchanged sharp remarks with Dotty until she cut him short.

'I agree with Camilla. We've looked everywhere for nearly two hours. It's time to call the police in – they will have dogs or something.'

'Dogs?' Felix laughed. 'They don't get dogs out that fast – it's got to be really serious for that, not just two girls who have fallen asleep in some den somewhere.'

'Dotty, they'll turn up,' Kate urged, edgy. 'Let's not bother the police, at least, not yet.' Hussain was still outside looking – she needed to find him fast if the police were coming.

Dotty looked at her strangely. 'You would say that,' she said cuttingly. 'I'm calling them – now.'

'You can't,' shouted Felix, suddenly assertive.

'Why on earth not?' she retorted fiercely.

Phoebe appeared briefly in a flowing silk dressing gown. 'What's the commotion about? Keep your voices down, or you will wake the other children again.' She disappeared back to bed.

There was a babble of voices as everyone began to argue and make suggestions as to the right course of action. Felix was whispering to Dotty. Kate, with a growing sense of dread, saw the expression of horror on her face. She suddenly realized that none of this was going to end well. Terrified, her mind froze. She stared at her hands wrapped round her warm mug. At that moment, Hussain came in from the garden. When he gathered the gist of the discussion, she saw his anxiety: she recognized the creased forehead, the finger on his lip; he was thinking, trying to decide what to do.

What cut through the hubbub was Camilla's appearance at the door.

'I've just rung 999 and the police are on their way.'

Kate began to shake. Felix was standing beside her and put his hand on her arm.

'Who's on their way?' asked Art, squirming past the ashen Camilla to stand beside his mother. He looked around at the frightened adults, alarmed.

Kate suggested he go to the TV room: the adults needed to talk something over. He didn't argue, recognizing the gravity in her voice; she took him across the hallway and arranged him on a sofa and put some cartoons on the TV. Back in the kitchen, she found Felix still arguing with Dotty, saying that someone needed to tell the police not to bother. Fauzia and Hussain were whispering – they were working out how to get him away from the Hall as quickly as possible. Dotty took Camilla off outside for one last circuit of the garden.

'You should go back to the cottage,' Kate said to Hussain.

'It would be better if he was further away – is there anywhere else he could go?' asked Fauzia. 'The police search could easily extend as far as the cottage. They will want to interview everyone. Is there a friend in a nearby village?'

Kate shook her head.

'I can stay out, spend the night on the hills somewhere – it's not that cold,' suggested Hussain. 'Then take the first train back to London. When is that?'

'Good idea. There's an early train at six from Champing Common station. It's nearly two now – I could drive you over. The first one from here is an hour or so later,' said Felix, turning to rummage in one of the kitchen drawers to find the timetable.

'You can't, Felix – you could bump into the police on the road,' said Fauzia flatly.

'How far is Champing Common if you walk over the hills?' asked Hussain. Kate realized with a shock that his hands were trembling. He was frightened.

'Well, if you go via the Iron Age fort, it can't be much more than five miles over the top. A couple of hours' walking at most. The boundary with the Ministry of Defence land is clear, and they put up flags when there are manoeuvres and so forth. I'll get a map for you,' said Felix.

He left the room and Kate reached out to touch Hussain's arm. He put his hand over hers.

'You would only have to wait at Champing for perhaps a couple of hours for the train back to London,' said Felix coming back with a map which he spread on the kitchen table.

The four of them leaned over it, Felix pointing out the track which led from the end of the village up the hill.

'I know the way,' said Art. Unnoticed, he had sidled back into the room, and was standing at Hussain's elbow. 'I can take him.'

'No, no,' said Kate quickly. 'Absolutely no way. You can't do that.'

'It's not a bad idea, actually,' interjected Fauzia. 'No one will notice if Art's not here, and if Dotty does, we can say he is asleep at the cottage.'

'Hussain doesn't know the way, and he could get lost,' insisted Art.

'He's got a point, Kate,' added Felix. 'It's not that far, and before long there will be some light. Dawn is early this time of year. Hussain and Art can hop on the train in the morning and head for home – well out of the way.'

Everyone's eyes were fixed on Kate as Felix muttered quietly to her, 'If something has happened to the girls, you don't want Hussain anywhere near here.'

Hussain was already moving to the back door, keen to be away. Kate looked at him. She trusted his judgement, he wouldn't put Art in danger.

'This seems a good plan,' he said. 'I'm not much good at reading this type of English map. I can carry Art if he gets tired. I'm not sure I would find my way without him.'

'What about I come with you instead?' suggested Kate.

'It's better if Art goes,' said Fauzia firmly. 'This could get more serious – it probably won't come to that, but, if it did, the police would want to know the adults' whereabouts, and we couldn't conceal the fact that both of you were missing. It's easier to cover up Art's absence than yours,' she repeated more quietly. She talked with authority, as if she knew how police investigations worked. Kate, shivering with a combination of cold and fear, knew just one thing very clearly: she wanted Hussain as far away from the Hall as quickly as possible.

'I suppose the worst that can happen is that they get cold. Art does know the way,' she said slowly. Everyone was looking at her. She turned to Hussain. 'I'll come with you to the cottage to pick up some extra clothing and a bit of food. You're sure you remember the turn at the top of the hill after the woods, Art?'

'Of course – we've been up to the fort dozens of times,' Art said emphatically, pleased to have such an important task.

'Hussain, take this map and a torch,' said Felix. 'And hurry.'

As they left the house, Kate saw Felix arguing heatedly with Dotty. She assumed it was about Hussain. She dreaded the aftermath to this already: Dotty's questions now she knew Hussain's immigration status.

Kate, Hussain and Art ran down the lawn and through the back gate to the cottage. Art seemed to see the prospect of staying out on the hills for the night as an adventure, and Hussain was trying to appear calm for his sake. Kate had a deep sense of foreboding. They could already see the blue flashing lights of a police car through the trees in the distance. Camilla must have exaggerated the situation to get such a quick police response.

As Kate put the kettle on to boil for the thermos, she told herself that Art knew the fort well, and he was a good walker now. He and Maisie often went out on their own – and the station was only slightly further than one of their usual expeditions. She made him put on his puffa jacket, and put some biscuits in his pockets. She gave Hussain all the cash she had and her credit card, and they checked his phone. Reception wasn't good in the hills, but once they were on the train, he could call the cottage landline. They agreed a code of ringing twice, and hanging up if there were still police about. Then she hurriedly kissed them both goodbye. She would follow them to London in the morning, once everything was sorted out.

'Ridiculous,' she muttered to Hussain, in an attempt to reassure him. 'The girls will turn up, I'm sure of it.' It was not the point, and they both knew that. He kissed her quickly.

'We'll have lunch together tomorrow back at the flat in London.'

She ran her fingers through Art's hair, and kissed his forehead.

After they had disappeared down the path through the woods, taking care to keep clear of the lane, Kate went back to the Hall.

Three police cars were parked on the gravel at the front, their car doors open, and she could hear the bleat of their radios. Police were everywhere.

She saw Dotty and Phoebe in the drawing room, talking to the officer in charge, and she ducked past them to reach the kitchen, where she found Fauzia with a large malt whisky. She offered her a tumbler, but Kate shook her head; she needed to keep a clear head.

'Why on earth are there so many of them?' she whispered.

'Turns out Camilla is the daughter of a certain former Foreign Secretary, one that took us into a deeply unpopular war in the Middle East,' Fauzia said sarcastically, as she finished her whisky. 'Whenever she is in a sticky patch, she has only to call Daddy and everyone snaps to. Tedious.'

Kate's heart lurched again with fear. Seeing Hussain and Art heading off at a brisk pace had brought a temporary sense of relief; now the dread closed back over her, worse than ever. Two of the people she loved most in the world were jogging up on to the hills in the dark.

'They know the path – they'll be fine,' Felix insisted, coming in and pouring himself a large whisky. 'Thank God Hussain is out of it all – we did the right thing to get him away. They've brought dogs, infrared sensors, everything –'

'It could get worse – what if this blasted girl has got herself drowned in a pond or something?' said Fauzia, fingering her tumbler thoughtfully. 'Where is your laptop?'

'My laptop?' Kate was confused.

'Well, if things go pear-shaped, we don't want the boys in blue digging into your laptop, given the research Hussain has been doing with me – it wouldn't help his application.'

Kate glanced at Fauzia and saw that some part of her was enjoying the drama of this – the suspense, the frisson of fear. 'What should I do with it?' she asked, panicky.

'Oh, help, I don't know – wiping the search history is probably not enough – hide it in the woods somewhere? Maybe Hussain should have taken it, but it's a bit late for that now. We'll just have to hope it all blows over, and that Camilla's little darling reappears.'

Kate sat down, anxiously plucking at the fabric of her dress. Her heart was thumping. She stared at her shoes, muddy after tramping around the woods in the dark. She felt a hand on her shoulder and looked up. Fauzia was stricken.

'I'm sorry, I was being tactless.' She knelt down in front of Kate with both her hands resting on her knees. 'It's going to be OK, I promise.' For the first time, Kate's eyes filled with tears, touched by Fauzia's sympathy. 'I promise,' Fauzia repeated, and she gave her a tight hug.

Dotty brought in a police officer. A slow man, he painstakingly took down all their details: date of birth, address, occupation, next of kin. It took over half an hour. Kate marvelled at how any crime could ever be solved with such ponderous bureaucracy. Just as he reached the question about Kate's next of kin – always tricky – there were shouts of delight from the front lawn. They crowded around the window: there, coming up the driveway were two policemen, each carrying a large bundle. They deposited two very sleepy and shocked girls on the front doorstep. The dogs had found them: they were safe.

*

After most of the police cars had left, Kate finally agreed to the whisky that Fauzia had continued to press on her. It was very welcome. Her nerves had been shot to pieces and the honey-coloured liquor slipped down her throat, relieving the tension. She wouldn't completely relax until she was back in London, with Hussain and Art in her arms, but at least now she could feel that was possible, and only a few hours away. There was some discussion as to whether Felix should borrow one of the estate cars and go over to Champing to see if he could pick them up, but they agreed in the end that with one policeman still finishing up with Camilla and Dotty, it was best to stick to the existing plan. Kate poured another small measure; she felt too alert to sleep. She overheard Felix say something to Fauzia, but his voice was too quiet for her to catch more than the odd word; it was something the police had told him about the army. She caught the word 'live'.

'What was that?' she asked, alarmed.

'Nothing, Kate, honestly.' Felix came over and put his arms around her. 'It's going to be fine now. Relax.'

The three of them even shared a laugh about Camilla's histrionic performance before Kate left the Hall to stumble across the garden, to the cottage and bed. There was light breaking over the hills. It was about 4 a.m., and Hussain and Art would be arriving at the station any time now. Perhaps Art would lie down on a bench and sleep; Hussain had an extra jacket in his backpack and he would put that over Art, and let him rest his head in his lap. She liked that image – it eased the anxiety which, despite the whisky, had not fully subsided. As she settled into bed, aching with tiredness, she set the alarm for 6.30 a.m.; she would catch the 7.30 a.m. train from the village. She told herself that there was no cause now for worry. She would pick tulips in the morning to add to those Phoebe had brought, and take a big bunch up on the train. They would look lovely in the flat as they all ate lunch.

*

Kate was woken by hammering on the cottage door. Immediately, her heart was crashing against her ribcage. She tried to pull a cardigan over her pyjamas, but struggled to get her arms into the sleeves. She called out that she was coming, but she didn't recognize her thin, wavering voice. Please, please let it be Fauzia or Felix on some crazy errand, she prayed, and she pulled back the old bolts on the door.

On the doorstep, she was confronted by an astonishing, horrific sight: two armed men in balaclavas, their machine guns held at the ready, their fingers on the triggers. Someone was shouting and a bright light was in her eyes, dazzling her. Between the trees, blue lights flashed from cars in the lane. They cast sinister, flickering shadows. She shaded her eyes. It was utterly unreal, as if someone was about to appear with a clapperboard and announce, 'Cut.' The men pushed past her into the house, and she could hear them thumping up the stairs, banging doors, turning on the lights. Two other men appeared from around the corner of the cottage.

'All secured,' one shouted to a woman, whom Kate now noticed for the first time.

'What's happened?' Kate asked, her voice little more than a whisper. She was shaking so violently she had to hug herself to keep standing upright on the threshold, her bare feet on the stone doorstep.

'Katharine Wilcox Smith, I am arresting you on suspicions of harbouring a terrorist and abetting an act of terrorism. You do not have to say anything, but it may harm your defence if you do not mention when questioned something you later rely on in court. Anything you do say may be given in evidence,' the woman rattled off, as she checked her mobile phone. 'You will have access to a lawyer. You need to dress and pack a small bag, and someone will accompany you.' She pre-empted Kate: 'I am not able to answer any questions at this time.'

Kate's wrist was grabbed by another woman, who clipped on a handcuff. How many times had she watched these scenes and heard these words in television dramas – only this time it was happening to her. Coupled together, they awkwardly went inside the cottage, and Kate was jostled up the narrow staircase to her bedroom. A policeman followed them, and waited outside the door. The handcuff was taken off, but the woman stayed close to Kate, standing beside her in the bathroom as she peed and brushed her teeth. In the bedroom, Kate pulled on the dress she had been wearing a few hours ago. She felt sick. She couldn't tie her shoelaces, and only managed on the third attempt, but the policewoman was impatient, urging her to hurry. She put her toothbrush, some pants and a spare cardigan in a plastic bag. Her mind was numb, but for the repetitive refrain that this had to be an awful mistake, that someone must sort it out very soon. Thank God Hussain was not here. She willed herself to keep thinking: I will wake up in the morning in the sunshine, and everything will be normal.

Several policemen were in the cottage and she could hear them moving around downstairs. Another lurch as she remembered her laptop and Fauzia's comments a few hours ago in the kitchen at Lodsbourne. The whisky and sleep had left her muddled, but she tried to scrabble her thoughts together. She needed to get a message through to Hussain. It was too dangerous for him to go back to the flat. He needed to drop Art off with a friend, and find somewhere to lie low for a few days. She slowed her movements down as she gathered a towel and shampoo and tried to give herself time. Could she call someone such as Felix or Fauzia?

'I need to make arrangements for my child,' she said to the policewoman. 'I need to call someone.'

The woman ignored her. She took Kate's bag and handcuffed their wrists together again. Kate was pushed down the stairs, out of the front door and along the path to an unmarked police car waiting in the lane. She glanced back over her shoulder and saw the cottage, its uncurtained windows full of light, with people in every room, searching the place. The next moment, she felt a hand on her head, forcing it down, and she was pushed into the back seat of the car.

'We're taking you to a maximum-security police station for questioning. You will be able to contact a lawyer at that point,' the woman in charge said, and she leaned down to add, 'Your child is being cared for.' Then she slammed the car door shut.

That was when Kate started to panic. She couldn't breathe, struggling to squeeze air into her lungs. Cared for? Your child? The words reverberated in her mind, bringing in their wake a proliferation of insistent questions: how did this woman know she had a child? What care did he need? What had happened to Art? She couldn't speak, the words wouldn't come into her mouth, or she might have tried to ask the woman sitting beside her, their wrists still handcuffed together. The frail, mad hope that everything could be sorted out quickly had been crushed by that woman's parting comment. Her mind raced on. She could feel her heart, the adrenaline surging through her.

No one spoke for the length of the journey back to London. They were driving fast and the car rarely slowed, using its blue light to force through junctions. The pale sky was strengthening into blue, and the sunlight was casting long shadows as they arrived in London. She recognised the flyover, and then they turned off the main road and headed down into an underground car park. The weather forecast for today had been good, she dimly remembered, as if in another life – they had talked of swimming in the pool.

Somewhere in the midst of her fear, she clung to the hope that, now she was back in London, she would soon be able to hold Art's skinny, restless body, to feel his sweet-smelling breath on her cheek, and his fierce impatience for life. She didn't dare to think of Hussain. It was too painful, like someone had ripped out something from deep within her.

14

Kate shifted on the narrow bed. Whichever way she turned, she was uncomfortable, her neck and back ached. She moved on to her side and fixed her eyes on the small window. It was too high to see out, and besides the glass was frosted – and dirty – but she could see a glimmer of light. Another day was breaking, one of these long midsummer days. It must be about 3 or 4 a.m. – she didn't have her watch, and she wasn't sure when dawn broke at this time of year. She remembered the pale sky in the east over the down as she was led out of the cottage to the police car, two days ago. It was as if that memory belonged to someone else: how could a life disintegrate so swiftly? How had she managed to construct such a flimsy life that a small domestic incident could bring in its wake these terrifying consequences?

She rolled over on to her back, and examined the pattern made by a large stain on the ceiling, and traced the line of a fine crack. She felt choked with multiple emotions – fear, anxiety, even anger, and already, the first intimations of grief – fighting chaotically for release. Her chest was tight, her throat strained and dry, as if she had been talking too much, but the long hours were painfully silent. Both nights she'd slept fitfully, waking at intervals, desperate to know where Art was, and when they would let her see him. She begged some unbelievable god that he was not in this grim building – he was only a child. All they told her was that he was assisting with their investigation in the presence of a social worker. Beyond Art lay the even more awful questions about Hussain, and she didn't dare ask them.

She told herself to keep calm, repeating that it was a stupid mistake, but she knew now that was not true: this would be disastrous. Then the shaking would begin again, and she would clench her fists to focus her mind: she would fight everything, for everyone. She must never give up. The shaking would slowly ease, but the overwhelming sense of dread persisted. To distract herself, she listened to the odd noises of this building: the occasional footstep and rattle of a bunch of keys. Once, she heard the low voices of a woman and a man, and she strained to catch the sense of what they were saying, then the sound receded, as if her cell were on a long corridor. She found some reassurance that there were people about; she told herself she was in Britain, where the police were usually polite and helpful – they would understand eventually that there had been a mistake. But she could see already that was absurd. When they'd led her to her cell, the two guards had been brusque, and suspicious. They treated her as if she were a convicted criminal already. She had never experienced anything like this; no one had ever doubted her innocence before.

'I work for a children's charity, I'm the office manager. This is a terrible misunderstanding – I can give you my boss's details, she can vouch for me,' she'd told them, and she could hear the pleading in her voice.

Such details only made sense in the life she had been living up to forty-eight hours ago. She had been plucked out of it, and tipped into this nightmare. She lay on the hard bed, trying to keep warm under the skimpy blanket. The cell smelled of a powerful detergent, and when she used the metal latrine in the corner, it flushed a brilliant blue. The sharp acid tone irritated her throat and she kept coughing.

She closed her eyes and imagined herself back in the cottage garden. One Saturday, a few weeks ago, she had got up early while Art was still sleeping, and walked to the line of ash trees at the end of the garden. A breeze rifled through the branches, which moved as if they were dancing, the stems of the leaves forming graceful curves as they dipped and swayed, an exquisite pale green against a precious blue sky. She stood there in her bare feet on the dew-silvered grass. She watched the leaves catch the first rays of the sun rising above the wood, astonished that the moment was utterly perfect, replete with riches of varying kinds – the beauty in front of her, Art's soft breathing before she left the cottage, and the early-morning text from Hussain in the flat in London, waiting for his coffee to brew. There was nothing, she had thought, that needed to be added or taken away, and she had chuckled to herself: who would have thought a year ago, that she could be this happy? In the last twelve months, she had felt herself coming to life with an exuberance she had never known. Thinking back to that memory helped calm her, but it also made the end to the magical train of thought even more painful as she opened her eyes. Cruelly, it appeared that happiness had been in direct proportion to its fragility. It had hung by a thread, and with one small snip of the scissors, it was gone.

They led her down into the bowels of the building for questioning, to a room without any natural light. Kate's solicitor, Ruth, was there, and they exchanged nods. Across the table sat a woman in her early fifties. She looked up briefly as Kate was brought in, and then resumed tapping on her laptop. Her complexion was poor, from too much smoking or drinking, and her hair was pulled back into a ponytail. She looked strained and had deep lines around her mouth; her job required a hardness, Kate saw immediately. It scared her. She waited; that was how it went during these strange days. And she waited in her cell as she listened to London's impatient traffic.

The woman turned to the policeman in the room and muttered something. Kate couldn't follow the bureaucratic jargon, but gathered that some paperwork was missing. The woman sighed heavily. 'Another of my colleagues will be joining us shortly. He has texted to say his bus is stuck in a traffic jam.'

Ruth tapped her fingernails on the briefcase balanced on her lap.

'Rather than return you to your cell, you will wait here. It should only be about a quarter of an hour.' With that, the police officer gathered up her papers and her laptop, and left the room.

Kate fiddled with the fabric of her dress; it was the same dress she had worn for Phoebe's dinner. She remembered how, in the cottage that evening, she, Hussain and Art had prepared to go over to the Hall, calling to each other from room to room. Hussain had come out of the shower with a towel around his waist, his hair dripping on the wooden floor, and Art had burst into their room with a request for a picnic the following day. She had chosen this linen dress because Hussain had once said the light blue suited her eyes. Now, after several days in a police cell, the linen hung limp and crumpled; she smoothed out the creases compulsively, even though it didn't make any difference. She felt shabby and filthy, and her hair needed washing. Would they let someone bring clean clothes? Who would try to visit? Perhaps Felix, but it was possible that the Wilcox Smith family would drop her and the chaos of her life. That would probably be Dotty's preferred course of action. Kate remembered Dotty's quick glance of horror when Felix had explained the danger of the police finding Hussain.

The woman came back with two policemen, and sat down across the table from Kate again. Without speaking, they all opened up laptops, and Kate watched their eyes fix on their screens, their faces pale grey from the brightness.

'Ms Katharine Elizabeth Wilcox Smith?'

'I only use Wilcox – Kate Wilcox.'

'We understand that you have been concerned about your son,' said one of the men.

She nodded.

'We can reassure you that he is safe and in good health. His father flew in from America last night, and has taken him to his grandparents in London. Arthur has asked after you and we have told him that you are safe and well.'

'Thank you,' said Kate flatly. At least Art was not in a police station.

'Social services have taken on his case and are working with the police and intelligence. At some point, I expect you will be questioned by a social worker, but I gather that we have had assurances from Arthur's father that Arthur will be resuming school shortly. It has, of course, been very stressful for the boy, but he is receiving support from a child psychologist.'

His manner was clipped and formal, but Kate was relieved to be getting some information at last, and felt absurdly grateful.

'Now, I'd like to turn to you and your relationship with the man you know as Hussain.'

Kate looked at him. He had pale-grey eyes behind his steel-rimmed glasses.

'I understand from the information you gave my colleague that this "Hussain" moved into your flat as a lodger in June of last year?'

Kate nodded silently.

'And that you knew little of his background?'

She nodded again. She listened to the emphasis he put on certain details; the story sounded implausible when reduced to such bare outlines.

'A rather risky thing to do, surely, Miss Wilcox Smith? To take a man you knew nothing about into your home, when you have a child?'

'Wilcox,' insisted Kate.

The man ignored her correction. 'We took your laptop and mobile phone from the Hampshire property. A team have been analysing your search history and internet use, as well as all your calls.'

He paused. Kate knew what would come next.

'It seems that you and "Hussain" were in an intimate sexual relationship.'

She raised her head and looked straight at him. 'Yes, we are in love,' she said, with deliberate emphasis. The present tense.

'Despite his wife and family in Bahrain? Despite his illegal immigration status?'

'He was waiting for his case to go through. He was trying to claim asylum – he wanted to use the proper legal process and regularize his position. That's what we were trying to do.'

'As we understand,' he replied drily. 'You don't feel you were used?'

Kate was jolted by this sudden turn in the questioning. 'No, absolutely not. I have complete faith in Hussain. You have made a mistake here. He is not –' and her voice cracked as she tried to say the word – 'not a terrorist. This can all be cleared up.'

'But various things are not clear-cut, are they? Just to make the seriousness of the situation absolutely plain, Miss Wilcox Smith, "Hussain" and Arthur were found in the middle of a high-security army training operation on Salisbury Plain.'

He paused for this detail to register with Kate.

'"Hussain" immediately gave us the information that you were the mother of Arthur and your address in both Lodsbourne and London. He has been helpful. Was he using Arthur as well as you?'

'No, he has shown Art nothing but love and –'

The other man interrupted her brusquely. 'Did he use your laptop?'

Kate hesitated. 'Sometimes.'

'We don't like the search history, Miss Wilcox Smith, to be blunt. It seems that someone on your laptop was very interested in the defence and security industry, and, in particular, in the dealings of a major British company – ZSKa – in the Middle East.' He paused. 'We assume that person was not you. Do you have an interest in Middle Eastern politics and the British security industry?'

He was crafting the interrogation so that the noose tightened slowly. The other man was typing, his head bowed, the woman was watching her closely. Kate felt that her every facial expression was being noted; more people were probably watching her beyond the mirror on the wall.

'To make the matter even more interesting, you are, of course, a shareholder in ZSKa. You inherited a stake earlier this year.'

'I was going to sell the shares,' said Kate miserably.

'Of course,' he replied equably. 'A sum was paid to a British legal firm to take on "Hussain's" case.'

'We gather you were on the anti-war marches in 2003,' said the other police officer, scrolling through something on his screen.

Kate started. Her laptop was only a couple of years old – how had they found that out? 'Everyone was on the anti-war marches in 2003,' she said stiffly. 'There were more than a million people on the streets. It was a disastrous war.'

'Not everyone attended meetings as early as 2001, Miss Wilcox Smith.'

Kate searched her memory, and dimly remembered joining Shirin at a meeting about the invasion of Afghanistan, before they went for a drink; she couldn't have been there for longer than twenty minutes. Was that what he was referring to? Ed had been threatening to leave her. How could these strangers know details of her life that she could barely recall?

'I have a friend who is British-Iranian, and we met for a drink.'

'As we understand. Your friend is currently in custody, also answering questions.'

This was spreading much further and faster than she had feared.

'There is no need for that,' said Kate angrily. 'Shirin has nothing to do with any of this; she has lived in this country for years, and is a British citizen. She is entitled to participate in British democratic politics.'

'Of course, it's just routine. I am sure she will be released shortly,' interjected the woman with oily calm.

'What has happened to Hussain? Where is he?' demanded Kate, incensed by these people in front of her. Ruth put a restraining hand on her arm.

'"Hussain", as you call him, is still being questioned on a range of issues. We have been in touch with international agencies and our partners in the Gulf region.'

The shaking had started again in Kate's leg. Every time they used his name, she could hear the inverted commas. She stared at the woman.

'Partners in the Gulf?' Kate repeated. 'How can you? Have you no idea? These people would murder him simply for having done his duty as a doctor. You can't extradite him: that would mean sending the man to his death. He has a right to asylum.'

She slammed a clenched fist on the table. Ruth's hand was on her arm again.

'I suggest you calm down, Miss Wilcox Smith,' said the woman, unmoved. 'An asylum application is inappropriate in the circumstances. This man passed private information concerning the commercial activities of ZSKa to other organizations here in the UK. We believe you have been targeted and used to gain access to private family property where this documentation was held –'

'No, no!' Kate shouted. 'You're wrong. Hussain is a good man and you are murderers – his blood will be on your hands. You know what will happen to him if he is sent back to Bahrain –'

'Miss Wilcox Smith, please, the Bahraini authorities have offered us guarantees that he will be subject to their usual judicial procedures. Providing he has committed no criminal offence, he has no reason to face prosecution or even custody –'

'This is outrageous hypocrisy,' Kate interrupted, her voice hissing with suppressed fury. 'What are you talking about – usual judicial procedures? Do you think that happens in Bahrain? You are choosing to ignore evidence that is staring you in the face –' She broke off, trying to catch her breath between sobs.

'It's worth reminding you that you have a lot at stake here in the UK,' added the man, unperturbed by Kate's distress.

'Is that some kind of threat?' she demanded.

'We wouldn't describe it in such terms,' he replied, stroking his cheek. 'We would see it as a reminder that your son's welfare has rightly been uppermost in your mind in the last few days. We would point out that his father has made it clear to social services that he will claim custody –'

'Claim custody?' Kate felt like an idiot as she kept repeating their awful comments. Ruth was making notes. Kate's voice trembled as she tried to speak more calmly, 'But his interest in my son is erratic – weeks can go by without a word from him. I'm the one who has brought him up.'

'Well, the desire for more engaged fatherhood and its responsibilities can emerge unexpectedly,' replied the man dismissively. Kate restrained the impulse to slap him across the face. His steady imperiousness enraged her. The man continued, 'And he has made a convincing case that he can offer the boy a stable home in Washington with his new partner. If contested, it will be settled by a family court.'

Losing Art was impossible: she had to do anything – and everything. She sat in silence. They were tapping and scrolling on their laptops, Ruth was scribbling on a document. Kate remembered the conversation when Hussain had warned that all he could offer her was pain, and she had put her finger on his dry lips. She had never imagined this, but he knew about these kinds of unimaginable pain.

'We need as detailed a picture as possible of your relationship, Miss Wilcox Smith. All the names and friends of Hussain that you met. His interests, politics, ideas: everything about him.' The woman's voice was brisk, even impatient now.

Kate was sobbing as she began to talk in broken sentences, and she frequently stopped to wipe her nose on the back of her hand. She felt each word was a betrayal as she told these strangers details of their relationship – and they wanted everything, no matter how trivial. She had to search her memory to relay every conversation to satisfy their relentless questioning. They pounced on some of her answers, and pressed her for the exact phrasing of Hussain's questions about Martin and Phoebe, and the comments he made about Edith's papers. Then they moved on to his research on ZSKa, and his relationship with Fauzia. They were comparing what Kate said with what they had found on the laptop. They asked about Khalid and the visits Hussain made at night for his surgeries. They asked why she had accompanied him, and what she knew about Maryam and Reem. When they asked about his visits to Iran, she tried to dredge up the details of his pilgrimage as a child to Mashhad and his Iranian relatives. Had he ever discussed the politics of Syria or Lebanon? Had he ever mentioned Hezbollah?

'Hezbollah? Lebanon?' she asked, bewildered. 'He never discussed either of them – not a word,' she insisted.

They simply switched to another line of questioning. She felt they didn't believe anything she was saying. They focused on those days of protest at Pearl Roundabout in 2011, asking her to recount where Hussain had been, who he had talked to and what he had done. Then they shifted to his escape to Saudi and his reasons for coming to the UK. Their last question was so absurd, it almost made Kate laugh: did he drink alcohol?

The next day, they started again, covering the same ground. Kate glanced down at Ruth's painted nails beside her, and then she looked at her own, a rime of earth under several from her gardening. She remembered trying to use the nailbrush to clean them before they went to the Hall for dinner. Art had been impatient and called up the stairs, 'Mum, Mum. Hurry *up!*'

'Miss Wilcox Smith?' asked the man, interrupting her thoughts.

Ruth touched her arm, and Kate pulled herself away from the memory. She found it hard to concentrate, on this fourth day of questioning. The sense of betrayal of Hussain made her full heart ache at night, but co-operation was necessary, they emphasized, if she had the best interests of her son at heart.

'He is a doctor. He tried to help people here in London who were too frightened to access healthcare.'

'I see.' There was a pause as the man looked back at his computer. Kate listened to the tapping of the keyboard. All her words were being transcribed, analysed, circulated; she tried to think carefully before she said anything.

'You asked him to come and live with you? Was that sexually motivated?'

Kate was startled. 'What?'

'You heard the question.'

'He needed a room. I am a single parent and have a big mortgage. For several months, we lived entirely separate lives, but, yes, a relationship did develop. We fell in love,' Kate repeated.

The two officers conferred under their breath. 'You had a sexual relationship with this man – the man, you say, was a doctor?'

'Yes, that's what I said,' replied Kate impatiently. She hated the way they managed to make everything she said sound ludicrous.

'The health check we have conducted here indicates you are pregnant. The first trimester. I assume you know.'

Kate stared at him, disbelieving; was this a trap?

'You are at the earliest stages of pregnancy,' repeated the woman. They were all looking at her.

Could it be true? Was that part of why she felt so nauseous?

She looked at Ruth, bewildered. Ruth was saying something to the officer, but Kate's mind was in such a whirl she only caught odd words: 'my client', 'medical attention', 'immediately'. They were arguing. Suddenly, two of the officers stood up, pushing their chairs back noisily. Ruth was insisting on a break in the interrogation. The next moment, Kate was alone with Ruth. Even the policeman at the door had retreated.

Kate stood up, looking around wildly, and began to pace the room, her hands clutching her belly.

'Can this be true?' asked Ruth, incredulous.

Kate shrugged. 'Perhaps,' she whispered.

'You are sure it's Hussain's child? You haven't slept with anyone else?' She stared at Kate with something approaching contempt.

Kate shook her head vigorously, not trusting herself to speak. They had taken samples of urine a couple of days ago as part of a routine check, but this had not occurred to her. She and Hussain had only had unprotected sex two or three times, and she hadn't thought much of it, given her age and her difficulties conceiving Art. She tried to recall when they had had sex, when she might have been ovulating, and why she hadn't realized this possibility before hearing the news from a stranger.

'I've asked for medical attention straight away,' sighed Ruth wearily. 'You'll have to decide about whether to keep it, given the situation.'

Kate was still too shocked to speak. How come this dream had materialized in the midst of the chaos? She felt herself to be the victim of a huge cosmic joke in which she might lose everything, and yet gain the baby she had wanted.

'We will keep it,' she said, emphasizing the plural pronoun. 'We planned a family. We love each other,' she repeated. Ruth raised her eyebrows.

The officers had come back into the room.

'Was this pregnancy planned with "Hussain"?' the woman asked.

Kate nodded.

With an intake of breath, the man said, 'You chose to have a baby with a man who had illegal migration status. Yet you yourself have acknowledged that you were financially struggling as a single parent with your first child.'

Ruth broke in: 'I don't see the relevance of this. It was a personal decision. It's not the role of the anti-terrorism branch to set themselves up as arbiter of a moral decision about a pregnancy.'

'I agree,' said the man, his voice softly sinister. 'I would just suggest that it won't look very good when the family court is assessing custody for your client's son. It was in passing – no relevance to the case.'

'This is blackmail – you are using Arthur to manipulate me,' burst out Kate furiously.

'Not now, not now,' Ruth urged her quietly.

'All we want is full co-operation. Your laptop history doesn't tally with the activities of someone working in a children's charity. You seem to have developed some new interests during your relationship.'

'That's true, but none of them had anything to do with terrorism,' argued Kate.

'That's my job to work out – not yours. Tell me what you know about Khalid. I gather he visited the flat regularly.'

'Not regularly, a few times at most. He came to collect food – I told you we had a charity called Secret Kitchen. You can find the fundraising page on Facebook.'

'Yes, we've found it. We saw that you had several large donations for your "lentil stews" from an anonymous donor.'

'Hardly large – a hundred and fifty pounds, once or twice.'

'Mmm . . . And you say you received cash payments from Hussain as well.'

'Those were for medicines – Hussain was treating people. He was a doctor. He saw a dozen or so people each time, and they came for all kinds of ailments, from broken ankles to pneumonia. He prescribed antibiotics, painkillers. That type of thing. I – we – he ordered medicines online with my credit card and sometimes patients gave him cash if they could afford it and he paid me back. That's not a crime. We were helping people.'

Kate swallowed hard. 'Listen, please, I know none of this was legal – many of these people were illegal, but they were desperate, and it had nothing to do with terrorism. I keep telling you Hussain was a doctor, a skilled surgeon, and he was arrested after the riots in Bahrain, along with lots of other doctors. You can read it all online. He is a political refugee and is trying to get asylum here, and all he was doing was helping other people caught in the same predicament.' She whispered, insistent, 'He is a good man.'

She clenched her fists tight, and hot tears trickled down her cheeks. These men didn't believe her: why couldn't she convince them? Was there anything they knew that she didn't? Could one of those young men in the garage have had links to terrorism? Why were they so interested in Khalid? Had Hussain been careful enough?

As if reading her thoughts, the man asked, 'Did you ever talk to Khalid?'

'No. I left it to Hussain to do the talking.'

'So, a man whom you didn't know came and went to your flat freely.'

'It wasn't that often,' she repeated.

'You work in an office five days a week, yes?'

Kate said nothing, irritated.

'My point is that you were often out. Hussain was in. Khalid was seen visiting the flat – including when your son was there.'

'How do you know?' she asked. 'Who told you that?' But she didn't need him to answer; she remembered how Jackie's eyes had hovered inquisitively over their heavy bags that night they had met her on the stairs.

Later in her cell, Kate lay on her bed and tentatively put her hands on her belly: a baby. A smile even crept across her lips. She felt a short surge of intense happiness at the idea that she was having Hussain's child. Lying in her dirty dress on the thin mattress, she closed her eyes to the glare of the neon light and luxuriated in the idea of her belly growing heavy with the weight of new life. She let her imagination creep as far as the birth, and the bloody flesh bundle fastening on to her breast, its blind red mouth searching for her nipple, and the satisfaction of feeling its urgent tugging as it drank deep, eager for life. 'It' had no pronoun yet, but the cells were rapidly multiplying and taking shape deep inside her.

That night, when Kate couldn't sleep, she asked herself whether she could have misread Hussain. Had she missed anything? She cast her mind back over the last year, trying to recall conversations she had had with him, everything he had told her. Then she asked herself – probing, as if with a scalpel: was there any doubt in her mind? Could the insinuations of her interrogators have any basis? Could Hussain have had terrorist links or sympathies? She remembered his anger and resentment about the role the British had played in Bahrain and Iran, the arms exports, the private-security companies. Did she fully understand his relationship to the Iranian side of his family? Could he have helped someone whom the authorities labelled as suspect or as part of a terrorist organization? Had he given them a meal, medication or information? During one interrogation, the officers had put photos in front of her, asking if she recognized anyone. Many were the grainy blur of CCTV images, and she tried to match them with her memory of people she had seen in Hussain's surgeries. She needed to be helpful, she knew that.

Ruth had told her that the best bet was to stress the romantic relationship: Kate had fallen in love with Hussain, she was naive and out of her depth. Ruth was constructing a story, and although Kate understood why, everything in her protested. She was not out of her depth; on the contrary, no part of her life had had such clarity, conviction and purpose. She had known the complications that loving Hussain entailed – his migration status, Maryam and Reem – yet she had loved him, regardless. They had known he could be detained at any time after his visa ran out, and they lived with that uncertainty, but as the months slipped by and she noticed how careful Hussain was, she had dared to hope that they could live like that until he was on a regular track to claim asylum. He was due to attend what they called a 'screening' in Croydon but a backlog of applications had led to delays. If that had gone according to plan, Ruth had told them he would then be assigned a caseworker and in due course, would have had an asylum interview. They had gathered the witness statements already. Given his politeness and courtesy to everyone he came across, he was simply too clever – and too honourable – not to win through in the end. The path to some future normality might be difficult, but it would emerge; had that been naivety or a touching faith in justice?

★

Felix was the first, and last, to visit. Kate was in a little room, barely big enough for a chair, and the prison officer stood behind. The ledge in front of her was scored with marks; someone had spent their visits scratching the wood. After a few minutes, Felix appeared on the other side of the thick glass partition, smiling encouragingly, but he looked strained. He put his hand on the screen and she put hers up to match it, fingertip to fingertip, only glass between them.

'How are you doing?' He spoke into a dirty grille, and the words were slightly muffled.

'Not so bad – considering,' grimaced Kate. 'Thank you for coming, for everything. How's Art?'

'It's a bit like one of those films,' grinned Felix nervously. 'I had to hand in my phone – finger prints, the lot.'

'I'm high security, apparently. How's Art?' repeated Kate.

Felix straightened his shoulders. 'He's fine. Ed got him from social services, and took him to Ed's parents. I visited and he seems happy enough, given the circumstances.' Kate could tell he was being reassuring rather than honest. 'We have told him that you will be home soon. He gave me a letter, and I've handed it in, so you should get it eventually. Ed didn't think he should come with me.'

'Yes, that's probably right,' said Kate. 'All this might alarm him.' She nodded, holding back tears. 'And Hussain?'

'Ed's a bastard – always has been. Sorry, had to get that off my chest. Hussain? We've heard nothing. Ruth is doing everything she can.'

'He mustn't be deported – it's not safe for him to go back to Bahrain,' said Kate, insistent.

Felix shrugged helplessly.

'I'm sorry, Kate. The whole thing is terrible – they even questioned Fauzia. Her company provided her with a lawyer . . .' Felix's voice trailed away.

Kate put her hand on the wooden ledge in front, feeling the dirty grooves of a pair of initials.

'I'm the one who has to say sorry, Felix.' Her voice was barely audible. 'They questioned Shirin too. I've brought this on everyone.'

'Don't say that – Fauzia is home now.'

'That's a relief at least,' murmured Kate. 'Felix, what happened that night? Has Art said?'

'We didn't want to press him. I think it was difficult . . .' Felix looked uncomfortable. He was holding things back. 'He is very insistent that they didn't take the wrong path, but they got picked up by the army with infrared night-vision equipment. I think they were hiding in a ditch.'

Kate didn't say anything.

'Fauzia thinks the laptop and the Secret Kitchen project won't be helping. There could have been people Hussain helped who –' He didn't finish his sentence. 'She's been doing everything she can on the media front, but it's been insane.'

Kate hadn't thought of that; she had assumed that cases didn't get into the news until there was a charge.

'They're calling Hussain "the garden bomber", and the cottage has featured on all the front pages. It doesn't make any sense, but I suppose a country cottage with a pretty garden makes a good picture; they claim he was hiding in the countryside, gardening.'

Kate forced a bleak laugh. 'He didn't even like gardening. I was the one who did the garden – he said he had servants to do that kind of thing at home. Anything else?'

Felix looked down at his hands in his lap. Kate could see he was twisting his wedding ring.

'They say he manipulated a British woman into a sexual relationship, and used her child as a cover for his movements around London, linking different terrorist cells. It gets lurid. Dotty did some reputation damage limitation for ZSKa and gave an interview to *The Times* claiming the family's hospitality has been abused. Best not to look at it – grisly stuff.'

Kate groaned as she rubbed her creased forehead. 'Ed must be reading all this. It'll help his custody battle.'

'Keep heart, Kate. We're going to get you out. Ruth is good.'

'Thank you for everything – getting the lawyers. Thank Fauzia too.'

Felix paused. 'There are a couple of things I need to ask – that we need to know.'

Kate looked up, his tone had changed. He leaned forward to whisper. 'You still trust Hussain?'

'Yes, completely. He is a good man.' Her sacred mantra.

'But good men can make mistakes – end up with the wrong people. Could he have helped someone who is not all they appear to be?' asked Felix.

'Hussain was clever and careful. He knew what he was dealing with. I trust him completely.' She paused. 'There's something else I need to tell you, Felix – I'm pregnant.' She couldn't bring herself to look at him. She heard him groan.

'You want it? Did he want it? Will you keep it?' he asked in quick succession.

'I want this baby,' she said stubbornly.

Felix put his head in his hands. 'God, Kate, this makes it complicated.'

'Well, that was always the case; a baby doesn't make it more so. I have never loved anyone like I've loved Hussain,' whispered Kate fiercely. 'I was not the naive idiot they make me out to be. The last year with Hussain has been the happiest of my life: we were a family, and, for both Art and me, that was a wonderful revelation. I went into it with my eyes wide open.'

'Kate,' said Felix, looking at her intently, 'you didn't convert, did you? Ed is jumping up and down saying that Hussain tried to convert his son – is that true?'

'No, of course it's not true. Art said prayers once with Hussain, and we agreed that was dangerous, given Ed's ludicrous views. We did talk of doing Ramadan together next year – it would be easier for Hussain. Perhaps one day, before we married, I would have converted. Hussain would have expected that of me as a wife, and I would have been happy to do it. We both agreed that Art could make that decision only when he was an adult.'

Felix looked stunned.

'The point is, Felix, that we loved each other and were serious about trying to find a future together – and for me, the baby was part of that. It's the one part which is coming true and it gives me hope that eventually the rest will come true too. I still have hope.'

He frowned. 'There isn't going to be a fairy-tale ending to this, Kate. The online stories are awful – a Somali man called Ali sometimes came for meals to that garage. He's on a terrorism suspect list.'

'It will be a girl, you know, Felix. A little baby girl,' said Kate doggedly, her jaw set hard. 'That's what I am holding on to: one day she will meet her father, and he will hold her in his arms. We will be a family.'

The prison officer moved over and snapped the handcuffs back on to Kate's wrist for the short walk back to the cell. 'Time's up.'

The intercom had been switched off. Felix had tears in his eyes as he put his fingers on his lips to blow her a kiss.

15

For several days Kate couldn't rally herself. She lay in her bed back at her flat, unable to sleep. She didn't answer the phone. She got up to pee, and once she managed to run herself a bath, and lay in the water until it went cold. Every movement of her limbs required a huge effort, almost more than she could bring herself to achieve. The idea of food made her wretch. She drank black tea after the milk ran out. The silence became a monstrous, terrifying thing. She found herself straining in the night for the soft, sweet sound of a body breathing beside her – Hussain or Art. If she fell into a light doze, she would jerk fully awake when she suddenly remembered – with gut-gripping fear – that neither were with her in the flat, and that she didn't even know where Hussain was. For hours after this abrupt awakening, she would lie staring out of the window at the shadows cast by the street light, her mind full of memories of their bodies. Art's wriggling limbs invariably used to poke her in the ribs or face, but she had never minded those swift stabs of pain, because if he was awake, they were followed by a heartfelt apology and a quick hug. Meanwhile Hussain woke like a cat: a sigh, yawn, his arms stretching above his head. He would turn over and kiss Kate, and stroke her hair. The memory was so powerful that if Kate closed her eyes, she felt she could almost will herself back to that time. But when she reached out her arm or leg, there was only a cold emptiness between the crumpled sheets.

Felix had brought her back from the police station; he stocked up the fridge with some ready-made meals and milk. The police searches had left the flat in a mess and he did his best to tidy things up. Then he sat her down at the table and told her she had to be strong for Art's sake. She had nodded, without following his words. He asked for the number of her boss, and from the room next door Kate heard him explaining that there had been a family emergency and that she would be off work for a few weeks. 'There have been no charges,' he repeated insistently. Her boss had read the story in the papers, Kate realized, with a groan. When he came back, all he said was that she would need a sick note from the doctor.

Then he'd added that he had to go to the States to give a paper at a conference, but would be back in four days. He would call every day to help her get up, and if Kate needed anything, Fauzia could bring it round after work. Art was at Ed's parents, and social services had said it would take a few more days to arrange a contact visit. Felix told her all this slowly, and she nodded her head at the relevant points. She assured him she would be fine. He gave her a hug and then he left, banging the door shut behind him, and she listened to the quiet humming of the old fridge.

She didn't charge her phone: talking required an organization of her thoughts which she couldn't manage. How could she answer questions such as 'Are you all right?' or 'How are you?' Even from people like Fauzia or Shirin. She shrank down deeper under the duvet at the thought, and turned her face to the wall – to where Hussain had once slept. She tried to smell him on the pillowcase and the duvet, but it had been over a week since he had last slept there. She remembered packing the suitcases for their weekend at Lodsbourne – swimming costumes and tennis rackets, walking boots and sun hats. The flat had reverberated with their chatter as they each hunted out essential belongings: books, games, trainers, phones and chargers.

She had been released pending further inquiries. They didn't tell her where Hussain was, but she was told that he was co-operating fully. With Felix, Kate had run through some of the questioning; he explained that Fauzia was worried the police had found the material relating to Edith's papers on the laptop – Hussain had been following up names with activists in Bahrain, and tracking the hire of British ex-police officers by the Bahraini government.

'But Edith died fifteen years ago,' remonstrated Kate. 'It would all have been very dated, it couldn't be important now.'

'It seems the stuff was still sensitive,' said Felix, and, embarrassed, he added, 'Remember that private-security company Dotty hired after the funeral, who questioned us all? Turns out a hard drive of Martin's had gone missing. The police were even involved, and the catering staff were questioned, but the study was locked and there was no sign of a break-in. Dotty is adamant that Hussain stole it – and she has said as much to the police.'

'Fuck. That explains it – all the questioning, their insinuations that I didn't know Hussain as well as they did.' Kate dropped her face into her hands. 'Fuck,' she whispered.

From under the duvet, Kate once heard someone knocking on the door. She wondered if it was Khalid, and knew she should open the door and explain; people might still be coming to Hussain's surgeries and wondering where he was – but then, she thought numbly, in that world it was probably not uncommon for people to disappear without word. Either way, she just lay there, her thoughts disconnected from the effort required to act on them. Several minutes later, the person left and she heard their footsteps receding down the staircase.

After three or four days – she had lost track of time – she forced herself to have a shower and wash her lank hair. She opened a tin of baked beans, but struggled to eat more than a mouthful. She sat on the sofa in an old T-shirt, plugged in her phone to charge, and lay back, listening to the texts pinging in, one after another. The phone finally went quiet, having harvested its crop of texts and missed calls. It sat there, silently waiting for her with all the emotions it would provoke or require. She looked at it, knowing that it entailed a re-engagement with life, agreeing in some way to the struggle: the fight for Art, the impossible fight for Hussain.

Another person was knocking on the door, only this time they were not giving up. She heard a voice calling her name. The knock became more like thumping as the door rattled in its frame.

Felix was shouting: 'Kate, Kate. Open up.' He sounded panicky. 'Kate, Kate, for God's sake, answer the door, or I'll call the police. I'll break the door down.'

Everyone in the block would hear. She grabbed a dressing gown and unlocked the first lock.

'Thank God you're there,' he said through the door. 'You didn't bloody answer the phone. Why the hell not? Kate, I've been so worried about you – why did I ever go to the conference?'

Kate was shaking. He sounded so angry.

'I'm sorry. . .' she stammered, tears running down her face.

'God, you look terrible,' said Felix, visibly shocked.

He hugged her as she sobbed, then led her back to the sofa. 'You don't look as if you have eaten in weeks.' He sat down beside her.

'You have to get dressed, Kate, and then I want you to eat something,' he said as if he were talking to a child. 'Fauzia is doing everything she can to find Hussain.'

The phone started pinging again with incoming texts.

'Do you want me to get that?'

Kate nodded, and Felix picked up the phone.

'See if there is a message from the social worker about Art,' she whispered.

'Blimey, three days of texts . . .' He was scrolling through. 'Half of them from Fauzia and me, a missed call from Phoebe, Shirin, Art's dad. A text from Dotty . . . and texts from someone called Maryam. Three missed calls from Maryam. Who is Maryam?'

Kate reached out to grab the phone. 'Maryam,' she murmured.

Felix stood there, in the centre of the room, waiting. 'Who is Maryam?'

'Hussain's wife,' said Kate flatly.

He sighed heavily. 'I thought the papers were making it up. Art said something about it to me once, and then insisted Hussain was divorced.'

'There's no need for drama, Felix. Of course Hussain is married. He is in his forties.'

'But, Kate, this makes so many things more difficult.'

'It doesn't,' she said fiercely. 'He never lied to me. He made it clear that his first loyalties were to Maryam, and that he loved her. I knew all that. But he also told me that he loved me. At least in Islam you don't have to leave one woman to love another. He told Maryam everything about us.'

Kate was feverishly flicking through the texts. 'I want to know why Maryam is calling. She may know where Hussain is.'

Felix said nothing. He went into the kitchen and she could hear him preparing food. She tried calling Maryam's number, but there was no reply. She had given nothing away in her texts. Just one line repeated three times in the last few days: 'Call me when you can. Salaam. Maryam.'

Felix persuaded Kate to eat some toast and honey while he tidied her bed. Then he suggested she sleep while he made some calls in the sitting room. She lay there listening to his steady, low voice. He had come straight from the airport, and only now was he able to get through to her lawyers, and talk to social services. She couldn't hear the words, only the persistence of his tone. Determined but calm, he was his father's son after all, Kate realized, and was surprised to find it comforting. He was someone who could make things happen, who knew how to make the world work. She listened to the pauses between his comments and guessed the responses.

'Yes, Dotty, I'm at her flat. She's OK – just about – very worried about Art, of course.'

He lowered his voice, and Kate strained to hear.

'As Kate points out, it was ridiculous to imagine Hussain wasn't . . . Good-looking, a highly respected surgeon, Muslim – of course he has a family. Anyway, Dotty, it doesn't matter much, does it?'

A long pause, and Felix's voice was sharp, as if interrupting: 'That's ridiculous. It was obvious – at least to me and Fauzia – that they loved each other. He wasn't using her. Dotty, he's *not* a terrorist.'

Felix had got up and was pacing the room, his voice loud and insistent now. 'The point is to find him: get human-rights groups involved, get the right media coverage if he is in prison or detention here. If he has already been deported to Bahrain, he is in real danger, and only international attention can offer any protection – and that's not much. Ruth believes that they haven't found anything to incriminate him on terror charges. He may have occasionally kept unsavoury company, and done some internet research, but those are not yet crimes. He can't be personally linked to anything more dubious than handing out the odd bowl of lentil soup –'

Kate held her breath.

'Dotty!' Felix was shouting. 'Dotty, listen. No, you listen to me: you have *no* proof he stole that bloody hard drive – it probably got thrown away with old newspapers, or something. The investigators crawled all over that one.'

Kate flinched. He'd kicked something – a kitchen cupboard, perhaps.

'You and your bloody company! Fuck the publicity. Lives are at stake. Is that all that matters to you right now? Your millions and your rich clients with their billions?'

Felix went quiet. When he spoke again, his voice was calmer.

'That's why she needs our help. Her solicitor says the custody case is not looking good. She may even lose access. It will kill her – you must understand that, you're a mother.'

Kate felt a rush of affection. Felix was trying so hard to fight her corner. It would be hopeless, she was sure, but she loved him for trying.

'I'm not sure Dad's guilt gesture after all these years quite wipes the slate clean – Kate has had a hard time of it, and Dad should have done more, in my view.'

When he spoke again, he sounded defeated. 'I'd realized that. I'll explain to her about the cottage. She'll understand – it would be difficult for everyone, I can see. If Sue can pack up her things, I'll bring them up here next weekend.'

*

A week later, Ruth rang Felix to say Ed had got custody, and would be taking Art to Washington, but if no further evidence emerged against Kate, Art would return three times a year for holidays. After much argument, Ruth had managed to get Ed to delay his flight by a few days so that Kate could say goodbye to Art at a family contact centre. She asked Felix to break the news to Kate. Fauzia insisted they both go round to Kate's: this was not news to deliver over the phone. They took food to cook a meal, and overnight things in case she couldn't be left alone and they needed to stay.

Kate was listless and pale, but she took the news of Ed's custody relatively calmly. 'Dazed' was the word Fauzia used later.

'Three times a year?' she repeated, shocked. She had hoped for half-terms. She picked at the food on her plate, despite Fauzia encouraging her to eat for the sake of the baby.

They could hear Kate pacing her room until the small hours. In the morning, she dressed carefully for the visit to the contact centre, with some help from Fauzia, who insisted she wash her hair and put on some blusher. She almost looked her old self, and when Fauzia and Felix congratulated her, she managed a compressed smile.

At the family centre, Art ran down the corridor, throwing himself into Kate's arms, his face strained after the weeks of anxiety. He hugged her tightly and then burst out, 'Mum, we didn't take the wrong path, I promise. I knew the way. We didn't get lost.'

She stroked his hair and whispered reassurances in his ear. She could see the relief; he had been carrying a punishing sense of guilt.

They sat side by side on plastic chairs, and Kate put an arm around him.

'I've missed you,' Art went on. 'I just kept on telling people that Hussain is a kind man. They wouldn't listen, so I had to keep on saying it. Dad says I'll come back to see you often. He says you've agreed to me going to America.'

Kate smiled, her eyes filling with tears. 'You did really well, and it helped. That's why I will see you in the holidays. We can talk on the phone every few days. Daddy and Mona will look after you.' She kept smiling in answer to the questions in Art's eyes, but she felt her heart was breaking.

'You won't be lonely without me?' he asked, his eyes fixed on her face.

'A bit, of course, but we will talk,' she insisted firmly.

Art described to Kate what had happened when he and Hussain had been found in the ditch on the hilltop.

'It was scary – like we were in a film, and these soldiers appeared with their guns pointing at us and their faces covered in mud. It was still a bit dark. They told us to put our hands in the air, and then they took Hussain. He tried to break away when the men separated us, but they grabbed him and he shouted to me that the police would fetch you soon. Then a woman soldier took me in a jeep to a police station. They made me hot chocolate and we watched television, and then special police came from London. Mum, why did they ask so many questions about Hussain? What do they think he has done?'

Kate tried to sound confident, telling him that Hussain was fine. Art looked doubtful but he changed the subject, recounting how his father had taken him to McDonald's and to the cinema. Kate couldn't follow his version of the film plot, but the sound of his voice was like a balm. They were sitting so close she could feel his body against hers – it was the most comforting thing she had felt in a long time.

Later, after Felix had read the social worker's report, he confirmed that Art had explained in detail their family life, saying he had grown to love Hussain because 'he is kind'. He'd told the detective and the social worker the same thing: 'Being a Muslim made people kind.'

*

In the morning when she woke, there was a brief pause before Kate remembered what she had lost, and then it rushed back, crushing her again as if for the first time, shocking and raw. After that, her days were like breathing broken glass: each tiny absence, each reminder of Hussain and Art, hurt. Shoes by the door, dirty laundry waiting to be washed in the basket, a book on the sitting-room table, a toy under the sofa cushions, the spices for Hussain's cooking in the kitchen, the backpack he used for his surgeries, still half full of medicines. It was slightly easier at the office, but concentrating on her work was an effort. She ignored the curious glances and kept her head bowed over her computer screen. The sympathetic gestures were the worst – a Post-it on her screen from a colleague on her return from lunch one day – they undermined her brittle determination that for Art's sake, for the baby's sake, she couldn't lose this job.

*

Still there was no word of Hussain's whereabouts. Fauzia's contacts confirmed that the police were trying to find enough evidence to bring charges on the grounds that he had passed on sensitive commercial information, and individuals under police surveillance had attended his surgeries. Kate had had to give details of the surgeries and their exact locations, and she feared illegal migrants would have been detained as a result. Meanwhile, Fauzia's reporting, her blog and tweets kept the case under close public scrutiny.

It took Ruth several weeks to get an answer out of the police: there would be no charges, and Hussain had been passed on to the immigration authorities. 'Is this good news or bad?' Kate demanded, but Ruth's evasive replies didn't reassure her. The immigration authorities were proving equally uncooperative, and Ruth complained that they were not following the standard procedure. She sounded worried. She was struggling even to find out which detention centre Hussain had been sent to. Every day Kate texted her for updates. Then she called Maryam to explain and discuss any new details on his case. Their conversations were kindly but guarded – they knew they wanted the same thing, and that it both brought them together and kept them apart.

It wasn't until ten days later that Ruth called her at the office to say Hussain was at Harmondsworth, near to Heathrow.

'I'm going there now. I want to see him,' Kate told Ruth with quiet resolve. She was already searching for a map online.

'In that case, I'm coming with you – you may need me,' said Ruth unexpectedly. 'We can meet at Heathrow, and get a taxi. I'll clear the afternoon's meetings, but, Kate, it's unlikely we'll be able to see him at such short notice.'

'I have to try,' said Kate fiercely, gathering up her handbag and her coat. 'And, Ruth, thank you.' She had thought her lawyer had lost patience with her.

She told her boss she had to go home as she was not feeling well – at least that was not a lie. She felt intensely nauseous most days; 'morning' sickness was a misnomer – this time round she felt tired and sick almost continuously. Only by nibbling dry biscuits did she get some relief.

As the tube emerged into daylight in the suburbs of west London, Kate noticed with a start that the sun was shining, and children were playing in the parks. She realized she had not been aware of mundane things like the weather. She had been enveloped in such intense confusion and despair that rain or sunshine had ceased to register, her mind consumed with anxiety about Art and Hussain. Sometimes in the evening, she lay down on the bed she'd shared with Hussain. She looked at the books he had been reading, and the suit she had had dry cleaned after the funeral. His Qur'an and the photo of Maryam and Reem had gone; at least he had them with him – unless the police had taken them when they raided the flat. He had told her that he never went anywhere without them.

She sent a message on WhatsApp to Maryam to say that she was on her way to see Hussain. Kate was almost at Heathrow, and she wished she had had time that day to pack up a few of his things – he would need them – with a photo of her and Art. Still, the most important thing was to see him as soon as possible and explain to him about their baby. She was nervous that he would be angry; she had taken risks, whereas he had made his view very clear. She could feel the anxiety rising. This meeting might be goodbye, and she couldn't bear the idea that it might be overshadowed by anger.

She sat down on a bench at Heathrow to wait for Ruth, and watched the passengers wheeling their suitcases, a steady stream of greetings and farewells enacted in front of her. Every nationality was represented in this flow of people. She thought back to the journeys she and Hussain had made in east London, and how they had come across the migrants, who inhabited the city's edge. Both were part of the same vast circulation of people around the world. Just a crucial paper separated the illegal from the legal, making it a smooth transition for some, and for others, a journey fraught with danger, their lives hanging in the balance – like Hussain. A flight could be a death sentence.

The thought brought that dull, intense fear, and she found herself retching with nausea. She had to run to the cloakroom, reaching the toilet bowl just in time. Afterwards, she stood at the sink and splashed water on her face, and dried it with a tissue. She looked at herself in the mirror under the neon lighting. She dug out some lipstick and foundation, dabbed them on, and brushed her hair: she needed to look as if she was managing. If she did see Hussain, she didn't want him worrying.

Ruth was her usual brisk and efficient self, ushering Kate into a cab and giving the driver directions to the detention centre. Something had softened in her over the last few weeks, and Kate had come to appreciate that her sharpness concealed a surprising warmth. The cab dropped them at the entrance. Kate looked at the barbed wire perimeter fence and bleak brick walls: Hussain was somewhere inside.

'Leave the talking to me, and, whatever you do, keep calm – for Art's sake,' hissed Ruth. 'We don't want him to have to deal with you getting arrested again.'

Kate nodded. If anyone could get her a visit with Hussain, it would be Ruth. The reception area had the anonymous look of any public building – it could have been an A and E department, or a benefits office. The rows of blue plastic seats were bolted to the floor, the walls were pale pink and scuffed, a noticeboard bore alarming posters about HIV, and warnings that anyone abusing the centre's staff would be prosecuted. In the corner was a drinks dispenser, and Ruth bought them both tea in plastic cups. As they sipped, Ruth admitted she had never visited the place before; she usually spoke to clients on the phone.

After about forty-five minutes, Ruth went back to the desk to ask again. Kate watched from her seat, her heart beating wildly. She feared she was about to be sick again – the tension was exacerbating her nausea. She held a tissue to her mouth. She could see that Ruth was getting exasperated. The receptionist shut the glass window that separated her from the public with an irritated bang. Ruth was left standing, mid-speech, but she turned, and, very unexpectedly, gave Kate a wink.

Then she heard her name called by a man standing at another door. She looked back at Ruth, who nodded encouragement. He checked her ID, then beckoned her to follow him. Kate noticed several large bunches of keys hanging from his belt. He stopped and unlocked a door; inside the room, one wall was lined with lockers. Kate put her mobile and Kindle in one, then added her bag after taking out a half-drunk bottle of water. She needed sips to curb the nausea.

'Water in the locker,' said the man, bored. Kate looked puzzled, but his face was impassive and she complied.

He unlocked another door and led her down a corridor. She had to go through a metal detector and a woman patted her down and gestured for her to put her forefinger on a machine reader. Then they went out of a door and in through another – more unlocking required – in an adjacent building. The third locked door gave on to a large empty room. Hussain was sitting at a table, hunched and expectant. He got to his feet as Kate entered. They were alone. He was thinner and paler than she remembered, but he smiled and came over to put his arms around her. She breathed the smell of him deeply as she buried her face in the rough cloth of a shabby – and unfamiliar – sweatshirt; it wasn't his usual scent of aftershave and soap, but an institutionalized smell of unwashed clothing and cooking. Tears were pricking her eyelids. She felt so angry and helpless; Hussain shouldn't be locked up like this.

He moved his head back to look at her, his arms still around her. His eyes were full of sadness. He wiped away her tears with his thumb, and then put it in his mouth, tasting the salt water as he gazed steadily at her. He was gently shaking his head. 'No tears, no tears,' he murmured.

Kate nodded, trying to smile as she cried. She pulled a tissue from her sleeve, and wiped her eyes and cheeks.

'How is Art? Where is he?' asked Hussain. The lines around his mouth and eyes were scored deeper than ever; he had aged.

She tried to keep her voice calm, but inside she could feel the panic welling up; she held his hand tightly as they sat down on plastic chairs.

'He's fine. He is in Washington with his father, but he will come back for holidays – he wants to see you. I talk to him on the phone. He asks about you all the time.'

Hussain rubbed his thumb as he clasped his hands. His knuckles were white. 'You've lost custody?'

Kate nodded.

'I'm not coming back, Kate, I'm sorry. You do know that?'

'No, no – Ruth is fighting for you. Don't say that, keep hope. Fauzia is doing everything she can. And there has been good coverage on social media – your friends from America have been helping,' said Kate desperately.

'They have told me they will put me on a plane in the next couple of days.' He paused, and Kate stared at him. 'This is goodbye, Kate. You managed that, and I didn't think you would. I'm so glad to say goodbye and thank you for everything.'

He was there in front of her but not there; he had already left. He was bracing himself for what might happen. She couldn't stop crying and, at the same time, she could feel the nausea rising in her stomach. How much time did they have? How much time to share this pregnancy: no more than a few minutes out of the nine long months? Beyond that, how much would this baby ever know of its father? Kate wanted to howl like some kind of wild, caged animal. She clenched her jaw tight; Hussain would hate such a loss of control.

'I have something to tell you,' she whispered. 'Something important.'

Hussain leaned towards her, his elbows on his knees.

'I'm carrying our child.'

He didn't say anything. He took her hand, and thoughtfully traced a circle on her palm.

'I'm sorry,' she blurted out. 'I'd stopped taking precautions. I thought I was too old to conceive – I never imagined I would get pregnant. But I'm not sorry: I wanted our child. I never thought it could happen, but I wanted that possibility.'

He put his finger on her lips. 'Shsh, never say sorry for the gift of a child. We have been blessed.'

Kate nodded as her tears fell.

'Promise me one thing.' He paused as he tried to keep control of his faltering voice. 'Whisper this prayer into the baby's right ear: *God is great, there is no God but Allah. Muhammad is the messenger of Allah. Come to prayer.* Can you remember that? Do you need me to repeat it? That is what the father should say to his new baby, and you must do it for me.'

She repeated the words after him slowly.

'If you forget, Shirin can help.'

'I think it's a girl,' added Kate. 'I have an instinct.'

Hussain nodded slowly and then said, 'Perhaps it could be Anas, if it's a boy – after my father – but if you're right and it's a girl, can we call her Labiba?' he suggested with a smile. 'It means "wise", a girl of intellect or quick understanding. Like her mother.'

'And her father,' added Kate, her heart relieved of one burden at least.

The door opened and the man who had brought Kate put his head in. 'Time's up, got to get you back to reception. It's about to close.'

They stood up and held each other. 'Be strong,' Hussain whispered in her ear. 'May Allah's blessings be upon you and our child.'

'We will be together again, one day. I know it,' Kate insisted.

She held his hand tight and he slowly stepped away, his palm slipping from between her fingers. He watched as the man hustled her out of the room, and when she looked back, his eyes were burning in his pale face.

ENGLAND
2018

16

Fauzia watched the thin sliver of moon slowly arc its way across the sky. Kate had followed her out on to her tiny balcony, and, wrapped in a blanket, they sat in the cool night air amongst Kate's plants, unable to sleep. Occasionally one or other would remember one of Reem's characteristics, and the detail suddenly became precious – her quirky sense of humour, Spotify playlists, and love of cake – then there were long stretches of silence as they each wrestled with a sense of guilt and sadness. After an hour, they were chilled, and made herbal tea, retreating to the sitting-room sofa to listen to Arabic pop music, turned down low. As the sound of traffic began to build up in the early morning, Kate turned on the lights, and made coffee. Only then did Fauzia see the pain in her face, how her eyes were puffy and red. When Kate brought the coffee through, her voice was unsteady.

'I may have made mistakes. Some might say Hussain and I should never have fallen in love – but I don't see how one stops something like that. Certainly, I blame myself for what happened that ghastly night – it was so stupid to send him off with Art. I should have gone with them. There were other things too – I should have questioned him about whether it was safe to do the surgeries or distribute food. I encouraged him – we had become so confident that he would get asylum. I was naive and I didn't realize how the police and security services could make up ludicrous allegations. I acknowledge all of this, but . . .'

Her voice had risen to a crescendo, then she came to a halt, her voice shaking with intensity. 'But my faults are trivial compared to ZSKa and how that family has lived off its profits for decades. Reem was trying to do what neither you nor I ever did – we didn't have the courage, energy or determination. She was trying to understand the business, and she believed that its history had a bearing on the death of her father. She was determined to prove it. That's what killed her. They may not have ordered the killing, hired the thugs or whatever, but somehow I'm sure her death was tied up with protecting ZSKa.'

'Maybe you're right,' nodded Fauzia uncomfortably, fiddling with the cuff of her sweatshirt. 'Kate, there's something I've been meaning to tell you for a long time.' She paused and looked away from Kate's attentive face, out of the window, where the sky had lightened. She wanted to be rid, finally, of this nagging sense of guilt and betrayal. She could have stepped in when Hussain was accused of taking the hard drive; she had been cowardly, still so anxious for the family's approval and fearful of how she might lose Felix – as she did in the end anyway. None of that was an excuse, only an explanation. She took a breath.

Kate, hearing the unfamiliar tone in Fauzia's voice, stopped pouring the coffee and turned to look at her, eyebrows raised.

'Do you remember Dotty's private investigators after the funeral?' asked Fauzia, and hesitated, trying to keep her voice steady.

Kate nodded, puzzled.

'And what they found on Hussain's laptop here in the flat –' She was interrupted by a shrill cry.

'There's no loo roll, Mummy,' Labiba called out from the bathroom.

Kate rolled her eyes at Fauzia in mock apology, and called back, 'I'm coming, sweet.' To Fauzia, she added, 'We'll have to talk about this later. I need to get her to school.'

'Of course. It can wait,' agreed Fauzia hurriedly, as she got up to put the bowls and cereal for breakfast on the table.

A few moments later, Labiba appeared in the sitting room, her face still bleary with sleep.

'Fauzia!' she cried with surprised delight, and a grin spread across her small face. She ran across the room to hug her. Fauzia, always uncomfortable around children, was suddenly over-whelmed with emotion; she could feel the tightness of those thin arms, so like her sister's, and the same intensity in the nut-brown eyes now looking up at her. The resemblance between the two sisters was striking, much to their mutual delight.

'Why are you here? Did you stay the night?'

'Fauzia has boyfriend problems,' interjected Kate swiftly.

Labiba's expression was almost comical as she rearranged her features into a suitably sympathetic expression, patting Fauzia's arm gravely before sitting down at the table to pour cereal into a bowl. Kate gestured over her head not to say anything.

'I need a cereal box for school,' Labiba reminded Kate, and she explained to Fauzia how they were going to be making models. Both Kate and Fauzia maintained the semblance of a normal day, but the brightness of their voices was strained. Kate hurried Labiba to finish eating and dress. Once she was in her bright school sweatshirt and trousers, Kate carefully brushed her thick black hair and tied it into two bunches with bright toggles. Fauzia glanced over at the two of them as she made Labiba's sandwiches; Kate was barely listening to the child's breathless and elaborate account of a dispute with a friend the previous day and the intervention of the teacher, but she intermittently managed to make the right sounds to satisfy Labiba. Fauzia had always admired Kate's patient, generous love for her children.

'I'll take her to school on my way to the tube – that will give you some time to get ready for work,' suggested Fauzia.

Kate gratefully agreed, and picked up Labiba's nightdress, folding it absent-mindedly.

'Reem left a drawer of things here when she left for Cambridge.

Some clothes and a few books and papers,' Kate said. 'She couldn't fit everything in her suitcases and the idea was that on one of her visits, she would pick the stuff up, but she never got around to it. She complained that the room in Cambridge had very little storage space, and I told her that until I rented the room out, it could all stay.'

'Can you look through it and call me if you find any notes on her research? Anything that might be relevant.'

Kate nodded. 'And we'll talk later about the other thing you were about to say?'

'Oh, it was nothing – just history,' said Fauzia as she smiled down at Labiba, tugging her sleeve and picking up her satchel. Kate was puzzled, but quickly distracted by Labiba's tight hug goodbye.

Once outside on the street, Fauzia paused briefly to catch her breath; she had stopped herself just in time. Kate relied on her – another betrayal would be too much. The least she could do was carry her guilt in silence. She felt Labiba's warm hand slipping into hers.

'Auntie, are you staying tonight as well?' Labiba asked as they set off to get to school.

Kate and Labiba had agreed that Fauzia was still an aunt after her divorce from Felix, and she was a frequent visitor, often bringing lavish presents. The crisis over Hussain had brought Fauzia and Kate close, and Fauzia had been a reliable source of support when Labiba arrived, and during the long gaps between Art's visits. And it was Fauzia who broke the terrible news to Kate of Hussain's death of multiple, unexplained injuries in prison. Since then she had continued to lobby the All Party Parliamentary Group on Bahrain to make representations on human-rights abuses to the Bahraini government.

Today, she found Labiba's cheerful enthusiasm deeply reassuring. Perhaps this was what children were most useful for: this urge to continue, to keep going forward, growing, learning and exploring, regardless of the tragedy littered around them. Fauzia suddenly realized that you could follow in their wake, their little determined personalities pulling you along, into the future. She would not have her own children now – she was past her fortieth birthday and single. When she had married Felix, she had assumed that they would have a family, but it was without any sense of conviction or enthusiasm. She had watched Kate's struggle – Labiba had been capable of screaming for hours – and shuddered with horror. Now, as they walked, Labiba's chatter was a welcome distraction from what had preoccupied her through the long sleepless hours of the night: that they might never discover the real cause of Reem's death.

Fauzia waved goodbye at the school and watched Labiba's dark hair and bright pink satchel disappear into the throng in the playground. She could feel her phone reverberate: a text from Tim that he was already on the train to London, and asking if they could meet. She texted back the name of a cafe by King's Cross. Afterwards, she could get home to change, and be in work by late morning. She emailed Jack to say she had a doctor's appointment.

*

Fauzia sat by the window watching the commuters hurrying by in the rush hour. She caught a glimpse of herself in a large mirror on the wall, and dug a comb out of her bag, and dragged it quickly through her hair. She was still wearing the tracksuit she had put on late last night. Another text from Tim: his contact believed the police would make an identification of the body by the end of the day. His train was due into King's Cross in ten minutes.

It was a small cafe and every time a man entered, Fauzia looked up expectantly. She had no idea what Tim Blatchford looked like, and while she waited, she tapped in his name and scrolled through some links: a list of articles on state formation in the Gulf and across the Middle East; keynote speaker at a recent conference in Copenhagen on the subject, and two books, one on US–Egypt relations and another on the relationship between Iran and Saudi Arabia. She found a couple of photos of him at a rostrum, gesticulating emphatically. She tried to imagine why a busy man like this, with students to teach and lectures to give, was taking time off to come to London in pursuit of one of his PhD students. Was this what being a conscientious PhD supervisor entailed?

'Fauzia?' asked an elderly man tentatively.

The online photos were out of date, and he was older – certainly late sixties, perhaps in his seventies. But what struck her was that he was shabby – there was no other word for it; his old raincoat was creased and one of the grubby cuffs was ripped. He was carrying a shoulder bag bursting with papers, and he didn't look like he had slept for several days.

They shook hands. 'Good to meet you.'

As he stood at the counter to get coffee, Fauzia looked at his thinning grey hair and stooped shoulders. He looked as if he had been punched: his body sagged.

He sat down opposite her, pushing her coffee across the table.

'We haven't got long, I've got a flight to Cairo this afternoon. I'm seeing a friend in the Foreign Office this morning, and then I'm heading to Heathrow. My visa is still valid.' He took a sip of his double espresso. Fauzia raised her eyebrows. 'The idea came to me in the early hours last night, when I couldn't sleep, and I booked this morning. I was talking to an Egyptian friend yesterday, and he pointed out that the body would not be repatriated to the UK, nor could it go to Bahrain . . . they'll want the body buried straight after the post-mortem . . .'

His voice faltered. Fauzia looked up, and to her astonishment saw that there were tears in his eyes. He cleared his throat noisily and rummaged in his coat pocket for a handkerchief.

'I'm very sorry. I – I couldn't bear the thought of her getting a pauper's burial – of no mourners at her funeral, and no one who had known her to say goodbye, or to make sure she is treated with respect and dignity. I was told that it can be brutal in these police stations – unless there are relatives with some money. I know Reem had family in Bahrain who will come for the burial, but I wanted to get out there as soon as possible. Speed enquiries up – do what I could to help.'

Fauzia nodded slowly; she didn't trust herself to speak. She looked at him, his pale eyes blinking rapidly behind their thick glasses. He was right: Reem deserved better than that. She remembered again her elegant wrists, and shivered at the thought of how easily they could be broken.

'Should I come out as well?'

'Can you get the time off work? You'll need a visa and, given your line of work, it would have to be a press visa. That will probably take a few days, maybe longer.' He had a nervous habit of pushing up the bridge of his glasses with his forefinger.

'It has to be a burial – cremation is not allowed – and I've been looking online,' he went on. 'The Latin Cemetery is probably the best option. I'm hoping the embassy will help on some of the practicalities, but I've not had much luck with them on the phone so far. Perhaps if I'm out there, standing in front of them, they will make a bit more of an effort. They keep insisting she was not a British national, and that it's nothing to do with them.'

He was trying to be matter-of-fact and practical, but the calm voice she had heard on the phone in the last couple of days had disappeared, and in its place was a man Fauzia could only describe as desperate. Why did he care so much? Perhaps the lack of sleep was not helping her to see clearly; she was confused.

'Did you ever read her MA thesis? She told me you had helped her with it.'

Fauzia shook her head. 'She offered to send it, but somehow

I never chased her up. I was busy at work, I got promoted.'

Listening to herself, she realized how lame her excuse sounded. The truth was that she had been scared of what Reem might have found out. She wanted nothing more to do with the Wilcox Smith family or their damned business. After the divorce came through, she decided to draw a line under her entanglement with them. The family had a way of drawing people in and subtly corrupting them, she had concluded; not the blatant kind of corruption which grabbed headlines and provoked government inquiries – although she suspected there might be some of that carefully hidden – but the kind of corruption which established a hierarchy of people who mattered and those who didn't. The judgements were instant and irrevocable, and were based on utility and power: a person had to be useful, decorative or entertaining. In the early days of her relationship with Felix, she had matched up: she was pretty enough to be decorative, successful enough to be an asset at their lunches. She had been stupid enough to be flattered, without registering how entirely dispensable she was; when she and Felix broke up, Dotty had made that very clear. She had warned Fauzia off a claim on Felix's family money with the threat of expensive divorce lawyers. Fauzia had thrown herself into long shifts at work, and a couple of affairs.

She looked over at this odd man. Did he know about the hard drive, she wondered. Did he know who had given it to Reem?

'I don't know how she had managed to piece it together,' he added, as if reading her thoughts. 'No one had been able to establish the involvement of ZSKa in arranging the Budaiya deal –'

'Was that the huge contract for Harrier jump jets and Chinook helicopters in the late 1970s?'

'The deal was a bit later, actually, early 1984, after the Falklands. But, yes, that's the one. Freedom of Information requests have been useless – the official documents are redacted. When I read Reem's MA thesis, I urged her to talk to a journalist, and she said she had tried, but it was too long ago, no one would be interested. I argued that the company was still in business, many of the individuals involved were still alive. Moreover, it set a pattern for brokering British arms sales in the Middle East which is evident today. She agreed, but said she needed more recent evidence to get media interest – I'm afraid that's what she was doing in Eygpt. Did she ever talk to you about it?'

Fauzia winced. 'I couldn't get my editor interested.'

'Her PhD research was even more important. She was unearthing new information about a big contract in the early 2000s. It was as if she had a source somewhere who was feeding her new information all the time. We had a plan to write a book together.'

Fauzia could feel her leg jigging uncontrollably under the table. She put a hand on it to hold it down. Tim replaced his empty cup on the saucer, and picked up the sachet of sugar and fiddled with it, working its contents from one end to the other. She watched his pale fingers, thinking how she hadn't really known Reem. Beneath the warmth and the polite charm, she had been a very secret person. Someone who knew to keep their thoughts private. Reem had learned young that few people could be trusted, and that the world was full of unexpected danger. She had been fifteen in the 2011 riots, and she had made references to how those events had transformed her family's life – how she and her mother had struggled after her father's arrest, and then his disappearance abroad. She never talked about the last months of his life, when her mother tried to get access to him in prison. She had never talked to Fauzia about Tim Blatchford: how much had Reem really confided in her?

'Her belongings in the hotel room in Cairo might give us clues. Hopefully, her laptop will be still there. I'm hoping I'll get to them before anyone else does; that's why I'm in such a hurry. If you can think of anything that might be relevant, *anything*, let me know.' He pushed back his chair and stood up. 'I've got to get going. Keep in touch. Call me if you decide to come out.'

As the two of them stood outside the coffee shop, he shook Fauzia's hand again with an hesitant formality. 'This is not just about an unfinished book project. I developed a very deep regard for Reem –' He broke off, his voice hoarse, and looked away. 'She is a remarkable young woman – one of the most admirable people I have ever met. The death of her father spurred her on. I've not seen that single-mindedness in a person before; she was quite fearless, as if she had already lost everything of importance that there was to lose.'

'That was only half true – her father was dead, but her mother will get out one day,' protested Fauzia vehemently. 'She has a half-sister here in the UK, grandparents and cousins in Bahrain. She has a lot to live for –' Fauzia broke off, fighting to keep her panic down, reluctant to let go of the present tense. 'She was on the brink of creating a life for herself here. I had such hopes.'

'But she was prepared to risk all that. How many of us in our comfortable lives do that?' He shifted his weight from one foot to the other, and added, so quietly that Fauzia almost missed it, 'I've never done that in either my professional or my private life. I couldn't help admiring what I had never witnessed before.'

Fauzia stared at him, startled by his strange intensity. He gave a small, sad smile. 'It can happen you know – even at my age. My wife died some time ago. It was unrequited, it was not even known; she didn't need the burden of that. I was never other than completely professional –'

Tears were rolling down his cheeks, and he turned to hurry down the street.

*

'Anything that might help,' Fauzia repeated to herself as she began walking back to her flat. That meant telling him about the hard drive: who had given it to Reem, and, before that, who had given it to Hussain. Fauzia felt sick, and she turned into a side alley, and, leaning against the glossy marble wall of the office block, felt her stomach heave with the coffee. This was how her stomach responded to anxiety. For five years, she had lived with the secret of the hard drive, and the fierce shame it provoked in her. She had begun to think she might never need to tell anyone what had happened.

The hard drive had contributed to the success of Reem's MA thesis, which won her the place at Cambridge, that much Fauzia understood. She knew the thesis had focused on security deals in the 1970s – stuff for historians, not journalists – but when Reem tried to explain to her, Fauzia hadn't followed all the details. What mattered was that the information that had destroyed the life of Reem's father had given Reem the chance of a new life – or so Fauzia reasoned with herself in the early hours when she couldn't sleep. She'd told her – and Reem later agreed – that there was material on the hard drive which British intelligence might regard as sensitive. She didn't explain how she knew that, nor how it had damaged Hussain's asylum application, and no doubt contributed to his death in detention back in Bahrain. By the time he was deported, he knew things which both the British and the Bahraini governments wanted kept quiet.

What those things were, she still didn't exactly understand. The hard drive had not provided direct evidence to prove that ZSKa brokered arms deals. In that fateful moment on the day of the funeral, when she'd seen that the door to Martin's study was open, she had imagined a possible scoop which could win her awards and propel her journalistic career out of the doldrums, establishing her as an investigative reporter. She would keep her source hidden, and she didn't think through the implications for her relations with her in-laws, beyond a vague belief that Felix would be on her side in the end.

But after Hussain helped her get access to the hard drive, Fauzia had been disappointed. When she impatiently scanned through the hundreds of emails, files and accounts, it was family stuff: business-class flights, hire of private limousines abroad – Paris, New York, Dubai, Milan and Cairo – huge shopping bills at places like Prada and Gucci, and enormous hotel bills. This was not the material for a scoop, despite her surprise at the scale of the Wilcox Smiths' wealth. What most people saw was the worn, exquisite taste of Lodsbourne, and Phoebe pottering around in her old cardigans and muddy Wellingtons, but it appeared the family had another life where they indulged their appetites for glamour and luxury. Dotty was not the only one; there were regular bills of up to £50,000 at the Paris Ritz, and hundreds of thousands in private school fees – could Dotty really have spent that much on her children's education? Then came the shock of Hussain and Kate's arrest, and Fauzia focused all her efforts on blogging in support of Hussain. After he was deported, an element of fear, combined with little spare time, meant she never went back to the figures to make more sense of them.

But the issue resurfaced in her furious rows with Felix as their marriage began to disintegrate. She would accuse his family of hypocrisy and absurd extravagance and interrogate him on the business. What exactly did it do? Who were the sinister characters from Russia, Ukraine and the Middle East who came to the shooting parties? What did ZSKa's tailor-made 'security consultancy' or 'communications expertise' entail for such clients? He was defensive, insisting that he knew no more than her, but Fauzia didn't believe him. The subject made him acutely uncomfortable; as she frequently pointed out, the business had enabled his parents to buy him a handsome flat off Ladbroke Grove when he was still in his twenties. As for fancy holidays and shopping sprees, he denied it all and said she was mad. She couldn't bear the dishonesty, the way he was prepared to look the other way. Felix made much of his own antagonism towards his father, but in their bitter arguments, Fauzia accused him of doing nothing more than posturing. He was as implicated as the rest of them.

She never confessed to him that she had stolen the hard drive, that she had passed it on to Hussain, who had made her a copy.

*

The house had been relatively quiet early on the morning of the funeral. Dotty was obsessed with compost and burying the body, and Phoebe preoccupied with flowers. Kate was in the kitchen, and Sue had been at the back of the house helping the catering-company trucks to set up. Fauzia was passing the door to Martin's study. It was the first time she had seen it open on her many visits to the house over the preceding four years. Weak sunlight was breaking through the heavy grey snow clouds and splashed a pale light on the handsome desk. Large pots of beautiful orchids were in bloom on the window ledge, and a handsome Persian rug was spread in front of the fireplace. She slipped in, shutting the door behind her, and walked around the room, scanning the titles on the bookshelves. She ran a finger along the fine grooves of the marble mantelpiece, with its carved cherubs at play. It was laden with photographs of the family: Phoebe as a young woman in a flamboyant jumpsuit, her hair back combed and her eyelids heavy with make-up, and in the background the sharp shadows and palm trees of a hot country. A photo of Phoebe with Dotty as a toddler and Felix as a baby by a swimming pool. Photos of dogs, Dotty's wedding day, the christenings of her children in the church where they were about to have Martin's funeral. Fauzia and Felix at the registry office in London.

Someone passed the window, and Fauzia shrank back against

the wall. It was Dotty, but she was intent on her task of organizing the day, and she did not glance in. Fauzia needed to be quick. She turned to the desk: someone had removed the desk-top computer already, and leads were scattered across its tooled leather surface. She tried the drawers – all locked. She sat down in the comfortable leather swivel chair and absent-mindedly swung one way, then the other. Somewhere in here, she was sure there was something interesting. She cast her eyes over the pictures on the walls, the sculptures on a side table, the scattering of magazines and a newspaper dated from a month ago, before Martin fell ill.

Then her eye fell on a pile of papers on the floor by the desk, and as she knelt down to look through them, she saw a hard drive. It had fallen – perhaps when the computer was removed – and had been concealed by the papers. She didn't stop to think; she picked it up and tucked it inside the old copy of the *Financial Times*. She could hear Dotty calling her name. She needed to hurry. She opened the door cautiously and the corridor was clear, but just as she slipped out, Kate appeared at the foot of the stairs. For an instant the two women confronted each other in the dimly lit space.

'Just looking for a hymnal,' lied Fauzia, impressed by the plausibility of her excuse. 'But no luck. Martin was obviously not the religious type.'

'There are a couple in the kitchen,' Kate replied, and it looked as if she was about to say something else, but Fauzia didn't give her a chance.

'Good. Just need to do my make-up, will be back down in a second.'

Only when she was in the bathroom and had locked the door did she realize that her heart was pounding. It was not in Kate's nature to be suspicious. The only risk was if Kate told Dotty that Fauzia had been in Martin's study. It was the one place in the house which had always been strictly out of bounds. She looked in the mirror, added some eyeliner and fresh lipstick, and after a few deep breaths, when the landing outside sounded quiet, she crept into her bedroom to tuck the hard drive into her handbag. She didn't want questions from Felix.

A few days after the funeral, she stayed late at work trying to access the hard drive with the help of a friend who regularly boasted of her hacking skills, but with no success. She needed Martin's password. It was fanciful, she realized, that someone whose company provided cybersecurity, would be careless with his own. She had reached a dead end. And then Hussain began to ask questions, and offered to help.

*

Back at her flat, Fauzia felt weak and nauseous. She poured a glass of water from the filter jug in the fridge and sat down on her sofa, hoping she would feel better. She watched an aeroplane vapour trail fade and disintegrate into wisps of white. A year ago she had vomited like this, in the early hours of the morning after she'd had a dream in which Reem was arrested and the police found the hard drive in her possession. It was what had happened to Reem's father, and that had been equally unlikely at the time. The guilt would be intolerable. She had called Reem early that morning, waking her up and making her promise, despite her sleepy confusion, to destroy the hard drive. While they talked, Fauzia trawled YouTube for methods on how to destroy it – cooking it in the microwave, soaking it in hydrochloric acid – and urged Reem to use the simplest: a hammer and screwdriver. She had wanted to stay on the phone to hear the smash of the little plastic box. Reem had been reassuring but firm; she didn't have a hammer or a screwdriver, but said she would borrow them that morning, and once the box was in small, indecipherable pieces, she would put it in a public bin. Finally satisfied, Fauzia had rung off and gone back to sleep. In the year since, Fauzia believed the saga was finally over. She hadn't vomited again, and she had been able to reduce her medication. Only now there was Tim Blatchford, and his word: *anything*.

She pushed the thought away. She would call Kate and tell her about the strange encounter with the old professor. She had a quick shower, then, still wrapped in a bath towel, she put the phone on speaker, and described the meeting.

'He asked us to tell him anything that might be relevant. Anything,' she concluded.

'I didn't get to work – I couldn't face it, I called in sick,' admitted Kate. 'Then I looked through Reem's box. It was mostly clothes, and just seeing them – a couple of scarves, a pair of jeans she used to wear – was hard. It felt like she might come through the door any moment and ask me why I was rifling through her belongings.' Fauzia knew Kate had been crying from the thickness of her voice. 'There were a couple of notebooks at the bottom. I flicked through them – they didn't seem to offer much – a few significant dates in Anglo-Bahraini relations. Some figures and lots of initials. The other notebook was full of her handwriting, but it was in Arabic.' Fauzia adjusted her towel, she was getting cold. Kate added, 'There was something else I remembered – it was stupid, I should have thought of it earlier. You said Phoebe mentioned on the phone that Reem had met a Lebanese businessman in Cairo who had been to Lodsbourne. This Cambridge professor needs the name, and if Phoebe doesn't remember, it will be in the visitors' book. It's kept in Martin's study.'

'You're right – he could have been one of the last people to see Reem alive.'

The visitors' book was always brought out at the end of a visit and placed on the hall table with an old fountain pen which used to belong to Martin's father. Either Phoebe or Martin would badger their guests to sign. It was a leather-bound book of thick, creamy cartridge paper, with marbled Venetian endpapers. Fauzia had once admired the cover, with LODSBOURNE tooled in gold, and Phoebe had explained how they had the books custom made by a bookbinder in Clerkenwell. Once when Fauzia was signing it, she had been left alone briefly, and rifled through the pages – she'd spotted the name of a former prime minister sprawled across a full page. After it had been signed by guests, it was always whisked away, back to Martin's study.

Fauzia began to dress as they talked.

'The two of us could go down to Lodsbourne. Tell Phoebe about Reem, and then persuade her to let us look through the visitors' book – if she really can't remember the name.' Kate had been thinking it through. 'My hunch is that she will know. Phoebe has an excellent memory.'

'Go down to Lodsbourne? When? I've got work.'

Kate was emphatic. 'I think Blatchford needs all the help we can give him. It's the least we can do for Reem.' Alongside her quiet gentleness, she was occasionally capable of a steely resolve; it was how Kate had got through those tumultuous times back in 2013. 'If we leave now – there's a train at 11.30 – we can be back by the time I need to pick up Labiba from the after-school club.'

'What if Phoebe isn't in?'

'I've called Sue already, and she said Phoebe is at home all day. I also want to talk to Sue. Whenever Reem stayed at Lodsbourne, she would visit her in the afternoon to talk about the family. Reem was very clever about things like that; she knew that there wasn't much in the Wilcox Smith family that Sue didn't know.'

'I'll call in sick, I'm coming. Meet you at Waterloo.'

*

It was several years since Fauzia had last been to Lodsbourne, and for Kate it had been even longer, but little had changed on the lane from the station down to the estate. When Fauzia had visited for the first time as Felix's new girlfriend, it had been this time of year: the same bleak, bare branches and sodden undergrowth. She had never understood the appeal of the English countryside; the shallow contours, and narrow colour range of muted greens, grey and brown. Only on a few rare days when the sun actually shone was the dullness replaced by buoyant colour. Then the flowers were pretty at Lodsbourne, and the lawns perfect. The rest of the time, winters were damp and muddy, and most summer days were overcast, with a maddening weight of grey cloud. Felix had liked weekends away in country hotels, but it was cities which made Fauzia's blood run, and it had been a recurrent source of friction: Barcelona or Burford for their anniversary? She had lived in London since she was a tiny child and its raucous rhythms of sirens and traffic made her spirits rise.

'We both fell for this family, didn't we?' said Kate, scuffling the dead leaves at the edge of the road, interrupting Fauzia's train of thought. 'Above all, I loved their sense of ease – as if they had never had reason to question who they were, or the place they took in the world.'

Fauzia took Kate's arm and squeezed it. The first time she'd met Kate was a hot weekend in June, and she'd had a habit of shrinking from every conversation. Art must have been about ten. It was before Hussain, and before Phoebe and Martin offered her that damp, dilapidated cottage. Fauzia had never seen its appeal – the place was too dark for her taste – but Felix insisted it was kind of his parents. Fauzia suspected it was a way to ensure Kate never raised objections to the uneven fortunes of the two branches of the family. She had pieced together the story from some of Sue's guarded comments about the way the brothers had been pitted against each other in a race to inherit that ended up warping both their lives. Ever since, Fauzia had seen the malevolent legacy of Martin's father implicit in every part of Lodsbourne's beauty.

But Kate was right, she had been seduced by Felix's charm and

Phoebe's beauty. She had been excited by Martin's reputation, and his intimacy with power. She had loved the dinners at the House of Lords or at his club, and how her father-in-law was greeted with respect. As she walked alongside him, she noted a nod to a senior politician, or a quick exchange with another household name. It satisfied that deep craving to be part of it all, to belong to this odd, damp country. She edged round the puddles – she didn't want to get her trainers dirty. She was unsure whether she had been right to accompany Kate. Phoebe had been gracious about the divorce, and had even insisted they stay in touch, but Fauzia knew that, deep down, she blamed her daughter-in-law for not holding on more tightly to her adored son. It had all been so different at the beginning.

★

Phoebe showed little surprise at seeing her unexpected guests on the doorstep. Sue must have told her they were on their way. She looked older, and for the first time that Fauzia had ever seen, she wore no make-up. Her hair was awry, one comb had slipped, releasing strands of her white hair. In place of the familiar self-assurance was vulnerability; she must now be well into her seventies.

'I'm so sorry to hear about Reem,' said Phoebe, her back to them as she measured out the coffee. Kate and Fauzia's eyes met; they heard the tremor in her voice.

She caught their exchange of looks as she turned to put the cups on the table.

'It's tragic. She was a splendid young woman, and so full of life and warmth. I loved her visits. She was so interested in everything. Is there any suggestion as to how she was killed?'

Kate shook her head. 'Hit by a car, according to the police, but it's too early to be sure. There will be a post-mortem.' Her eyes were still red and swollen from crying.

'And Labiba? Is she all right?'

'She doesn't know anything.'

'What a horrible business. And there's a mother in Bahrain?' said Phoebe. 'Is there any way of getting news through to her?'

'She's still in prison. The next of kin are probably her grandparents – her Cambridge PhD supervisor expects the identification will be confirmed soon. He's flying to Cairo this afternoon.'

Phoebe pulled herself up straight and sighed, her lips tightly pressed. 'I appreciate you both coming down to give me the news in person. Sue said you were on your way, and sadly we guessed you had bad news.'

There was silence. All three felt the loss of Reem keenly, each mourning their very different relationship with her. The only sounds were the ticking of the clock, the hum of the fridge and the heavy breathing of the dogs in their basket. Outside, just by the window, a blackbird began suddenly to sing. The sound was jarring, and Fauzia longed for a strong whisky. It was unlikely Phoebe would offer, but she knew where the decanter was kept, on a tray in the drawing room. She tried to think of a way to extricate herself from the kitchen, but Kate had begun to talk.

'Phoebe,' she began hesitantly. 'Reem's professor at Cambridge has asked us if there is anything we might know that would help him piece together what happened in Cairo – her movements, and why she was found in a shabby suburb of the city.'

Phoebe looked surprised. 'What could I know?'

Fauzia continued, trying to keep her voice level. Of all the people in the room, Phoebe was the best informed – she was, as Reem had established in a Companies' House search, a director of ZSKa – but her appearance of innocence was flawless. 'I think you mentioned that she called you? You may have been the last person we know to have spoken to her. Can you remember any detail of the conversation, however small? It could help.'

Phoebe looked down at her worn hands and their silver rings.

When she raised her eyes, Fauzia detected an agitation in her face that she had only once seen before, when Martin was dying.

'Well, she talked about visiting the pyramids, and asked if I remembered the Gayer-Anderson museum,' she began slowly. 'When she was here last summer, we had long conversations about my Iranian textile collection, so she wanted to tell me about the Persian Kashan on the main stairs. It's a style of carpet with a diamond-shaped medallion in the middle of the Shah Abbas field –' She could see their impatience, and switched tack, but Fauzia noticed she was struggling to focus. 'Reem told me about some of the meals she had had – we had a very good meal in a Lebanese restaurant in Mayfair only a few weeks ago. So she was comparing it with the food in Cairo –'

Kate interjected gently, 'And you mentioned to Fauzia her meeting someone you knew?'

Phoebe frowned. 'No, I don't think so. Did I?'

'Yes,' said Fauzia firmly. 'You said Reem had met a Lebanese businessman who had been to Lodsbourne for a shooting party. Can you remember his name?'

'I don't remember. It's my memory – it's shocking these days,' said Phoebe, pulling her cardigan around her shoulders. 'You must stay for a quick lunch. I'm sure Sue can rustle up some soup and salad.'

'Even if you have forgotten Reem talking about this, perhaps you can remember a Lebanese guest who came to a shooting party?' Kate pressed.

Phoebe bristled. 'I wasn't involved in the shooting parties after Martin died. Dotty took all that on. We are talking about parties which happened more than six years ago, and we had dozens of guests. I can't be expected to remember the names of all those people.'

'Perhaps the visitors' book would help jog your memory?' Fauzia said.

Phoebe turned to stroke one of her pointers, who had come to nuzzle her knee.

'Can we go through the visitors' book?' asked Kate bluntly.

Phoebe looked from one to the other. 'Is this some kind of ambush? I don't think Dotty would approve.'

'Well, she's not here,' said Fauzia crisply.

Kate interrupted, her tone deliberately gentle, 'No, it's not an ambush, but we did hope that if both of us came, we might persuade you to help. We both want to know how Reem died. The tiniest thing might help.'

Phoebe got up abruptly. The colour had drained from her face. 'The dogs need a walk, and the rain has eased. Perhaps you could help Sue with lunch. She'll be here in a minute.' She raised her hands, as if in a gesture to stop them. 'I'll think it over – see if I can remember anything that might be useful for poor Reem.'

As she ushered the dogs out of the kitchen, Fauzia turned to Kate and shrugged, annoyed. She watched Phoebe, in her long raincoat, head across the lawns. She walked slowly, the dogs circling around her, before they raced away to the edge of the grass where the woods began, and then doubled back. The first daffodils were coming out, offering small splashes of colour. For the first time, Fauzia noticed that the gravel on the drive looked unkempt. It had not been weeded, and the low box hedge which lined the stone path had died. Something was slipping; the garden used to be immaculately maintained.

'One could almost feel sorry for her,' said Kate coming up behind her. 'Her empire is coming to an end.'

'As Phoebe says, Reem was so interested in everything,' said Sue, as she set down carrots and onions on the table for Fauzia and Kate to chop. 'She would come over to the cottage in the afternoon – or help me prepare vegetables in the morning for lunch. She always asked questions. She wanted to know what it had been like to grow up on the estate. I was ten when my parents began working for Martin in 1972. That's when he took on the estate, after his father went into a care home, and then he did the major renovations. She asked so many questions about it all. I told her that no one lived at the house for two or three years, because the place was a building site: scaffolding and diggers. They redid the roof, landscaped the gardens, dug the swimming pool, put in the kitchen. As a child, it was fascinating to watch the workmen and see it slowly take shape. The house was transformed. Martin was doing well in business by then, and money was no object. Phoebe would come back every few months and stay in the hotel down the road. Sometimes she came with the children, and the nanny looked after them in the garden while she turned her attention to the renovations. I remember, because she used to give me a pound if I helped the nanny keep the children entertained – that was a lot of money in those days.'

Sue laughed and straightened, pushing her hair back from her forehead with the back of her wrist. There was a quick catch of breath as if she had suddenly remembered the reason for their visit. 'I always felt Reem knew what she wanted. It wasn't idle curiosity. She needed all this family history for some reason.' Sue looked uncomfortable, and she lowered her voice. 'Of course, over the years I've had my own questions about what Martin's work was and where all the money came from. It certainly wasn't from his family – his father was almost bankrupt when he died. I've asked myself who their guests were at the fancy lunches and shooting parties, and why Phoebe got caterers in. But it was never my business or Bill's to pry. Sometimes, when he was driving them up on to the hills for the shoot, Bill overheard conversations, but he's not a man to repeat gossip. I don't think even Reem got far with him, although she tried. She would ask him about the estate and the farm, but he never took to her. He doesn't like women who ask questions.'

'When Reem called Phoebe last week, she mentioned a

Lebanese man she had met. We think his name is in the visitors' book,' said Fauzia.

Sue sidestepped the comment. 'A lot of Reem's questions were about the farm. When had they bought it? How much had it cost? That kind of thing. I explained it was a wedding present for Dotty. They wanted to protect the view, because there had been some question of building affordable housing on the land. They've done a grand job with it, I'll say that. It's won these environmental awards since they abandoned the farming. Bill thinks it looks a mess, but the butterflies, beetles and so forth have come back – there was an article about it in the parish magazine.'

'When did Dotty get married?' asked Fauzia, suddenly curious.

'Must have been about 1998. The farm cost millions, I know that,' interjected Kate. She had finished chopping the vegetables. 'I need some air. Let's walk down to the woods. We might catch Phoebe on her way back.'

Sue looked relieved.

They walked across the lawn to the gate which led on to the downs, and Fauzia felt her mobile vibrate in her pocket. It was a text from Tim: 'Foreign Office notified. Identification confirmed from dental records. Next of kin informed.'

'Reem's dead,' whispered Fauzia.

Kate nodded, her eyes filling again with tears.

Fauzia put her arms round her and under the bare branches of the copper beech, they hugged. 'This shouldn't have happened,' said Fauzia bitterly. 'It didn't need to happen. If Reem had understood the risks . . . she was too young to understand.'

Phoebe saw them on her way back to the house from her walk, and changed direction to meet them. The ground here was scattered with crocuses and wood anemone. Small buds of green were breaking out on the bushes.

'You've heard?' asked Phoebe. Fauzia nodded.

They walked on in silence before Phoebe continued,

'Nadim – his name was Nadim. A tall plump man with a beard, if I remember right. He worked with Martin in the nineties. He visited several times after that. Perhaps the last time was in 2010 or 2011. I remember he came to Martin's funeral, which was good of him. Flew in specially from Beirut, I was told. We can look at the visitors' book if you want. The surname might be there – although some of Martin's guests preferred initials or first names only. I hope it's useful.'

Fauzia and Kate walked back to the house with Phoebe, past the empty swimming pool where the leaves lay rotting, uncleared.

'Poor Reem, this terrible tragedy reminds me of someone I once knew – another brilliant life cut short. My life might have been very different if he had lived,' she said on the doorstep, but pre-empted any questions by turning to call the dogs. As she opened the door, she muttered as if to herself, 'Dotty will never forgive me.'

17

Fauzia heard the phone vibrate on her bedside table through her confused dreams. As she picked it up to answer, she saw the time, just past eleven – 1 a.m. in Cairo. After the previous sleepless night, she had taken a couple of sleeping tablets and gone to bed early.

'I'm sorry if I woke you,' said Tim. He sounded agitated.

Fauzia propped herself up on her pillows, immediately awake.

'I went straight from the airport to Reem's hotel room this evening.' There was a pause and Fauzia could hear the muffled sound of traffic. She remembered the roar of Cairo, the car horns, and how the noise barely paused at night. 'I had to bribe the night manager. I wasn't the first – someone else had already been.'

Fauzia misunderstood; she thought he meant a cleaner.

'Someone had been through her belongings. Clothes and papers were scattered all over the room, and her laptop was gone. They had pulled out her suitcase, opened drawers, ripped off the bedding.' She could hear his irregular breathing.

'Fauzia, it was the work of a very determined person, who was looking for something. It wasn't a chance burglary – a pair of pearl and gold earrings was lying on a bedside table and they hadn't bothered to take them.'

Fauzia rubbed her forehead with the heel of her hand. 'Did you ask the hotel staff?'

'The night manager said he knew nothing. When I gave him some money, he still said he knew nothing, but to come back in the daytime and ask for a cleaner called Abdul. I'll go in the morning, after I've had some sleep.'

For the first time, Fauzia felt frightened. She glanced around her familiar flat, her bedroom door open on to the corridor. She listened to the quiet of the block at this time of night, when the soft thuds and movement in the floors above and below eased. She didn't know her neighbours, beyond an occasional encounter in the lift, but they were there, within reach of a shout or a scream.

'Fauzia? Are you still there?'

The connection between her and Tim across a continent and a sea felt very delicate; bad reception could cut them off at any point, and someone could be listening in to Tim's phone. Was anywhere safe? She thought of Reem knowing all this, feeling this fear and yet making her way to Heathrow, sitting at the departure gate, boarding the plane; she would have done up her seatbelt, sat back, and perhaps, if it was clear, she might have looked down on the muddy fields of southern England – perhaps even on Lodsbourne itself – as the plane circled round before heading in the direction of North Africa. She had been a brave woman.

'Yes, I'm still here.'

'It makes me think this wasn't just police thugs. It's too well organized.'

'Tim, we got the name of the person Reem saw in Cairo – Nadim Ayoub. He went to shooting parties organized by Martin Wilcox Smith. It may be relevant.'

As she said this, Fauzia suddenly questioned whether Tim could be trusted – and then dismissed the thought as paranoid. Her mind felt unsteady.

'Good – that's good.' Tim's voice brightened. 'I'll make enquiries. I should be able to track him down. Fauzia – can you do something? I should have searched Reem's room in Cambridge, but I was in too much of a hurry yesterday to get to London and catch the plane. If I call the college and arrange permission for you to get into her room, can you go and gather her notes and files – anything relevant to her work?'

'What? Tomorrow?'

'As soon as possible. I looked up the trains, and if you get the 9 a.m., you would be in Cambridge shortly after ten. By then, I will have sorted out the permission. Go straight to the porter's lodge at the college, and they'll take you up.'

An image flashed into Fauzia's head of Jack's scowl if she rang in sick again, but she put it quickly out of her mind. For years she had been doing twelve-hour days; she was owed time off. After Tim hung up, she couldn't get back to sleep, and scrolled through possible flights to Cairo. She could be there tomorrow evening if she went on a tourist visa. She texted Tim that she was coming and would bring the notebooks Kate had found as well as the papers from Reem's room in Cambridge. He replied immediately: Good. Neither of them was getting much sleep.

She pulled the notebooks out of her bag which Kate had found in Reem's box: an A5 notebook, which was half empty, an A4 notebook with various papers inserted, and a printout of a report on Anglo-Bahraini relations. A lot of writing in Arabic, some in English. She found pages of figures in columns under initials. Of more interest was a timeline Reem had compiled since 2011 in her distinctive, neat handwriting: the cancellation of Formula One in 2012; the king of Bahrain's invitation from the queen to attend the horse trials at Windsor in 2014; the gift of a horse to the queen; Prince Andrew on a visit to Bahrain in 2016; Prince Charles opening the new naval base in 2017. The dates and names began to swim, and she turned the page, to find a small photo of Rebecca Wilcox Smith at a reception in London of the Bahrain Society in 2018: Dotty in elegant evening dress, standing between Prince Andrew and a member of the Bahraini royal family. Champagne glasses in hand, they smiled fixedly at the cameras. With those kind of connections, Dotty could help them find justice for Reem – if she wanted to. What if Fauzia stood in front of her and asked: would that work? There was no love lost between the former sisters-in-law, but Reem had been of great comfort to Phoebe when she had stayed at Lodsbourne last summer, and, for her sake, Dotty might respond to a direct request for help.

Or was this the mad musings of the early hours? Fauzia would decide in the morning, after a few hours of sleep, when her mind was clearer. She put down the laptop, pushed the papers aside and slid under the duvet. Even if it led to nothing, something in her wanted to see Dotty's face, the tiny movements of eyes and jaw muscles, when confronted by Reem's name; and to hear what words she would use if she refused to help.

Sleeping tablets always made Fauzia's dreams vivid. In the morning, they came back to her in sharp detail: she had been back at Reem's birthday dinner at the Lebanese restaurant in Harlesden. As she made herself coffee she recalled leaving the tube station on the busy road and the astonishing rich aroma of baking which hung over the whole neighbourhood – a smell normally associated with the cosiness of a kitchen or a tantalizing bakery. Through the railings of the bridge, she had spotted a biscuit factory, its brand name glowing in the rainy evening. Inside the restaurant, Reem was already seated at a large table of university friends and family. Kate and Felix were there, and even Phoebe had been invited. In pride of place, tucked in beside Reem, was Labiba, her cheeks flushed with excitement. The little girl was wearing an elaborate pink party dress with sequins – a present from her grandparents in Bahrain, she told Fauzia breathlessly. Reem was finishing her MA and had a place at Cambridge. She was glowing with pleasure, her arm often around her little sister while she posed for photos. Fauzia watched the beautiful sisters. The restaurant was full of Arabic chatter, with large family groups at the other tables, the air rich with the smell of grilling meat and vegetables. She exchanged a nod with Felix and his girlfriend at the other end of the table and introduced herself to friends of Reem's – one young woman was studying medicine and another engineering. The restaurant had made a large cake and everyone – diners and staff – joined the chorus of 'Happy Birthday'. Reem even managed to get her grandparents on FaceTime and flourished her phone around the gathering as the Arabic speakers voiced greetings to the blurred, elderly faces thousands of miles away.

Fauzia roused herself from her reverie and hurriedly dressed. Her phone vibrated with another text from Tim: he was making progress on Nadim Ayoub and would tell her more when she got to Cairo. He gave her his hotel address.

*

Fauzia stood sheltering from the rain outside the porters' lodge in Cambridge as she checked her phone. She had missed calls from Kate and Jack.

A porter peered through his hatch at her. 'Can I help?'

'Professor Tim Blatchford asked me to come, I need to visit Reem Hameed's room.' Fauzia looked at the man's plump, friendly face, hoping she sounded confident.

He shut the window while he conferred with colleagues and she could see them talking animatedly. Another man came to the window.

'I'm to accompany you. The professor said it was to gather some notes needed for their work in Cairo, is that right?'

She nodded.

Fauzia followed him along the stone path next to a flower bed brimming with primroses and daffodils.

'The professor said it was twenty-five degrees in Cairo this morning. We could do with some of that sunshine here, couldn't we?' the porter commented cheerily. 'So what kind of work is the professor doing with Ms Hameed? Some people have all the luck – trips down the Nile and call it work!'

'Indeed,' laughed Fauzia, wondering how she would be able to keep up with his chatter whilst trying to concentrate on sorting out Reem's notes.

After climbing several flights of an old wooden staircase, they came to a door with Reem's name. In the room, it felt strange to see her things as she had left them: the little jewellery box on the bedside table, several of her scarves hanging over the back of a chair, the boots she often wore in winter discarded by the door. As Kate had said, it was as if she might appear at any moment, surprised and delighted to see her.

Fauzia sat down at the desk where Reem had arranged her papers in neat piles. She pulled one towards her.

'I'm afraid this is going to take some time – perhaps half an hour or so?' she said to the porter waiting at the doorway. He looked uncertain. 'I could drop the keys off at the porters' lodge on my way out – or you could come back in twenty minutes?' she pressed. 'Professor Blatchford told me not to rush, and Reem has explained in some detail what to pick up.'

To her relief, the porter agreed, confessing that they were understaffed in the lodge. As his steps echoed down the staircase, Fauzia closed the door and looked around. The room smelt of Reem's perfume. She sat down on the bed and felt overcome with sadness. On the white pillowcase, she noticed a stray black hair, and picked it up to hold it against the light. When Reem took off her headscarf at home, the thick coil of black hair would unfurl down her back, almost to her waist.

Above the bed, a photo was pinned up of her as a little girl with her father. She must have been about seven or eight – a little older than Labiba. Hussain was crouched down, with his arm around her, as they both smiled at the camera. Perhaps Reem's mother had taken the photo, because both of them had such warmth in their eyes. Fauzia looked closely at Hussain. She had liked him; if she was honest with herself, she had even been attracted to him. Apart from family events at Lodsbourne, they had met twice to discuss ZSKa at a coffee shop near Fauzia's office. The first time, they'd discussed the material they had found on the web, including ZSKa's long-standing relationship with the Bahraini government. She mentioned the hard drive, and Hussain understood immediately its significance. She never explained how she had got it, nor did he ask, but when she said she hadn't managed to get into it, he offered to have a go. He had a friend, a computer engineer, who could help. On their second meeting, he gave her a copy, with the password, and they planned to meet again to compare notes on what they discovered. That was only a few days before the fateful night at Lodsbourne. Fauzia presumed that the police found the hard drive in their search of Kate's flat, and they certainly would have found material on her laptop. What part had it played in Hussain's deportation? She would never know, but when Dotty accused Hussain of stealing it, she could have confessed – and that could have helped his case.

Her eye moved to another photo above the bed, of Hussain, Maryam and Reem with, presumably, her grandparents. Reem was a little older, perhaps fourteen. Two of those smiling faces were dead, and the mother was in prison; the grandparents had experienced so much grief and loss. Fauzia shifted her gaze uncomfortably to the window, where she could see the tower of a church across the street, and stared at the grotesque leering of a gargoyle. In the street below she saw a crowd of students on bicycles. Only a short while ago, Reem might have been amongst them. This university was other-worldly; its quaint routines and pretty buildings offered an unreal fantasy, unlike the shabby modern campus where Fauzia had studied. Reem enjoyed the ceremony of the place, she'd confessed – she liked the candlelit dinners and camaraderie of college life.

Fauzia's phone pinged with a text from Kate asking her to call. First, she needed to get to work. Reem was a meticulous researcher, and one pile of journal articles was marked up with annotations. On the top was a loose page, a handwritten poem, and the words, 'Dear Reem, thought this would interest you . . . Love you, Sam.'

'Homage to a Government' by Philip Larkin (1969)

> *Next year we are to bring all the soldiers home*
> *For lack of money, and it is all right.*
> *Places they guarded, or kept orderly,*
> *We want the money for ourselves at home*
> *Instead of working. And this is all right.*
>
> *It's hard to say who wanted it to happen,*
> *But now it's been decided nobody minds.*
> *The places are a long way off, not here,*
> *Which is all right, and from what we hear*
> *The soldiers there only made trouble happen.*
> *Next year we shall be easier in our minds.*
>
> *Next year we shall be living in a country*
> *That brought its soldiers home for lack of money.*
> *The statues will be standing in the same*
> *Tree-muffled squares, and look nearly the same.*
> *Our children will not know it's a different country.*
> *All we can hope to leave them now is money.*

P.S. See? English PhDs can be political!

Did Reem have a boyfriend, Fauzia wondered, she would ask Tim. Beside the poem was an open notebook, where Reem had scrawled the name 'Edith G.' and, underneath, a time at the Institute of Archaeology for next Tuesday; the name was familiar, but she couldn't place it. The notebook was full of Arabic writing. She put them both to one side to take. Next, she sat down at Reem's desk and opened the drawers, rummaging through old computer leads, printer-ink cartridges and stationery: nothing of significance. She went into the small bathroom and cast a quick eye over the bottles of shampoo, shower gel and the towel still lying on the floor where it must have fallen after Reem left. She rifled through the dresses and trousers in the wardrobe, and then a chest of drawers by the bed, where she found piles of knickers, bras, socks and T-shirts. It made her feel uncomfortable, this intrusion into the intimacy of another person's life. It reminded her of the time when she had to clear her mother's flat after her death.

The porter could return at any point. She took a quick breath – she could feel something, a book of some kind, beneath the knickers at the back of the drawer. She pulled out a leather-bound notebook: an old-fashioned diary with a gilt lock and key. The pink leather had faded and was worn along the spine, and, without hesitating, she wrenched open the strap – the lock was little more than decorative. The pages were dense with Reem's handwriting in Arabic. Impatiently Fauzia flicked through to check: no English. A small photo fell out on to the floor, a copy of the family photo Fauzia had examined on the wall.

She felt guilty: do the unexpectedly dead lose all right to privacy? They have had no time to prepare their belongings. She immediately suppressed the question. It had too many possible answers. Trying to find out why Reem was dead justified snapping the lock on the diary, but she would have to wait for Tim to translate its scribbled secrets. She filled Reem's sports holdall with the annotated journal articles, in case any offered a clue. On the top she placed the diary, the poem and the notebook with the appointment at the Institute of Archaeology. She could hear the heavy footsteps of the porter coming back up the stairs.

She quickly left the room, closing the door behind her and heard the click of the lock. The sound had a finality, as if she was saying goodbye to Reem.

'Got all you need?' asked the porter, breathing heavily. Fauzia nodded, not trusting herself to speak. 'You'll give my regards to Ms Hameed when you get to Egypt? A very polite lady, if I may say so. Always says good morning as she passes the porters' lodge. The kind of student who is no problem.'

He paused on the landing to chat, but Fauzia cut him short: 'I've got a train to catch if I'm to make my flight. I'll pass on your regards.'

She wondered if he could hear the break in her voice as she lied.

Back at the railway station, she found a bench at the end of the platform where she could sit and call Tim while she waited for her train to London.

'I've found a diary written in Arabic and a half-empty notebook – looks like her research, most of it is also in Arabic.' He sounded pleased. 'Oh, and a note of an appointment at the Institute of Archaeology for next Tuesday, with the name 'Edith G.'. Does that mean anything to you?'

His voice was muffled, and Fauzia wondered again if someone was listening to their conversation.

'Yes. She's significant. Edith was the wife of Roderick Grant, who was the king of Bahrain's personal security consultant for over twenty years, and she was his secretary. Reem wanted to be the first to write a full account of the man's career and business dealings. He was known as the "butcher of Bahrain" and trained a generation of policemen in interrogation techniques. Edith Grant was Phoebe Wilcox Smith's aunt, and Phoebe introduced Roderick and Martin. The Grants helped Martin set up ZSKa. But I don't understand the connection with the institute – are you sure the words are linked?'

'Yes, definitely,' said Fauzia, looking at the piece of paper. She could imagine Reem on her phone, jotting down the name and time. 'I understand now a comment Reem made the last time we met: she told me that Phoebe had "set the ball rolling". She was going to explain it all to me. She sounded so excited.'

There was a pause on the other end of the phone, and a sigh. 'It's tragic. She was so talented. I'll make some calls to friends in Cambridge and see if we can work out what Reem thought she might find out about Edith Grant at the institute.'

'And I found a poem by Larkin – copied out by someone called Sam. Does that mean anything?'

'"Homage to a Government"? It's apt for her research . . . Sam? Could be a postgrad in college. I saw her a couple of times with another student, and wondered . . .'

'What about you? Anything come up on the room?'

'I found Abdul, the cleaner at the hotel, and he told me that three men – Westerners, not Arabs – used the key from reception to get into her room. He saw them leave with a bag. It's much as I expected, after seeing the state of her room. Someone didn't like Reem. The conclusion is really unpleasant.' Tim sounded tired but he continued hurriedly, 'My research into Nadim Ayoub has thrown up some helpful leads. He's a businessman with extensive interests across the Middle East, and he's the subject of plenty of rumours. One contact told me that he is supplying arms to a country in West Africa – it's not clear whether it's Burkina Faso or Chad. I can't think how Reem managed to get a meeting with him. I'm seeing someone this afternoon who might be able to help. How soon will you get here?'

'I want to see Dotty – Rebecca Wilcox Smith – before I come, so it may not be until tomorrow or the day after. I'll come on a tourist visa.' Now Fauzia had said the words, it sounded right: last night's thoughts had settled into a resolve, both about confronting Dotty and about flying to Egypt. She had spent many years picking her way around Dotty, and she had had enough of it. If Dotty was going to refuse to help, she would have to do it to her face – and explain why.

'Rebecca Wilcox Smith is a tough character. I've heard her speak at conferences, and I didn't trust her. I said as much to Reem.'

'What about the body?' Fauzia asked hesitantly. She still found it hard to believe it belonged to Reem.

'It's in a police morgue for a post-mortem. They say they won't release it for several days, but I've spoken to undertakers because it needs to be buried the day it's released. We're applying for a burial plot through the usual bureaucratic procedures. I gather her grandfather and uncle have booked flights from Bahrain for tomorrow.'

Tim rang off and Fauzia sat staring at her phone's screen saver of the Greek beach where she had been on holiday last year. Then she texted Kate, 'Know of Edith Grant?' The reply came back almost immediately: 'Phoebe's aunt. Dead for years. Why?'

'What did she have to do with archaeology?'

'A hobby, why?'

★

Fauzia sat in ZSKa's offices in Mayfair, waiting. She had not called ahead and on her arrival, the receptionist had assured her that Dotty was very busy with back-to-back appointments, but Fauzia insisted she would wait. The receptionist had shown her into an empty waiting room and made a point of shutting the door behind her after she brought coffee. It had now been about an hour, Fauzia had read the copy of that day's *Financial Times* and was halfway through the *Economist*. There was silence except for the occasional click of the front door and the sound of footsteps on the marble floor of the hallway, but she didn't see anyone. The room was stuffy. Another hour passed. It was almost lunchtime, and she assumed Dotty would go out for a business lunch. Then she heard the unmistakeable sound of high heels approaching, and Dotty flung the door open.

'Fauzia – what a surprise! I suspect I know why you are here. My mother told me you had made a visit. You're quite doing the rounds – although I'm sure Felix isn't on the list. At least you didn't bring the rest of your delegation with you on this occasion – I've no wish to see my cousin.' Her smile conveyed a deep distaste. 'Let's see if we can sort things out swiftly. I have an appointment in ten minutes.'

Dotty led the way to her office. Fauzia had been here only once, when she and Felix had come to meet Martin on the way to a reception at the Athenaeum. It had been early in their relationship and Fauzia had been impressed by the smart office and the chauffeur-driven car.

'How can I help you?' said Dotty as she looked through papers on her desk and began to pick out some to put in her briefcase. 'I gather Reem has been killed in a car accident in Cairo. Poor Mummy is very upset, she was fond of the girl.'

'The Egyptian police are doing little – we are not convinced it was an accident. Someone broke into her hotel room and took her laptop. You have contacts who could help ensure there is a proper investigation.'

Dotty straightened and looked at Fauzia, and then spoke with chilly calm. 'I would have thought it was clear, but evidently not, so let me point it out: as I see it, I know very little about this young woman and what she was doing in Cairo. If she was anything like her father, then I can conjecture various scenarios, none of which inclines me to pursue the matter further. Meanwhile you are an ex-sister-in-law who is in league with a cousin I haven't seen or spoken to for five years, after the shambles of a misguided affair which nearly destroyed my company, so I'm not disposed to go out of my way to help either of you. Quite apart from the fact that this death, while tragic, is straightforward – I've had someone look into the figures for fatalities in road accidents in Egypt and it's over twelve thousand annually, and twenty per cent of them are pedestrians. You and Kate may have cooked up conspiracy theories in your overheated imaginations, but there is nothing to investigate. Sad but true: life in Egypt is cheap. This has been a fool's errand.'

Fauzia, tight-lipped, tried to keep her voice even. 'It's simply a few phone calls, some questions in the right places, and we might make headway – a bit more police engagement. Reem was twenty-two, she had her life before her –'

Someone knocked on the door and Dotty called for them to come in. An assistant brought in some papers and they exchanged murmurs. Fauzia heard something about flights and a hotel booking. After the assistant left, Dotty was silent for a few moments, twisting a ring on her finger.

'Well, my mother was fond of the girl. For her sake, I'll see if the body can be released soon and that she gets a decent burial plot. I'm not doing this for you or Kate – you have both treated this family shabbily. Now, let me make something clear: I very much hope our paths don't cross again. And I would urge you to steer clear of insinuating that Reem was murdered. It's a deranged notion, not appropriate in a sensible journalist, a point I *could* make to your editor, a close friend of mine. I think that wraps things up – I have to go.'

'I don't think this wraps anything up,' said Fauzia, so angry she couldn't help raising her voice. 'Don't think you can shut me up with cheap threats –'

A security guard opened the door – he must have been waiting just outside – and glanced at Dotty for direction.

'I'm leaving – I don't need to be hustled out,' Fauzia said with more composure. She turned back to Dotty. 'I don't know what happened to Reem, and I don't know if you had a hand in it – or one of your business associates – but I do know that one day, the truth will come out.'

'Ridiculous,' murmured Dotty as she stepped past Fauzia and left the room.

The security guard moved forward.

'I'm coming,' Fauzia said, shrugging his hand off her arm, enraged.

*

'Have you booked your flight to Cairo yet?'

Fauzia was walking back to her flat from the tube, holding her mobile to her ear, jostled by the rush-hour commuters.

'No.' She felt flattened by the bruising encounter with Dotty.

'Good.' Tim's voice was more robust and energetic than it had been the previous day. 'I've had a change of plan: I'm going to Istanbul for forty-eight hours, and I've booked a flight for first thing in the morning. The police say they won't release the body before the end of the week, so I have time before the funeral. Nadim Ayoub is a keynote speaker at a conference there the day after tomorrow, and an assistant at his Dubai office said he would be happy to meet and help with our enquiries. I'm sceptical that we will get much out of him, but I want to try. I've arranged a pass –'

'I'll come and join you, and I'll bring the notes and diary for you to look at. Besides, I'd like to see Ayoub – he has done a lot of work with ZSKa over the years. What kind of conference is it?'

'Global security and development. I've done this kind of thing before – businessmen, politicians, a few academics and journalists in a five-star hotel, with plenty of networking and side meetings. To all appearances, very respectable, and the perfect cover for a wide variety of wheeling and dealing. It's our best chance of tracking him down – he's elusive. I've been calling several of his offices – Geneva, Dubai, Cairo – and it has taken a while for anyone to return my calls, and all they've then said is that his diary is full. I'll book a hotel and text you the details. And bring everything you've got.'

'I picked up the papers Reem left at Kate's. They look like research for her MA. Some in English and some in Arabic.'

'Keep everything in hand luggage – we don't want it lost. I'll try and read it all before the conference. We can get it translated in Istanbul – I know a good agency who are quick – and then you will have copies. Text me your flight arrival time, and I'll be waiting at the hotel. And, Fauzia?'

'Yes?'

'Thank you for coming.'

ISTANBUL
2018

18

In the taxi from the airport, Fauzia rolled down the window and let the warm breeze ruffle her hair. The brightness of the light almost hurt her eyes after the February-grey light of London's short days. The road ran parallel to the coast, and between industrial units she glimpsed the sea beyond – a deep, vivid blue. A line of container ships punctuated the horizon, waiting in a queue to pass through the Bosporus. She had visited Istanbul once before, with Felix, shortly after their engagement. They had been with a group of friends and celebrated their announcement in a fish restaurant by the water, with copious amounts of Lebanese wine. She had worn a new silk dress, she remembered, suddenly nostalgic for that hopefulness of a life starting.

Tim had chosen a modest guest house in the old city, and the taxi wound its way through the narrow lanes before depositing Fauzia in front of a dusty façade. In the foyer, two plastic sofas were arranged in front of a large television screen tuned to a recent lingerie show by Victoria's Secret. The receptionist's eyes kept sliding over to the images of bronzed thighs, glossy hair and wisps of underwear in danger of disintegration as the models sashayed along the catwalk.

Tim came down from his room.

'You're wondering why I chose this place,' he said when he greeted Fauzia. 'It's cheap – but that's not the only reason. It has the redeeming feature of a roof terrace with a view of the Bosporus. I'll order tea and get to work on the papers immediately.'

Fauzia handed over the holdall. 'I didn't let the bag out of my sight. I feel it contains more of Reem now than the corpse lying in the mortuary in Cairo.'

Tim made an odd expression, and Fauzia was about to question him, but he forestalled her.

'Go and have a shower or maybe catch some rest. You must have had to get up very early to catch the flight. I'll look through this stuff and then I'll have a much better idea, and we can talk over dinner. I want to hear what Rebecca Wilcox Smith had to say.'

Fauzia showered and lay on her bed listening to music on her earphones while she watched the light shift to dusk; maybe it was a wild goose chase coming out to Istanbul, as Kate had suggested in one of their hurried calls over the last few days. But the trip satisfied Fauzia's need to do something, to make some gesture, to help establish why Reem had died. She felt she owed her that. If a busy, ageing professor like Tim could wander around the Middle East trying to find answers, then coming to Istanbul was the least she could do. She got up and dressed, keen to hear what Tim had discovered.

*

On the terrace Tim had chosen a table in the corner which faced the sea. He was bent over, intently reading the diary, and a lock of his grey hair had fallen forward. His cream linen jacket was badly crumpled. Beyond the terrace the rooftops of the tightly clustered houses ran down to the sea. Ferries were criss-crossing the water, ducking between the huge ships as they made their way along the straits to the Mediterranean, or up towards the Black Sea. On the Asian side, lights blinked on in the densely packed neighbourhoods. The streets nearby appeared to be full of small hotels similar to this one, and their roof terraces were strung with lines of coloured lights. Fauzia heard the murmur of music from the restaurants in the street below, snatches of loud laughter, and, a ship's horn reverberating around the city. Out in the Sea of Marmara, the lights flickered on the waiting ships.

When Tim raised his head and saw her, his expression changed. He looked eager – he had things to tell her.

'The diary takes the form of letters to her father,' he said. 'Reem began it shortly after his arrest in 2011, and the early pages describe her experience of the revolution and her visits to the Pearl Roundabout with her mother during the protests.' The waiter brought beers, feta cheese, olives and pitta bread. 'The dedication is very moving. I'll translate it for you – it's important for understanding how she used the diary.' Tim pushed the food aside and spread the book out to read to Fauzia.

'*Dear Father, I want to understand what happened and why. You have disappeared and it makes no sense. You were just a doctor doing your job. Yet mother tells me that you are in prison. I vow that for the rest of my life I will search to understand how such a thing could happen. I want to understand who and why these people could do this to you. It is so obviously a monstrous injustice, and I need to know why it has happened.*'

Tim read slowly, his finger moving across the page. 'She was almost sixteen at the time she wrote that, but at a couple of other points in the diary she picks up on that "vow". Like this, here –' He thumbed through the thin pages and Fauzia noticed the little stubs of paper he had used to bookmark specific places.

'In 2012, when Hussain has fled abroad for asylum, she writes, *Dear Father, I understand why you had to leave, but it makes mother and me so sad. I will keep writing to you as if I were speaking to you. One day, I hope you will describe your journey to Iran on the boat and your flight then to America. Are you very cold there? I hope you have warm clothes and somewhere nice to live. Mother tells me that in the next few days we should get a call from you, and you will be able to tell us what the country is like. I look at the tanks on the street here, and I want to know why they are here, who made those tanks and where they came from. I need to understand why these things happen to good people. It's like a chain with many links and I want to understand each one: the people far away who give the orders as well as the men in the prison who beat you.*

'I tell you all this because I have made a big decision and I hope it will not be a disappointment to you. I don't want to study medicine any more. When I go to university, I want to study how people do terrible things to others and believe it is justified. I want to study politics and international relations and history. This decision makes Mother very nervous, so it may take some time. Perhaps I will start my studies in economics and only later change to politics. I don't care how long it takes, I will get there. I need to study these things somewhere like England or America, so I will work extra hard on my English. Only there will I find the freedom to reach the answers.

'She gives vivid descriptions of the repression after the protests in 2011. At one point her mother was arrested and Reem stayed with her grandparents, terrified for both her parents. She says that after a burger in McDonald's at the mall, they could smell drifting tear gas and burning tyres as they went back to their car.'

Tim pushed the diary over to Fauzia. 'Look, she doodles flowers and palm trees along the margin.'

'I don't understand the reference to the journey to Iran. I thought Hussain fled to Saudi and then took a flight to England.'

'Some dissidents in Bahrain fled across the Persian Gulf to Iran by boat – perhaps Hussain's family were told he had taken that route in case they were arrested and questioned.'

'I remember Kate telling me that Hussain was very proud of Reem's grades. Now I see how she channelled her grief and anxiety into her studies,' Fauzia said as she examined the swirls down the margin of another page.

'She doesn't write regularly. I would say her entries are about once or twice a month. Sometimes they are very short, and they always start in the same way, "Dear Father". The saddest entry is the one in 2013, when she has learned that her father has been deported back to Bahrain. Here it is:

'*Dear Father. It is very painful to know you are so near and yet we can't see you. Mother has been to the prison every day this week but no one will tell her anything. We think of you all the time. I wish we could sit together and talk and you could describe England to me, where you lived and whether you liked it there. It is now nearly three months since I heard your voice, and I worry that I will forget the sound of it. I should have recorded you on my phone.*

'A few months later, she repeats her promise: *I want to understand why England sent you back. So many other people are getting asylum there, so why did they reject you? It makes no sense, nothing makes any sense to me. I have another question now that I need to answer. I have decided that I must go to England to study. That is my goal. There I can find the truth about why they sent you back when everyone knew the danger you would be in.*

'I've only skim-read some of it, but you can see how a teenager's distress develops into a powerful, settled determination.'

'When did she hear about Kate?'

'When Labiba was born, Maryam told her about Hussain and Kate. She was very distressed. She was angry with her father and accuses him in one entry of betraying her mother, but I think Maryam persuaded her to see the relationship in another light, as a form of comfort for him at a difficult time. By 2015, Reem refers to Labiba frequently as her sister – they must have been on FaceTime regularly – and writes that she wants to meet her. Then comes the extraordinary achievement of winning the scholarship to the London School of Economics – you know that those things are like gold dust? – but it doesn't cover all the costs. Reem works out she can afford to come to London if she can live with Kate, and her great-uncle in America also offers to help.'

Tim turned to the middle of the diary, and read, '*I was right to come to England, Father. Everything seems to come back here, to this place. I can't quite see how it all fits together yet, but I am working on it. I know now that I will be able to tell our story. That makes me so happy, because I can glimpse my goal and you always told me that it was important to have a goal.'*

'This is Reem's story,' said Fauzia thoughtfully.

'There is much more – in places it's repetitive – but I will get it translated so you can read it in its entirety. The agency says they can translate everything in three days. They seem reliable,' said Tim, as he finally closed the book and put it back in the bag at his feet.

'What about the papers and the other notebook?' asked Fauzia, taking an olive from the bowl in front of them.

'They are like pieces of a jigsaw puzzle,' Tim replied. 'Gradually, I will be able to see how they fit. Alongside the academic research into the Budaiya deal, Reem took copious notes on conversations with Kate and Phoebe. She was trying to assemble the details of their lives. She wanted to know how Kate had come to love her father, and to understand their relationship. It is as if she is reconstructing it – he started as a lodger, then grew close to Art, and so forth. She had told me a little of this, but there is a lot of intimate detail, so Kate must have confided in her. The notes on Phoebe are also detailed, and I don't see why Reem was so interested in her life in Iran – apart from curiosity – but I haven't read them all, and I may see a link. There are a lot more notes on Kate than on Phoebe. She has little to say about Rebecca Wilcox Smith. It was as if she needed to learn about every aspect of Phoebe and Kate's lives to see how they related to her father's. Did Reem spend a lot of time with Phoebe?'

'They grew close when she spent two months at Lodsbourne last summer. The housekeeper, Sue, was in hospital for a hip replacement, and Phoebe doesn't like being in the house alone. Kate suggested it as a way for Reem to earn some money while she finished her MA. Phoebe had liked Reem on the couple of occasions they had met, so it sounded like a reasonable plan, and it proved a great success. Despite the differences in age and background, they formed a close friendship.'

Fauzia paused to watch a passing cruise ship, its windows ablaze with light. Tim waited for her to resume.

'When Kate and I visited Lodsbourne before I flew out here, Phoebe made a couple of comments which now make more sense. She told us that Reem had been so interested in everything. It was the way she said it, with the emphasis on "everything". Sue made much the same point; she remembered Reem asking about the renovation of the estate.'

'Ah, yes, there are notes about that – the acquisition of a neighbouring farm and completely rebuilding the farmhouse,' interrupted Tim. 'Reem must have been tracking the Wilcox Smith family finances, and how they relate to ZSKa's activities. She made a note of the dates of big arms deals, compiled from public data, and you can see her drawing links between those deals and the figures in the notebook she left at Kate's. They are from ZSKa's accounts, in columns under initials, itemized as "accommodation", "school fees", "shopping", "travel", and so forth. She added them up. The year before the Wilcox Smiths bought the farm was particularly busy. I couldn't see the link between all these different things – arms deals, these figures and the family, but then –' he paused, looking at the jottings he had made on a napkin. Fauzia leaned forward, fixing her eyes on Tim's face. 'I'm guessing that the spending on shopping and hotels were sweeteners paid to other parties to secure deals, and a ZSKa subsidiary – their business travel company, probably – was given a budget by the arms companies to pay the bills. At this stage, some of this is conjecture, but I think this is the direction Reem was taking.'

'So those figures don't refer to Wilcox Smith family expenditure?' exclaimed Fauzia, 'It was a form of bribery?'

'Yes. Some official in the defence procurement department

of, say, a Gulf state is offered an all-expenses shopping trip to Paris or a nice apartment in New York in return for favouring one arms company over another. For example, a total of $6,568,000 went from ZSKa to one set of initials, N.O.Z., over a period of a few years in the early 2000s. That could have bought N.O.Z. a comfortable house in the Surrey commuter belt, a couple of nice cars and a china dinner set to boot.' Tim peered at his napkin to decipher the scrawl. 'I need to examine the material much more systematically – and, of course, we need to try and identify the initials, but an arms company doesn't want to come anywhere near property, shopping, hotels, yachts and school fees – their auditors would be all over them – so they hide the totals in some "marketing" budget and hand the money over to ZSKa, whose watchword is discretion, and, for a handsome fee, it settles the bills. Everything looks above board, and the sums escape detection by anyone looking out for illegal payments. Martin Wilcox Smith would have known the players, been privy to all the big arms deals, and then positioned ZSKa to tidy things up and ensure a smooth transaction, for a service fee of fifteen or twenty per cent. That's the going rate on this kind of arrangement, I was told by an insider a few years ago. On that $6.5 million account, twenty per cent would be $1.3 million, and that's just from one client.'

'Clever. The arms company pays ZSKa to pay the sweeteners.'

'Exactly. ZSKa's subsidiary company does plenty of bona fide corporate security and travel, entertaining and relocation, but meantime it channels millions of dollars in benefits to individuals. On paper, it looks respectable. From the figures in Reem's notes, I estimate ZSKa's takings at well above £10 million per annum, just from these figures, and I suspect the real sum is higher. The company is owned by family trusts, and Martin Wilcox Smith probably salted away a lot in offshore tax havens, so it will be hard to track the family's wealth. We know the Budaiya deal involved

$30 billion in arms contracts over twenty years – and it would have needed a lot of sweeteners to ease that through. That much came out when the Serious Fraud Office closed down their investigation.'

Fauzia nodded. 'A colleague worked on that – he was furious that the British government just caved in, declaring any further investigation was against national interests.' She sighed. 'I should have been quicker off the mark – Felix once talked of a family trust fund in Bermuda which would cover school fees for any kids we might have. But when I pressed him on how big it was, he joked: "Squillions."'

The significance of the hard drive was becoming clear: this was the shabby secret at the heart of Martin's business, one that had to be managed by him personally to ensure the utmost discretion. Fauzia remembered the exorbitant shopping bills, the motor-boat hire in San Tropez and Sardinia. They served to oil the wheels of commerce. She felt a thrill of excitement: finally, they might have something they could use to destroy the family. She shook herself, Tim was saying something.

'The bit I don't understand is where this information came from. Someone must have been feeding it to her,' he mused, fingering his empty glass.

Fauzia didn't reply, and for a few minutes they watched the lights, and listened to the feral cats screeching and fighting in the nearby street, and the hum of the city's traffic.

'I know where she got the information,' said Fauzia, subdued. 'I gave Reem a hard drive which I took from Martin's study at Lodsbourne, the day of his funeral. I didn't intend to steal it – the study was out of bounds, but on that day Dotty must have forgotten to lock it. I ended up wandering in and poking about, and found the hard drive – it had fallen off his desk and was lying with some papers on the floor. I was curious, I admit. I always felt that family had something unpleasant to hide. Beneath all the perfect hospitality and immaculate manners, something was rotten. You could smell it.'

'Reem never told me. But there are a couple of references in her diary to you giving her some very expensive perfume. She said she wanted to work out the ingredients; it must have been a code she used.'

'I never told her how I got the hard drive – I've never told anyone before. I gave it to her and made her promise not to breathe a word about it. Later I got so nervous I told her to destroy it, and she assured me she had. When I went up to Cambridge, I didn't find it in her room, so hopefully she kept her word. I didn't tell her the rest of the story – I don't think she would have forgiven me if I had.'

Fauzia came to a halt. She couldn't form the words, she could feel her heart racing. The mint tea Tim had ordered arrived, and she measured out two teaspoons of sugar into the glass of hot brown liquid.

'I told Hussain about it, and he offered to help me get past the password. He made a copy for me and kept the original. He was as interested in the contents as I was, and he was working his way through it on Kate's laptop before his arrest. I've blamed myself ever since – perhaps I could have done more to warn him to be careful.'

'And you think it was a factor in his deportation?'

Fauzia nodded. 'There were other issues – he had not claimed asylum when he first arrived, and had ended up overstaying his visa. He had Iranian relatives, and perhaps one of them was on intelligence databases, and then he was helping illegal migrants in Walthamstow, one or two of them were on a suspect list, or so I gather – but plenty of other Bahraini medics got asylum. I don't know why they sent him back. Perhaps it all just added up and they didn't like the look of it – and neither did the Bahraini government.

'Like me, he could smell the rot in the Wilcox Smith set-up.

At Martin's funeral, he saw a senior figure in the Bahraini security services. Between us we identified a couple of the other guests – a Saudi and a Russian – who were peripherally involved in a corruption case in the UK back in 2008. Perhaps he had information on them too. I don't know. We were beginning to piece a few things together.'

'Hussain had all this on Kate's laptop?' asked Tim. 'And you took the risk of giving the hard drive to Reem?'

'Yes, I did.'

Tim didn't say anything, and after a while Fauzia continued, 'I didn't tell her that her father had seen it. I haven't told anyone any of this before. I felt guilty about Hussain. He had helped me, but neither of us had thought how dangerous it might prove for him. Then, three years later, Reem comes along and starts asking questions. I gave it to her, on an impulse. I thought it might be useful for her MA. I also thought that someone needed to look into ZSKa, and Reem was clever. Perhaps she could do something I hadn't managed to do. I never understood the significance of what was on the hard drive. Only now, listening to you, does it begin to make sense. Stupid of me.'

'Some of what she was working out might have been on her laptop. If it was too sensitive for the British, it would have been sensitive for some other countries.'

'Reem was careful, she had the story of her father to remind her of the danger, even if she didn't know all the details. I can't believe she would have run the risk of taking a laptop to Cairo with that information on it. That wasn't Reem.'

'No, I agree. But someone understood that she was investigating things that a lot of people did not want her to know. She might not have realized how ruthless some can be in getting rid of anyone who asks inconvenient questions, and it's not hard to do in Cairo. The police insist it was a hit-and-run accident, and it's impossible to prove it was deliberate.'

Fauzia nodded. 'It was as if Dotty had worked all that out when I visited her. It was so odd, she had got someone to look up the figures on road deaths – as if she had her defence prepared, and knew how hard it would be to prove a murder.'

'Convenient.' Tim frowned. 'Few cases are investigated or followed up in Egypt. People blame bad driving, others blame poor quality roads, and the police can't keep up. You should have seen their offices – crowded, dirty, shelves of old files gathering dust. The chances of them investigating anything are negligible, unless they are under pressure from a wealthy family or a foreign government.'

He sat back and looked straight at Fauzia. His voice was strained, and she struggled to catch his words: 'The body was very badly injured. It's impossible to know how she actually died.'

Fauzia blinked back tears. Reem would have fought with every last breath for her life.

'Did Ayoub meet her somewhere?' Tim went on. 'At one of the big hotels at the pyramids, for example – and then offer his car and chauffeur to drive her back to Cairo? That would explain why she was in that neighbourhood.'

Fauzia was tearing her napkin into tiny pieces.

'Is it my fault?' she blurted out. 'The hard drive contributed to her father's death – and perhaps to Reem's? I never dared tell Kate . . .'

There was a brief silence and Tim straightened, rubbing his back as if the flights in the previous few days were taking their toll.

'I don't think telling Kate was necessary,' he said, with unexpected firmness, and, shyly, he reached out to put a hand on Fauzia's arm. 'I don't know her, but I imagine Kate has had enough to deal with. Leave it as a traffic accident for Kate, Labiba and the family in Bahrain. It's not your fault – Hussain and Reem wanted the hard drive, both were up against something much bigger than they realized. You've been a good friend to Kate from what I gather; that has to be enough.'

Fauzia gratefully held his hand for a moment. It was dry and warm, despite the cooling evening – the hand of a kindly father. For the first time in years, she felt a degree of relief that the issue could be laid to rest. He had absolved her, like an old-fashioned priest might have done back at her Catholic primary school. She smiled at him, touched by the gentleness evident in his face, despite his sadness. Her thoughts turned back to Reem. She had been on the verge of a breakthrough which would have exposed everything. Poor Reem. She had worked assiduously to gather the details for her story, and had been cheated of her chance to tell it.

*

Fauzia was woken by the call to prayer and opened the windows of her bedroom. Dawn was breaking, the elegant minarets pierced the pale sky, and across the city the call to prayer started up, one echoing another. She had never been so close to the speakers amplifying its cry, and the hotel reverberated with the sound. She found it moving, despite her dogged agnosticism, and thought of her devout grandmother when she was a small child. On a visit from India to see her grandchildren, she had been baffled by the cold and the size of London. Fauzia remembered they had shared a room, and in the early mornings she would half wake to hear this gentle, quiet woman getting up to pray. She hadn't thought of her for years; she didn't return for another visit. Fauzia felt Istanbul stirring, its millions of inhabitants woken for a few minutes for a practice that looped back over centuries of human hopes and fears, and projected forward into the future. She liked the definition it provided of this moment usually missed in sleep, when the first light seeped into the night sky. Another ordinary day beginning of busyness, endeavour and striving: the relentless motion of time. Yet it called everyone backwards, as if time were rewinding to the first call to prayer in Mecca, summoning the Prophet to his prayers. A thread of continuity across time and space, for thousands of miles across this continent, the exact same call, the same prayers echoing in dusty, narrow streets and across motorways. She shook herself – today promised to be an important day – and slipped back to bed for a few more hours of sleep.

They had agreed to meet for breakfast on the terrace at eight. Fauzia woke late and dressed in a smart suit; today she needed to be taken seriously. She was relieved to see that Tim had done the same – he looked a different man, clean-shaven, a dark suit and tie.

'I know,' he said, seeing her surprise. 'Today I have to play the Cambridge don if we are to make any headway.'

*

The conference was in one of Istanbul's biggest hotels, a massive cream complex that squatted in its own terraced gardens leading down to the water. A huge plate-glass window in the foyer gave a vista of the Bosporus. They arrived in the midst of the usual morning bustle of an international five-star hotel, guests were checking out and the taxis queued up to take them to the airport. Meanwhile, attendees were gathering around the lifts to go down to the conference centre for the opening event. Everywhere, attentive staff ensured that all was ordered and calm. A magnificent display of irises and mimosa dominated a marble centre table. Everything gleamed and glittered – brass, marble, glass. Tim greeted a colleague from Istanbul university, and Fauzia stood beside him, scanning the throng. Amongst this well-dressed crowd was perhaps the last person to have seen Reem alive. She had googled Nadim Ayoub, but found no image on the web: he was a man who usually kept out of the public eye. Several times Tim was greeted by people he knew, and exchanged a few words in Arabic or English. He didn't introduce Fauzia and she hung back. One of these contacts was the person who would introduce them to Ayoub.

'Fauzia. How unexpected.'

Fauzia spun round – she recognized instantly the irritation and crisp authority.

'I can't imagine what you are doing here.' There stood Dotty, dressed in a scarlet silk suit, her blond hair immaculate. She was waiting for an explanation.

Fauzia, just as surprised, recalled the PA in Dotty's office, talking about flights and a hotel booking for a conference. By way of reply, she scrambled a series of disjointed sentences together: 'Research . . . a series for the website on global development . . .' Her eye happened to land on a long banner advertising the conference, an image of a beautiful African girl filling a container with water from a standpipe. 'And water,' she limply concluded.

Dotty looked her up and down coldly, clearly sceptical.

'I didn't know you were interested,' she said lightly. 'ZSKa is one of the conference sponsors. We strongly believe in the relationship between security and development.'

Her eyes flicked away from Fauzia, and she nodded a greeting, before murmuring, 'As long as you aren't still pursuing those odd ideas about the girl in the Cairo car accident.' She turned to greet someone else, but flung over her shoulder, 'Charlie is our press officer. He'll help you.'

Fauzia found herself facing a young man in his late twenties; his good looks and smart suit made her think of a watch advert. He put out his hand, launching into a description of how Rebecca Wilcox Smith had been a pioneer in bringing the aid and security industries more closely together in a series of conferences and award-winning publications.

'No country can develop without security, so the two things are interdependent. Strong states can develop strong economies,' he said, smiling pleasantly, his expensive education evident in his articulate self-confidence. Fauzia could envisage his public-relations experience landing him a safe Conservative seat in parliament in a few years. He put a press pack in her hands and offered his card. 'I have to go, Rebecca is on the opening panel.'

Fauzia watched Dotty move across the room, steered by a gentleman who seemed to be in charge. She had never seen her at work: everyone wanted to meet her, and whichever way she turned people tried to catch her eye or shake her hand. She was famous in this world, and powerful. It brought to mind one of those portraits of Elizabeth I: this was a court, and Dotty was queen. The bland conference facilities and corporate suits were different, but the power plays and intrigue were not, and Dotty clearly thrived in this milieu.

Fauzia looked down at her pack of information about state aid programmes and the potential for companies to win lucrative consultancy contracts, on subjects as diverse as female genital mutilation and infrastructure development. A press release from ZSKa announced that it had opened a new division specializing in the use of social media in public health systems. As she flicked through the brochures, Fauzia realized that this presentation of ZSKa's activities didn't correlate with her earlier impressions and certainly gave no hint of Tim's speculations the day before. She began to suspect that Dotty had presided over a carefully orchestrated repackaging of the company inherited from her father. She had recast ZSKa as a company that arranged deals and public relations not just for security contracts but for well-digging and vaccination programmes. As she read the promotional literature more closely, it looked as if Dotty's strategy had been to ensure that the lines were so blurred between aid and security that campaigners – and government regulators – would not be able to target ZSKa. The discretion of Martin's era had been replaced by this slick operation, which ensured that she could attend a conference such as this as a respected public figure.

Fauzia had to steel herself to listen to Dotty's performance, and the ingratiating responses of fellow panellists. She felt sick: what chance did she or Tim have of ever proving that the great edifice of Dotty's business and her international reputation was rooted in bribery and corruption going back decades? People like Hussain and Reem were trivial collateral damage, easily disregarded as the juggernaut of prestige, power and money pressed on.

'He is outside on the terrace,' Tim murmured in Fauzia's ear, as Dotty graciously inclined her head at the end of her address to accept the loud applause from hundreds of delegates. Thousands more were watching online, the press release announced.

They got up and squeezed past the crush of delegates who had been unable to get a seat. Ahead of them Tim's contact led them through a set of double doors on to the terrace. Small clusters of attendees were drinking coffee, and, slightly apart, stood a tall, plump man, talking on his phone. Fauzia guessed he was in his early sixties, sizing up the colourful tie and crisply tailored suit. As they approached he rang off, and shook hands with them, but was clearly distracted and kept glancing at his mobile until Tim mentioned Reem.

'We believe you were the last to see Reem Hameed alive?'

Ayoub turned and stared intently at Tim. 'Sorry, I didn't catch your names.'

They repeated their introductions as a Cambridge academic and researcher – they had agreed that Fauzia's press credentials were best concealed – and he looked briefly agitated, his eyes flicking around the other people on the terrace, but the moment passed so quickly that afterwards, Fauzia wondered if she had imagined it, and he assumed the overbearing manner of a man in charge. With a hand on Tim's arm, and a nod of acknowledgement to Fauzia, he suggested they join him for coffee and led them to a quieter part of the terrace.

'I want to offer my deepest condolences for the death of your colleague,' he said smoothly. He beckoned to an assistant, and added, 'She came to see me a few days before the accident at my office in Cairo. She was a highly intelligent young woman and clearly had a great future ahead of her.'

'Why did she come to see you?' asked Fauzia, suppressing her irritation at his platitudes.

He waited while the coffee was brought to the table.

'I'm sure I remember your face. I have a very good memory for faces – particularly of attractive women.' He laughed, and Fauzia gave a guarded smile, anxious to keep him on side but concerned that he could have seen her at Martin's funeral.

'No, you're right. It is not the time for jokes – or flattery.' He glanced at Fauzia's legs. 'You are right to ask these questions. Let me see if I can remember the details exactly.' He paused, as if he were trying to recall the meeting. 'She said she had found my name on ZSKa company documents. I explained that we have had a long relationship with the company. I have a lot of clients in the region, and we have used ZSKa's services on a number of occasions. I think she told me she was doing an MBA, and had decided to do a case study on ZSKa's remarkable growth in the last decade. She approached me in my hotel lobby and asked to meet, and of course I agreed. She was a very pretty lady – if I may say so – and obviously a very determined researcher. I was intrigued.' He smiled at them both as he took a sip of his coffee. 'I would have offered her a job when she finished her degree.' He laughed again.

'We've seen some of those documents,' lied Tim. 'We're interested in your dealings with ZSKa back in 2000s.'

'That's nearly twenty years ago, and I'm afraid I've not got a good memory, but I can put you in touch with my head of corporate relations – they can run through the history of my organization with you.'

'There was a Ritz hotel bill in 1999 which we believe was

yours – to the tune of £46,243 – which was paid by ZSKa. That's a lot of champagne. Why would they pay your bill?' Tim kept the tone of his voice calm, almost nonchalant.

Ayoub smiled. 'Professor Blatchford, I'm afraid your research has led you astray. I have no recollection of any such bill.'

The two men looked at each other; Fauzia noticed Ayoub had a slight tremor in the muscles of his left eye. Then he turned back to Fauzia.

'I heard about Ms Hameed's death in Cairo. Tragic for such a young person. In fact, Rebecca and I had an idea – and we are about to put out a press release. It will serve as the perfect way to commemorate the death of your colleague. Cambridge have been delighted to help set it up.'

Fauzia ignored the comments, ploughing on with more questions. Had Reem said anything about her plans for the rest of the visit? Had she mentioned anyone else she was seeing? But Ayoub waved them away with a gesture as if they were irrelevant. Fauzia noticed a heavy gold ring on his little finger.

'I think your friend was a little naive. No serious commercial operation discusses details of its business publicly; I'm not sure what she expected me to tell her. But we parted on very good terms and I offered to meet her again in London if she had more questions for me – I was in a hurry, and couldn't spare her more than fifteen minutes.'

He beckoned to his assistant and murmured a few words in his ear.

'I've asked for the press release to be given to you now – it will come out in a couple of hours in London, so it's still under embargo. I appreciate you were fond of this young woman, and I think you will be pleased.'

He smiled at Fauzia and she noticed how his eyes moved up and down her body. Tim was trying to ask something, but Ayoub spoke over him, talking about the importance of the conference and the excellence of Rebecca Wilcox Smith's contribution. Tim had been disconcerted by the reference to Cambridge being 'delighted to help'.

Ayoub stood up, buttoning his jacket over his prominent stomach. 'The press release will make it clear. My assistant will be a minute or so, if you wait here, but I must leave you – I have another appointment. Here's my card.'

He had the manner of someone who had done them an immense favour. As he smiled again, the baring of his teeth looked more like a threat than an expression of friendliness. Whatever Reem had asked him, this man was well used to deflecting the curious. Fauzia watched him make his way across the terrace. In the doorway, he stopped to talk to one of the security men, and briefly glanced in their direction. For a fraction of a second he caught Fauzia's eye; his heavy face now wore an expression of tough impassivity. Fauzia felt certain that he had been lying throughout their exchange. She was about to say this to Tim when the assistant arrived and handed them each the press release. Topped by the logos of ZSKa and Cambridge University, it announced a major gift from the company to endow three postgraduate fellowships for women from the Arab-speaking world.

'ZSKa Analytics recognizes the invaluable role of the highest-quality postgraduate education and is keen to develop the opportunities for a new generation of young women . . . Delighted to announce this ground-breaking initiative with Cambridge University in memory of Reem Hameed . . .'

The phrases danced in front of Fauzia's eyes. She looked at Tim and his eyes were closed, his lips compressed with fury.

'This is how the whole thing gets covered up – generation after generation,' he said bitterly.

'Ah, Fauzia, Tim,' the press officer, Charlie, called out, making his way over to them. 'Rebecca asked me to make sure you have all the information you need about the fellowships. Isn't it wonderful? It was all Rebecca's idea. They will be known as the Wilcox Smith Fellowships.' He was full of excited self-importance, and Fauzia realized that he really believed in Rebecca's ambition to integrate security and development. He thought he was assisting in the unfurling of a bright new future.

★

Still clutching their press releases, they left the conference and walked down through the gardens to the Bosporus. Fauzia felt hollowed out; the self-assurance of the event and its participants had left her exhausted: was this how the world worked? These arms salesmen not only made huge amounts of money – and she assumed Ayoub was one – but they managed to manipulate the system so that they could pose as statesmen and philanthropists. Those who challenged them ended up looking like cranks and conspiracy theorists. Fauzia glanced over at Tim. His shoulders were rounded, his back hunched. She put her hand on his arm briefly and he looked at her, appreciative. They were too angry to talk much.

'I'm glad I came. I wanted to confront the man. Did you hear how he talked of using "ZSKa's services"? I think Reem had got to the heart of it: he was one of the big contractors, and ZSKa sorted the bills for him. My task doesn't stop here, it starts,' concluded Tim as they reached the water.

'Task?'

But Tim ducked the question, suggesting they take the ferry across the Bosporus. They joined the short queue to board. On the boat, it was crowded, but they found a place on the wooden bench at the side, and Fauzia craned her head to look back over the water to the Golden Horn, Hagia Sophia and the mosque of Sultanahmet. They sipped sugary black tea from small glasses bought from the boat's tea seller. The smell of diesel and the lurching of the boat in the choppy strait made her feel queasy, but it was a relief to be away from the hotel and its spectacle of power-broking.

Once they reached the Asian side, they walked along the promenade at the water's edge. They were an incongruous couple – thirty years between them, both in smart suits, as if for a business appointment – but the stout mothers with their headscarves and gaggles of children, the teenagers in jeans and leather jackets barely looked their way. As they left the ferry terminal behind, the diesel fumes cleared, and they breathed more easily, tasting the salty tang of open sea. This stretch was busy with day trippers, and the street vendors sold ice creams, nuts and helium balloons. They watched an old man buy his small granddaughter a balloon and an expression of delight spread across her astonished face. Further on, the crowds thinned, leaving only a line of men fishing. Boxes of tackle and equipment sat at their feet, while the rods extended out over the churning, dark sea. The men's faces were hard, and intent; this was fishing with a purpose – not the pleasurable dawdling of English angling, but the studied determination of men who needed to bring protein home. Fauzia peered into the tubs beside them, where the gills of the silver fish gaped, gasping for water.

The sun bounced off the sea and the white stone of the promenade, and both of them shaded their eyes to look across towards the Topkapi Palace rising above the trees, and, beyond, the mosques' clusters of domes and minarets against the bright blue winter sky.

'You could write Reem's story,' Tim said, as if he had just thought of it. 'You're a journalist. You've got an imagination, and you'll have her notes and her diary. She has gathered most of the story already, it simply needs someone to write it up.'

'Me?' Fauzia prevaricated: 'I don't have the time – the day job is enough.'

'You know the people Reem was interviewing, and you knew

others she never met, like Martin Wilcox Smith. Kate can help you. I can see how the book could work: that's the way to get people to listen. Lightly fictionalized, of course, change a few identifying details to dodge the libel lawyers – they will be biting at your heels – but it's worth the risk. For now, it's the only way to get the story out there.'

'But when am I supposed to have the time? Why me – why not you?'

'Take a few months off. I'll help, but you're the one to write this story of Reem's. I'm an academic – and I have another task. By the end of this week, Reem will be buried, and then I will work on her notes, piecing together the names and transactions in Martin's accounts. I want to work out the people behind the initials, such as Ayoub, and see how they link to other commercial contracts. If I'm right, and ZSKa's role is to handle the bribes on behalf of arms dealers, I want to untangle the whole complex structure – several different holding companies will be involved, probably registered in different tax havens. My suspicion is that ZSKa is a very small cog in a much bigger operation. Ayoub's tone towards ZSKa was patronizing; the likes of Rebecca Wilcox Smith are window dressing compared to the biggest players. Plus, I want to find out what on earth Reem thought would be interesting in Edith Grant's papers at the Institute of Archaeology, though my hunch is that that's not a big part of the story –'

Fauzia interrupted. 'Kate said that she and Hussain looked through some Grant papers and found case notes of young men tortured in Bahraini prisons in the early 1970s; she told Reem that there could be more material amongst her archaeological notes.'

'Ah, so that was it. A friend at the institute is looking out Grant's papers for me, and I'll check them over – they might help me establish how much Martin knew about police brutality. Like Casaubon in *Middlemarch*, this will be my life's work from now on.' Tim laughed. 'More seriously, I will put in some freedom-of-information requests, although I don't know how successful they will be. Since the Serious Fraud Office investigation was closed down in 2006, the sector has become very difficult to research.'

They turned round and headed back towards the ferry terminal.

'Did you know that the UK's arms exports have grown by nearly forty per cent in the last four years?'

Fauzia shook her head. 'Why so steep an increase?'

'Rebecca Wilcox Smith has a lot of friends in this government – she made a hefty donation to the party last year, I saw – and she and her chums have set the country in this direction. For what it's worth, my efforts will be a memorial to Reem. I may become an eccentric crank in the process and be dismissed as obsessive, but I'm too old to care. Your job is no easier. This is not a tidy story with a clear ending – it's all still going on. The baddies are not yet done for. We will never know what Reem really talked to Ayoub about, where they met, whether he persuaded her to let his chauffeur drive her back to her hotel – a lift which left her dead on a backstreet. Nor will we ever know who ordered the break-in at her hotel and took her laptop. As soon as she got to Cairo, she was out of her depth.'

'Publishers won't like that . . .'

Tim sighed and shrugged his shoulders. 'You may be right, but give it a try.'

The sun was dipping and Fauzia shivered in her thin suit. Later, sitting on the ferry, her eye fell on a young woman seated opposite, texting on her phone. Her head, covered in a scarf, was bent over the screen, so Fauzia couldn't see her face, but her wrists reminded her of Reem. The cuffs of her coat were turned back, accentuating the slimness of her arms, the muscles in her wrists vibrating as her thumbs quickly tapped. She was wearing a delicate gold chain bracelet similar to the type Reem used to wear. The resemblance was striking, and Fauzia's eyes filled with tears. She thought back to that first call from Tim in the newsroom just over a week ago, and each of the intervening days had been intense with memory and grief. She couldn't shake the feeling that she had brushed up against some vast, hidden evil at work; she had felt its breath, smelt it, and several times it had left her palms clammy with fear. She thought of Kate's blotchy, swollen face as they parted at the flat the day before she flew to Turkey; she thought of little Labiba in her new school uniform that morning she stayed at Kate's, just starting out in life, reception year at school, her sister and father already dead. Absent-mindedly, Fauzia stared at the wrists of this stranger opposite her.

From the ferry terminal, they wound through the backstreets of the old city, dodging the tourist-shop owners' persistent requests to look at the piles of coloured pottery and jewellery glowing under the bright lights. Ahead, they glimpsed a street lined with restaurants, and they turned off into a side alley. It was darker here, the houses were shuttered as if abandoned, and the pitted surface of the street was lit up only in the pools of light cast by the street lamps. In a gap between two buildings, there appeared to be a ruin, and they paused, their attention caught by something glittering. Then, as their eyes adjusted, they saw that the dark was shimmering with dozens of pairs of eyes. They glimpsed the outlines of innumerable stray cats climbing over the broken masonry, as if every surface was moving, with more animals perched in vacant window frames, staring down at these interlopers in their secret world. The night before, they had heard them as they sat on their hotel terrace. Fauzia scanned the extraordinary scene with her phone torch, revealing hundreds of cats.

Later, sitting on the terrace with a last drink, she held the image in her mind of this life teeming in the city's ruins, exhilarating in its wildness and fecundity; above all, in its sheer tenacity. Life which clung fiercely to itself, to its own determined survival.

ISTANBUL
2019

Epilogue

Fauzia plugged in her laptop at the desk. To one side sat the file containing the translations of Reem's notebooks and diary, and on the other she laid out the sketch plan she and Tim had compiled of the lives of Phoebe and Kate, and the additional details she had chosen to fill the gaps. On the wall beside her, she had taped three images. The first was of Reem's grave in Cairo. Fauzia had planted a mimosa tree, and given the caretaker money to water it. She would come back to visit, she told him. She remembered the heat on the day of the burial, the early morning flight from Istanbul, and how the hearse passed parts of the cemetery where families lived in shacks amongst the tombs; ragged children had stopped their game to watch them pass in their air-conditioned cars. The concrete plaque with Reem's name bore an inscription from the Qur'an, chosen by Maryam: *To Allah we belong, and to Him is our return.*

The other two images Fauzia had downloaded from the web: the first was of Dotty with the king of Bahrain, Nadim Ayoub and the queen at the Royal Windsor Horse Show in 2014; the diminutive white-haired monarch wore the delighted grin only evident on occasions involving horses. In the second Dotty was with the young press officer, Charlie: he had been given an award by the Bahrain Society in the House of Lords for his biography of Martin Wilcox Smith. Now Fauzia stared at the photos, at Dotty's face with its professional smile; was it just her imagination or could she detect an edge of anxiety in the tightness around her mouth? She remembered Felix quoting Yeats, laughing at his family's 'ceremony of innocence'.

And there was Reem's innocence. Fauzia took a deep breath and felt a great calmness settle: she had three months of unpaid leave, and this rented room with a view of the Bosporus; all she had to do now was write. She took a sip of mint tea and opened the laptop, with its desktop screen saver of Lodsbourne in the summer of 2012: the deckchairs and lawn, the front door standing ajar, with the dogs lying in the shade on the terrace. It was partly a joke, she had explained to a surprised Tim when they had been working one day in the British Library, but it also served a purpose, and reminded her of what she needed to write: how a family like the Wilcox Smiths survived, how they were able to insulate themselves from the violence they inflicted on other lives they regarded as cheap. She fingered the keyboard, and began to type, the horns of the ferries below her window punctuating the reassuring tapping of the keys.

Acknowledgements

All the characters and events of this book are fictional but they draw deeply from history. In one place only, I used direct quotes involving real historical figures when describing Roddy Grant's papers: John Stonehouse's speech to industrialists in 1964 and Harold Hubert's letter to the British embassy in Tehran in 1966; this material is quoted in Nicholas Gilby, *Deception in High Places*.

I have found particularly helpful the following books on the end of empire in the Middle East: Anthony Parsons, *They Say the Lion*, and *The Pride and Fall of Iran 1974–79*; Frank Heinlein, *British Government Policy and Decolonization 1945–63*; Glen Balfour-Paul, *The End of Empire in the Middle East*. On the UK arms trade, Open Democracy's site OpenSecurity has some excellent reporting. Human Rights Watch and Salam for Democracy and Human Rights monitor the situation closely in Bahrain. Of the wealth of material on the web, Adam Curtis's blog on the history of British-Bahraini relations includes fascinating BBC archive footage: *https://www.bbc.co.uk/blogs/adamcurtis/entries/a317e502-5bb9-39b4-9f7e-94f91e6365c4*.

Of help on Iran was *A Mirror Garden* by Monir Shahroudy Farmanfarmaian and Zara Houshmand; on the Shiraz Arts Festival, Robert Gluck's article in *Leonardo*, vol. 40, no. 1, 2007; and on Dylan Thomas' visit, Professor John Goodby in *Dylan Thomas News*, 2017.

Thanks to Neil MacGregor and Joanna Mackle, then at the British Museum, for an inspirational visit to Iran in 2007. An even older debt I owe to Professor John Lonsdale, Trinity

College, Cambridge, for his teaching on Mau Mau, and the bitter processes of decolonization, and for subsequent encouragement of my columns in the *Guardian* which tackled the neglected legacy of empire. I owe the idea of the Happy Family cards to my mother's beautiful creation as a young art student in the early 1950s. My thanks to my friend Martina Klett-Davies, who articulated the question with characteristic accuracy: 'Why have I, as a German, been expected to come to terms with and acknowledge my nation's historical record, and you British have not had to do the same with your empire?'

I am very grateful to my former colleague Ian Black for introductions to Ali Alaswad, and several other Bahrainis who did not wish to be named. Ala'a Shehabi helpfully corrected various details. They all offered insights into their home country of Bahrain. I have drawn on the written work of Shehabi with co-author Marc Owen Jones, including their excellent *Bahrain's Uprising*. Owen Jones gave me many helpful suggestions and introductions at a very early stage of the novel, as did Christopher de Bellaigue, whose writings on Iran have been invaluable. My thanks for details on walnut jam and other delicacies to an Iranian who did not wish to be named. Much appreciation to my friends Shahedah Vawda, for an important and insightful reading, and Gillian Hughes, for key details on Harmondsworth detention centre. And gratitude to my son Luke, one of my first readers, who brought his fascination with storytelling and sharp analytical mind to bear on a draft; his detailed comments on the plot were invaluable. We share the drive to tell stories we believe to be important, and I watch with admiration as he develops his craft.

As ever, my deepest appreciation to my editor, Bella Lacey, and my terrific copyeditor, Daphne Tagg; their wise and dedicated advice is invaluable. A writer could not wish for a better team than the staff at Granta, which includes Christine Lo, Pru Rowlandson and Lamorna Elmer; their passion for books is evident in all their hard work. I owe a huge debt to my agent, friend, and advisor on matters professional and personal, Sarah Chalfant. It is a privilege to have her support and attentive oversight.

Keep in touch with
Granta Books:

Visit granta.com to discover more.

GRANTA

Also by Madeleine Bunting and available from Granta Books
www.granta.com

THE PLOT

A Biography of My Father's English Acre

WINNER OF THE PORTICO PRIZE
SHORTLISTED FOR THE ONDAATJE PRIZE

'Grippingly readable . . . among the very best non-fiction to have been published in a long while about what it means to be English'
Simon Schama

Keen to understand her complex father and the plot of land he loved, Madeleine Bunting makes an extraordinary journey deep into the history of Yorkshire and of England itself. From medieval ruins to ancient droving paths, through to the tiny stone chapel her father built himself, Bunting reveals what a contested, layered place England is, and explores what belonging might mean to any one of us.

'This is a seriously good book: a borehole history of both an acre of England and Bunting's complicated father . . . a wonderful excavation of what a "sense of place" might mean – and of the delusions and fulfilments that landscape can inspire' Robert Macfarlane

'Through the prism of a single acre, she plays witness not only to the moors, but to England and its people – how our lives have transformed over the past thousand years, and how our connection with the land has itself changed' *New Statesman*

LOVE OF COUNTRY

A Hebridean Journey

For centuries the remote beauty of the Hebrides has attracted saints and sinners, artists and writers. Journeying through these islands, Madeleine Bunting explores their magnetic pull, delving into meanings of home and belonging, and uncovers stories of tragedy, tenacious resistance, and immigration – stories that have shaped the identity of the British Isles.

'A magnificent book, a heroic journey that takes us as far into the heart as into the islands of the north-west'
Richard Holloway

'Excellent . . . I cannot think of a more intellectually challenging or rewarding travel book in recent years'
Mark Cocker, *New Statesman*

'Moving and wonderful . . . the author and reader of this book end up losing themselves not just in politics and history and the details of nature, but a sense of wonder'
Amy Liptrot, *Guardian*

'A luminous enquiry . . . an exquisite and realistic account of life at the edge . . . Bunting [is] a shining companion through the tangle of the isles'
Candia McWilliam, 'Best Books of the Year', *Herald*

Also by Madeleine Bunting and available from Granta Books
www.granta.com

LABOURS OF LOVE

The Crisis of Care

LONGLISTED FOR THE BAILLIE GIFFORD PRIZE AND THE ORWELL PRIZE FOR POLITICAL WRITING

'Caring is what makes us human, Bunting argues. Quite so
. . . [Her] interviews capture the elusive blend of attentiveness,
compassion and kindness that we know, intuitively, is the essence
of care' Rachel Clarke, 'Books of the Year', *Observer*

'An urgent, searching and vital overview of the landscape of care . . .
sometimes angry, often tender, always illuminating' Gavin Francis

Care work has long been underpaid and its values disregarded. In this
remarkable and compassionate book, Madeleine Bunting speaks to
those on the front line of the care crisis, struggling to hold together a
crumbling infrastructure. A combination of extraordinary first-hand
accounts of caring with a history of care and its language, *Labours of
Love* is an impassioned call for change at a time when we need it most.

'A tour de force . . . an unbearably poignant tapestry of history,
literature and economics, alongside strands of Bunting's personal
biography . . . [elevated by] the intellectual and emotional depth
Bunting brings to her subject' *Financial Times*

'Moving, forensic and historically grounded' David Kynaston

'[A] masterpiece. Humane, perceptive, honest, compassionate,
wide-ranging, and erudite, it is a profound inquiry into the most
important social issue of our time' Raymond Tallis

'Moving, essential . . . thank you, Madeleine Bunting' Philippa Perry

Also by Madeleine Bunting and available from Granta Books
www.granta.com

ISLAND SONG

'Vivid and engrossing' Claire Messud

'Striking . . . The irresolvable mystery of this story, in common with all great fiction, is the human heart' *Observer*

In 1940, Helene – young, naive and recently married – waves goodbye to her husband, who has enlisted in the British army. Her home, Guernsey, is soon invaded by the Germans, leaving her exposed to the hardships of occupation. Forty years later, her daughter, Roz, begins a search for the truth about her father, and stumbles into the secret history of her mother's life. As Roz discovers, truth is hard to pin down, and so are the rights and wrongs of those struggling to survive in the most difficult of circumstances.

'A wonderful evocation of wartime secrets and hidden histories, and a moving exploration of the far-reaching consequences they can have' Catherine Hall, author of *Days of Grace*

'A very fine piece of storytelling and a highly intelligent examination of the difficult, indeed painful, choices that people have to make. This is the kind of book that draws you into it, one in which you want to know what happens and how the characters make out' *Scotsman*